W9-CLN-254

Unnatural Acts

Also by Dylan Jones

Thicker Than Water
Outside the Rules

UNNATURAL ACTS

Dylan Jones

ST. MARTIN'S PRESS ♏ NEW YORK

Library of Congress Cataloging-in-Publication Data

Jones, Dylan
    Unnatural acts / Dylan Jones.
        p.   cm.
    ISBN 0-312-14753-8
    I. Title.
PR6060.U5117U56   1996
823'.914—dc20   96-27966
                                                         CIP

First published in Great Britain by Century,
a division of Random House UK, Ltd.

First U.S. Edition: December 1996

10   9   8   7   6   5   4   3   2   1

For my mother, Beryl Noreen,
who read to me before I could talk,
and for Ken, who makes it all happen

Yet each man kills the thing he loves,
By each let this be heard,
Some do it with a bitter look,
Some with a flattering word.
The coward does it with a kiss
The brave man with a sword.

(Oscar Wilde, *The Ballad of Reading Gaol*)

'. . . Defaced, deflowered, and now to death devote!'

(Milton, *Paradise Lost*, Book 9)

Saturday, November 5

THE 38 SLUG took her low in the back on her left side. It struck the curving arc of her hip bone, shattering the lip of her iliac crest and ricochetting outwards, miraculously sparing all the vital organs. But at twenty yards the impact hit her like the kick of a crazed mule, jerking her sideways, combining with the momentum of her running form to flip her like a discarded doll to the ground. She lay there for long seconds, winded from the fall, waiting for something to happen, waiting for death.

The asphalt was hard, its caress on her cheek a gritty, unpleasant kiss. Shock numbed her senses, then fear kicked in with an adrenaline blast that drove her to her feet. Grunting, her breath heaving, she staggered upwards.

The pain came then, burning and clawing at her left side as she ran, her feet clattering unevenly against the hard blacktop, the noise muted against the November gale screaming in off Lake Michigan. She looked down and saw numbly that she had lost a shoe. Realisation dissolved in the pain that was now a hot spike beginning somewhere in the small of her back and shooting down the rear of her leg. But still she ran, her ears straining for another gunshot. It came, but this time there was no jolting impact. Missed, you bastard, she thought.

It spurred her on towards the domed building that loomed ahead. There, perhaps, was shelter and escape. The wind gusted her forward, a welcome ally against the blooming obstacle of agony that grew with each stride and mingled with the fog of lethargy that sucked at her will. She fought them both as she had the maniac who was pursuing her, who had shot her in the back, who was stalking her now, in the darkness.

Thought of him brought a further spurt of panic. She tried to increase her pace and almost stumbled. She slowed, focusing her mind, grinding her teeth. Anger helped. Anger at being in this predicament. This was not meant to happen to her. She had a life and she was going to get back to it. She would not *allow* this to happen.

But it was.

In the dark night of a strange city, Dr Catrin Jacob, abused, shot and half drugged, was fleeing for her life.

The Planetarium walls curved huge and dark in silhouette against the glow of North Lake Shore ahead while the squat rectangle of the first-floor entry level reflected uneven ripples of street light from its smooth glass surface. A squall burst above her driving needle pricks of freezing rain into her bare neck. She was still twenty yards from the building but no lights shone inside as she scanned it in wild desperation. The city was half a mile away, awake still, lights burning in every street. But in between were eight hundred yards of darkness that may as well have been eight thousand and she knew with a wretched certainty she would never make it that way.

Above, a light aircraft thundered in thirty yards over her head. She waved her arms in desperation, but it flew over towards the airfield a few hundred yards behind leaving her screaming in frustration. She was almost at the roadway now, the looping drive that led to and from the city. She lurched towards the nearest vertical surface, a black iron archway with mesh doors. She rattled and shoved but they were unyielding. Cursing, she fumbled around the side and behind and saw that the archway was shallow, leading to nowhere. Then her hands found the buttons and she realised that this was an elevator. Bare and practical – designed for freight, not passengers. She stabbed at the buttons until her fingers hurt and her mind kicked in. She remembered entering at ground level and descending. That was why they needed freight elevators – to get down into the building. If that was the case then there must be some way for human traffic to emerge, emergency exits at least. She looked up and squinted through the rain. There, five yards away, was a glass and steel shelter that she had mistaken at first for a bus stop. She hobbled across to it, her left leg now heavy and unresponsive, slapping jarringly as she drove herself onwards. She couldn't prevent one more terrified over-the-shoulder glance which showed only black night and the hammering rain. She couldn't see him but she knew he was there. She dragged her head around and forced her mind to forget his rough, filthy hands upon her.

She had feigned unconsciousness after he had made her drink the laced coffee and the flailing kick she had levelled at his crotch had hit home and taken him completely and totally unawares. She had not waited for his reaction, she had merely thrown open her passenger door and fled, head back in a cheek-blowing sprint until his lucky shot had knocked her flat.

Rain ran in rivulets down her face and into her eyes. She paused and the sudden cessation of movement made her head reel. A wave of nausea brought her to her knees in a cold sweat. She gulped in air, put her head down, cursed, counted to three and then looked up again. She was kneeling in front of a doorway, the kind with a press bar for opening from the inside only. Except the doors were not flush. Someone had wedged something between the two to prevent them from springing shut and locking.

Without a second thought for the reason for this minor miracle, she thrust herself upwards and stumbled and staggered through the doors and down the steep stairs towards the dense blackness below. She clung to the side-wall for support, but managed nevertheless to miss the bottom step and fell onto hard concrete, panting like a dog, her injured side screaming in protest. She lost her second shoe in the fall.

She lay for one long moment, listening to the wind moaning and the rain clattering against the glass above. To be out of it was bliss. She risked shutting her eyes and regretted it immediately as the world began to whirl around her in a giddy spiral. She snapped her eyes open and the whirling stopped, but she felt the seductive lethargy of the drugs and the warmth of the building creeping over her like marsh gas. It was pitch black. She dragged herself to her knees, her hand flying involuntarily to her left side, touching a warm wetness there. She put her fingers to her mouth and tasted the coppery, salt tang of her own blood.

A fresh geyser of anger and fear engulfed her again and she hauled herself upright, pushing her back against a wall, sliding up it until she was on two feet. Slowly, she began inching forwards, groping out with her hands. Two yards along, she felt a handle, tried it, a moan of frustration oozing out of her mouth as whatever door it guarded failed to budge to her thrusting weight. Above her, the glass and steel exit rattled again, but this time not from any gust of wind. Instead she heard a grunt of effort as someone large and bulky attempted to navigate the treacherous stairs. A bright lance of terror shot through her brain. She fumbled further along the dark wall, found another handle, depressed it and almost fell forward into a room. Even warmer now, a few dim lights throwing green and red glows onto glittering surfaces, LEDs reading forty minutes after midnight. She vaguely registered that they were microwave ovens as she moved forward along the narrow gangway, realising dimly that she was in a large kitchen. Ahead, in the gloom, she could make out a double door. She reached forwards, pushing the doors open with a crash. Ahead beckoned another vestibule and another set of doors. She staggered through these and without warning found herself in a huge open space. She stood there, momentarily in awe of the large shadows that loomed about her, squat and silent like sleeping giants in the glow of security-lit exit signs along the walls. In the centre, a huge ball occupied the floor space and she recognised it immediately; a giant globe of the earth in all its glory.

She had been here before. Had it truly been only a few hours before? She had sat in this room eating and drinking and admiring the blue-green illumination of this same globe. She had dined near a wall, but in the dim glow of the security lighting, all she could see was that the room had been cleared of tables and chairs. She shouted out. Her voice echoed around the big room before fading away into the silence again. Behind her, she heard a door clang open. There was no attempt at concealment on her pursuer's part. He was crashing along after her and he didn't care who knew it. Her eyes scanned the room for somewhere to hide or a way out. Now she remembered the given name of this room: the Hall of Space Exploration. She'd been in it barely five hours before but now she found herself desperately trying to remember the layout. There was a corridor that wound upwards to the entrance . . . there might be security guards there. Behind her there came a metallic clatter. Her pursuer was in the kitchen. She ran into the hall, looking for somewhere, anywhere to hide, groping blindly to her left away from the door and slumping behind a large pyramidal shaped booth. She remembered it as one of four designed for demonstrating the night sky. She sat, trying to breathe evenly, trying to make as little noise as possible. The exit lights bathed everything in a surreal softness, casting deep shadows around the large oblong shapes of the exhibits. She shut her eyes and tried to remember where the exit corridor was.

After a long moment, she risked a glance between the night-vision booths and saw that the door to the kitchen she had come through was swinging gently shut on its spring. There was no sign of her pursuer, but she knew that he was there.

The corridor. Where in God's name was the corridor? She forced her doped mind to think. They had got up from the tables and wandered slowly off to the corner of the Hall. She had stood there and looked back at the exhibits and . . . her gut suddenly churned. She had looked back from the far side at the cafeteria door she had come through. The corridor was on the other side of the room.

Another sob threatened, but she bit down again on her hand and peered across at the huge expanse of floor that faded into darkness across the hall. That was where she needed to be.

She risked another glance around at the door and did a double take. It seemed to be swinging slowly closed again, as if her pursuer had had second thoughts and gone back into the kitchen.

She pulled her head back and squeezed her eyes shut. She couldn't be sure of anything any more. Her mind was as sluggish as a mud-filled creek. A vast dark pool of seductive drowsiness seemed to fill the space between her ears. Velvety warm and welcoming, all she needed to do was yield to it and it would be over.

She bit her hand harder, welcoming the pain. It brought her back to consciousness with a start. That wasn't the way it was going to be. She was going to fight. Fight for herself and for her people so far away.

She forced herself to look around her, to find something, to think. Behind her, the wall was a dark expanse dotted with shallow partitions. Earlier she had stood there and pressed buttons and stared through peep-holes in the booths separated by these partitions. The planet wall they called it, but now it was a featureless landscape of half-shadow. She ran her eyes over it in the dim half-light and there, at the far end, she saw her salvation. A small orange light glowing in the darkness. Obtrusive and conspicuous. A fire alarm.

It stood halfway up at eye level no more than twenty yards away. She got to her knees and began to crawl in the deep shadow towards the wall to her left. It was taking her away from where she wanted to get to, but it offered the best cover. She reached an adjacent L-shaped booth and crouched low, staring up at the glass screen, making out the mottled surface of the moon in the baleful orange light. The planet wall with its waist-level bar of visual displays was no more than two yards away. She squatted beneath the Moon exhibit, looking back at the way she'd come, seeing nothing but shadows before turning back to her objective. The alarm was at the end of the wall, fifteen yards along its exposed length. There were two square pillars between that she could hide behind. They were narrow, but they were the only real cover she could use.

Catrin Jacob took a deep breath and darted towards the first pillar in a low crouching run. She took two more deep breaths and made a lunge for the second pillar, banging her leg into an unseen obstacle in the process. The pain blossomed, deep and nauseating, bringing with it a vasovagal surge that nearly tripped her into a faint. She staggered back, pushing her hands deep into her mouth to quell the scream that threatened, waiting for the pain to abate.

Come on, come on.

With another supreme effort, she forced herself to move again, into the dim light of the room. Another lunge toward the next pillar, her hand sliding gratefully around it for support. But instead of cold plaster, she felt something warm writhe and move under her grip. She fell backward, stumbling onto her backside, staring in dumb horror at the pillar. A hand emerged from behind it, long white fingers trembling as they reached forward. And then a face swam out of the black shadow and Catrin Jacob screamed.

She clambered backwards, turning and scrambling to her feet, escape driving everything from her mind. She careered into a stall, the jolt stunning her momentarily as she tried to reorientate herself. And then she was lurching across the hall, all pretence at concealment gone.

The face . . . the face . . . different from the one she remembered from her ordeal in the taxi. A gaunt countenance reflecting as much fear and confusion as she herself felt. And there had been no beard. Were there two of them then?

Whimpering sobs of denial and fear gurgled in her throat as she hobbled away.

Two of them . . . dear God, no . . . . She was almost toppling forward, the exit light within clear view when she was hit heavily from behind. A big hand gripped her shoulder, clamping onto her flesh through the material of her jacket. She stumbled from the impact, her hands flying out to stop herself from falling. And then the body was upon her, the big hand almost encircling her neck. A fist smashed into her lip and nose, squeezing pincer fingers cut off the air from her lungs. Her bulging eyes took in his face, saw the close beard as the darkness in her brain grew into a dense mushrooming cloud.

Weakened from loss of blood and the drugs, her last thoughts tainted with confusion and doubt over the terrified face she had seen under the Planet wall, Catrin Jacob died an unlawful and unnatural death in the Hall of Space Exploration.

2

JACOB BEK HAD been in the Planetarium for three consecutive nights. The drugs that held his schizophrenic mind in check had all but dissipated and his grip on reality, tenuous at the best of times, hung by a gossamer thread. It had slipped disastrously that evening when he'd first set eyes on the woman. He'd fixated on her immediately, followed her and waited for her outside in the darkness, watching her emerge and look despairingly for a taxi. But Solidarity Drive had been empty, the usual line of cabs absent at a time when the Adler had normally long shed its daily quota of tourists. She had begun walking briskly onwards towards the city when the cab appeared from nowhere, gliding out of the dark street. For a moment it looked as if it would pass her but then its light flicked on and it had slowed, as if it had been waiting for her and her alone. Jake had begun to run forward, unsure of what to do. A numbing, dreadful sense of loss paralysed him as he saw the cab pull away. But as he watched, the taxi doubled back and drove in towards the car park. Hope had flared again in Jake and he'd followed in a low crouch, furtive and cautious.

The taxi had drifted around and parked in a corner away from the street lights. The driver had emerged and walked once slowly around the vehicle, crouching at the offside wheel, then he'd straightened, gone back to his seat and Jake had seen him reach down and hand something to the woman. Jake had stared across from his hiding place. There was little light; what he saw was mainly silhouetted against the glow from the airfield through the cab windows. He saw her put something to her lips, saw the driver's movements become more animated and urgent, pointing insistently. After a few minutes, the driver got out and quickly got in again next to the woman, still pointing. Then nothing. Behind him, the other Planetarium guests all left via the convoy of taxis that appeared not ten minutes after the woman had taken it upon herself to depart. Jake had huddled against the crumbling walls of an abandoned beach house and restaurant on the Michigan shore, fifty yards from the main building and the same distance from the dark and silent cab. Huddled and shivered for long, dragging minutes which stretched into an hour or more until the night exploded to the sound of the woman charging out through the flung-open passenger door. It was only then that his confused mind appreciated that there was something badly wrong. It happened so quickly; her running, the muzzle flash of the gun, the impact throwing her to the ground.

He had moved then, following the big shadow of the driver in front of him, slipping down the exit stairwell that he himself had left open. In the kitchens, he had squatted behind a table and heard for the first time the high-pitched whistling noise that brought the flesh on his back up in ridges of gooseflesh. Ahead of him, the man had tilted his head from one side to the other, the signal changing in intensity as he did so. Jake knew then that this man was hunting her. Silently, he'd followed into the Hall and crept to his hiding place behind the pillar where the woman had sensed him and found him.

Jake had seen her recoil from his outstretched hand, yet her touch had thrilled him. So normal, so *human*. But there was panic in her face, horror, revulsion. He'd tried to speak, his mind thudding back into focus from the dizzy heights her touch had induced. He'd tried to warn her, tried to help her, whispering her name, *their* name. But it was drowned out by her screams as she'd turned and stumbled in her fear. Jake had emerged from his hiding place but it was too late: The Whistler appeared like a phantom, falling upon her as she ran.

Jake had stood, paralysed. The thin whistling trill had pierced his mind above the noise of muffled struggles. He'd seen The Whistler's hand come up to his head and abruptly, the high-pitched keening ceased. Almost instantly, the girl's screams too were cut off and for a few breathless seconds, silence descended before her struggles redoubled.

In the sudden quiet, Jake had felt naked fear. A conviction that The Whistler would hear his pounding heart. Panic overtook him and he had fled, a shadow amidst the deeper shadows in the Hall with which he was so familiar. He'd run with a gawky, loping stride. A tall, emaciated figure with eyes that glittered with fear in a haggard face, headed for the upper levels, the sound of the girl's drumming feet as she died, a distant tattoo.

Now, in the Observatory on the second floor, he sat with his hands around his knees under the huge telescope, rocking back and forth, his voice a barely audible mantra hum.

This was his favourite place in the Planetarium. The wood-panelled walls and the huge heavy iron and brass telescope were imbued with life. He had a name for the dummy with the hat that kept looking through the eyepiece in the hope of seeing a star. Sometimes, as he gazed across the room at the life-size model of the sailing ship *Swift* and its navigation table, he saw it pitch and roll.

The outside world, the one his brother called 'reality' had begun to fade and slip days ago. *This* was Jake's reality; the dummy and his stars, the *Swift*'s never-ending voyage on the ocean. For the third time in consecutive nights he had stayed until the last moment, until the attendants had begun ushering people out. It had been easy to find somewhere to hide in the upper-level renovations. For two nights after the lights had dimmed and the attendants had all made their jokey farewells, he had had the vast halls to himself. He had been free to wander and respond to the questions the stars and planets posed in that echoing voice in his head, without the blatant stares and the strange glances that 'real' people gave him during the day. He walked the exhibits as a pilgrim in this Cathedral of Space, seeking solace in the heavens, all the while hoping for a sign that the voices in his head were there for a purpose. That there was a greater intelligence. And that night, that magical night, it had come. That night the exhibit halls had closed earlier than normal. An event that in itself had helped Jake's purpose in the confusion the announcement brought. There were more people around than normal and it had been easier for him to slip behind the boarded-up area on the second floor. The small army of cleaners had hurried through and Jake had waited for the lights to dim. But this evening they had not. Instead, from the lower levels, a thin trickle of men and women began to appear. They were not like the people that he normally saw in the Planetarium. There were no hordes of riotous children, no open-mouthed tourists. Instead, through cracks in the wooden partition walls, what he saw were men in jackets and ties, the women in cocktail dresses. They wandered amongst the exhibits like exotic birds with a reverence that puzzled and pleased him. They spoke in strange tongues, with accents that matched the crystal glasses they carried from one exhibit to the other. They might have been aliens, or ghosts.

Then, he'd seen their Queen; a pretty girl in a simple black dress and a dogtooth jacket. Unbidden, she walked across the hall and stood opposite where Jake was hidden, inspecting the Observatory exhibit, her back to him. A trim figure with an upright confident posture. She seemed alone, separate from the crowd. As Jake watched, a man approached and spoke to her. They talked for a while, the polite banter of strangers. The man had a sticker on his breast pocket – TECHRIM. An alien name that fitted Jake's perception of these visitors perfectly. After a few moments, the man glanced across the room towards someone waving at him. He excused himself.

'Hope you find who you're looking for,' he said and held out his hand. 'And I hope you enjoy the rest of your trip.'

The girl watched him go and turned towards Jake. It was then he saw that she too had a name. His name.

JACOB – Dr C. Jacob.

In that instant, he knew he was looking at an emissary from another world. A kindred spirit. A Jacob, just as he was a Jacob.

And she was looking for him, that was obvious. Looking for her fellow Jacob to return with him to their world of origin. God, it felt good to know that he had been right all this time. Isolated for all these years amongst a people he had never understood and who had never understood him. Revelation. Vindication.

It was impossible for Jake to explain how ' or why this unshakeable belief arose. It simply existed, intransigent, impregnable to logical discussion or interpretation.

He had watched while the room filled and then emptied as the travellers were ushered up to the Sky show. He waited until it finished and then snuck back down to the Hall of Exploration and out via the stairs adjacent to the freight elevator, noting the trestles in the lobby laden with urns full of coffee and hot chocolate and petits fours. He felt light-headed and exuberant, pacing around the rear of the entry-level building, thinking of all the things he was going to tell her, someone to share all the words that wanted to spill out of his head, words that told of his incredible life, the one only he knew about, far removed from 'reality'; the upbringing on the plains of Eastern Africa and then the tunnelling expedition under the Amazon and the dreadful destruction of his condo in El Salvador (after his true biological mother's death), that had left him with the dust mote in his head. And his designs, the designs that were so 'intricatable' and only understandable by the super-intelligent. There would be so much to tell on their journey home. So much.

He strode backwards and forwards in the shadow of the building, his fantasies rampant, the gale tearing at his tufted hair. After a while, his mood had descended, the euphoria abating into dull despondency. She had failed to communicate any telepathic message all this time. The silence between them stretched into long minutes. It had begun to rain by then, sharp spits of driven water that spiked into his face and through his padded White Sox jacket. He could see the lights above in the lobby, see the faces staring out in wary disbelief as the Chicago night played its capricious mischievous ace. He was beginning to resign himself to mild panic when the first travellers began to emerge. They ran down the steps, their collars turned up, crouching under umbrellas in trench coats, the women in tottering heels as they ran towards Solidarity Drive. Their fellow passengers watched from above, saw how the weather tore at their clothes and threatened to invert the umbrellas and drove them back into the building. Few after that first handful ventured out.

But she had come. The rain died for a moment and she emerged alone, looking vaguely lost, head down against the wind. He watched her leave, sure that she was aware of his presence, wondering when she would give him the signal. If only he had made contact then . . .

Now, as he sat with his hands around his knees, as his tortured mind replayed the events over and over and the dark river of despair that roared in his head rose to a raging torrent of noise, Jake clamped his hands over his ears. He didn't want to hear that white noise. He sat under the telescope choking back the sobs.

See him cry. Crying like a child. The voice was a sneering one tonight. Full of acid mockery that grated and twisted in his head like rusting barbed wire. He felt cheated and frightened and angry and achingly alone. She had come to find him and she had been brutally, horribly hunted down and destroyed.

Bet your life.

He cried for her, big tears of grief spilling off his chin onto his knees. He knew then he had to leave and never come back to this place. Leave before The Whistler found him. But he couldn't go without her.

Go find her. Find her you chicken shit.

It took him almost twenty minutes to get back to the Hall of

Exploration. He tip-toed down the corridors like a man on a thin ledge above a thousand-foot drop, the voice in his head now taunting.

Whistler man is there.

He crept along, his hands flush against the wall feeling his way, his ears alert for even the slightest creak of wood or tick of expanding metal in the walls while all around him, the solid building reverberated dully to the buffeting wind.

Whistler with the big wolf's face and the huge teeth.

Every ten yards he would stop and stand still, listening for several seconds for the high-pitched whine to begin.

It'll jump on him and suck his brains out. Jump on him and suck his brains out of his nostrils.

She was not where he remembered the attack had taken place, but there was evidence of her presence. In the dim light he could see the polished floor slick with her blood. He fell to his knees and ran his fingers through the brown smudges before bringing it to his lips and tasting it. It was like his, warm and salty. He followed the trail back out into the kitchens.

She was naked, stuffed under a steel preparation table like a piece of discarded meat, her limbs awry, her face, that pretty face, swollen and suffused in death. Jake knelt, whimpering now, and pulled her out gently, his mind filled with guilt at what he had allowed to happen here. Her body was cool but not yet cold, heavy in death, flesh and inanimate bone lolling in his hands. Her abdomen was covered in blood that still glistened and stuck wetly to his White Sox jacket as he propped her into a sitting position and held her, rocking, like a child in his arms. Then he stood slowly, bowing under her weight as he carried her inside to the Hall and placed her between the planet booths; Mars, Jupiter, Saturn and the Moon to guard over her soul. He found her clothes discarded in a corner and covered her with the black dress, wiping the blood from between her legs and placing her arms across her chest. From the lapel of her jacket he took her name badge and noticed on the other an elegant pin. A simple red spinel bar brooch which he took as well.

He heard the wind outside again, hissing and moaning around the big building, mocking him with its howls and rattling shutters and windows in its anger. It seemed to be growing in strength and suddenly, paralysingly he was afraid again. More afraid than he had ever been. He held her hand for one last time, mourning his dead Queen. Then he turned and made his way out through the kitchens. He crouched low behind the doors of the exit shelter, hearing the mocking tones in the wind's message. It threatened him with its ululations and its elemental anger in that dark space. Reminding him that The Whistler was out there waiting for him.

That The Whistler was a hunter.

Trembling, he emerged from the exit, his eyes wide, searching, seeing nothing but the looming shadow of the Planetarium dome and the incessant rain.

He scrambled out and crouched, a frightened animal in a hostile environment.

He's here.

Behind him, the wind gusted anew and rattled the doors, whistling through cracks in the framework.

Don't look back.

For once he welcomed the voice's counsel. He ran across the empty car park without a backward glance.

Don't look back or The Whistler will get you.

He ran much as a rabbit might with a hell-hound baying for blood on its tail.

3

'Lou? Lou?'

Lewis Bek clutched the phone automatically to his ear and with both eyes still closed answered in a sleep-laden, bull-frog voice.

'Jake? That you?'

'Lou, please . . . I . . .'

Bek opened one eye and glanced at the bedside clock. 'Hey, Jake, it's two a.m. What's the matter?'

'She's dead, Lou. . . .'

Bek opened the other eye and propped himself up. 'You been having those bad dreams again?'

'The Jacob. The Jacob is dead.'

Bek sighed. 'You're not dead, Jake. How could you be dead and still be talking to me on the phone?'

'The Jacob, Lou. The Whistler. . . .' A sob. 'You have to help me, Lou.'

'Jake, listen to me, you at home? Go get Mom and put her on.'

'She's dead, Lou.'

'Jake, you're beginning to scare me here. I hear street sounds in the background. Where the hell are you?'

'East Twenty-third.'

'East Twenty-third? What the hell you doing there at two a.m? Where've you been?'

'They came tonight, Lou. I saw them arrive, I saw them all arrive. They came to fetch me. They were all dressed up like at a captain's party . . . I was scared. I hid under the planet wall. She touched me . . . Lou, she was looking for me until The Whistler . . . Oh Jesus, Jesus. Her face was so swollen, blood all over her stomach.'

'Where have you been, Jake?'

'The Planetarium.'

'Are you telling me that someone died at the Planetarium?'

15

'She was a Jacob, Lou. Like me. But he smelt us. The Whistler smelt us . . . he's searching us out, Lou. He knew who she was and he's going to find me too. I need you and the other cops to stop him from finding me, Lou. I wanted to help her but I couldn't. The whistle stopped me, I couldn't help it . . . They know I'm phoning you. It'll be in the newspaper tomorrow. He hears what I say to you now. He bounces into my head and sucks it all out. Everything that I know.'

'Jake, this is crazy shit. I want you to go home.'

'I put her neat and tidy, Lou.'

Bek was awake now, his brain fighting to decode Jake's rambling.

'Jake, go home. I'll see you there. Go home.'

'Lou, help me. Will you help me?'

'Yeah, Jake, I'll help. OK. I'll fucking help.'

Bek put his phone down and sat up, his body aching with fatigue, his mind accelerating away from the blissful ignorance of sleep. It was not the first time his brother had rung him in the early hours, but it was the first time he'd heard him so out of control.

No one had offered Bek any explanation of why Jake's fertile imagination fed on the astronomical sciences in general and the Adler Planetarium in particular. In his controlled state, when the drugs kept whatever neurotransmitter imbalance that plagued his brain in check, Jake had been a devotee. At the Adler, the blend of pure science and show-business that softened and sweetened the dry academic message of astronomy was beautifully done. At the Adler, he could examine a real used space suit and then go to fantasy land with Captain Kirk and his crew. Jake had loved it there, the razzmatazz of the skyshows, the moonsuits, the Trekkie homage that had run for so many months.

So, OK, chances were that this was another one of Jake's nightmares, but why did he have such a bad feeling about this one? Jake was out on the street and losing it, maybe had lost it already. Groaning, Bek picked up the phone and dialled the familiar number. It rang half a dozen times before his mother picked up the receiver.

'Mom, it's Lou.'

'Lewis, what is it? What's wrong?' Bek pictured her, hand up to her face, fingers touching her cheek in anxiety. She would have picked up her robe and thrown it on, refusing to have the phone at her bedside, insisting on the old model in the hall that had been there as long as he could remember.

'Where's Jake, Mom?'

'He isn't back yet . . . What is it, Lewis?'

'He just rang me, Mom. He sounded crazy. . . .'

'Lewis, don't say that. . . .'

'How has he been the last few days?'

Her momentary hesitation set alarm bells ringing in Bek's head despite her reassurances. 'He has good days and bad days. I don't need to tell you that, Lewis.'

'Did you ring Keller? He wanted to be told of any change, Mom. This new medication . . .'

'Jake is fine. . . .'

Bek cursed inwardly. 'When he comes home, keep him there.'

'This is his home, Lewis.'

'Mom, just keep him there. I'll come over as soon as I can.'

'You're overreacting, Lewis. . . .'

'Just keep him there, OK?'

He rang off and threw on a shirt with two days worth of sweat rings under the armpits, found his trousers, holster and jacket and left his warm apartment. He had a thermal jacket in the trunk of his car. He hooked it out and put it on before getting into the driver's seat. The Chevy's heater was shot. It was ninetieth on Lou's long list of things that needed doing. It took twenty minutes to heat up enough to even make a difference these days.

Twenty minutes.

By that time, he would be at the Adler. Traffic was two a.m. light and he didn't need to clamp the magnets of the portable bubble to the roof. Thinking about it he realised he probably wouldn't have anyway. OK, he had his badge, but this would be family business until or unless it had to be otherwise.

Family business. Bek snorted.

Lou had been sixteen when it first happened; Jake had been thirteen and a half. Jake had always been a joker, what happened had at first seemed like nothing more than Jake's exuberance getting a little out of hand. In the ninth grade, his persistently anarchic behaviour had his classmates in fits of laughter as he scampered around the room on all fours making animal noises, but the teachers saw it all in a different light. His disruptive behaviour and his tendency to indulge in regaling anyone who would listen with fantastic stories in which he would play as many as a dozen parts each with its own voice, led to a psychological evaluation. The term 'fragmented ego structure' was one that Lou would always remember. It was the first in a whole list of terms which he didn't at first understand but which added up to his brother's slow, inexorable fall into chaos.

At the beginning, Jake slept well, but as Lou's teenage years advanced, Jake became a creature of the night, wandering around, obsessed with the multitude of pulp Space fiction that Hollywood began turning out in the late seventies with spectacular success. It was not uncommon for Jake to wake Lou up to show him his latest 'invention' made of balsawood and broken watch parts. Lou would have to sit and listen, his eyes half open while Jake explained and justified his design with pages of complex mathematics which consisted usually of nothing more than simple repetitions of basic addition, multiplication and division.

Sometimes, Jake would need something, a 'phase modulating synchroniser', or a 'matter transducer' and Lou knew that no one would get any sleep until he found some suitably obscure tool in the garage which would satiate Jake's bizarre imagining. But Lou would always find *something*. Jake was his brother and that was all there was to it.

It was only much later that they started understanding that Jake's head told him to do things that he had no control over. That what they'd seen had been schizotypal behaviour. But for weeks after that first incident when Jake had been removed from his school barking like a dog to the delight of all his classmates, Lou had quietly cursed Jake on all counts. As if the social embarrassment of the act wasn't enough, he had to go and get himself diagnosed as suffering from a mental disease. Lou's love for his brother made him despise those misguided and disloyal thoughts. But still they haunted him, fizzed away on a slow fuse inside Lou everywhere he went. Were still fizzing away, even now as Lou approached the lake.

The Adler Planetarium's listed address was 1300 South Lake Shore Drive. It sat at the end of a finger of Chicago shore that jutted out accusingly into Lake Michigan, linked to Lake Shore Drive by the looping spur of Solidarity Drive.

To the south, the tower of Merril C. Meig airfield sparkled. Not a busy airport, but its proximity to Downtown had attracted a couple of major airlines that ran successful shuttles to and from the Midwest. To the north, the lights of Navy Pier blinked through the trees as Lou headed east on the finger. Behind to the west, the

Chicago skyline peered down, dominated by all 96 floors of the John Hancock building. But ahead to the east, there was nothing but the black waters of the lake and the ever-present threat of the weather coming off it.

Lou parked in the lot, got out of his car and stared up at the rain that was driving across the ground between the lake and Planetarium in horizontal sheets. He was not a tall figure, his battle with booze and pizza gaining the upper hand in the form of a moderate gut. His gaze took in a street light as the road looped round the rear of the building. The rain danced and weaved against the light like a shoal of startled sardines as the wind tore outwards in howling gusts. Beyond, to the left, at the edge of a poorly lit parking lot, some stunted trees bowed and scraped to the squall's raw command. Further out was the black vastness of the water. It was a desolate spot at two-thirty on a November morning.

He hurried towards the building after noting that there were only three other cars in the lot at this ungodly hour. Two of them were vans with the Planetarium's logo and phone number on their sides. He walked up the steps to the main entrance, found it locked and heard no response to his knocks and rattles of the door. From there, he circled the building on foot twice and found nothing. Shrugging, he headed back towards his car. He was ten yards away when the beam of his flashlight picked out the wet shape of a woman's black pump in a pool of water. He walked over and squatted on his haunches, not touching it, letting his eyes follow the logical line to the nearest structure. Rain pooled in slick puddles everywhere. A gust of wind tore at his face as he got up and wandered over to the glass shelter of the exit. He allowed himself the luxury of thinking that maybe some kids had thrown the shoe out of a schoolbus window. It sounded unconvincing. When he reached the shelter, he shone the flashlight into the blackness of the stairwell and there, at the bottom, he could make out the shape of a second shoe. It lay on its side, like the first; a black pump with a two-inch heel. It was then that Lou's gut rippled with the first stirrings of real anxiety.

He pushed gingerly on the door and wasn't totally surprised to find it open. He pulled his gun and slipped down with practised stealth. He knelt and shone the beam directly on the shoe. The label pasted to the insole said that it was a size five and that the manufacturer was Russell and Bromley, London. So these were English shoes, OK, but where were the feet that should have been in them?

He flashed the beam around. He was in a large open room stacked with boxes and cleaning equipment. And then his flashlight picked out the streak of drying black blood. It started a few inches off the floor and ran up as a dark smudge to about hip level. There was a bloody handprint on the wall and on the first and second door handles. Bek fished out a paper napkin from his trouser pocket and using one finger, depressed the lever on both doors in turn. The first one was locked, the second swung silently inwards into a kitchen. Someone had been through the place either in a hurry, or with violent intent. Big stainless-steel ladles and spoons lay on the floor with upturned cauldrons and pots. There were blood stains in long smudges over the tiled floor and more pooled under a preparation table in the middle of the room. It was as he was kneeling down to inspect the area that he heard the door at the far end of the room creak open and the beam of a powerful flashlight caught him square in the eyes, blinding him.

'Don't move,' said the voice above him. 'I have a gun.'

Reflexively, he fell into a crouch behind the preparation table and yelled, 'Police.'

'Put the gun down and lay on your stomach,' ordered the voice.

'Listen, man,' protested Bek.

'On your stomach, legs spread.'

Reluctantly, Bek capitulated and heard a metallic scrape as his gun was kicked away.

'Now, nice and slow, show me your badge.'

With one hand, Bek reached for his shield from his back pocket and felt it snatched away from him. He saw the beam waver as it was inspected.

'OK. Roll over and let me get a look at you, detective.'

Bek rolled and squinted against the full force of the beam in his face.

'You can get up, now,' said the voice.

Bek stood and brushed himself down, retrieving first his shield and then his gun.

'Sorry about that . . .'

'Could you get that thing out of my face?' said Bek. 'There any lights?'

The flashlight wavered and wobbled away. Then the kitchen was filled with light from three big overhead fluorescents. Bek finally got a look at the guy. He wore the blue serge trousers, grey shirt and blue tie of a security guard. He was black with a grizzled moustache and still held a small snub-nosed revolver loosely in his hand.

'Mind putting that thing away?' asked Bek.

'Sure. Saw your light from outside. Figured you were doing something you shouldn't have been.'

'I got a call half an hour ago. Guy said something bad was going down here.'

'Here at the Adler?' the guard smiled. 'I been here ten years and I've never seen anything. . . .'

Bek pointed to the pool of brown liquid under the table.

'That isn't coffee under there.'

The guard stared at the stain.

'The door outside is open, you know about that?'

'No,' the guard was defensive now. 'Caterers may have left it open. Caterers are always leaving doors open. It was shut when I came on duty, that's all I can tell you.'

'What time was that?'

'Ten-thirty.'

Bek gave him a sour look. 'Looks like someone got in that way,' he said.

'Isn't anything here worth stealing 'cept some moonrock.'

'I don't think whoever was in here was a thief,' said Bek. 'We better take a look around. Careful where you step now.'

The guard led the way in, Bek dripping rain after him. It wasn't a difficult trail to follow. From the pattern of the bloody skid marks, it looked as if something had been dragged in and then out of the kitchen. In a moment, they stood at the entrance to the Hall of Space Exploration. The guard flicked on the light switch.

'Doesn't look like much has been messed with in here,' said the guard moving off. 'Least ways nothing I can make . . .' He stopped short of finishing his observation and Bek heard a muffled expulsion of breath.

'What?' he barked.

'Sweet Jesus. . . .' was all the guard managed.

Bek joined him behind the planet booths. She lay on her back, clothes covering her like sheets, her face exposed, the head tilted at an angle so that her eyes looked upwards towards the ceiling. The face was swollen, the lips bruised and misshapen, the eyelids puffed, the nose ugly and broken.

'What the hell happened to her face?' asked the guard, his

21

voice high-pitched, his eyes staring from a face furrowed with disgust.

Bek felt his own heart beating in his chest, felt his throat constricting. 'She's been beaten and strangled. Get to a phone, OK? And don't touch anything. You got that?' Bek's voice echoed in the huge room.

The guard walked shakily across to a small office, muttering to himself. As he dialled 911, he turned back to stare at the cop. He was leaning against one of the booths, one hand out to support himself, the other entwined in the thin hair that covered his head, his face a mask of pain, as if mourning a long-lost friend. The sight of the corpse had unnerved the guard, but he'd never seen this kind of reaction from a cop before. And they said that cops had no feelings?

Fifteen minutes later, the night homicide team turned up. Bek had spent most of the time pacing backwards and forwards along the corridor outside the Hall of Exploration. He didn't want to be inside, didn't want to see the girl's blackened face or the dirty bruises on her body. The guard had been bold enough to stick his head around inquisitively once.

'Don't you want to start doing something?' he had asked.

Bek had turned on him.

'Listen, Columbo, we don't touch anything until the crime lab gets here, you understand that?' Bek's finger was pointing accusingly.

'I could ring the catering people if you like. See if they know anything.'

'Just keep out of it, you hear?' Bek was shouting, his frayed nerves close to spontaneous combustion.

'OK, OK. Jesus, who the hell rattled your cage?' The guard had wandered off, muttering, leaving Bek to work out a way of getting out of there as quickly as possible.

And as the night dicks breezed on, Bek had his story set. Sergeant Mike Gibbon ran a health food store called The Nut House with his brother by day. He'd opted for the night shift for the last three years and despite the hours, he looked fitter and leaner than Bek had in ten years despite only six months of difference in their ages.

'Hey, Lou, what you got for us?' asked Gibbon.

'You seen her?'

'Sure. ME's taking a peek right now, but my guess is rape strangulation.'

'I took an anonymous call at two a.m. Not one of my regular snitches and I don't know how he got my number. Said there was a dead girl at the Adler. Sounded flaky but . . .'

'Think it was the perp having pangs of guilt?'

'Maybe, who the hell knows, right?' He massaged his stomach and grimaced.

'What is it, Lou, you OK? Come to think of it you don't look so hot.'

Bek was faking the pain, but the film of sweat on his brow was real enough.

'Think I picked up a bad chilli dog from that Guatemalan place over on Clark.'

'You want some Pepto? I got some in the car. . . .'

'No, it's worse than that. I need a favour, Mike. The guard saw everything I did. You think maybe I could get out of here? I'll pick it all up in the morning. Truth is I think I'm gonna throw up any minute.'

'Go,' said Gibbon with a wave of his hand. 'ME will be half an hour, crime lab another forty minutes. Ring me in the a.m. around eight. I'll be at home. I'll brief you then.' Gibbon's face was full of concern. 'Lou, you look terrible.'

'I'll be fine,' said Bek over his shoulder.

Yellow police tape had cordoned off the scene and he had to thread his way through half a dozen uniforms who were there because it was dry and warm and beat the hell out of being on the street on such a filthy night. He left via the lobby and was about to push open the door when he heard a shout from Gibbon behind him.

'Lou, we've got an ID.'

'Yeah?'

'The mark is an MD name of Jacob. Dr C. Jacob. Has a British Medical Association ID card. Shot in the back, strangled and raped.'

Bek squeezed his eyes shut.

'Sorry, Lou,' said Gibbon. 'Just thought you'd want to know.'

Bek waved and pushed open the door. He felt his breath coming in gasps. As if to give truth to his lies, he suddenly did feel nauseous, his mind spinning.

He ran to his car, head bowed against the rain, but still it found its way into his eyes and down his neck. It kissed his skin with freezing wetness. A corpse's kiss. He leaned against the car door and vomited until bitter bile filled his throat. Finally, he got into the car, feeling his armpits damp with sweat that had nothing to do with his run across the car park. He squeezed his eyes shut, praying in the darkness that when he opened them again he would see the cheap Chinese willow-patterned wallpaper of his apartment. Instead, the waving branches of the trees writhed like black snakes on the other side of the parking lot and he knew it was all for real.

Breathing hard, he gunned the engine and roared away until he saw a phone-booth. His mother answered on the third ring.

'Is he back yet?' gasped Bek.

'Lewis?' Her voice was trembling and odd. 'Yes. Jake is here now.'

'How is he?' His concern was for her, not for his brother.

'Your brother . . .' she paused, 'I need you to come over.'

'Keep him there.'

'Lewis . . .'

'Just keep him there.'

Two minutes later, Bek was on the up ramp of I 94 on the 43rd Street entrance, heading south on the Dan Ryan expressway. Heading home.

4

BEK PULLED IN to his mother's driveway without any recollection of the journey along the expressway, or the streets that led to 103rd and western at the edge of Evergreen Park on the borders of south and east Chicago.

One thought, and one thought alone had preoccupied him on the drive down: that Jake was tied up in a homicide.

He stopped it there, not letting it go any further than that. Not allowing himself to consider the possibility that Jake had actually . . .

A wave of self-loathing at these shabby thoughts washed over him like the tide on some polluted shore. Thinking of Jake did that to him. Thinking of what Jake had become. Whenever he did, the memory of what Jake *used* to be kept coming back. And all the anger and frustration and cursing would give way to a deep, desperate yearning for what could never be. Remembering the roguish, exuberant Jake of old always gutted him. No matter what happened, Jake was still his brother, wasn't he? *Well, wasn't he?*

He sat and stared at his mother's house; a solid, three-bedroom greystone in an area where they still managed to keep the streets clean and the residents held tenaciously on to old Eastern European village traditions. With a sigh, Bek got out of the car. The garage door stood open, Jake's beaten-up blue Mazda sitting squatly inside with a hint of warmth on the hood and the occasional popping tick from the still hot engine beneath. He opened the driver's side. Slick brown smudges of blood glistened on the wheel, on the handle, on the seat.

'Sweet Jesus,' he whispered to himself.

He got out and entered the house through the side door. It was after three-thirty a.m., the very middle of the night. The dark houses around showed no sign of life and as he stepped across the threshold, he felt suddenly, utterly alone. He was no stranger to this feeling. It had visited him often in the small hours, even when there was someone to share his bed. He could never explain the reason for his loneliness to anyone. It was a complex amalgam of grief and anger inextricably tied up with his responsibility towards Jake. He was alone because Jake was not really there any more and his absence was a dark foreboding shadow that hovered always in the recesses of Bek's mind. All he really *knew* was that the ache inside burned there like an ulcer in his gut, flaring sometimes into a red angry pain.

Inside, he could hear his brother's voice coming from the bedroom. Loud, exuberant, impassioned for the moment. He knew that within seconds it might plummet into a secretive whisper for no good reason.

Bek made no noise, but stepped into the bathroom. Clothes floated in the tub in a swirl of pink liquid. A sleeve from a JC Penny shirt had clogged the bath plug. He leaned in and shut off the faucet. In the sudden silence, his brother's voice sounded louder.

He picked up a toothbrush from the rack above the sink and held the bristled end as he used the handle to tease out the tangle of pants, shirt and a Cubs sweat shirt. The sweat shirt should have been royal blue. Now it was a stained plum colour, mottled and splashed with congealed blood.

Flecks and droplets of pink water had splashed up the side of the tub from the faucet's gush. Cold water for blood stains. He could hear his mother saying it. One of the rules by which she lived and she lived by a thousand of them. They had helped her survive and he had never questioned them. They were all part of her, his, *their* existence.

She'd stripped Jake as soon as he had walked in through the door. Stripped him and piled the clothes into the bathtub and him into the shower before allowing herself to think of the implications. That was her way, of that he had no doubt. Strong-willed, single-minded, even in the face of impending disaster. Disaster. The word echoed in his head. Yeah, that was what this was. He ground his teeth together.

'*Shit.*'

This was a mess. A God-awful mess. He stared down at the clothes again and felt the room begin to close down on him. For a moment, his anger evaporated and fear crept back in its place. He slumped onto the toilet seat and let his head fall into his hands. He looked up at the four walls of the spotless bathroom he himself had repainted not twelve months before. He had sat on this seat a thousand times and seen the walls green then blue then yellow and now eggshell rose. He was bound to this room and this house with ropes of devotion that were a hundred times stronger than steel, but suddenly he felt that they were choking him to death, drowning all sense of right and wrong in a sea of confusion.

Outside in the freezing November air there was tomorrow and the rest of the world. Inside there was now. And in the now were the bonds that had held him and his family together for forty years, the last twelve of them without Art Bek, the head of the family – Lou's friend and ally in the great battle.

He pushed himself up, the sudden movement, the proximity of the ceiling lamp to his eyes and the spacy feeling that came with the hour sending a sudden pain through his head. He put two fingers to his temples and squeezed. The pain seemed set to blow his skull open. He pressed his fingers inward until the pressure hurt more than the pain inside and then let go.

His mother was in the kitchen, a slight figure in a candlewick robe and long straight grey hair which was only ever let down at night. Sometimes Lou worried that if she went outside, the wind might blow her away like a piece of thin ribbon. She confronted him now with her lips compressed and her face set for the fray.

'He was in a fight, wasn't he?' Her tone was dismissive, making light of it all.

'It wasn't a fight,' said Bek.

'He doesn't lie to me, Lewis.'

Bek snorted, 'He doesn't know what the truth means, Mom. Haven't you got that yet, after all these years?'

She shook her head and smiled sadly. 'You cannot say that. His truth might be the only real truth. He sees what he sees, hears what he hears. What he knows might be beyond our understanding.'

'So now you're telling me you believe him? You think he really had dinner with a delegation from Jupiter or some Goddamn place? There's a dead girl at the Planetarium.' He made to move past her but she stepped in his path and put her small hand on his arm and squeezed.

'He is your brother,' she whispered harshly.

Bek shook his head and bit back a retort. He didn't need any reminders, but this was not the time for another tired argument. He pulled her hand away, but did it gently. 'He needs help, Mom. Maybe we should call Dr Keller right away.'

'I spoke to Dr Keller two days ago.'

'What did he say?'

His mother looked away. 'He said the long-acting drugs take a while to adjust to. It's been three weeks since his last dose. He didn't want to boost it just yet.'

Great, thought Bek. And in the meantime we have to sit back, watch him go ape-shit.

'Fine. Let me talk to Jake alone, OK?'

Bek walked into the bedroom remembering the conversation he himself had had with Jake's psychiatrist two months before. The efficacy of his medication had waned over the hot summer and Jake's progressive lack of insight had led to poor compliance. The answer was, according to Keller, injected depot preparations. Long-acting phenothiazines that were meant to exert control for up to a month at a time. Keller was keen to try a new one, a piperazine just on the market. But they would have to monitor it closely for the first month or two, he had said.

Jake sat hunched in the corner, his knees drawn up, staring about him like a visitor from a far country. Occasionally, a tiny smile crossed his face and he laughed softly, his eyes darting from one place to another as he communicated with whoever or whatever he imagined he heard or saw.

'What happened, Jake?'

Jake cocked his head.

'Tonight. What happened?'

'The Whistler . . .'

Bek saw his mother slide past him with surprising speed. He saw her hand come up and crack across Jake's head with a resounding slap.

'Jacob,' his mother's voice crackled with anger, 'answer your brother, do you hear?'

Jake whimpered and Bek squeezed his eyes shut, thinking for the hundredth time that his mother had been looking after Jake for too long. She had accepted the responsibility without question, but Bek was never sure how well she had accepted the illness. The emotional toll had been great and Bek had an uncomfortable conviction that there had been a mental one too. She was torn in her reactions to Jake's disease. One minute understanding and excusing, the next dismissive and over-reactive, treating him like a child in a man's body.

'That isn't going to help, Mom.' He stood and pulled her back, firm but gentle. Then, he knelt in front of Jake and held his face, putting his own near to his brother's. 'Jake, I'm sorry. I'm really sorry. But you have to talk to me.'

Jake's eyes slid away and he turned his face to the wall. Bek sat back on the bed, his expression heavy with defeat. His mother stood in the doorway. Light from the living room threw her face into silhouette, making her expression unreadable. Bek looked back at Jake, but his words were aimed at his mother.

'He's ill.'

'Lewis, you are sure . . .' she began in a small, contrite voice. It fell on Bek's ears with tinkling familiarity. Her voice was still thick with the accent she'd brought with her fifty years before from the ghettos of Warsaw. But all he could do was shake his head and laugh mirthlessly. In the quiet bedroom it sounded more like a cackle.

'He called me, Mom. He rang me and told me somebody had killed Jacob. He fixated on some poor girl with the same name as his. Jesus, you saw the blood too, didn't you?'

She stared at him defiantly.

'Didn't you?' he insisted.

This time she flinched from his words and he found himself regretting the anger.

'I'm going to ring Keller, now.' Bek got up and started towards the door.

She grabbed his hand, clutching it in both of hers and turning her face up to his.

'Lewis, this is your brother. Your beautiful little brother . . .' He looked across at Jake. He'd tried cutting his own hair and the result had been patchy with several thin spots that were only just filling in. He was rake thin, hollow-faced, ears too big for his gaunt features. The hair and the dark haunted eyes lent him the look of some crazed, rabid dog.

'Look at him, Lewis. My beautiful boy. He can't help himself. He doesn't know how lucky he has been to have a brother like you.'

Bek squeezed his eyes shut, her words contradicting her own actions of a moment ago. He didn't want to hear any of this. They had both lived with Jake's schizophrenia for many long years and they had both heard Keller's warning that its brittle nature in Jake's case made an acute relapse possible, despite full and expert medication. But the pleading in his mother's expression checked Bek's progress and he turned back towards the bed. Jake watched him approach with wary, slitted eyes.

'Hey, Jake.' He paused momentarily, hating himself for sounding too patronising. 'So what happened?'

Jake frowned and half turned his face away.

'What happened, Jake?' Bek asked again.

'You're good. You even look like him.' The voice was sly and grudging.

'Look like who, Jake?'

'Like Lewis.'

'It is Lewis, Jake,' said his mother, irritation threatening to erupt again.

Jake smiled and shook his head. 'He sounds like Lewis. He looks like Lewis, but he isn't Lewis. You know that. You know that because you brought him here.'

Bek stared. This was new stuff. Added to all the rest, it was scary. 'He doesn't even know us. How long has this been going on?'

'A few days. He often has a bad couple of days.'

'Why didn't you tell me?'

'You're busy, Lewis. You're a busy man.'

'Mom, for Chrissakes.' Lewis turned to Jake. 'Jake, listen to me, what happened tonight?'

Their mother answered. 'He went to the Planetarium. The Comet Collision show.'

Bek felt as if the skin was crinkling and beginning to peel off his neck. He tried to keep his voice even. 'He drove there and back?'

'He has a permit, Lewis.'

Bek nodded, forcing himself to remember that just last week they had celebrated the fact that Jake had held down a job as a packer in the basement of the Save on Bags warehouse in Hinkley for two years. It had killed Bek to know that his brother had an IQ fifty points higher than the guy he worked for, but hell, it was a job.

He turned to his mother, his face full of sick, sad emotion.

Jake began speaking again, answering Lewis' initial question, but speaking softly and almost to himself.

'Whistler came, he could smell her, sense her with his whistling. He had a Chariot of light. I watched her break the door open. She was so pretty and a Jacob.' He was crying now, big salty tears running down his face. 'I went to her and saw what was done but there were no communicators and The Whistler stopped me.'

'Jesus,' said Bek hopelessly. He got up and walked out of the bedroom. 'We have to tell Keller. I have to call it in . . .' Jake stood then, his face suddenly full of terror.

'Where is my mother?'

'Jake sit down.'

Jake sat warily, his eyes shifting between Bek and his mother's face.

'Will he be locked up?' she asked suddenly.

'A girl is dead,' explained Bek slowly.

'People die in this city every day for a hundred petty reasons. Jake can't help himself. To him this is no different to taking a walk on the beach.' She spat out the words, an ugly expression on her mouth.

'Mom . . .' said Bek warningly.

'I have stood in this room and heard you promise that you would help me keep him out of that place. I have heard you promise your brother. Doesn't that mean anything to you, Lewis?'

Bek stared across at Jake, but his mother wouldn't let go. 'And don't bring what you do into this. This is family business,' her voice was hard, her eyes shining.

'He's a danger to you and other people, Goddamnit. Can't you see that?' he said.

His mother pulled herself erect. Five feet six inches of will-power in a candlewick robe.

'Jake loves his mother,' she said above him. 'This will pass. He will be well again. These things he says, they are all in his head. If you listen, really listen . . .' She saw the sad doubt in Bek's face and her anger flared. 'He is a good person, Lewis. Doesn't that count for anything?'

Before Bek could answer, he saw movement out of the corner of his eye as Jake suddenly stood and loped towards the door. Bek lunged for him and grabbed him in a tenuous hug, ripping Jake's shirt, feeling a fist plough achingly into his ribs. In seconds, it had escalated into an ungainly, vicious brawl, Jake like an animal, scratching, kicking, wild.

'Mom, ring for help, you hear me?' yelled Bek breathlessly over his shoulder. She was watching them struggle, obviously in two minds as to what to do. They were in the corner of the room now, Bek trying to pin his brother to the wall with his hands, but Jake was wiry and strong, filled with a desperate strength.

'Get help, Mom. He's gone crazy.'

But she was coming across the room, her face drawn and white, her hand outstretched as if to try and calm the beast that Jake had become.

31

'No, Mom, no. Don't come over here,' yelled Bek, 'you can't do anything.'

One of Jake's legs lashed out, catching her on the hip. She fell back across the room and onto the edge of the bed. There was a loud crack of snapping bone and a heavy thump as her head hit the wall. Bek let go of Jake and ran across to her. She'd yanked the bedsheets off as she'd fallen and they lay scattered on the floor half covering her slumped form.

'Mom, Mom!' He fell to his knees and heard her moan. He didn't see the chair until the last moment. Its legs smashed into his shoulder and head, sending him sprawling with a dull ringing in his ears.

He felt his weight collapse onto his mother, heard a sickening scrunch before her scream. He tried to get up, but his struggles brought fresh groans from her. He got onto his elbows groggily, his breath coming in ragged heaves as, from the direction of the garage, he heard a car start up.

'Jake,' he yelled, but as he made to stand, he heard his mother groan again and he knelt, gingerly taking the covers off. One leg was bent under her, the other was straight out, but the angle of the foot was all wrong, turned almost backwards on itself. The sight of her foot brought bile to his throat, but she pulled his face down close to hers, her voice weak with pain and shock.

'Lewis, I'm an old woman. He pushed me, just a little push. My balance is not what it was,'

'Jesus, Mom.'

'I think my leg is broken.'

Lewis glanced at the foot and felt like screaming out at her.

You bet your ass it's broken.

'Where is Jake?'

'He's gone.'

He saw her face contort with pain.

'I'm going to call for an ambulance.'

He felt her grab his jacket. Her grip was not hard, but he knew what an effort of will it was for her to hang on and he stayed where he was, pinned by the gaze of her washed-out blue eyes.

'He is your brother, Lewis. He loves you in his way. I didn't mean to hit him.'

He nodded sickly, his eyes closed, tears pooling there.

'If I die, you will look after him. Promise me that?'

'You're not going to die, Mom.' Bek gritted his teeth.

'Promise me.'

'I promise,' he hissed. 'Now, *please* let me get an ambulance.' She let him go then, sinking back onto the floor, her voice paper thin. 'You're a good boy, Lewis. Always such a good boy.'

5

D R RHYS JACOB stood back from the incubator and admired his handiwork. Could he come and put up an IV? the Special Care Baby Unit had asked. Of course, he'd replied and the tiny butterfly needle was, at last, taped to the baby's foot. A nurse fed the infusion tube into the casing of a Danby-DCR volume infusion pump and turned on the small reciprocating shuttle that drove the fluid. Its steady rhythmic beeping confirmed that the needle's plastic cannula was indeed in baby Liam's vein.

His armpits were damp as he stripped off his gloves and tossed them expertly into a nearby bin. There was pure concentrated anxiety in that sweat. And he had sweated the whole of the twenty-five minutes it had taken him to put up that IV. He fished out a pen from the pocket of his white coat slung over a nearby chair and glanced about the SCBU before letting his eyes come to rest on the incubator that baby Liam Andrews was occupying. He lay, twenty-nine weeks old, plucked from his mother's womb twelve weeks early, wizened and wrinkled but alive and well in a room full of similar medical miracles.

In mitigation, Rhys knew that in two months time he would have completed that same simple task in one-tenth of the time. He'd learned in the six years since qualifying that it was always thus; the nuts and bolts of medicine were learned on the job. And there was some consolation in the realisation that there were few things he had so far attempted that had defeated him.

Around him, half a dozen quietly efficient nurses attended to the incubators. A Chinese girl with a West Country accent had stood and calmly watched his efforts without commenting and he was grateful for her patience. However clumsy she had found his ministrations, she was that rare, wise animal who knew that the difference between observing and doing was huge. Nurses were not expected to perform the duty themselves, but many became armchair physicians of the most intolerant kind and bristled with impatience at inexperienced doctors. New senior house officers appeared once every six months and he knew that some never got the hang of sticking the prems.

He wrote up the fluid chart before donning his white coat and leaving the SCBU. One wall was adorned with Polaroid prints of the children that had been through the unit and grown into normal, healthy toddlers. The predominant colour of the walls was pink, and dotted here and there were Health Education posters advertising the benefits of immunisation against the panoply of childhood illnesses, brazenly manipulative in their use of doe-eyed innocent children in their efforts at getting messages across. He still wasn't used to the quiet, environmentally controlled atmosphere of the place yet. These premature infants were in a way a daunting medical challenge but he had another five and a half months to get used to it, he mused. As usual this early into a job, he couldn't quite decide if he was going to enjoy it or not. It was very different from the twelve months' psychiatry he'd just done. But then, the psychiatry had seemed light years away from the O & G he had done prior to that.

He quashed the doubts by reminding himself that this was the last leg of a long journey; a sustaining thought during his long hours of duty. Once this six months was over he would have completed the hospital side of the mandatory three years vocational General Practice training.

Since qualifying, Rhys had been driven by a burning ambition to get from A to B as quickly as possible. The end point of this journey was a spot in General Practice somewhere. At present, after twenty-eight years, he had no real idea where that somewhere was. As long as he was there doing his own thing and being his own man it really didn't matter.

In his heart, there nestled just the smallest shadow of a doubt. The one that suggested that perhaps it might not be such a terribly bad thing to take a year out, have a look around before committing himself to a life of General Practice. One that also suggested that perhaps there might be an alternative to this straight and narrow path he had chosen. But prevarication was not his style. These were thoughts that were fleeting and largely ignored. He was a driven man, moulded by an upbringing which demanded success as a means of survival and a ticket to a different life and broader horizons.

Since Emma and he had split up nine months before, this vague

35

wanderlust had all but faded into nothingness. It was she who had really cultivated the little germ of doubt. She who had almost convinced him that a working trip around Australia and New Zealand would do no harm to his career prospects. But that was quick water under a high bridge by now. Without anyone else's wishes to consider, Rhys was pressing on with his head down; he wanted his master's ticket and he wanted it as soon as possible. He had given little thought to anything beyond that.

Emma had accused him of pusillanimity and lacking spontaneity both in his expression of feeling and his attitude to life. He had fretted, hurt by an attack on his character. But since their break-up, he'd fallen back into old, comfortable ways. When he and Emma spoke these days, it was with the polite disinterest of ex-lovers, not as friends.

One day, he supposed, there would be a mortgage and kids and a Volvo but they were over his horizon. He was still unfashionably committed to medicine and his personal life was something that either happened or didn't.

His pager went off as he neared the doctors' mess. He read off the number and gingerly touched a kettle sitting on a table at the rear of the newspaper-strewn room. It felt reasonably hot and he poured himself a lukewarm cup of coffee before answering the paged number. Wendy, the paediatric ward clerk, answered on the third ring.

'Hi, it's Rhys.'

'Two gentlemen to see you. They look terribly official, so don't dawdle.'

'You intrigue me.'

'Flat feet and truncheons, you know the type?' she whispered.

'Really?' he whispered back.

She mumbled something mildly derogatory, but Rhys had already put the phone down. He wasn't the slightest bit perturbed by Wendy's news. His previous job in St Anthony's psychiatric hospital – a mere stone's throw away from the high-rise block he currently worked in – had, almost by definition, brought him into frequent contact with criminal behaviour. He had been interviewed by the police on numerous occasions during their investigations into minor disturbances of the peace, assaults and occasionally drug-related offences involving individuals in his care. And just because he'd left St Anthony's three weeks before for the panoramic views offered by the Gloucester Infirmary, didn't mean that the wheels of the county court had stopped grinding.

He breezed into the ward and almost tripped over a tiny little girl of four in Jurassic Park pyjamas pushing a dilapidated pram containing a mutilated doll. The little girl, whose name badge announced her as Rosanne, wore an eye patch stuck on with Sellotape.

'I thought you were supposed to be having your operation this afternoon?' asked Rhys.

'I've 'ad it, silly,' she said pointing to the pad.

'Oh. I see. What about a rest in bed?'

'Bored. Can I take the pad off?'

'No. Not 'til the morning.'

'Pleeease.'

'I'll be shot.' Rhys feigned a bullet in the chest.

Rosanne giggled and shot up the corridor at a rate of knots towards the play room.

He stuck his head around the duty office door and saw an apple-cheeked Wendy filing notes. An efficient mother of four, she was the ideal liaison between hard-pressed staff and anxious parents and sick kids. She took it all in her comely stride, organising ward outings, Christmas parties and leaving do's with good humour and pleasure.

'Where are they then?' asked Rhys.

'In Sister's office. Why aren't you worried?' There seemed a genuine twinge of anxiety in her voice.

Rhys laughed. 'The innocent have nothing to fear,' he announced dramatically and favoured Wendy with a knowing stare under lowered eyebrows.

Both men stood as Rhys entered. He was mildly surprised to see that they were both plain-clothed.

The taller of the two, rake thin and stooping with sparse hair and heavy lids, said, 'Dr Jacob?'

'That's right.'

The policeman held out his hand. 'I'm Superintendent Gilby and this is Detective Constable Canton of Gloucester CID. Thank you for coming so promptly.'

Rhys nodded and sat in one of the office's uncomfortable blue vinyl-covered chairs.

'I'll come straight to the point, doctor. You have a sister by the name of Catrin Jacob, Dr Catrin Jacob?'

'Yes, I do.'

'Your sister has been attending a medical conference in Chicago?'

The first dim rumblings of anxiety began dragging at Rhys's gut then. This was not what he had expected. He'd anticipated having to give a statement on the mental state of some junkie up for disorderly conduct or a bout of shoplifting from one of the manic-depressives.

'Look, what's all this about?'

Gilby was doing all the talking. 'Sir, we received a call this morning from the consular department at the Foreign Office. I'm afraid it was bad news.'

'An accident?'

'I'm afraid it's worse, sir. There isn't any easy way to say this so I won't try.' He paused and then said, 'Your sister is dead, Doctor Jacob.'

Rhys stared, feeling an inappropriate smile crawl over his face. This was surely a setup, wasn't it? Candid camera? A scam thought up by someone from the mess? Loomis, maybe. He was always fooling around with diuretics in your tea, plastic turds in the take-away. One of these serious men was Loomis's brother, surely? Setting up old conscientious Rhys Jacob for a big laugh. Drag him up to the ward and tell him his sister is dead. Ha, ha, ha. Huge hoot that. Any moment now, some patronising berk in a false beard and wig was going to come in through the door and pretend to deliver some mail before thrusting a microphone into Rhys's face and grinning, wasn't he?

But why weren't they smiling back at him? Surely they could see that he had twigged.

Stop the joke now, gentlemen, it's gone far enough . . .

But the room stayed silent as Gilby and Canton stared at him with expressions that held nothing but ragged sorrow.

'Dead?' whispered Rhys, his eyes at odds with the inappropriate smile.

Gilby nodded slowly. 'Details are sketchy, sir, but there is no doubt that foul play is suspected. Chicago are treating it very definitely as a murder investigation.'

Rhys felt his chest suck the stale air from the room into his lungs. He felt suddenly as if the inhalation would never stop until his lungs might burst. But finally it peaked and reversed itself in a trembling exhalation. Gilby told Rhys as much as he knew. It was patchy and sparse and most of it sped effortlessly passed Rhys's ringing ears.

Things seemed oddly out of focus, all his senses numbed, the room dull and flat, the policemen shadowy figures from his imagination as the shock set in. There were a hundred questions he knew he should ask, but his brain had stalled. Fragments of memory kept surfacing. He still had his sister's jump leads. He had meant to give them back months ago but they were still in the boot of his car with the WD40 and a spare set of plugs. Why the hell hadn't he given the damn things back! He chided himself; jump leads weren't important. But at that precise moment, they seemed the most important thing in the world. Something left undone, something he regretted not doing as part of his relationship with Catrin.

The now dead Catrin.

The policemen left fifteen minutes later after some easily forgotten words of condolence and written instructions for Rhys which contained contact numbers in London. Rhys sat, stunned and numb on the chair staring at a wall-planner dotted with uneven rows of coloured adhesive stickers denoting staff leave, barely aware of their departure, nodding a cursory thanks in their direction.

After a long moment, Wendy put her head round the door. Her mischievous face fell at the sight of him.

'Rhys? You alright? I saw them leave . . .'

He dragged his face up to acknowledge her, his expression a mask of confusion and pain.

'Whatever is it?' asked Wendy.

'My sister,' he shook his head, refuting his own words. 'She's dead . . . killed in Chicago. . . .'

He saw her face drain of colour, felt the terrible unfairness at involving her in this moment of personal grief. But the wave of immense relief that engulfed him at having shared this harrowing secret with someone swept away his misgivings. Wendy walked across the room and put a consoling hand on his.

'Oh Rhys, I'm so sorry . . .'

'They want me to go out and identify the body . . .' he looked away, his frown deepening, 'I only spoke to her last week. . . .'

'Was it an accident?' Wendy enquired in hushed tones.

Rhys shook his head, his eyes squeezing shut with the effort of controlling the emotion that suddenly threatened to erupt.

'They said she's been murdered. They didn't say how or. . . .' He let out a hiss of ironic laughter. 'She loved the States. High flyer, my sister. Youngest senior registrar on the Professorial unit in Nottingham. They thought the sun shone out of her. . . .' He checked himself, still shaking his head. 'She was planning to go out there for a year or more. She was in Chicago for a satellite meeting of immunologists. Some bloke at the Johns Hopkins she wanted to work with,' he paused, his face frowning with confusion. 'I still have her jump leads in the boot of my car.'

'Shall I get you a cup of tea?' said Wendy.

Rhys nodded dumbly and watched her go with unseeing eyes. He was glad Wendy had found him. It meant that word would spread and that was fine. He didn't want to have to keep explaining. It hurt too much. He wanted to crawl away into a corner and be alone with his thoughts, but some blown trip-switch in his head made even the thought of any physical movement completely impossible at that moment.

The paediatric unit were used to dealing with tragedy, but it was a credit to them that they had never become inured to it. And so they were kind and gentle with him, staff and administrators alike. Their words, simple and heartfelt, acting as a balm that soothed away the day.

There were things that needed to be done, details that needed sorting out . . . but he couldn't bring himself to do any of them in the numb limbo of shock. It was evening before he could drum up the courage to ring his sister's boyfriend. It had been a two-month relationship that had, in his sister's words, a moderately permanent feel to it. Richard's sobbing, moaning grief knocked the stuffing out of Rhys. Up to that point, he had been too preoccupied with amorphous thoughts to feel the deep pain that was growing inside him. But as he put the phone down on Richard, the well-head blew and he sat in his room and wept.

His sister had been two years older than he. A bright academic extrovert who Rhys had emulated and admired. As children they had fought like all cubs but once childhood disagreements passed, they had become friends. Their father's death before either of them had reached their teens had brought the family closer, their mother's death five years ago had been an emotional burden they had shared openly.

Alone in his mess bedroom, Rhys found himself regretting the fact that he hadn't seen Catrin for almost two months with an aching, inconsolable sorrow. Both had been busy carving careers for themselves, both had interests and friends that occupied much of their leisure time. They usually met up four or five times a year; both lured home to relatives and roots at Christmas by a need to savour a morsel of the family life that still bound them. It was more than mere sentimentality that drove them to sit in tiny back rooms with aunts and uncles and the excited, uncontrollable noise of half a dozen offspring of their extended family munching mince-pies. It was a reaffirmation. A pilgrimage almost.

Other times they'd juggled leave to make a week of it on a skiing trip or a Sunday lunch party at which Catrin would inevitably try and gently pair Rhys off with one of her innumerable friends. It had always been that way. She had, since leaving home before him, adopted a distinctly maternal attitude towards him which he had found amusing and oddly comforting. The more so since his mother's death. She had been forgiving of his reticence, always generous, always there for him. And he, God forgive him, had expected it always to have been thus.

Now, forced to contemplate life without his big sister, he realised with dismay that the feeling of emptiness and loss which had so abruptly come upon him since the police had gone stemmed from love. They had been undemonstrative siblings; a legacy of their mother's reserved emotional nature. He had never told Catrin he had loved her, it was not a word either of them used or even thought of lightly, let alone voiced to one another. But it had been there, inside them both, mingled in with a quietly fierce pride in one another that some had mistaken for arrogance. But they had willed one another to succeed because it had been their parents' wish, something that had been instilled into them by a thousand small acts of proud encouragement and reinforcement.

Catrin had indulged her adventurous spirit, her impulsive nature the antithesis of her brother's pensive conservatism. Rhys had watched uncritically and without envy, marvelling at her seemingly endless energy. It seemed impossible to believe that such a spirit had been taken away. She had always appeared virtually indestructible to Rhys.

He slept fitfully, his mind fretting and troubled over what was to come. He awoke with a raw, thumping headache and eyes that blinked resistingly against the shaft of cold November sunlight that pierced the gloom of his mess room. He got up and threw open the curtains. The crystal, frozen clarity of the morning seemed to mock his grief. His mood was one that needed lowering clouds and drizzle, not brightness. But in a second, he was chiding himself for his self-absorption. Nature, as he well knew, was immune to such mundane matters as death.

He phoned the Whitehall number given to him by Superintendent Gilby and was put through to the consular office. On his knees was the crumpled fax from Chicago Police Department that Gilby had left him. In it was a request that he, as next of kin, formally identify the body. The British consular department in London were efficient, kind, knowledgable and surprised him by informing him that the Chicago authorities – they weren't sure who specifically – had insisted on picking up all the costs of his flight and accommodation. When he asked if that was usual, the reply was that it was not, but that it had been something they had insisted upon. He hadn't even thought of expense up until that point, he had merely accepted the fact that it was something he had to do.

'Then I'd better start trying to sort out some flights,' Rhys said half to himself.

'There are some already available in actual fact,' said the consular official, rustling through some papers.

'Really?' asked Rhys.

'We retain options on most transatlantic flights for emergency purposes. Ah, here we are. American Airlines direct to O'Hare at eleven p.m. this evening from Heathrow.'

'Doesn't give me much time,' mused Rhys.

'There is a number to ring should you wish to rearrange the flight.'

'No, no. I'd rather get on and do it.'

'You're also booked in to a hotel in Chicago, details are at the American desk. The Hotel Geneva, I think. Someone from the authorities will contact you there tomorrow.'

'Is it worth me ringing them?'

'I wouldn't recommend it now. It's just after three in the morning out there.'

'Of course.' Rhys cursed his own stupidity before thanking the helpful voice and put the phone down. It was nine-fifteen a.m. He had fourteen hours to do what he had to do. He was not the seasoned traveller that Catrin had been, but he had been Stateside a couple of times. Once to Boston for a weekend with an old girlfriend and once to Killington with Catrin on a skiing trip. But unlike Catrin, he had avoided the big cities like New York and Los Angeles and all their attractions. He harboured a nameless anxiety about big cities. He even disliked London despite spending five years there as a medical student. There was simply too much grime, too many people, too many concrete acres, too many strange, preoccupied faces. Now, contemplating the trip, the horror of Catrin's fate fed and reinforced his anxieties ten-fold.

He threw some things into a suitcase, rang an understanding boss and a less-understanding administrator to announce his imminent departure and by ten, he was walking out of the hospital entrance to his car.

He took some money from his bank and did a few menial tasks before setting off west for his home town knowing that he simply could not put off seeing his mother any longer.

He travelled through the Forest of Dean, through the acres of wild woodland with the cool sun dappling the largely empty A 4136. At Monmouth, he headed west through Abergavenny to the heads of the valleys road which led home.

Gradually, the landscape changed and gave way to a windswept expanse of grass and bog that in its own way held a stark, bleak beauty. The unhealed scars of years of industrial rape blackened the mountains above the towns and villages with their toytown rows of terraces perched at improbable angles on the steep hillsides.

His mother lay where he and Catrin had put her, in the sunniest corner of a secluded graveyard behind a freshly painted chapel with the word 'HOREB' picked out in shiny black above the huge doors. Both he and his sister had escaped the area that had once been a slave to coal and steel and which now eeked out an existence on the meagre pickings of bland factories that made washing machines and car components. Both his parents were in the graveyard, but it was to his mother's grave that Rhys walked alone on this cold autumn day.

There was no self-conscious hesitation in the words he spoke to her, although they were soft. That was his nature, the way he had spoken to her for as long as he could remember, even as a child. She had possessed a serenity that had encouraged quietness and sincerity. He had always come back to tell her about the important things, although he knew in his heart that somehow she was aware of it all before he had uttered a single word. And a part of him realised he was there purely for his own peace of mind. Nevertheless it was a ritual he needed and never questioned.

He laid flowers, as he always did, knelt and then stared at her name. Mair Sian Jacob; a simple name that had never seemed to do justice to the enormity of her achievements but that could neither, somehow, have been anything else. He knew how much she had looked upon his sister and himself as her crowning glory. Not in a proud way, but in a quiet, self-satisfied way that was humble and fulfilling. Theirs was not a vicarious success, that was too simplistic. In their mother's eyes, they had stood for winning against the odds in a country where unemployment and poverty were no strangers even in the fifties and sixties. A country whose government two hundred miles away had conveniently forgotten its ravaged working communities.

'I'm sorry about Catrin, Mam.'

It was all he managed to say for a long while. All that seemed necessary. He didn't know enough to discuss it but as he stood there, the gravestone seemed to stare back at him accusingly.

'Don't worry,' he whispered. 'I'll bring her back.'

In his mind, he saw her smile then. The smile she kept for when one of them had done or said the right thing without being asked. And he knew too what she would have said after that smile and to some it might have sounded old-fashioned, presumptive even. But coming from a woman who had refused to lower her standards in the face of widowhood, it should have come as no surprise. Food, clothes, text-books, bicycles; they had always been found even when it appeared that money was nowhere to be had. She had given freely too of her wisdom and had asked only for honesty in return. He remembered vividly the day he had returned home with his medical degree. A brilliant June day, the street full of children playing and dogs sleeping on the hot pavement. He had found his mother alone in the cool, dark kitchen where so much of his life had been lived. She had watched him come in without speaking, a faint smile on her lips, and bade him sit down and listen to her. Her manner had been oddly solemn, the language ancient but still alive in the west and north of the principality, still rich with feelings and emotion. His mother had come from the black hills of the west and she had spoken nothing but her own mother's tongue to her children, committed to seeing it survive another generation.

'There will be people who will try to take advantage of you because it will be their nature, their weakness. Your accent and your background will set you apart and the truly ignorant will consider that a failing because they listen to the noise and not the content. Respect yourself and your family. Your blood is strong and will bind you to your father and me, even after we have gone.

44

Be true to yourself and your sister and be proud of who you are and where you come from. Remember that.'

She delivered this prepared speech before allowing herself a word of congratulation, as if it were some necessary rite that denoted his passage into a new existence. He had laughed about it later with his sister as she admitted that she too had received this formal warning when she had qualified. But the quiet power of those words had remained with him as a vivid memory. And both he and Catrin kept their family pride locked safely in their hearts as they moved through the very different society that medicine had given them access too. A simple but unbreakable bond that had kept them all close through the good and the bad.

Rhys stood up and stared at the gravestone. He would go to Chicago and try and ensure that they would do right by Catrin. It was all he could promise her. But he did so with a solemnity that burned his cheeks.

Turning from the grave, he toyed momentarily with the idea of visiting one of his many aunts and shied away from it. Time was pressing but the truth was he simply couldn't face the emotional storm it would inevitably whip up. Instead, he decided to ring a cousin of his from an M4 service station later and let the news filter through that way. It was a cop-out, he knew, but there was also the trip to the airport and money to exchange and . . . feeble excuses, but ones to which he clung.

By eight, he was in Heathrow, wandering around the Duty Free, trying to tire himself in readiness for the journey.

The plane left on time and he ate a passable dinner. Afterwards, he found a relaxation channel on the in-flight entertainment and settled down under a blanket. The tape was a continuous loop preaching relaxation and tension-relieving exercises. Its hypnotic quality mingled with his flayed and raw emotions and ninety minutes into the flight, he fell into a deep and exhausted sleep. He dreamed only one dream. He was climbing a mountain with his sister ahead of him. There was laughter and joy. But when he crested the summit and reached out for her, she was gone. Below there was nothing but the quiet landscape of his childhood and an awesome and terrible loneliness.

6

A S RHYS LEFT his mother's graveside to begin his journey to reclaim his sister, Lou Bek stood in a cramped office in the Eleventh Street station, unshaven, his eyes red and raw from a sleepless night. The cause of Bek's insomnia lay on the desk in front of his boss; a carefully worded statement detailing his version of the previous night's activities. There was no mention of Jake in the statement. He was conscious of Lieutenant Finch watching him with the air of a man used to making difficult decisions in lousy situations, but not liking it one bit. He saw Finch cast a wary eye over the dark stubble on his chin and the sheen of grease on his unwashed face. Bek knew he looked like shit, but there was something about the way Finch was looking at him, something that made Bek want to slide his eyes away from Finch's piercing gaze. Maybe Finch had an in-built guilt detector. Maybe the thing had the needle way over in the red zone.

'We're all sorry about your mom, Lou.' Finch's condolence broke Bek's paranoid musings.

'Thanks, Matt.'

'The thing is, Lou, the Superintendent is giving me a lot of heat on this one.'

'Why?' Bek feigned surprise. 'What's different about this tourist?'

Finch sat forward, his lithe frame with the arms folded in front of it took up almost the whole space. He raised a wrist and held up his index finger.

'This isn't just any tourist, this was a foreign conventioneer who happened to be a doctor. A lot of people come to this city to conventions. The Superintendent doesn't want anyone to get jittery. Press are already making a banquet out of it.'

Finch waited for Lou to respond, but all he got was an impatient shake of the head.

'Lou, I am really sorry about your mom, but the fact is that

I have three men away sick and you are the most experienced investigator on the violent crime team. I need you to clear this case.'

Bek stared at Finch, his mouth suddenly arid, his mind spinning at this cruel twist. He blurted something out, buying time to think. 'This is a real bad time for me, Lieutenant. Besides, I'm already up to my eyeballs in the Randolph Street killing. Why don't you give it to Valdez?'

Finch kept on grinning. 'Kiss the Randolph Street case over to him.'

'To Valdez!' exploded Bek.

'Give it to Valdez,' repeated Finch quietly, noting Bek's hypocritical response to his suggestion with an ironic smile. He stood up; his favourite and most effective ploy. At six four, there were not many detectives in Violent Crime that stood any chance of eyeball to eyeball contact with him. He peered down through Ferragamo glasses that heightened the clean-cut, bookish air he favoured.

'Clear this case and take some vacation time. There's an election on Tuesday, the department is up for financial review in six weeks and the paperwork is driving me nuts. Also, I have three men off sick. Everything else is cotton candy except for the fact that I would also like the perpetrator of this crime nailed, in case there was any doubt about my losing perspective here.'

Bek tried to keep a poker face, but couldn't stop his jaw working. The Lieutenant was a fair man. He would understand and make sure that Jake was dealt with squarely if he came clean now. So why not? If he gave the word they would flush Jake in maybe a matter of hours.

Promise me, Lewis.

A good attorney would swing a diminished responsibility plea, wouldn't he?

Promise me you will not send Jake to that place.

He could get Dr Keller involved, do the right thing by Jake . . .

'Lou?' asked Finch softly, leaning in close. 'Are you getting all this?'

He's your brother.

'Lou?' asked Finch again.

'Yeah, yeah, Matt.'

'Good. The victim's brother is in from London tomorrow, right?'

'I guess . . .'

'I've decided to assign Mackie.'

Bek's tortured mind felt a surge of relief. Mackie had been with the squad for only a month, a transfer from Jefferson Park in Area 5. She was still learning her craft, still a little in awe of hard-nosed vets like him. This was good, this was perfect, but he played it out the way he felt Finch ought to hear it. A little pissed, a little attitude.

'Nothing like giving me experienced help,' he said drily.

'Mackie's OK. I'm getting good vibes from everyone she's worked with so far. She's a good cop.'

'Yeah, I've heard. You want it by the book, she's your man.'

'Nothing wrong with ambition.'

'Ambition,' Bek snorted. 'Took me ten years to make second grade. This lady takes a class at school and makes it in two.'

'While you were moonlighting with a little bodyguard duty, she was taking criminal psychology at the University of Illinois. The wheel turns, Lou.' Finch was grinning.

'Yeah? Well, I heard she couldn't hack it over in Area 5.'

'A little health problem, that's all. But that's history. I took her on because I know she does a good job.'

'You're the boss.'

'She's been on a victim rehab programme. She can look after the brother.' Finch paused before adding, 'I'm cutting you some slack here like I always do. Get on top of it.'

'Sure, Matt.'

The interview over, Bek left with his mind racing. He walked right out of the station house and drove back to the hospital in Oak Lawn, on the way toying with the idea of explaining it all to his mother. Explain to her how he couldn't shield Jake when the whole thing was becoming a high-profile case, getting way too big. He sat at her bedside, holding her hand. A dozen times he meant to say it. Then she opened her eyes and spoke.

'Jake? How is Jake, Lewis?'

'He's fine, Mom,' he lied. 'He's staying with me for a while.' She was in pain, the drugs keeping her half-asleep, but her face broke into a wide smile at hearing what Bek had said.

'You're a good boy, Lewis. Such a good boy.' Her hand had felt cold on his wrist. He had stared at that hand and tried to crush the miserable, demeaning thoughts that kept knocking on the door of his mind. Up there out front was the big one.

Why?

He'd read all the theories about the role of family in the schizophrenic process, about contradictory messages from parents, about lack of mutuality and consensus of approach and poor communication and of how an unrealistic pattern of behaviour is triggered. But none of these answered the big question.

Why?

He'd quizzed his mother on their family tree. No big bad crazy people hiding in the genealogical closet. No mystery drugs taken during Jake's pregnancy. No answers to the big one.

When Jake had first been diagnosed, they had sat down and talked about it as a family, had absorbed it and dealt with it as best they could. What no one had told them was how much the damage would spread. The casualty list had grown with time. His ex, Rita, was just one of many. His mother's friends had polarised, the circle ever shrinking. Their father had suffered it with an iron will, putting Jake first always, finding him jobs, finding the right doctors . . .

Why?

They had all lived with it as one might under an overhang that was geologically unstable. They had all known that rock was going to fall someday. Knowing it had not been any consolation, was not any consolation now.

He knew guys who had thrown cases, covered things up for friends or relatives, fixed fines, fixed jobs, but he hadn't. Lou Bek had despised those that had, had hated the petty favours asked for by politicians and heavyweight crime bosses and cap-in-hand friends who grovelled and conveniently forgot that there was no smoke without fire. He had prided himself for never having allowed himself to be drawn into that quicksand.

But suddenly he was contemplating doing exactly the thing he most despised and yet it seemed the only real option. And maybe he could find a way to get Jake some help through all of this, to make sure it wouldn't happen again. The important thing was to find him. Keep the hounds off his back until he could find him. Yeah, that was all, just hold things back a while. He couldn't see any great harm in that.

A grinning clown face popped up in his head sporting a plastic smile.

Bullshit, said the face.

'Jake's a good boy, Lewis.' His mother's whisper chased away his daydream. Her sincerity seared his heart. That belief was central to the core of her existence. The steel support at the centre of her will; a will that had held the family together. And his own doubts about Jake felt base and cheap in the light of that conviction. Jake was his brother, not some crazed rape-murderer, not until there was proof. And all he had at that moment was circumstantial. No weapon, no gun, just blood and crazy talk and a presence at the scene. OK, people had been arrested for less but this was Jake. Lou Bek made a pact with himself at that moment. He would keep what he knew to himself for the time being, pursue the investigation and try and get to Jake. If evidence came to light proving that it was Jake that had done those terrible things, he would not stand in the way of the process.

The clown face popped up again, but Bek zipped its mouth shut and clung to the reasoning of that pact. He clung to it as he showered and changed in his apartment before getting back to Area 4 and beginning his investigation into a homicide, the only lead in which he was going to have to keep from his colleagues.

The clown face was still grinning gleefully when Bek sat down at his desk.

Mackie was briefed by Finch in his office mid-afternoon.

'Mac, thanks for coming in.'

'That's OK,' she said. Nonchalant, like it was no big deal, like she hadn't just been sitting in her apartment watching TV and eating nachos, trying not to remember what the date was. Trying not to remember what had happened twelve months before and failing abysmally. Finch wasn't to know that she would happily have come in to type up the duty rosters for the next four months. As it was, he was looking at her with that apologetic way of his, building up to something big, she could feel it.

'I'm getting hassled, Mac. Mid-term elections are usually sluggish affairs, but suddenly our incumbent congressman Kervesky has realised that his usual strategy of ignoring the opposition has backfired. Polls show Kervy ten points down and the Republicans smell blood. The Grand Old Party is funding their boy Sheehan to the tune of sixty thou and in case you hadn't noticed, he's been blitzing the incumbent with both barrels on TV and radio.'

She kept her eyes pinned on his as he spoke, making herself concentrate. Nick had worn glasses like Finch's. Tortoiseshell frames with big lenses whenever he took his contacts out. Had been wearing them that November morning when he had walked out, bags packed, so casually, so maturely, willing her to be sensible and brave. And she had tried to hate him then and since, tried and failed.

Her face gave nothing away. She had put her black hair up at the back in braids, brushed a little make-up over the good bones and the olive skin, a mask behind which the emotions flowed. She'd come in wearing a straight skirt over thick tights and polished but not new pumps. When she spoke, the generous mouth and her big, grey-blue eyes mirrored Finch's expression of barely restrained disgust.

'Kervy's actually sitting up and taking notice? Must be the first time in what, thirty years?' Her voice sounded surprisingly normal in her own ears.

Finch nodded and smiled, glad of their little shared joke.

'Kervy's like Christmas, only his festivities come every other year with re-election. This time, though, he's under pressure from the term-limitation lobby.'

'Plus the federal indictment over misuse of campaign funds,' added Mackie with one raised eyebrow.

Finch laughed. 'Kervy'll ride out that storm, no sweat. No, his problem this time is mid-term apathy. He may not get enough people off their asses to vote and that leaves him wide open to the "kick the old fart out" school of political thinking.'

'God, I'd love to see that flimflammer lose, but you think it's likely?' Mackie's tone was sceptical.

'All I know is that some people in this town are not happy to sit back and wait, unlike Kervy himself has been up to now. The mayor's office has been leaning in all directions. Kervy and he go back a long way.'

'An old uncle/nephew Democrat thing?'

'The mayor's old man and Kervesky were old buddies. Anyway, Kervy has had to appear at some press conferences. When he's not biting the heads off reporters, he's ladling out the pork on transportation promises, libraries and crime.'

He laid out the details of the case. It was the distraction she needed and she fell into the routine of it, feeling herself become that other Susan Mackie she had to be to deal with all the horror and the violence, letting it envelope her. 'We and the Adler are both in Kervy's district, in case you needed any reminding. He and the mayor and the whole Democratic machine want this one done smoothly and by the numbers. They're even sending Hopper across on containment detail to handle the press.'

'I get the picture,' said Mackie with obvious distaste.

'I want you in on this, Susan. I'm putting you with Lou.' Mackie grinned then. So here it was at last. For a month she'd tagged along with the squad members, not exactly extra baggage, but not entirely in the game, doing as she was told, watching and listening, learning the ways they did things here at the Eleventh Street. A new assignment always took a while to ease into and she wanted to be able to start on the same page as these guys. But Lou Bek? He had hardly said two words to her since her arrival on the violent crime squad. Don't mind Lou, they all said. Always delivered with narrowed eyes and that slight knowing grin that was kept for the good ones, the ones that took no shit. Bek was a maverick, but a stand-up one.

'Lou's the primary, but I want you to concentrate on the victim's brother to start with. He's coming over to ID his sister's body tomorrow. I want you to pick him up and take him through it. Also, with Lou's mother in the hospital, maybe he'll want you to do a little extra leg work.'

Mackie nodded. 'Thanks, Lieutenant.'

Finch didn't smile. 'Don't thank me yet, Mac. This is going to get a little crazy now that Hopper's involved. All I can say is try not to get caught up in his bullshit mindgames. Just do your job and you'll be fine. Lou's preliminary report is on your desk.'

She went downstairs and bought coffee from the vending machine, took it back up to the squad room and read Bek's report. It could have waited till morning, but she didn't want to go back to the apartment and mope over the past and a defunct relationship that she had never gotten over. She picked up the report and started reading until she remembered that she still hadn't wrapped her father's birthday present and groaned inwardly at the barrel full of rabid monkeys that memory suddenly threw up. The anniversary of Nick's leaving and her father's birthday – what a start to the week. Working with Lou suddenly seemed like a welcome challenge.

Finch watched her go and shook his head. Not tall, thinner now than when he'd interviewed her two months ago. Child-like face that couldn't quite hide a little personal pain. Mac was the product of Scottish and Italian grandparents; a second generation Michigan girl with three brothers and a father with a Napoleon complex. Something, which she had never explained, had led to a rebellion against her siblings' law-school/med-school and business degrees. Finch liked Susan. Oh, he knew what some of her colleagues thought; that she was playing at being a dick and if things got really tough she could hand in her shield and go running back to daddy and his money. But she was better than that and he knew it. He also knew that she was motivated by something that was powerful and emotional rather than fiscal. A lot of her contemporaries were already spending a lot of time planning what they were going to do with their retirement cheques over beers in their favourite watering holes. But not Susan. Well, that was OK, but it made her a very hungry barracuda indeed. Susan needed challenges and, all credit to him, Finch did always try to oblige. But in this case she was the only one suited to the job and once in a while everyone had to take a little latrine duty, didn't they? He sighed and turned back to his paperwork, trying to suppress the bad feeling he had about this case. A very bad feeling indeed.

O'Hare was a sprawling conglomeration of buildings and lights that seemed to stretch for miles from the window of the 747 as it taxied to a standstill. Inside, the immigration hall was the biggest and best staffed that Rhys had seen but when he crossed the yellow line and handed his passport to a smiling and immensely corpulent black girl at the booth, he was momentarily lost for a reply when she asked if he was there on business or pleasure. He toyed with telling her the truth, discarding the idea as tasteless and settled for the inappropriateness of 'business', relieved when she didn't ask him to elaborate. He took her well wishes and the passport and headed for his luggage.

Outside, it was cold, but not perceptibly worse than when he'd left Heathrow. He wasn't sure quite what he'd expected but snow and howling winds where high on the agenda. He stood for a long moment scanning the approach to the terminal, watching the twenty or so flags from as many countries on tall, vertical poles across the road, flap in the wind. Around him, limousines, taxis and courtesy hotel coaches rolled by. He felt disorientated and distinctly odd. The five hours of broken sleep he'd snatched on the plane had left him groggy. His body told him it was rise and shine time, but the airport clocks told a different story and the paucity of traffic and the relative quietness of the airport gave the place a definite small-hours feel. Now that he had arrived, the prospect of what was to come palled on him. He suddenly felt the urge to turn around and get back on the first available flight.

He didn't want to be there at all, didn't want to have to face any of this.

Pulling his coat around him, Rhys walked resignedly to a taxi rank, stepped inside a yellow cab and gave the driver the name of the Hotel Geneva. On the dashboard, a mug-shot of the cabbie was pasted above the name, Tariq Mrquatif. Tariq was not a conversationalist.

Forty minutes later, the cab deposited Rhys at his destination. The address was unimpressive; East Wacker did not resonate with the same ringing tones as Park Avenue or Park Lane, but the building, and all those surrounding it, had a huge vertical presence that was certainly imposing.

In the lobby, he signed in and followed a busboy with a heavy Vietnamese accent up to his room.

One hour after leaving the airport, he stood at the huge window of his room staring out across at Lake Michigan a block away. From twenty storeys up, the lake was a dark mass with no horizon that stretched into infinity. Large cars, silent from the sealed room, sped below on three-tiered roadways the width of motorways. It all looked so alien, so complicated.

He turned into the room, his head light and off kilter, his hand straying to the rough feel of his beard. The room was pleasant enough, rich dark wood, king-size bed, all very comfortable. But it irritated him. He didn't want to feel comfortable knowing why he had come. His brain wanted to get on with things, get it all over with as soon as possible. But his brain also knew that it was impractical at two-thirty a.m. in a strange city. So he climbed out of his sticky clothes and showered, found some *Bonanza* reruns on the TV and lay on the bed sipping a Coors from the mini-bar trying not to remember the things he had never said to his sister.

Across the city, to the north, Lou Bek awoke in his two-room apartment on Mason Avenue to the insistent ringing of his bedside phone. He snaked an arm out from under the covers and expertly tilted the handset up from its cradle and into the palm of his hand without raising his head from the pillow.

'Yeah?' he croaked.

'Lewis . . .' the name was spoken tentatively in a small timorous voice. It brought Bek instantly awake and up onto the edge of the bed pawing sleep from his eyes.

'Jake? Where the hell are you?'

'I had to warn you, Lou. I saw them. . . . They looked just like you. Just like you and Mom.'

'Jake, listen to me . . .'

'Don't go over there, Lou, the other Lewis might meet you there . . .' His voice trembled with strain.

'Jake, where are . . .'

'I can't . . . I can't say anything. The Whistler is listening. Shit, Lou, The Whistler.'

Bek knew enough to realise that Jake was spiralling out of control again. His ears strained to make sense of what he was hearing, the disjointed ramblings chilling him and tearing at his heart.

'Jake,' he croaked, fighting off the torpor in his voice, 'who is The Whistler?'

'The Whistler is The Whistler is The Whistler.' The words rushed out in a staccato burst. 'I wanted to talk to the Jacob at the Planet house but The Whistler watched. . . . The Whistler used his beam on me.'

'Jake, Mom's in the hospital, Goddamnit. She broke her leg. She wants to see you. . . .'

'See me? No! No! No one must *see* me . . . if The Whistler *sees* . . . Lewis . . . Lewis, help me hide.'

'Jake . . . Jake. . . .' The phone went dead. Bek slammed it down and afterwards sat for a long moment with his back against the cheap padded headboard. He looked at his watch. Three-ten. He faked an intellectual debate as to whether it was either too late or too early for a drink. The debate lasted fifty seconds. His mouth felt thick and furry from the heavy session at Calhoun's earlier that night. He'd gone there desperate for a drink after visiting his mother at Christ's Hospital for the second time that day. She'd looked frail and helpless on the bed. Some doctor had told him that they wanted to operate, but there was an appreciable risk. He'd understood most of it but had pretended not to; something about spiking temperatures and the possibility of a clot in her lungs from the fracture. Bek had exploded then, flying at the doctor, pinning him to the wall, demanding that he fix it and not make dumb fucking excuses. The doctor, a thin, bearded Bengali had blinked at him, his eyes strangely devoid of fear. Bek had read pity and understanding there and it had shocked him. Understanding was not a commodity that he stumbled across too often on the street.

He pushed himself off the bed, joints aching after a misguided hour of raquetball three days before, pretending he was ten years younger than he was. The bourbon was on a table next to the coffee-grinder in the tiny kitchen. He glanced at them both and almost laughed at the thought that there might be even the slightest possibility of competition between the two.

He poured himself three fingers of amber liquid and wandered into the living room to stare out at the silent street below. He had moved out to the apartment three months after he and Rita had split up. It hurt him to think that it was almost ten years since then. They still spoke on the phone, but she had moved to San Diego with some computer analyst and they had two kids now. When the first kid arrived, it had nearly driven him crazy because it was the thing that had driven them apart. Rita had been baby mad. After two years of marriage it was all she ever talked about. But Bek hadn't played ball.

He laughed at the pun his mind had thrown up. They *balled* well enough, he and Rita. But he had practised the withdrawal game and became an expert at it. So good she didn't even notice. She'd even started to have tests. But in all that time, in all that long, torturing time he had never sat her down and told her the real reason why he didn't want kids.

It was no surprise that he hadn't told her because for a long, long while, he hadn't even dared admit it to himself.

Cramp our style, honey!

No more Easters in Acapulco!

We're still young, babe!

The excuses he'd tried on her sounded stale and phoney and stank like the crock of shit they were. A hundred times after a dozen large ones at Calhoun's he'd lurched to the phone near the washrooms, pressed all the digits of Rita's number except the last one. Desperate, with tears running down his face, to tell her the *real* reason why. The one that tore him to shreds because he kept it all bottled up inside.

He'd talked to half a dozen doctors about Jake. Some of them listened and shrugged, others were more definite. One had taken him to one side and explained the things he had not wanted to hear. Yes, they thought that there were certain hereditary factors. There had been twin and family studies. They were still looking for the genetic markers but they were sure that they existed. It was controversial ground and some people kicked against it, but like the tide, it seemed inevitable. If there was a chance, if there was the slightest chance that he and Rita could end up with a kid that started to go bad before he really started to live . . . The genetics of it were beyond him but it didn't matter. He had the simple wish not to put anyone, victim or carer, through what he himself had lived through.

He had never told Rita for the simple reason that he was scared she would have tried to talk him out of it. He scanned the street, his eyes seeing nothing. Vaguely he was aware of the dull thud of a boom-box through the walls from an apartment on the same floor. A young couple, Puerto Rican and Salsa crazy. They were probably high on something, getting their shit together at three a.m. in the morning. There was a time when he and Rita would do that. Just roll over in the bed and find each other awake and hungry. Just roll into one another with the radio on low. Bump and grind to the soft rock stations. He felt the smile on his lips and it tasted sour. He didn't know the PR couple's names, hardly knew any of his neighbours, using the apartment as nothing more than somewhere to sleep and eat. Weekends he would escape north to what he had come to consider his real home, spiritually and physically. It was a seventy-mile drive but out there was water and trees and emptiness and a chance to breathe and be someone else for a while. He had plans for that place. Plans that had included his mother and Jake, but now . . .

The bourbon caressed his palate with a warm maize mouthwash. It hit his stomach with a welcome charge, but already his mind was beating out the same old rhythm that drummed at his nerves during every waking hour.

And the song it played was a sad one.

7

ON MONDAY MORNING, Rhys awoke with a fuzzy head and a furred tongue, his body clammy from the heat of the hotel room. He got up and padded across to the window that made up one wall and seemed even larger in daylight. Grey clouds edged with a pale orange glow crawled sluggishly across the sky. Below him, he saw that the block between the hotel and the lake was being converted into a pitch-and-put course and driving range. Large puddles dotted the landscape, the bunkers dirty and grey, looking just like the way his face felt.

The cars below still had their lights on as they sped by in the early morning rush. Ant people in coats, hats and gloves gave a hint to what the temperature was like. Stretching, he glanced at the bedside clock. A red digital seven a.m. glowed back at him. He showered, read the hotel guide, saw that there were three restaurants in the basement and then, as he put the guide back on the table under the phone, he saw the message lamp glowing redly. He rang down and got an automatic answering service which asked politely that he press number one to receive his recorded message.

'Dr Jacob, this is Detective Susan Mackie with the Chicago Police Department. Sir, I realise that you have had a long journey and I trust it wasn't too tiring but we would like to proceed with the formal identification procedure as soon as is convenient. Could you call me at 706 8885 any time after eight o'clock tomorrow morning.'

Realisation of why he was in this city, dulled and unfocused by the mundane routine of morning ablutions and hunger, crowded in on him again.

Identification.

Was there even the slightest possibility that they were wrong? Would he gaze down at a dead stranger's face and feel a bubble of relief as the absurdity of it all burst inside him?

He shook his head. His instinct told him that there was no error.

He must have been too tired to have noticed the message light the previous night. In truth, he hadn't even been aware of the system's existence.

He glanced across; the clock said ten before eight. He decided to gamble and studied the phone again.

He dialled the number he'd scribbled down and got another calm female voice:

'The number you have dialled has not been recognised. Please try again.'

He cursed, and this time dialled a nine for an outside line.

'Mackie,' she answered at the fourth ring. He introduced himself and the voice softened.

'Thank you for returning my call, sir.'

'I'm a little early.'

'That's OK.'

'So,' said Rhys after a brief tremulous pause, 'what do I do?'

'Whenever you're ready I think it would be wise to proceed with the ID.'

There was a long silence before he said, 'Is it bad?'

'The injuries were extensive, sir,' Mackie answered.

He exhaled, not expecting the candidness of her reply. Again there was a long silence.

'Sir?' she said eventually and was that a tinge of impatience he detected there? 'We could always put this on ice until this afternoon.'

'No, there's no need. I'll do whatever you want me to,' he said stiffly.

'In that case I could pick you up in twenty minutes?'

'Fine.'

'Hotel Geneva, right? I'll meet you in the lobby. I'll be in a silver Buick.'

Rhys took the elevator down to the basement and bought coffee from a mock-up of a Swiss street cafe complete with authentically dressed waitresses. He stared at a bewildering array of six different glass coffeepots and plumped for Colombian regular.

There seemed to be a whole subterranean subculture down in the basement. Large airy corridors led off to a variety of destinations, the heated passageways thronging with people on their way to work, the women in coats and suits, the men in trench coats, freshly shaved, both sexes balancing coffee cups, newspapers and briefcases in a precarious high-speeed juggling act. Office-bound people on the make, blind to Rhys's pain, oblivious to everything but the pressure of the clock, unaware of the dreadful violation their city had effected.

Unaware and uncaring.

This was a different world. Strange and alien. Rhys sipped his coffee and eyed the rush-hour scene for a few minutes before wandering back up to the lobby where he sat next to some large burgeoning pot plants, trying to massage the odd rubbery feeling that came with travel and disrupted sleep out of his face while he waited for Detective Mackie.

8

S HE PARKED RIGHT outside the entrance of the Geneva, got out
of the car and flashed her shield at the huge doorman. She saw
him pirouette and give her a vulpine grin as she walked passed. He
let fly with some smart comment that she didn't quite catch, but
the grin remained friendly and she didn't bother turning around.

She walked in through the hotel's revolving doors and stood
scanning the lobby. She saw him stand and look in her direction
expectantly. Her eyes took in five-ten, maybe eleven, of lean, spare
frame beneath wide shoulders that suggested time spent at some
athletic endeavour. The face was square, the features almost a little
too fine for the body. He came towards her and she saw two black
spots of congealed blood on his chin where he had cut himself
shaving. Either he hadn't noticed them or had and considered them
an irrelevance. She manufactured a smile of greeting.

'Dr Jacob?' She came towards him, offered her hand. His
felt cool and dry. 'I'm sorry that we have to meet in these
circumstances, sir.'

He gave her a perfunctory nod, pain hooding his eyes. She took
in the aesthetic, clean European lines of the hotel, her lower lip
jutting out appraisingly. 'I've never made it to the Geneva before.
Looks comfortable.'

Rhys shrugged.

'I guess you're in no condition to notice, huh?'

'Not really.'

'No, I guess not. Car's right outside if you're ready.'

They headed east on Wacker, the sound of rubber on asphalt
the only noise in the car for a while as they doubled back towards
the city. After two blocks, Mackie pulled out a pack of cigarettes
and offered Rhys one.

He shook his head without speaking.

'Forgot, you're a doctor, right?' She rehashed the smile and
hesitated before putting the pack away, half hoping that he might

say he didn't mind if she indulged herself. But he kept his face forwards, his expression set.

'Ever been to Chicago before?' asked Mackie lightly, tucking her menthols away.

Rhys shook his head.

As they sped towards the Loop past the Wrigley Building, she tried once more to get a response out of him. 'It'll take us fifteen minutes to get to the ME's office. Traffic's not so bad this time of the morning but . . .'

'Detective Mackie,' said Rhys interrupting her, turning in his seat, his voice low and insistent, 'what happened to my sister?'

She looked across at him with a searching glance. 'How much do you know?'

'I've been told virtually nothing.'

She nodded. 'We haven't released many details yet. We won't until the ID . . .'

'You found her purse and her passport. There can't be much doubt can there?'

'The law says we must have a positive ID.'

'The law says, does it?' asked Rhys, eyebrows arched, his mouth quivering on the edge of a forced, irritated smile. She glanced over, hearing the pain in his voice, seeing the indignation on his face.

'This is tough for you,' she paused waiting for him to respond. When he didn't, she sighed into a reluctant precis.

'The body was found in the Hall of Space Exploration at the Adler Planetarium. We've established that your sister was a guest there. A drug company called Techrim hired the hall, bussed in caterers and threw a dinner for invited guests. Some Public Relations hotshot's idea of a fun thing to do. Everyone at the dinner, barring Techrim employees, was a doctor. All of them attendees at the International Congress of Immunology at McCormick Place. The victim had been shot in the back. We think the shooting took place in a parking lot, but she managed to struggle back inside the Planetarium, was caught there and was strangled.'

Rhys sat with his thumb and middle finger of his left hand rubbing his temples without speaking.

'Someone found the body and called in anonymously. Could even have been the perp.'

'Perp?'

'The perpetrator of the crime.'

Rhys grunted out a sardonic laugh. 'She wanted to come and *live* out here.'

'Excuse me?'

'How many murders do you get in this city a year?'

'Seven, eight hundred.'

'My sister actually wanted to come and live out here.' Rhys shook his head in disbelief.

'Believe me, it could be worse. This isn't Miami,' said Mackie defensively. 'Chicago is safe as long as you don't go looking for trouble.'

'Like visiting the Planetarium, you mean?'

'No,' said Mackie with exaggerated care. 'The Planetarium is a Chicago institution. Nothing like this has ever happened. . . .'

'Really?' said Rhys.

'Sir, we are taking this case very seriously.'

'Should I be impressed?'

'I think maybe you should.'

'I'll take your word for it.'

They lapsed into silence. Mackie could see the guy was hurting. OK, better he got it over with and disappeared back to wherever the hell he was from. If her conscience gave her a hard time later, she could send flowers, what the hell.

The thought, trite and ugly, grated in her mind and she chided herself. It was the easy way out, depersonalise the victims, be cool and professional and detached. But it was oh so easy to let it spill over into callousness. OK, she was aware of it which was more than could be said for some of her colleagues, but she knew too that it was more than her cop mind-set at work here making her crabby. She had begun the day with a promise to herself that she wasn't going to let the date get to her. November 7th was one of several blocked out in red on her calendar on the refrigerator. Reminders – as if she needed reminding – of just what a swell couple of years it had been. September 5th was another; the day she woke up with the cramps and only just made it to the bathroom, sitting there, feeling it all flow out of her, yelling for Nick who just stood at the door with that look of horror on his face at the sight of her, knowing what it meant, his mouth open, unable to reach out and take her hand. That one moment was frozen in her memory. The way he wouldn't, couldn't just reach out and touch her fingers.

September 6th when they finished the job at the hospital with a D & C, making sure nothing was left inside to rot or bleed.

September 8th when Nick came to pick her up and told her it didn't matter and that maybe it was for the best.

The best?

November 7th when Nick the public relations whizz kid announced that he was taking up a job offer in Denver and that maybe, *this* was the opportunity they should both take to grab a little space. A little time out after two years of bliss and three months of hell.

And tonight, just to cap it all, I have to attend my father's birthday dinner at the Dupont en famille and boy, is that something I look forward to about as much as root canal work. So, from my point of view, you picked one hell of a lousy weekend for your sister to get whacked, Dr Jacob.

She let her eyes slide across from watching the road and sagged inside at seeing the anguish in his face.

God, what was she doing letting this get to her? How many times over the last months had she got up in the morning telling herself it was all over and that it was time to get on with her life? And here she was, running the same tired old emotional video-tape in her head. She was pissed at the fact that it was getting to her. Messing up her mind and her day, making it unpleasant for this poor guy. Pissed but at the same time impotent in the wake of its constant presence.

Cook County Medical Examiner's office sat two blocks away from the greystone and marble mausoleum that is Cook County Hospital on Harrison. As they neared, they passed a steady stream of ambulances, some crawling, some hurrying with lights and horns blazing. Outside the hospital entrance, sitting or huddling against the cold, some thirty or forty people hovered in an odd kind of listless limbo. Almost all of them were black. Mackie saw a faint light of interest kindle in Rhys Jacob's eyes.

'That's Cook County,' she said trying to jolt herself out of her negativity.

Rhys nodded and surprised her by saying: 'Friend of mine came out here to learn about management of gunshot wounds. He's a medic in the army and they were sending him to Belfast. He could have gone to any number of war-zones to get some practical experience but he chose to come here.'

Mackie snorted. 'I'd say he got all the hands-on experience he'd want and some. This joint gets a dozen or more shootings on a quiet Saturday night.'

Rhys shook his head.

'I ever end up in there, I hope to God I'm D.O.A.' There was something shivery in her tone that made Rhys look across, but her expression remained inscrutable as she drove past the front of the hospital and took a left on Leavitt Street and parked in front of a modern, low, two-storey building of glass, steel and concrete that was the ME's office. All around them, steel railings fenced off other modern buildings in stark contrast to the stained facade of the hospital they'd just passed.

'Research Units for the Illinois medical centre,' said Mackie without being asked.

9

A N ATTENDANT IN a white coat and a nameplate with 'Andy' written on it led Rhys and Mackie to the rear and down some stairs into a small ante-room with glass walls. No one spoke as he opened a steel door and beckoned them in to a refrigerated, white-tiled room redolent with sickly disinfectant and the sweet odour of decay.

One wall was lined with vertically arranged steel doors. Andy opened one and slid out a drawer containing a corpse. The drawer made a noise like a heavy, well-oiled filing cabinet and Rhys was struck by the analogy. Here were the city's victims, neatly stacked like so many paper files.

A white plastic body bag completely surrounded the corpse. Andy moved to one side and looked at Rhys enquiringly. He nodded and Andy began to peel open the zipper. Catrin's skin was pallid and grey, the lids swollen but not quite shut showing the whites of her eyes now a waxy yellow in death.

Rhys tried to swallow but there was nothing there.

'Is this your sister, Dr Jacob?'

He heard himself mouth an echoing 'Yes', and then Andy was pulling up the zipper again. It was over in a few seconds, the drawer sliding back with a resounding clang, Mackie's hand on his arm leading him out, his pulse hammering with a dull unfocused anger at the senselessness of it all. His sister was dead and violated. There would never be another Christmas Eve in the pub followed by carols and hymns and early mornings bristling with excitement. No more downhill races. No more trading insults over the phone. It had all gone with that metallic clunk of the drawer sliding home. All the feelings that they had both taken for granted, a bond that was never spoken but which ran silent and deep.

He felt his breath rasping, the room suddenly overbright and glaring, the white walls dazzling his eyes, the noise of a running faucet reminding him of a riverbank that they'd played beside twenty summers before. A whispered aside from across the room became a remembered conspiracy between himself and Catrin under winter blankets, giggling in the torchlight over smuggled candies when they'd been kids.

He couldn't remember walking through the building, but suddenly found himself outside with cold November air on his face and in his lungs.

'You OK?' asked Mackie, and this time the enquiry sounded genuine to Rhys.

'No.'

'I guess not. I'm sorry for your loss. Come on, let's go sit down someplace.'

Rhys sat in the Buick with his eyes staring straight ahead but seeing nothing. They drove for no more than ten minutes along rutted roads before they parked on a street which seemed cluttered with blue and whites. There were so many that Rhys assumed they had arrived at a police station. A few blocks away, the huge looming presence of the John Hancock building reared above. Across the street, an abandoned building still had a battered sign that read Tyro Club hanging at an odd angle. He saw that they were on Delaware and when Mackie held a door open for him to enter, he saw a neon sign above which glowed out the name 'ELVIRA'S'.

A dark youth wearing an apron handed them a couple of menus and a large woman in bulging trousers and sneakers with severely listing soles led them to a booth. Glancing round, Rhys saw that the place was full, and amongst the diners were at least a dozen uniformed patrol officers. A couple waved to Mackie as she made her way to a booth with brass rails and red upholstered benches on which they sat.

A waitress upended glasses already on the table and poured in fresh iced water before disappearing. Looking around, he saw that it was her sole function. He looked at the menu with unseeing eyes, his mind four thousand miles away in a graveyard. The image that he saw was unnerving. A small group of mourners; the knot of family tied with blood gazing with respectful eyes. But there were two coffins being lowered into the ragged holes in the earth. The viewpoint was strange and fleeting and unfocused. The scene he could understand – his mind anticipating, facing the reality to come, the details of faces unclear but familiar. But there were two coffins being interred to join his mother and father. He felt no fear at this enigmatic image, just a vague puzzlement. Two coffins?

Mackie's voice broke in on his reverie.

'You'd better eat something.'

'I'm not hungry.'

'Believe me it helps.' She added, 'It's likely to be a long morning.'

Rhys shook his head distractedly.

'I recommend the omelettes. Should see you through until dinner.'

'Whatever,' he said putting down the menu and sipping at the water while another waitress poured coffee into their cups and took their order.

'You and your sister were close, huh?' asked Mackie.

'We were as close as most, I suppose. I'd never even thought of it in those terms before.'

'What about your folks? How are they handling all this?'

'They're both dead. There was only Catrin and me.'

'It's tough.'

'Yes, it is.'

They sat in silence until the food arrived. Rhys put one forkful into his mouth and then pushed his plate away.

'That good, huh?'

'I'm sorry,' he said.

Mackie shrugged and sipped her second cup of coffee.

'She was very bruised,' said Rhys finally. 'What caused it?'

Mackie let her eyes drop and then brought them up to meet his, judging just how much she thought he could take.

'There were extensive injuries and some mutilation, mostly inflicted after death.'

'Mostly?' Rhys exhaled and shook his head. 'What happened for God's sake?'

'Like I said, we think that your sister was attacked in the deserted lot at the Adler Planetarium. We think she somehow managed to get away but was shot in the process. It looks as if she staggered towards a service entrance and got inside where she was caught and strangled.' She paused, aware that she was repeating herself, keeping her gaze steadily on him and then said quietly, 'She was severely beaten. I've seen it before. Usually indicates a loss of control on the part of the assailant, a kind of frenzy.'

Rhys didn't speak, his mind too numbed with pain and bewilderment, the food in his stomach feeling leaden and unsettled.

'Have you any idea who did this?'

'No, but it's my job to find out who did.'

Rhys's mind flooded with a thousand questions, but they were left unvoiced as two uniforms got up from a table fifteen feet away, one of whom began peeling crumpled notes from a trouser pocket. The other walked over to their table, levering himself into the bulky leather jacket that completed the uniform of blue shirt and serge trousers.

'Hey, Mac, how'd that Delgado case pan out?' He was smiling, the question heavy with sarcasm.

Mackie turned towards him, her reciprocating grin a parody of sweetness. 'Don't sweat it, Gunderson. It'll be wrapped up in two weeks.'

'Yeah? Me and Rix reckon it'll run and run with you on the case. We're getting odds on it maybe getting to court by *next* Thanksgiving.'

Rix, still counting out his money, nodded and grinned without looking up.

'Shouldn't you two be getting back out there? Or is the Batmobile in for a muffler job today?'

Both men grinned delightedly at Mackie's response to their baiting as they walked out, automatically reaching down to their truncheons to stop them from inadvertently knocking into tables.

'Sorry about that,' said Mackie. 'They put their uniforms on and think they're Clark Kent and Steve Martin all rolled into one.'

'Is that what they call you? Mac?'

'It is.'

He nodded, storing the information, his eyes penetrating hers.

'Mine's Rhys,' he said after a long moment.

She cocked her head and let a thin smile cross her face.

'OK, Rhys. We'd better get rolling. Some people want to talk to you at the station and I need to get you there.'

They drove to the Eleventh Street station. Mackie found a space on the street behind two squads and Rhys got out, staring at the shabby, six-storey high-rise of dirty black glass and steel. Behind him, a train roared by on the El and the noise made him flinch. The street was pot-holed, the building surrounded by abandoned lots. The whole area looked like a set from a post-holocaust sci-fi movie. He looked up and saw that Mackie had already gone.

Quickly, he crossed the street and followed her inside. The hall was fairly quiet at this hour as Mackie waved a greeting to the desk sergeant perched up behind a narrow wooden admissions desk. He acknowledged her with a cursory nod and immediately buried his head in the paperwork that occupied him. As Rhys followed Mackie through a swinging door, they passed two women being led out.

One of the women returned his stare defiantly. She was rake thin, with a fake fur jacket over a bright blue leather skirt. Her legs shimmered in holed tights and ankle-high spike-heeled boots. As she passed him, Rhys heard a deep spasm of bubbly coughing spring from her chest. Her companion, a shorter black girl sporting a blond wig, didn't make any eye contact. She seemed half asleep.

Mackie watched Rhys's curious stares with mild amusement.

'Last night's hooker haul. Dazzling sight, huh?'

They continued into the building through corridors thronging with uniforms, up some stairs and finally to a lobbied area. Mackie offered him more coffee from a steaming pot in the corner. Rhys declined and watched her knock on a door with 'Lieutenant' etched on the glass. Seconds later, he heard a booming voice say, 'Come.'

The Lieutenant's office looked about as big as a store cupboard which is what it once had been. There was room for a desk and two folding chairs chosen primarily for their discomfort value. Finch stood as they entered and the room immediately shrank as a six-foot-four frame towered behind the desk.

Mackie made the introductions and Finch spoke into an intercom on his desk, leaning low with one hand on his tie to stop it hanging untidily. He asked the same questions about travel and the hotel that Mackie had and made smalltalk until someone knocked on the door and a man entered.

Rhys took a guess at mid-forties, but the receding hairline and the nose surrounded by a ragged flower of booze-blown veins made the guess difficult.

'Come in, Lou,' said the Lieutenant.

Mackie shuffled her chair into the corner, ending up with her head just beneath a shelf that sagged with the weight of a hundred files. Rhys pushed his chair back as far as he could and watched Bek hoist a hip onto the Lieutenant's desk.

'Dr Jacob, this is Sergeant Bek. He's the primary investigator in your sister's case.'

Rhys stood and shook hands with the paunchy detective, accepting Bek's condolences with good grace despite the fact that they were mumbled and hesitant. He'd missed a patch of beard when he'd shaved that morning and Rhys noticed a white flare of shaving cream under one ear. There were dark rings under his eyes and he shifted restlessly on the edge of the desk, looking everywhere but at Rhys. The middle finger of his left hand kept worrying at the small patch of beard on his chin. To Rhys, he looked like a man trying to remember all the words of a speech he was about to deliver and not succeeding.

Finch sat down again.

'Detective Mackie will have told you that the Department has given this investigation considerable priority.' He paused and leaned forwards, both hands together on the desk. 'We don't like homicide in this district, Doctor, especially homicide perpetrated against a guest of this city. I take it very personally. You can take it from me that we are doing everything possible. Sergeant Bek would like to talk to you about your sister's background. It's important that we know something of her habits, anything that might throw some light on what has happened.'

'Of course,' said Rhys automatically. He glanced at Bek. The man's eyes were focused downwards, his face fixed in an expression of preoccupied pain.

'And if there is anything I can do personally, just let me know.'

The interview room that Bek took them to had bare walls of flaking magnolia paintwork, a linoleum floor, a desk, three chairs and a two-way mirror that sat reflecting darkly in one corner.

'Sorry about the venue,' apologised Bek. He didn't smile, his tone flat, eyes downcast.

Rhys looked around and shrugged. Mackie was sitting behind, smoking and jotting things on a yellow legal pad.

Bek felt raw. His head thumped with throbbing intensity. He hadn't slept much after Jake's phone call, his head too full of guilt and worry. He'd got up at six and spent a couple of hours cruising in his battered Chevy through the lightening streets, his mind trapped in a maze of quiet desperation. He sensed that the logic of what he was doing was flawed in the extreme, but found no other choices open to him. Doing something was better than sitting around thinking about what

Jake might be doing. Whenever he did that a great void of panic opened up in front of him into which he felt he could topple at any moment.

Seeing the victim's brother in the flesh like this was making it all the harder. He'd done this same interview a thousand times before, had always managed to retain that delicate mixture of detachment and sympathy that made a good cop. But he was acting now and it all felt phoney and bad.

Bek cleared his throat and said, 'Has Detective Mackie filled you in on what we know?'

Rhys nodded.

'Doctor, I'm not going to waste time with the routine aspects. I think we should just get to the point here.' He was conscious of avoiding Rhys Jacob's gaze, pretending to refer to his notes unnecessarily. Finally, he dragged his eyes up and forced himself to look into Rhys Jacob's face. The guy looked back at him, half-expectantly.

'The autopsy listed the cause of death as strangulation. Your sister was shot once in the back with a .38 calibre slug, but it was not enough to kill her.'

'Was she robbed?'

'No, sir, her money and credit cards were still in her purse.'

'Then why did this happen?'

'Your sister was attending a function at the Planetarium. The drug company involved issued invitations from their stand at the conference in McCormick Place. Your sister was one of a hundred and twenty guests.'

'Is that significant?'

'Did she know anyone in Chicago, Doctor?'

'Not as far as I know.'

Bek changed positions in his chair, hunching forwards slightly and speaking low.

'The autopsy revealed that the attack was brutal. In addition to severe beating, it showed that your sister had been sexually molested with evidence of vaginal and anal penetration. Toxicology also showed significant levels of drugs in her blood. Was your sister on any regular medication?'

'No,' said Rhys after a long pause. 'Not that I know of. No, definitely not.'

'You sure, sir?

'Yes.'

72

'The drugs appear to be a cocktail, downers mainly. Sleeping pills and Lidoxine.'

'Lidoxine?'

Bek didn't expand. 'You don't recall any medical history, Doctor?'

'Catrin was perfectly well.' Rhys's confusion made his tone petulant.

'I'm just looking for an explanation, Dr Jacob.'

'This doesn't make sense. She'd just attended a dinner. Why would she have taken sleeping tablets?'

'Could be she needed to calm herself down,' offered Bek.

'Calm herself down?' asked Rhys, still bemused. 'Catrin didn't take drugs,' he added.

'When we searched your sister's room at her hotel we found some . . . materials. Some powder residue and a half-full pack of baking powder hidden up above the john behind a jemmied panel. The residue tested positive for cocaine.'

'Catrin didn't take drugs,' insisted Rhys, his eyes huge with indignation.

'Sometimes,' said Bek slowly, 'drug-users will pop downers to take the edge off the downside of stimulants.'

'What are you talking about?' Rhys asked in a voice edged with menace.

'You and your sister were close, Doctor?'

'What are you getting at?' said Rhys, getting out of his seat.

'Look, I'm only reporting the facts,' Bek said holding up his hands peaceably. 'I'm only suggesting that you may not have known everything that there was to know about your sister.'

'Jesus Christ,' said Rhys indignantly. He vacated his seat and started pacing the office.

'Maybe she didn't do drugs when she was at home being a responsible medical professional,' persisted Bek. 'Maybe her habit was recreational.' He knew he hadn't kept the accusational tone out of his voice but it looked as if this girl had been stoned. Bek didn't like junkies, especially ones who played at it. It made him feel better about the whole thing to believe that Catrin Jacob had got high and maybe took something to bring herself down. In so doing she had lain herself open. In Bek's book, junkies got everything they deserved whether they were pipe-heads doing ten-dollar bottles in the projects or assholes with Lamborghinis and Lincoln Park addresses doing weekend lines of coke. Bek, as

73

a salve to his conscience, had conveniently placed Catrin Jacob in the not-so-innocent victim category.

Rhys stood in the corner of the room, as far away from Bek as possible, staring into the mirror, his chest heaving. 'You're lying.' He hurled the accusation at Bek, his face livid.

'I'm just giving you the facts, Doctor,' Bek said, cautious now, reading the anger in Rhys Jacob's eyes.

'Lou?' said Mackie.

'What?' asked Bek, still with his eyes on Jacob.

'Could I speak to you alone?' Her tone was calm but insistent. 'Rhys, could you excuse us for a moment?'

He didn't answer. His angry gaze was locked on Bek.

She opened the door and Bek got up reluctantly and followed her out, his expression sour and unrepentant. They stood in the room adjacent, a place full of battered filing cabinets and econostore cardboard boxes with scuffed corners. 'Lou, what the hell is going on?' demanded Mackie angrily. 'I didn't know anything about the drugs.'

'We tossed her room this morning.'

'And found what, exactly? Evidence?'

'Yes, evidence. Goddamned evidence. You think I made it up? Meesman was with me. Jesus, Mac, why are we all walking around this as if it's some big deal? I'm sorry that the guy's sister got whacked, OK? But this is a shitcan if ever I saw one. A hundred boozed up medics and their practice nurses on a drug company junket. No one sees anything, no one hears anything. Maybe the little lady had a habit. Maybe she saw the opportunity for a little "R and R", huh? Maybe saw a way of getting to do the things she always wanted to here in Chicago. I have a theory about this killing. The night before she was at some sleazy strip joint, wasn't she? Hardly a shy and retiring Girlscout, our mark. You want to know what I think? I think she met someone at the Planetarium and they start talking sex or drugs or both. They go out to this guy's car, pop a few pills and things go badly wrong. She wants out – get's zapped.'

'Lou, why are you so mad?' interrupted Mackie.

'Come on, Mac. The minute they touch down at O'Hare, they see this big playground. They come here and they get a chance to do things they only ever dreamed about in their offices. And conventioneers are the worst. Conventions just give people the excuse they didn't even need. A little social gathering of strangers who know that the whole crap shoot has no history and no future, just one huge go for broke present.'

'What is that supposed to mean?'

Bek held her gaze for one moment only before letting his eyes drop to the floor and then back again. 'We aren't going to find this guy around here. He's out of state, I know it.'

'You don't know that. How can you know that? Even if it's true it's no reason to. . . .' Mackie put her hand on his arm.

Bek shook it off like it was a hot coal, his voice bitter with barely restrained fury. 'Mac, I've had it with you and the Lieutenant and this shitty case. The lady was loaded, read the report. I'm up to my shirt collar in paperwork and I'm due over in Cicero to make a social call on a scumbag that was seen hanging around the Metzels' apartment building the day Jo-Anne Metzel went missing. Remember her? Four years old, dumped in an alley behind a market with the fish-heads and rotten vegetables? And she didn't even have the consolation of flying high on mind-altering anything when it happened.'

'That isn't fair, Lou.'

'No? In case you don't remember, we're two weeks into that investigation with a big fat zero to show for it. Now, I suggest you get Dr Jacob here to take his sister and get the hell out and let us get on with this before it gets really ugly.'

He turned and walked out of the door, leaving her open-mouthed and confused.

Outside, Bek went straight to the locker room and locked himself in the john, breathing hard, his knuckles white as he leaned on the cistern. It had been more difficult than he had dared imagine, but it was done. The gloves were off. He felt like a man in an avalanche clinging to an outcrop. All around him the world was falling and he had no idea how long he could hold on for. He forced the image of Rhys Jacob's hurting face from his head. Perhaps there was an element of truth in what he had suggested. Perhaps the guy would be better off away from the jungle. But this was a matter of survival. There was no room for remorse, at least not yet.

Mackie waited a long ten seconds, took a deep breath and went back to Rhys.

He looked up as she entered, his face now pale with fury. 'The walls in this place are very thin,' he said in a trembling voice. She could see that his hands were shaking.

'Rhys, look . . .'

He interrupted her. 'Are you seriously telling me that he's the one trying to find my sister's murderer?'

'Lou's a good cop – very experienced. His mother's in the hospital. She broke her leg. . . .' It sounded like a cheap excuse to her ears and she knew it sounded a hundred times worse to Rhys.

He didn't respond, he could only shake his head in disbelief.

'We have to go upstairs now,' she said gently. 'There's a press conference. I told them it was a lousy idea but . . .'

'Wake me up and tell me I'm dreaming,' Rhys interrupted her. 'Please.'

She didn't answer.

'He's made his mind up already, hasn't he?'

Mackie shook her head. 'Look, forget this. Let Lou do his job. Let me do mine. We'll find the guy, I promise you.'

'I think I'm going to vomit.' Rhys dropped his head between his knees.

She groaned and fetched some water in a conical paper cup. Rhys put his head up and sipped from it, his colour returning as he gulped it down.

'Look, I'll try and get you out of here, take you back to your hotel. You don't look so hot.'

Rhys stood up shakily, a zombie look in his eye.

'You OK?' Mackie couldn't help the concern in her voice.

'Fine,' he said with an unpleasant smile on his face. 'Absolutely fine.'

IO

MACKIE TRIED TO usher Rhys out. At the top of the stairs, she paused to glance in through the glass panel of the door which led to the lobby outside the Lieutenant's office. Inside, a small army of reporters bristling with the weapons of newsgathering jostled for position. At the far end, Finch's huge frame stood to one side as the cream of Chicago's media listened attentively to a lean, bald black man with smooth skin and heavy-lidded eyes. He seemed to be enjoying the attention.

Rhys peered over her shoulder to catch a glimpse.

'Come on, let's go,' said Mackie turning away and placing a hand on Rhys's arm.

'No,' said Rhys harshly. 'I want to hear what they've got to say.'

'No you don't.'

'I think I do,' he said defiantly and shrugged his arm free of Mackie's hand.

Below them, the stairwell erupted in an explosion of noise as two uniforms pushed and dragged two handcuffed and swearing youths down to the lower level.

Mackie put her hand back on Rhys's arm.

'You want my advice? Go back to the hotel room, ring a mortician and arrange for your sister's body to go back to England on the next available flight with you.'

'Your colleague has just accused my sister not only of abusing drugs but of somehow bringing what happened to her upon herself, or did I just hallucinate that little conversation I heard through the wall?'

'Lou isn't himself,' said Mackie sheepishly.

'What's a shitcan?'

'Just a phrase. . . .'

'Which means?'

Mackie sighed. 'A homicide with a low likelihood of being solved.'

'You have no idea how wonderful that makes me feel,' said Rhys bitterly.

'Rhys, I won't lie to you. This has all the hallmarks of an ugly investigation which isn't helped by the political attention it is generating. The media are calling it the conventioneer killing and they're eating it in handfuls.'

'Why? Why so interested in my sister?'

'It's election week, Rhys. OK, there'll be two, maybe three, black kids murdered today in the projects on the east or south side just for wearing the wrong kind of sneakers. They won't make the inside page. But your sister was a white doctor at a convention. Worse, the security guard at the Adler claimed his sixteen seconds of fame with a graphic description of the victim's injuries. It sells newspapers and prime-time TV.'

'Christ.' Rhys exhaled.

Mackie put her hand back on his arm. 'If you go in through this door you're going to be walking right into the firing line. I can't help you in there.'

'I can't go home with things like this,' he fumed. 'Catrin didn't do drugs.' He circled the small space, his eyes bright with indignation. 'Jesus, you people have no idea what she was like. Catrin looking for trouble? . . . It's bloody obscene.'

Mackie eyed him without speaking. Rhys suddenly stopped and gave her a challenging stare. 'I'm going in to talk to them.'

'That is your prerogative,' she said resignedly and opened the door for him.

There were twenty or so people arranged in a rough and unsteady semi-circle including two TV crews complete with cameramen shouldering their weapons and soundmen with boom mikes, all avidly listening to the black man's speech. Finch looked distinctly uncomfortable next to him. None of the reporters turned around as Rhys and Mackie entered. Finch caught their entry, but apart from a slight narrowing of the eyes, his expression remained impassive.

'I can only reiterate,' said the bald man with an expression of well-practised sincerity, 'that this incident is a tragic and appalling example of exactly the kind of thing the mayor has pledged to deal with. Visitors to this city should and must feel safe to walk the streets and enjoy Chicago's artistic and scientific heritage without fear.'

He paused and a barrage of questions exploded from the floor.

'That's Hopper, from the Superintendent's office. He deals with news affairs,' whispered Mackie.

Hopper was holding his hand out, trying to quell the questioners as he peered over their heads towards the rear of the lobby and Mackie and Rhys. Then he was on his toes indicating to Mackie to come forward.

The reporters swung around in unison, their eyes alive with inquisitiveness. Mackie took Rhys's arm and led him through the tight knot of people to Hopper's side.

Hopper's face took on a pained expression of stricken grief as he addressed Rhys with one eye very much on his audience.

'Dr Jacob?'

Rhys eyed him with a tight mouth.

'Sir, I understand from Lieutenant Finch that you have positively identified your sister's body. This city offers you its sincere condolences.'

'Thank you for that,' said Rhys. Instantly, the cameras whirred and flashbulbs popped as the reporters started clamouring at once, yelling questions.

A male voice rose above the others, firing out a question at Rhys, hoping for an angle outside the official line. 'Are the Police Department keeping you informed about the progress of the investigation, Dr Jacob?'

Rhys felt his lips pull away from his teeth in a plastic smile.

'Oh, yes. I've been reliably informed that everything points to this turning into just another shitcan investigation.'

'Sir,' shouted a woman near the front of the jostling press, 'did you just say, shitcan?'

'Yes, I did,' said Rhys grimly.

'I assure you . . .' Hopper tried intervening but it was as far as he got. The barrage of questions drowned him out.

'*Dr Jacob? Dr Jacob? . . .*'

It finally came down to a blonde woman with overdone make-up and a CHTV logo on her microphone who screamed the loudest.

'Sir? Sir? Are you saying that it was suggested that this homicide is not solvable?'

'If that is what shitcan means, yes.'

'How does that make you feel?'

The plastic smile was still plastered to Rhys's mouth. 'As delighted as I'm sure you would feel had you heard that said about your sister's brutal murder.'

From the rear, cutting through the clamour, came a dry rasping voice: 'Dr Jacob, Tom Bellasco, *Chicago Chronicle*. There are rumours going around that this was a drug-related crime? Do you have any comments on that?'

'My sister didn't take drugs,' said Rhys categorically.

Hopper finally managed to recover himself. 'Ladies and gentlemen. Dr Jacob has had a traumatic morning, I don't think that specific questions of this nature . . .'

'My sister did nothing to bring this on herself. I'd like that made clear,' said Rhys again. It triggered another burst of celluloid activity.

Hopper's eyes were blazing at Finch. The latter took his signal and moved forward, his hands outstretched. 'OK, folks, that's it. We have work to do.'

'*Why do your men consider this an unsolvable crime, Lieutenant?*'

'I have no comment on that.'

'*Is there any evidence to suggest that Catrin Jacob was a drug user?*'

'No comment,' said Finch, his anger barely restrained now as he began herding the press out, making himself the barrier between them and Rhys, Hopper and Mackie. As he passed, he turned his head to Mackie and through clenched teeth hissed, 'Get him out of here, now.'

Mackie grabbed Rhys's arm and took him out through a back door and down to a rear entrance and into her Buick. She ushered him in and gunned the engine. As they drove around the block, Rhys saw the press encamped at the front door like vultures awaiting the death throes of some sick animal.

'That was some performance,' said Mackie, tight-lipped.

'I trust it was a better one than the Police Department have put on so far,' he replied acidly.

They drove on in silence for a couple of blocks.

'For what it's worth I thought you were pretty ballsy in there,' she said finally, breaking the silence.

'It won't stop my sister's name getting dragged through the mud.'

'We can't ignore evidence, Rhys.'

'God forbid.'

'It's my job.'

He didn't answer, preferring instead to stare sullenly out of the window at the strange streets. It was a ten-minute ride to East Wacker, the day still as grey and cold as when he'd stepped out that morning. People hurried along huddled inside their coats, their faces blanched by the bitter wind.

'What about Catrin's belongings?' he asked as they approached the hotel.

'Forensics are almost through with her clothes. You can pick up the rest as soon as you're ready.'

The big doorman at the Geneva opened the door for Rhys and he got out.

'What are you going to do?' asked Mackie craning her neck out of the back window.

'Bit of sightseeing, I expect.'

Mackie didn't appreciate the sarcasm. 'I don't think the press knows where you are. Keep your head down and I don't think you'll be hassled.'

'Is that an order, detective?'

Mackie shook her head. 'Just a little advice.'

McCormick Place sits like two huge grey concrete and glass building blocks thrown down haphazardly east of Lake Shore Drive, a mile south of the Adler. The convention centre is split into north, west and east buildings, each one a huge monument to modernism, with McCormick Place East the biggest. Purpose built in 1971 after fire destroyed the initial single hall and added to in 1986, it is the site of countless meetings, conventions and congresses throughout the year. For the biggest, shuttle bus services ferry passengers to and from the city's hotels, alighting and departing from a huge underground drop-off area on the lobby level which in itself is the size of several football fields.

Security was elaborate but not tight, concentrating mainly around the technical exhibits in the main halls. Attendees wore badges; all colour-coded allowing access to different parts of the building, technical exhibits, lectures or teaching sessions. With over four million visitors annually, dropped and lost badges were very common.

Jake had found two in the corridor leading from the shuttle drop-off area to the lobby itself where the first real security check occurred. One had a purple band at the bottom, the other orange. The purple badge had 'Gordon Opello MD' emblazoned upon it in black and 'FELLOW' written underneath in white on the purple band. This was the one Jake chose to pin to his lapel. The security guard at the entrance to the lobby had glanced momentarily at the badge and then his eyes were already straying to the next attendee with Jake inside the huge building staring about him at the thronging, milling crowds.

Above him, huge banners hung from the exposed girders in the ceiling thirty feet high. Jake saw the lettering, but to him it meant nothing. 'AAO', in maroon, 'TECHNICAL EXHIBITS 1–701, ON-SITE REGISTRATION'. . . .

He went with the flow and found himself in a massive exhibition hall lined with hundreds of exhibitioners, some hugely elaborate. He wandered along the gangways, staring at the booksellers, the surgical instrument manufacturers and their glittering, silver trays. Above him, the big companies had suspended brightly lit high-tech constructions from ceiling girders, enticing purchasers and other interested parties. Names like INTRALAB, LASINC, DIAMOND INSTRUMENTS; multi-million-dollar corporations that supplied one of the most popular medical specialities in America. Unbeknown to Jake, he was attending the Annual American Academy of Ophthalmology meeting – current in a line of medical conventions that had included the much smaller International Congress of Immunology at which Catrin Jacob had found herself and which McCormick was hosting that year. But unlike Ophthalmology, immunology had been a very much smaller speciality until AIDS had reared its ugly head.

Jake gazed around him, his disturbed mind now completely disoriented by this self-contained, glittering world. He walked around for half an hour picking up leaflets and garishly logo'd bags, watching looped promotional videos until he found himself back at the entrance to the hall, his mind buzzing with the noise – the constant barrage of conversation that crowded the air around him, forcing him to walk ever faster, turning this way and that, losing himself in the gangways, the noise chasing him, pursuing him with its unending, reverberating persistence.

Finally, he found himself at an entrance. A space opened out in front of him, people sitting, drinking coffee and eating doughnuts as they watched the video theatre display of operative techniques. He stood and watched the images of eyes being cut open, tilting his head as a dog might at a strange noise. The pictures seeped into his head, compounding the impression he had that he was in another world.

A memory of the purpose of his visit stirred inside him. All around him people wore badges. It was the thing that had drawn him here in the first place. The badges. This was the place that the badges all came from and to, the place where the people who had been with the woman had come from. For Jake, McCormick had become a huge port where people departed to and arrived from their worlds; the stars and planets. Here, he felt would be an answer to how *they* had found the woman and destroyed her. He found an escalator and wandered up, the crowds thinning as he progressed upwards. On the upper level, there were still some people, and so he stayed on, riding the stairway to its upper limit, reading the signs that said 'MCMAHON ROOM'. At the top, it was quieter, only a few people talking or sitting or hurrying to rest-rooms.

Huge bronzed windows from floor to ceiling looked out to the south. Jake wandered over and stood next to a pillar gazing out, orientating himself, letting the buzz of noise abate in his head.

He was still there two hours later, his trench coat on the floor next to him, his gaze directed downwards to the slowly moving line of taxis below. They wound from 23rd Street onto the ramp that led up and then angled down to the taxi-loading gate. Despite the free shuttle-buses, taxis did a roaring trade at conventions carrying a steady stream of people back to the city to lunch, bars and any of the other delights the city could offer.

Of the tens of people who noticed his presence, no one thought to comment on his motionlessness, no one interfered. Jake was lost in his task, his reason for being there in focus now that he had found his viewing platform.

It isn't safe.

He stood far enough away from the top of the escalator for people not to hear the constant whispered mantra he chanted to himself as he watched, his eyes darting in a motionless head with feverish concentration and intensity.

It isn't safe.

Searching for the Chariot of light. Searching for The Whistler.

It isn't safe. It isn't SAFE.

Bek was cruising through the darkening streets, his eyes staring at shadows in quiet desperation. He'd spent the whole afternoon nosing around Jake's haunts to no avail. Finally giving in to his headache and thirst, he pulled up in front of Lacy's on Wells. Across the road a banner hung draped over the door of a dingy restaurant next to Mr Dawg's take-out joint, its facade blackened by traffic exhaust. The banner announced a rib dinner for seven ninety-five. He debated getting some food, but his appetite was shot. He walked into the bar and ordered a Jack Daniel's and went straight to the men's room while the barman was pouring it. As he washed his hands in the basin he caught sight of himself in the mirror. His face glistened with a day's dermal ooze. It looked big and pale from late nights and crap food. He hardly recognised it. The thought brought him back to Jake's weird words of the previous night.

'*I had to warn you, Lou. I saw them. . . . They looked just like you. Just like you and Mom.*'

What the hell did that mean? Did Jake not know his own brother?

At the bar, he put the first one away without tasting it and ordered another before sliding across to the phone at the rear. It was gloomy back there, the place virtually empty. He took out his diary and phoned a number he found listed under K.

'Dr Keller? Hi, this is Lou Bek.'

'Lewis, how are you? What can I do for you? Is it Jake?'

'No, no,' Bek forced out a little reassuring laugh, 'it's police business. I need to pick your brain. You got a few minutes?'

'Sure. Fire away.'

'We picked up a suspect. Tried to push someone under a train at the El station on Clark. Victim wasn't killed, but it ties in with an MO on a seventy-four-year-old man four days ago who took a dive in similar circumstances. Everyone assumed it was suicide except for the grandchildren, plus there was no note.' Bek found himself falling into the lie easily, embellishing it as he went along. 'The suspect has no rap sheet but he does have a medical history an inch thick. Turns out he's a chronic schizophrenic and he's waxing kinda lyrical in the interview room.'

'Go ahead,' said Keller.

'This guy's brother came down from Wisconsin. When they met, the suspect went ape-shit. Said that the brother wasn't who he claimed to be. Swore that he was a stranger. Thing is the brother brought photographs that prove he is the real brother.'

'Capgrass syndrome,' said Keller.

'Say again?'

'Capgrass. One of the misidentification syndromes. Not exclusively a schizophrenic syndrome but commoner than in any of the other psychoses. It's one of a whole range of misidentification states. Usually occurs with someone the patient has close emotional ties with. Usually the ties involve ambivalent feelings, like admiration and jealousy, or dependence and irritation. Other misidentification can occur uh, Fregoli's syndrome for example, where identification of familiar people occurs in complete strangers or even subjective doubles where the patient believes that another person has been transformed into himself.

'Does it tie up with why this guy started pushing people under trains?'

'Maybe. But in schizophrenics some innocuous gesture on the part of a stranger can be misinterpreted in bizarre ways without any of the misidentification overlay. There is much more commonly a persecutory element to their delusions and so this innocuous gesture is seen as in some way threatening. Hence their response can be seen as a self-defence mechanism.'

'Jeez. I don't know how the DA is going to swallow a self-defence plea in this case.'

'It's likely that your suspect's attorney would not let him plead. I'm sure his psychiatrist would back that up,' Keller paused. 'You're not offering a consultation fee here now, are you, Lou?'

Bek let out another forced laugh. 'Sorry, Doc. Lucky we caught this guy when we did, huh?'

'Probably. Sometimes these delusional states can persist. Usually it's a sign of deterioration.'

'Wouldn't there have been some warning signs?'

'Not always. Sometimes the delusions do not necessarily influence all feelings and actions. Your suspect could have had a double orientation, could have been otherwise living quite contentedly but still be prey to whatever triggered off these attacks on the El.'

'Why is it you always make me feel so comfortable, Doc?'

'Come on, Lou. You know most schizophrenics can and do function in society on medication. I mean, look at Jake.'

'Yeah, Jake's a good example, isn't he?' He heard the lie catch in his throat. 'But that doesn't mean he might not go off the rails one day?'

'Let's not be pessimistic, Lou.'

'Na, look on the bright side, huh, Doc?'

There was a pregnant pause. 'Lou, is everything OK?'

'Yeah, fine. Tough day is all. Thanks for the information, doc.'

'Any time, Lou.'

He went back to the bar and sank the second Jack Daniel's in one. His brother didn't believe in him anymore. Didn't recognise him. Jake saw him as a stranger, an alien, a monster.

On a stool at the end, a woman sat smoking. He'd seen her around, a working girl with better legs than most and a hundred-dollar tongue. He toyed with the idea of spending a few hours with her, screw away some time to avoid the thoughts that beat in on him. She looked across, her gaze phlegmatic, smoke spiralling up from her cigarette and out of her painted mouth. He could see she was there for the taking. One nod from him and . . . He turned his face away and finished his drink, slid off his stool and walked out alone.

I I

Susan Mackie was late for her father's birthday party. He always booked a room in a restaurant if they had one, sometimes the whole restaurant. So that everyone would know that there was something *special* going on in there. He insisted on dining early, or maybe drinking early would be a better way to describe it. The Dupont on LaSalle Street was more than happy to oblige. She stood in the entrance, knowing she should be rushing in there to make her apologies, but instead here she was in the street, reading in the light spilling out from the restaurant, her attention focused on that evening's flysheet edition of the *Chicago Globe* just picked up from the street vendor.

The main story was the arrest of yet another anti-abortionist for the shooting of an abortion clinic doctor – the second in six months in Florida. But it was the column next to it that had caught her eye. The press conference had made the front page but Mackie was disappointed to see that it was unimaginative, knee-jerk copy.

CONVENTIONEER KILLING –
POLICE SPECULATE ON SORDID MOTIVES.

Police today confirmed the identity of the victim of the Adler Planetarium slaying as that of Dr Catrin Jacob, a British immunologist who was visiting Chicago for a medical convention. Speculation that the motive for the brutal slaying may have been drug- or sex-related continues to escalate. A spokesman at this morning's Area 4 press conference refused to confirm whether illegal substances found in Jacob's hotel room were linked directly to the dead immunologist, but the victim's brother, Rhys Jacob, stringently denied any allegations that his sister abused drugs. Brought into a press conference fresh from identifying his sister's remains, Rhys Jacob went on to attack the authorities over their insensitive handling of the investigation. Boyd Hopper, News Affairs Officer with the

Superintendent's office was quick to respond to the criticism. Both he and Lieutenant Matt Finch, who is heading the homicide team, refused to comment on Jacob's suggestion that Chicago Police were already labelling the killing as insoluble. One suggested scenario is that the victim had been drawn into a drug deal that backfired or a sexual liaison that went out of control in the deserted car park of the Adler Planetarium following a dinner thrown by the Techrim corporation. Despite Rhys Jacob's insistence that his sister is an innocent victim, a source at the Eleventh Street station suggested that investigating officers remain quietly sceptical.

'The lady was at a convention, probably letting her hair down, doing all kinds of things she wouldn't normally do. At present, we have to keep all our options open.'

Speculation that female conventioneers may be at risk from further attacks were refuted by Hopper and dismissed as unsubstantiated alarmist rumourmongering.

Mackie exhaled and shook her head. Unquoted sources, the worst kind of conjecture. It all made the department look bad whichever way you looked at it. She tore out the article and folded it into her purse.

Inside the Dupont, it was all gold light fittings and flowers, pink tablecloths and aproned waiters. She adjusted her hair in a lobby mirror and went in to meet the family. They were all seated, and a small ripple of applause and a couple of hoots from her brothers greeted her entrance. It seemed good-natured enough and Susan was pleased to see that they hadn't started eating.

'Sorry,' she announced.

'The city's underworld keeping you busy, Susan?' her father boomed, deep and cutting. She walked up to the head of the table and offered her cheek first to her mother, bird-like, eyebrows raised in silent condemnation and then to her father, wondering how much the sarcasm was pure mood and how much had been stoked up by the booze. He wasn't a big drinker; like the rest of his life, he controlled it absolutely. But on his birthday, he usually tied one on with a vengeance. He glared up at her now, heavy eyebrows under greying hair, the chin jutting forward in that challenging way of his. A big man with a big ego.

She sat next to Linda, Michael's wife. Her middle brother worked in the city's financial district not five blocks from the restaurant, but Linda had decided their home should be twenty miles north. Susan was relieved to see Audra, Scott's wife, opposite her. She liked Audra. She was an antidote to the feckless, insensitive Linda. Even so, it was impossible to ignore the fact that both women were pregnant, and Susan risked a glance at her mother to see if she was getting any pleasure out of this. She tried to put it out of her head, not be so irritable, so damned hung up about it. But with Linda seeming incapable of talking about anything other that the difficulties of her first trimester and of how she'd read that dieting during pregnancy wasn't an entirely *bad* thing, it wasn't easy.

When Linda wasn't bending her ear, her father dominated the conversation with incessant reminiscences about the younger days of the family or of his own childhood. Occasionally, he would ask a question of one of the boys – designed to flatter, to make a point. Susan read them for what they were; all barbs aimed at her.

Finally, when Linda made a trip to the bathroom, Audra leaned across and gave out a loaded sigh. Susan reciprocated, but in truth they couldn't blame Linda for being an idiot. She was just one of these people with no insight.

Come on, Susan. It was eighteen months ago. Maybe it feels like yesterday to you, but it's ancient history to someone as preoccupied with herself as Linda.

Mackie rearranged the cutlery in front of her, eyes downcast. There were red roses in delicate cut-glass vases on the tables.

Red-letter days were what she termed the dates on the calendar, the colour she associated with that day. September 5th blocked out in red. The colour that had poured out of her. . . . Lest she forget. That was a good one. As if. . . .

Mackie had only been sixteen weeks pregnant. They had been kind in the hospital and said it was a spontaneous miscarriage, just one of those things. Nothing to suggest that there was anything to worry about in the future. But that immediate future, in the months after the miscarriage, had been bloody. Susan had told just a few people in the department, her bump hardly showing. But afterwards, people hadn't known what to say. Commiserations but not condolences. She had been thirty-one then and Nick had taken it so strangely, unwilling to talk about it for weeks and then dismissing it with a ghastly forced cheerfulness. She knew she should have brought it all out into the open, but that was with hopeless, bitter hindsight.

'So how are you really doing, Susan?' Audra's question took her by surprise.

'I'm fine. You?'

'God, you don't want to hear another pregnant lady story, do you?'

A little laugh, Audra sympathetic and nice.

'So, is there anyone at present?'

'Audra,' protested Mackie.

'Well, if you don't ask.'

Mackie smiled. 'No, no one special.'

She saw Audra's expression soften. 'You should come up one weekend. We could go riding while I still can.'

Mackie nodded. Scott, her eldest brother, and Audra had five green acres on the shores of a private lake outside Milwaukee – suitable accommodation for the corporate lawyer.

'I will. Soon.'

Audra looked at her in that way of hers. Sceptical but compassionate. Understanding perhaps better than Mackie did herself what was going on.

Her beeper took them both unawares. Mackie found a phone near the coat-check and rang in the familiar Eleventh Street number.

'Mac, that you?' The voice was Ryker's, a night shift detective on the squad.

'Yeah, what's up?'

'You near a TV?'

'No.'

'Get to one. Your guy's on *Eyewitness News*.'

'What guy?'

'The Adler victim's brother.'

She mumbled a thanks and grabbed a passing waiter. No, there was no TV in the restaurant, but she could try the bar across the street.

She ran across without her coat. 'Langley's', in neon over the door, mainly couples in booths, a few city types with their ties loose at the bar. She flashed her badge and asked a girl bartender to change channels. A blonde woman with heavy make-up appeared on the screen beneath a logo for CHTV *Eyewitness News*. Mackie caught nothing of what was said before the scene switched to the usual interview format of two seats angled at forty-five degrees in front of a lit backdrop of the city at night. But Mackie wasn't taking much notice of the scenery, she was concentrating on the face of the interviewee. It looked wary and solemn, the face of a grieving angry soul. Rhys Jacob's face.

Adjacent to him sat a girl with jet-black hair and Asian features that Mackie recognised instantly. Sue Cheng had a nose for a story and was on the street almost as often as she herself was.

Sue Cheng gave the camera one of her serious but dazzling smiles, glanced down to her lap at her pristine and probably empty info sheet and then turned to Rhys.

'Dr Jacob, we've just seen footage of the press conference at the Eleventh Street station this morning and this evening's *Globe* is running the story. For our viewers can I confirm that you positively identified the victim of the Planetarium slaying as that of your sister, Catrin?'

The close-up on his face showed Rhys's sombre nod.

'Your sister was a physician attending a medical convention here in Chicago, at McCormick Place, am I right?'

'Yes. It was her first time ... first time in this city.' The dry swallow halfway through the sentence accentuated his hesitation.

'And she knew no one here?'

'No.'

'Was she hoping to come and work in Chicago?'

'No, Baltimore – Johns Hopkins.'

'Dr Jacob, the police are desperately searching for some motive for this killing. It was suggested that this may have been drug-related. What is your response to that?'

'Catrin didn't use drugs. She was a doctor. They told me that some substances were found in her hotel room.' He rummaged under his seat and held up a battered leaflet in his hand and waved it at the camera. It looked like a stagey, phoney gesture. 'Today I found this in the wardrobe of my hotel room. It's a Parisian restaurant guide written in Japanese. I didn't invent its presence, but neither is it mine.'

Sue Cheng beamed at him momentarily and then her face became serious again.

'We know that this murder was particularly brutal. The other suggestion has been that there may have been a sexual angle here.'

Rhys was shaking his head, the pain evident in the lines on his forehead.

'Catrin was bright, intelligent . . . she didn't come to this city to indulge herself. She trained in London, spent a year in New York as a medical student. She wasn't some country bumpkin.' He paused, his expression confused and lost. 'To suggest that she was caught up in some . . . some sort of sleazy sexual encounter is offensive in the extreme.'

One of the guys at the bar murmured, 'Ever heard of playing the field, pal?'

Mackie swivelled around and shushed him angrily.

'So what would you like to see happen, Doctor?'

Rhys didn't answer for a long moment. He seemed to stare at the camera vacantly and then to gather himself, his eyes refocusing. Mackie found herself riveted to the screen. What they were witnessing was a grieving, traumatised relative, lost and confused by the harrowing strangeness of it all. And so far it had been painfully compulsive to watch.

What the hell had he agreed to go on for? she found herself thinking. But then Rhys Jacob took a deep breath and answered her question.

'So far,' he began, 'this investigation seems to be doing nothing but cast aspersions at my sister. I have to keep reminding myself that she is the victim here. Something dreadful has taken place but all that seems to be happening is that the reason for it all somehow gets thrown back at Catrin. That can't be right. Why isn't everyone worrying about who did this? There's a monster out there, isn't there?' He spoke earnestly, his eyes on the camera, the words now full of raw feeling. Sue Cheng took her cue.

'The mayor's office has been quick to allay fears that visitors and conventioneers are at risk. How do you respond to that?'

'I know that this murder is only one of hundreds in your city but I find it hard to accept any reassurances while this crime remains unsolved. It's pure political rhetoric, isn't it? My sister was attacked and killed in a public place by someone who is still at large.'

The camera cut to Sue Cheng's sincerely nodding head. She didn't speak. Being the pro that she was, she knew when to let a fluent guest have his head. And didn't he have just the most *incredible* accent?

'The authorities have offered to foot the bill for my stay here, offered to help with shipping costs. I'm grateful, but I also would like to know why. What are they trying to prove here? The fact remains my sister was killed while attending a convention. She was a doctor who trusted this city's authorities to provide some security for visitors. I presume that is what the city is trying to reassure everyone over. But my sister's reputation is being smeared all over the pavement. I'm not going to take that lying down. I'm a visitor here, I don't know how things work, but I'm beginning to think that making Catrin somehow responsible for what happened to her is very convenient. If it wasn't such a despicable thing to contemplate, I might even start thinking that it was a deliberate ploy to detract from the fact that there is a killer out there attacking innocent citizens.'

Someone whistled behind Mackie and she heard:

'This guy is one angry hombre.'

'Hope Congressman Kervesky is watching this.'

'The mayor must be having a coronary.'

Muffled laughter died away again as Sue Cheng milked Rhys for all he was worth.

'So you believe that whoever did this might strike again?'

Rhys shook his head. 'I'm no criminologist but until whoever did this is caught, that must surely be a possibility.'

'Dr Jacob,' said Sue Cheng as a closer, 'what would you like to see happen in this investigation?'

'I'd like to appeal for witnesses. Someone must have seen something. I'll be happy to speak to anyone if they'd prefer not to talk to the police. I'm staying at the Geneva . . .' Sue Cheng cut across him then. Revealing addresses was not a good idea in any city. Mackie winced, but at least there was a switchboard at the Geneva. She wondered how long it would take for them to realise they'd made the six o'clock news. She gave it about ten minutes until the operators blew a fuse. She'd better speak to them as soon as this was over.

The camera closed in on Cheng's face and pearly smile. 'Anyone with any information can contact the *Eyewitness* hot-line on 780 6675. All calls are confidential.' She pointed the smile in Rhys's direction for the last time. 'Dr Jacob, thank you for coming on at this difficult time. I hope CHTV *Eyewitness News* can be of some help. Now back to Leanda.'

The blonde woman's face filled the screen again and Mackie thanked the bartender who said, 'You're welcome,' before flicking the TV back to a *Chicago Hope* rerun.

Mackie ran back across the street but her beeper went off before she reached the door. She rang the number and got Finch's strained voice in answer.

'You see it?'

'Yeah.'

'Any comments?' Finch asked drily.

'The guy was angry after this morning. I couldn't believe Hopper expecting him to perform in front of cameras like that.'

'I have no control over Hopper,' snapped Finch. 'I didn't like it any more than you did. When is the body going to be released?'

'Tomorrow, I think.'

'Check it out. Where are you going in the investigation?'

'Running checks on Planetarium staff, looking for anyone with a sheet. Lou is chasing up the guest list I think.'

'OK. Meantime, I want you to go see Dr Jacob. Help him arrange the shipping. Keep him busy, keep him away from CHTV.'

'He's pissed off, Lieutenant. What if he doesn't want to go home?'

'Convince him, Susan.'

She walked back into the party, preoccupied, the muted roar of the audience's forced response to one of her father's jokes throwing her for a moment. She hurried to her chair, but not before her father fixed her with his baleful stare.

'Don't let us interrupt you, Susan.'

'Sorry, I had to call in.'

'Another major traffic violation?' He was motoring under a full head of steam now. 'Or has someone stolen all the paper clips from the mayor's office?'

Normally, she might have backed down, taken everyone else's feelings and embarrassment into consideration, but she was pumped up from seeing Rhys Jacob, her mind still at work.

'No,' she said evenly. 'The brother of the Planetarium rape-murder victim was on TV. It's my case.'

'I read about that,' said Scott, impressed.

'You mean they're actually letting you play at being a real detective?' Her father's smile was predatory.

'Looks like it. . . .'

Scott was about to say something but their father silenced him with a glance.

'And you consider this a token of your success, Susan?'

'It's nice to be in the game, sure.'

'What is it exactly that appeals to you? I'm sure everyone here would like to know. We can all understand Scott's attraction to the law and Michael's financial dealings. Even Richard's fascination with medicine is excusable but, homicide?'

'Dad, haven't you had enough to drink?' said Susan.

'What are you going to do, arrest me?'

Someone tittered, but mostly they stayed silent, watching this ritual sparring, wondering when Susan was going to back down.

'No indulge me, do,' said Ewan Mackie. 'Regale us with tales of the dreadful deeds perpetrated on the hapless occupants of the city. Conundrums that you unravel with consummate intellectual ease. Come, girl. You have a captive audience. Is it the camaraderie between you and your fine fellow officers 40 per cent of whom, according to last week's *Chronicle*, eat and drink in this city for free? Or perhaps it's the violence? Some streak in you that craves the beast?'

'Can't we just enjoy the party?' Susan spoke in a low flat delivery.

'Oh, but I am enjoying myself immensely. I simply want to know what it is that makes the criminal psychopaths you deal with every day so attractive?'

'There's nothing attractive about it. It's a job that I do so that people like you can sleep safe at night.'

'You hear that everyone, she's doing it for us. How touching.'

'Oh, for Chrissakes. Spare us this bullshit. You want photographs of the dead girl? I have some in my briefcase.' Silence fell like a heavy blanket. Eyes turned in her direction.

'Watch your language, young lady.' Her father's brows lowered. 'It's obvious you're mixing with people who don't mind blasphemy, but I will not stand for it.'

It was then that it blew. Her father's carping, pious, put-downs the pin that burst the bubble of pressure that had been simmering away inside her all day.

'No? Well maybe we should all get up and curse instead of sitting here like a bunch of wooden dolls listening to this crap.'

The room was silent as Ewan Mackie stood. Not as tall as his sons but taller than his one daughter. 'Plainly, you are either drunk or intent on ruining this evening. You have forgotten your values, abandoned respect.'

Susan got to her feet. 'Respect? For what, this make-believe ritual? I respect what I am, which is more than you do. Look at us,' she waved a hand around at the audience. 'Do you think any of us enjoys this? At least when I'm at work I feel that it's real. This is just a sham. Playing at happy families.'

'Susan,' her father growled.

'I'm sorry, OK? I'm sorry for being what I am and I'm sorry for ruining everyone's evening. But I don't have to sit here and listen to you belittle me any more. In case you hadn't noticed, I grew up and became a person.' She looked down at the faces around her, some downcast, most flushed with embarrassment. 'At least now, you may all get a chance to go home early.'

She turned and walked away. No one followed her. The room stayed silent. She walked to her car and drove back to the station house, anger stemming the tears that threatened to erupt. The previous year she had sat at a similar table in another restaurant at the same celebration, mutely drowning her sorrows the night after Nick had gone, her parents and siblings blissfully unaware of her melancholia, listening to the same old tune from her father, but staying quiet, letting it all flow over her, putting up with it all as she had done over the years.

As a kid, Susan had pitched for a little league team, played soccer, read *Batman* like her brothers. All the while with one eye on her father, the big man, the successful businessman with two companies, the patriarch.

They had lived in the big house overlooking the lake all their lives. The Mackies; sounded like a family soap which is exactly what it was. An opera, a staged existence where the outside world hardly ever intruded, where claustrophobic repression reigned. As children, they had all the trappings – huge grounds to play in, summers in Maine, prep school, Chelsea Day School. But more than anything, Susan remembered the house. It had a name, Portland House. A good name for a sturdy house. There were spacious kitchens that were warm in winter and smelled of baking pies and attic playrooms with shafted light beaming through the porthole windows in the early mornings, and her father's study, dark with mahogany like bitter chocolate and the rows of books that they had never been allowed to touch, were still not allowed to touch. Always this emphasis on property and sacred cows and forbidden pleasures that had always to be earned.

Susan had loved that study. She had stood for hours on the threshold staring in, seeing it as the closet door that led to Narnia. Except there was no lion on the other side, just her father. The man she wanted to be with, to tell about her exuberant day in eighth grade, about her collection of twigs, the frog-spawn in the pond, the million things that he was too busy to listen to. When she asked for time, as children do, the reply came always as *inconvenient*.

The only time she could guarantee his complete attention was when they went through the ritual of examining her grades. When there were As his eyes would glitter. Then at last he would hold her, chastely, but with genuine affection. She remembered those magical moments as so precious but so few.

And always, always as she watched the November storms hiss and boil across the lake from some high place in Portland House, she would wonder if somehow she had been secreted into this family by mistake. As if the faerie queen had brought her from another place. A changeling, craving an emotional something that had eluded her for so many frustrating years.

She took her head. These were old as the hills thoughts. No beginning, no end, just a crazy pathway full of holes she so easily fell into.

Rhys was sitting watching an infomercial when she phoned. It had taken him ten minutes to realise that this was just a huge, long and elaborate commercial mocked up to look like a talk show. The woman, a doctor, but not of medicine, was selling a personal relationships guide and kept bringing people up from the audience to tell everyone how they had benefited. The remaining seated members of the audience hooted and clapped at each clichéd truism and Rhys wondered who the hell was taken in by these things before realising that he had been watching it himself for ten minutes.

'Evening,' he said into the receiver, recognising Mackie's voice.

'Nice performance,' she said.

'I wouldn't expect you to understand.'

'Try me.'

'What do you want me to say? That I'm sorry for criticising the way this is being handled?'

'This is a free country, Rhys. I just wondered if you knew, really knew what you were letting yourself in for? Giving the name of your hotel was a dumb move.'

'Everyone knew where I was staying anyway. At least the press all did. Five minutes after I got back this morning I had six different newspapers and news agencies begging me for photographs and details. That, I could cope with, I've been in the world long enough to know one man's tragedy is another's titillating inside story. But an hour later, one of my uncles phoned from home. Some press agency floosie had actually been around asking for photographs of Catrin. But not just snaps. They were after something out of the ordinary. Something of her in a bathing suit for God's sake. They're decent people my family, you know? It wouldn't occur to them that these bastards are looking for something to spice up a story.'

'Did your uncle give them anything?'

'No. Not even after being offered pin money. He said he wanted to speak to me first.'

'I'm sorry you're getting hassled. But there have been no cranks?'

'Not yet. Just Bellasco at the *Chronicle* asking for an interview.'

'Rhys,' Mackie's tone was full of patient exasperation, 'this town has its share of whackos. They peek out from under stones and see their prayers answered when someone like you pops up.'

'Thank you for the lecture, detective. I'll just go back and lock myself in my glass cabinet, OK?'

The line was silent for a long moment. Mackie's voice when it returned held just a hint of contrition. 'I didn't call to chew you out.'

'No? You do surprise me.'

'If you want to know, I feel bad about this morning. No one deserved what they did to you. Hopper is a jerk. The Lieutenant is kinda jumpy right now . . .'

'Really?' Rhys's voice reverberated with cynicism.

'Look,' snapped Mackie, 'this is not an easy call for me to make. They all want me to hustle you on to the next plane back to England. But it so happens that I think you deserve a little better.'

Rhys didn't answer.

'Before I joined violent crime, I worked in victim support. What I'm saying here is that maybe it would do some good to talk. Let me take you for a drink. Start over. What do you say?'

'So that you can police my activities, is that it?'

'What do you want from me?' said Mackie exasperatedly.

'OK, I'll come out with you for a drink. But on my terms. I'll come if you take me to wherever my sister went before she died.'

'The Planetarium?' asked Mackie with distaste.

'No, before that. She was in this city for two days before she died. I want to know what this drug-addicted sex maniac did.'

He heard Mackie sigh and begin ruffling through some papers. 'The night before, she ate at the Saloon with a couple of medical reps and doctors. Another pharmaceutical company freebie. Then, according to statements, they went to a blues club and then on to the Nelson Theatre.'

'Let's do the same.'

'Now hold on . . .'

'I'll pay . . .'

'It's not the money.'

'You don't like blues?'

'No,' protested Mackie, 'I mean sure, but . . .'

'Then what? I want to know what my sister did before she died. Is it a lot to ask under the circumstances?'

He heard her sigh. 'OK, I'll pick you up at nine-thirty. Will you call for a reservation, or will I?'

'Do you have any influence?'

'A little.'

'Then why not use it.' He hung off before she had a chance to tell him to take a hike.

Jake was alone too. He sat in a room at the Honolulu Motel on the southern fringe of O'Hare's airport district. A crime-ridden area of failed housing projects and ailing industry. The room was a mess of discarded soda tins, deli wrappers from the Seven-Eleven across the road, clothes and newspapers. But it was the sort of establishment where no one was going to complain too much and the housekeeper visited once a week. A battered TV sat chained to the wall on a rickety table. Balanced on the TV was a pile of quarters ready to be fed into the payslot bolted to the wall.

Jake sat on the bed cross-legged, eating from a purple bag of mesquite-flavoured kettle chips, his eyes glued to the TV. He had left McCormick Place as it had started to empty, walking quickly to his car and driving back to his motel directly.

Around him, pasted to the wall were sketches and elaborate doodles. Most had a robotic motif, fantastic machines with huge antennae, but most were unrecognisable and meaningless to anyone except Jake.

There was a dead person talking to him on the TV. The features were the same as were burned in his memory; fine and dark, the voice with that similar odd accent.

He knew with absolute and unshakeable certainty that this was the Jacob. On the bed in front of his knees was the badge he'd taken from the dead girl at the Planetarium. The white plastic was splashed with dark blood, but still the name was readable. Dr C. Jacob.

And as he looked, a subtitle flashed up the interviewee's name on the TV: Dr R. Jacob.

The face on the TV screen was the same. Bigger yes, broader undoubtedly, gender transformed but with the identical expressive brown eyes, the same full mouth.

Fear flooded into him, engulfing him in its stranglehold. The kettle chips fell like petals from a decaying rose onto the bed as Jake's eyes beheld the face of the girl that had come to fetch him moulded into the harder features of a man. The fear came from the knowledge that others would be watching this. Others would see and know he was a Jacob. The Whistler would see and know . . .

He has to tell what he saw.

A scream began in Jake's throat but he bit it back and tried to speak, to drown out the broadcast.

He straightened his legs and reached for a pillow as he slowly let himself down on the bed and placed the pillow over his head so as not to see the shadows that threatened and hear the words that fired a hundred rounds a second into his head. Beneath the material, his hot breath moist and cloying, he felt the glare and muffled tones of the TV reach for him through the pillow. *But if he thinks about it, it'll find him. It'll find him and suck his brains out. The Whistler.*

In his mind he saw the innocent wave of the motel manager who had been outside when Jake had arrived home. He saw now that the wave was full of horrifying meaning. Any minute he expected the door to fly open and to see the manager standing there, his fingers pointing accusingly, his hand to his ear with a mocking grin, letting Jake know that all the other residents in the motel could hear Jake's every heartbeat, assimilate his every thought, sucking the air from the room and analysing his very breath for what he knew, what he feared, his filthy thoughts.

It isn't safe.

He couldn't be sure of anyone or anything. His brother, his

mother, they were not as they were. Perhaps The Whistler had got at them first, replacing them with his own demon-kind.

Memory of the horror at the Planetarium played again in technicolour, bursting in on him with an echoing roar. And he was there, in it, staring around in the Hall of Exploration, seeing his own open-mouthed figure cowering under the Planet Wall, seeing the huge frame of The Whistler squeezing the life out of the Jacob, seeing her feet dangling, her futile struggling. And then he saw himself running, away from that place. Relief came then. He was escaping, getting away, but in his mind, the echoing footfalls of his own body died away and he was left, watching. He saw The Whistler fall to his knees over the girl, squeezing with both hands, hearing the dreadful high-pitched whine that emanated from his head.

It isn't safe.

He wanted it to end now, didn't want to see any more.

How could he be seeing this, how could he possibly be seeing this?

She had stopped moving under the throttling power of those hands still around her neck. Jake was right behind them, not two yards away. He couldn't move, paralysed to the spot as he watched The Whistler's head begin to turn towards him, swivelling easily, the features in black shadow, all except the eyes which glittered redly, piercing him, peeling back the skin and bone from his head, exposing the raw surface of his brain, pillaging his very thoughts.

Jake screamed and the image shattered, leaving him sweating and trembling on the bed. For an hour, he plunged into the depth of a black chasm of hopeless paranoia until gradually, the swarming bees of his terror settled and he emerged onto a plane where he could at least exist and function in a semblance of partial reason. That reason was narrow and focused. He was known to them, that was clear. They were injecting the hallucinations into his head and he knew that they would surely destroy him if they went too far. He didn't want to see what The Whistler had done to the Jacob, he didn't want to know. He couldn't let that happen again. He couldn't allow the monster to roam free. Purpose, dreadful in its implication and forged by a twisted, misshapen logic, reasserted itself into Jake's head. He had to help even if it meant facing him again. . . .

The Whistler.

It isn't safe.

His task was to find it before it found the Jacob and him. The thought filled him with dread. He got up and began placing tin foil over the windows to deflect the penetrating, probing beams. And all the while the chanting mantra went on in his head.

It isn't safe.
It isn't safe.
It isn't safe.

12

THE SALOON BUZZED with noise and activity. It was not a big place, but all the tables were full with at least a dozen hopefuls at the bar salivating over their Martinis and pretzels and praying for a cancellation.

Mackie and Rhys were shown to their table immediately, squeezed in between a couple with an almost painfully slow Texan drawl and four Japanese teenagers who chattered and giggled inanely. There was barely enough room behind the seated diners for the white-aproned waiters to strut with their overloaded trays. After the inevitable glass of ice water, their own waiter, a freckled, well-muscled youth with an efficient hustling nature which seemed to suit the atmosphere perfectly bustled over with a plate of raw meats coated in clear plastic wrap as examples of what was available.

'I take it this is a steak house?' said Rhys drily after he'd ordered an eight-ounce rump.

'It's OK,' said Mackie indifferently. 'Definitely on the tourist route but I've eaten in a lot worse places. It was recommended to the medical reps that brought your sister here by the concierge at their hotel. A lot of entertaining goes on at these conventions. Both reps were also at the Planetarium and gave statements.'

'Same company organised the Planetarium dinner, did they?'

'Techrim.'

'Did the reps do drugs?'

'Not as far as we could ascertain.'

'So, when they came here they were just enjoying a meal?'

Mackie nodded warily. 'Your sister, two other doctors and the reps. One female, one male.'

They lapsed into silence, Mackie content to let Rhys make his point, judging that it was important to him, sensing the anger boiling away beneath the surface.

'From your phone call, I suppose your Lieutenant didn't appreciate my TV performance?' he asked eventually.

'Great ratings.'

'Has the TV station received many calls?'

'What do you think?'

'Anything useful?'

'Too early to say.'

Rhys nodded. 'You don't sound too hopeful.'

Mackie shrugged.

'I want to know what happened the night she died.'

'At the Adler?'

'Yes. And not just the edited version, everything.'

Mackie took a swallow of beer and wiped a froth moustache from her upper lip. 'The last sky show at the Planetarium was at eight p.m. Doors closed to the public at seven-thirty. Before and after the dinner in the Hall of Space Exploration, guests were allowed to wander around the exhibits and up to the second and third floors. Adler staff were meant to have cleared all the public out of there by nine-thirty. After the dinner, there was a special showing in the Sky Theatre dome for guests followed by hot chocolate and coffee in the lobby. Problem was, come eleven p.m., there were a hundred and twenty guests waiting to go home and no cabs. No reason for there to be any out at the Adler that time of night and someone had forgotten to tee up the cab companies beforehand. It took the staff twenty minutes or more to realise they had to rustle up some transport and by that time, the cattle were getting a little restless. It was a lousy night, rain and storm-force winds but even so a few people decided to risk it and began walking towards Solidarity Drive, hoping for a stray cab.'

'Is that what my sister did?'

'It's a possibility.'

Rhys took a sip from a chunky glass of draught Coors, its sides dripping with condensed moisture. 'So what then? She meets somebody she immediately gets the hots for, jumps into his car and they take a barrowfull of drugs, is that about the size of it?'

Mackie's eyes narrowed; her patience wearing thin. 'We're not speculating on what happened then.'

'You mean Detective Bek is still actually trying to find out?'

'Yup,' she said.

Rhys nodded. 'He struck me as a man with a truly open mind. Did I mention that to you?'

'I think you just did.'

Rhys took another hit from the beer and smiled challengingly. Mackie leaned forward. 'I know a little about how you feel.'

'Really. Someone in your family get throttled and sexually molested?'

'No,' said Mackie slowly with exaggerated care. 'But I do have family.'

'Nice for you.'

She pushed away her beer and sat back, both hands on the table.

'Maybe we should do this another time,' she said pushing her chair back.

'I'm not going to have another time, Detective Mackie.' Rhys stared at her.

Mackie hesitated and then let out a sigh of resignation. 'After eating here, they went to a blues club on North Halstead.'

'Fine,' said Rhys. 'Then that's what we'll do.'

He toyed with his steak and watched impatiently as Mackie ate a green salad, the little conversation they attempted frugal and strained. After twenty more minutes, he paid with a credit card and they took a cab, sitting in the rear without speaking.

They pulled up in front of a narrow building with a stone-dressed frontage around a large mural of blues players and their instruments. Two large black men in reversed baseball caps and gloves guarded the door.

Inside a tiny ante-room another black man and a minder stood behind a counter and took thirty dollars from Rhys as an entry fee for both of them.

The minder leaned forward and let them squeeze past through a second door into a room crammed with people, smoke and music. On the tiny stage to the left of the door, a black girl was belting out a song in competition with an electric guitar and drums. People were jamming the narrow passage to the bar and the room beyond. Mackie took a right and led Rhys into a second room, dark, but less crowded. She led the way to the rear where it opened out into a larger area well back from the second stage which mirrored the room they had first entered. Several high tables were bolted to the floor in this area and a few empty bottles still stood uncleared upon them.

'They alternate sets,' she explained, peeling off her coat. 'Look.' She pointed to a TV screen above the stage at the front; it showed the girl and her two-piece accompaniment from a high-angled camera. A circulating waitress in black jeans and a white T-shirt approached them almost immediately and they ordered two beers. Rhys looked around. The walls in the rear were plain whitewashed cinder block, the roof strung with exposed wiring and piping. He could see no exit indicated and mindful of the crush at the front entrance wondered how this place ever got approval for fire regulations.

Rhys wandered around, looking at the customers and seeing people with too much beer on board making a lot of noise. They stayed fifteen minutes and he didn't say more than three words to Mackie the whole time they were there.

She had been right about the dug-out. The blues was unspontaneous and too raw, the place losing out in its attempt at portraying the poverty from which the music was spawned.

'So, what do you think?' asked Mackie as they sat in the rear of another cab.

'The dug-out? I was not accosted by dope fiends, or did I miss something?'

'No. The dug-out is squeaky clean. They make their money from selling videos of the night's sets to the tourists.'

'So what next?'

He saw Mackie's eyebrows arch. 'After the dug-out, they all went to the Nelson Theatre, which is where we're headed for now.'

'Why the strange look?'

Mackie shook her head and simply said, 'You'll see.'

They drove through windswept neighbourhoods, devoid of the tall buildings that characterised Downtown. The streets were littered and bleak, the bars shoddy with red neon signs and an aura of better times. The Nelson Theatre was on West Lawrence. It stood out, an awning decked out with glowing bulbs and banners announcing the:

All New Nelson Theatre
For more than twenty years presenting the finest
in Adult entertainment.

The taxi stopped outside and they both got out, but Mackie turned to the cab driver and told him to wait.

'What's going on?' asked Rhys.

'I don't think I'll come in with you. I'll go get a coffee in a deli somewhere and pick you up in half an hour.'

'Why?'

'Wait and see.' She ushered Rhys in through a pair of big wooden doors. Inside, a man in a tuxedo glanced at them curiously but said nothing. The lobby was large, well-lit and carpeted in turquoise. Another tuxedo stood in an arched chest-high booth. On the walls, information boards detailing the Nelson's illustrious history were proudly displayed.

'Evening, sir,' said the man in the booth. He was young, clean-shaven. 'Admission is twenty-five dollars. That includes one free drink, but you must buy one more inside.'

Rhys paid and glanced around at Mackie who was tucked in behind him out of sight of the ticket-seller.

'Coat check to your left, sir.'

Rhys swivelled and took his coat off. Mackie moved in to the ticket-seller's line of sight.

'Evening, ma'am.' The booth man's face took on a surprised, slightly disapproving look. 'Thirty-five dollars.'

'I thought you said twenty-five?'

'You must be mistaken, ma'am.'

Mackie took out her shield and flashed it. The booth man's face turned ashen and he swivelled and whispered to some-one behind him. A new face appeared, older, more swarthy complexion.

'Detective, what can we do for you? I think there may have been a misunderstanding over the admission price.'

'Why don't you jokers just put a sign up saying men only. Then we can all stand back and watch the city close you down for good.'

'Anyone can come in here officer, you know that.'

'Yeah? You remember a party coming in last Thursday night? Three guys and two women?'

A look of intense concentration crossed the man's face.

'Come on,' said Mackie. 'The women came because the men dared them to. You should remember 'cos you asked them to leave.'

'Oh, sure. Yeah, I remember. Lady was kinda excitable.'

'At your prices she had every right to be.'

Rhys came back without his coat. 'Problem?'

'No, no problem.' She turned to the swarthy man. 'This is my brother. He's visiting.'

The man nodded. 'Sure. We'll take good care of him.'

Mackie grinned at Rhys. 'I'll come back in half an hour to pick you up. OK?'

'But I still don't understand why.'

'Enjoy,' said Mackie over her shoulder in a tired voice.

In mild confusion, Rhys watched her go. He walked past the booth and saw that behind it was another area sectioned off and guarded by a turnstile. Further on, the lobby funnelled down onto a shallow ramp that led to a black curtain from where people were emerging. Another tuxedoed minder appeared and spoke to him. He saw that the man, indeed all of them, were equipped with small two-way radios which they held in their big palms.

'Lost, sir?'

'This the way in?'

'Down the ramp and to your left. There are plenty of seats.' Rhys walked down the ramp and pushed open the door. The music hit him immediately, loud, rocking, the bass beat turbo-charged. The light was dimmed but not dim enough for him to avoid seeing what was going on on stage. To his right, along one wall, a group of girls sat watching the audience. They were all young, early twenties he guessed. From the glance he saw they all wore short skirts and high heels, all with their legs crossed. The stage area was large, jutting out into the room which was full of tables, some in the rear raised up on a dais. It seemed darker back there and Rhys couldn't see too well. He found himself a seat and eased in to it uneasily, his eyes taken with the spotlit girl on the stage. She looked Spanish or Mexican. An olive flawless body in a long trailing dress, her hair decorated with a red rose which matched the dress perfectly. But her dancing had nothing to do with Flamenco as she strutted and posed. Almost immediately a waitress appeared and asked him what he wanted to drink.

'A beer,' he said almost automatically. The waitress smiled patiently.

'Sorry, no alcohol.' She pointed behind her to a large sign to the left of the stage.

ILLINOIS STATE LAW PROHIBITS NAKEDNESS AND THE CONSUMPTION OF ALCOHOL IN THE SAME ESTABLISHMENT.

'Uh, Coke will be fine.'

She laid out a coaster and disappeared just as the music changed and went up tempo. The girl on the stage took off her dress and danced in a G string.

Rhys dragged his eyes away and looked around. Opposite the stage and slightly higher was a glass booth with a DJ wearing cans. A TV screen played videos of previous 'exotic dancers'.

The place was two-thirds full, tables occupied by groups of two or three men, occasionally one man alone like him. He saw only two women at the tables not dressed as if they worked in the joint. A steady stream of girls wandered to and from the wall where they were sitting and loped slowly to and from tables. There seemed to be a lot of activity behind him. And then he saw a tall dark-haired girl in a pink Lycra dress lean in and whisper something to a couple of youths with faintly Asian features and wispy moustaches at a table adjacent to him.

The men nodded and brought out some paper money. The girl turned her back on them and Rhys and slowly, teasingly began to take off her dress. She wore nothing underneath. For three, perhaps four minutes she pouted and postured, positioning buttocks, breasts and thighs inches away from the avid gaze of the youths who must have known all the rules as they sat mesmerised by the flesh on offer. Rhys watched the performance in something bordering on amazement. The expressions on the faces of the men were difficult to interpret. A mixture of guilty indulgence and lust. The reason for all the security became obvious. Here was flesh being shown and offered, but in a sanitised way. Touching was definitely not allowed.

A blonde girl with perfect teeth and dazzling eyes approached Rhys.

'Hi, I'm Lucy. You want a table dance?'

'Uh, no thanks,' said Rhys.

Lucy pouted.

'No really,' said Rhys.

Lucy shrugged and moved away to find someone else. Rhys watched her go, her skirt two inches below the cheeks of a round bottom, legs long and smooth in the heels. The waitress returned with his drink and he sipped it from a straw, relishing its coldness. He saw that the glass was packed with ice, the ounce of Coke already watery.

Above, a siren wailed and search lights flew across the stage. He realised that the Spanish girl had gone. The DJ's voice came over the p.a.

'OK, it's party time. Where is Jacky? Jacky, twenty today. Come on, man, own up. It's your lucky night.'

The wheeling spot picked out a kid in a Bulls T-shirt and jeans.

'OK. Here comes Patsy to escort you to the stage. Oooweee you're in for a triple header, my man.'

Another blonde in a black mini-dress took Jacky to the stage and proceeded to tie his arms and legs to a chair. She and two other girls then proceeded to strip in front of him, Jacky grinned incessantly as the DJ offered a running commentary on the presence or absence of the bulge in Jacky's crotch. It was an attempt at humour that the audience seemed to enjoy. But Rhys got the impression that most of the men just wanted to ogle the girls.

After Jacky's ordeal, the DJ announced a dollar dance. Each girl would come to a table and dance for a dollar until the music changed before moving on to another table that held up a dollar.

It was then that Rhys realised that this whole sanitised soft porn was geared to making the suckers in the audience cough up as much money as they could.

The watered-down drinks, the dollar dances. He guessed that to participate, you would need to spend upwards of fifty to a hundred dollars. The absence of alcohol and the forced humour was totally alien to Rhys. He had never seen anything quite like this before and it left him feeling strangely apprehensive.

The girls were stunning. Many of these were centre-fold material and he could imagine being here with a few mates. Good, clean, masculine fun? Maybe. But he didn't know where the hell Catrin had fitted into all of this.

He left after twenty minutes and went into the area behind the pay booth. There stacked on shelves were the more hard core magazines and videos. But they were kept out of sight, hidden from the main stream of customers. All wrapped in Cellophane and as untouchable as the girls inside.

He emerged from the theatre and breathed in the night air, confused and woozy as he came down from the rapidly ingested beers of earlier. After a few minutes, Mackie turned up in the taxi and he climbed in.

'Interesting place,' he said feeling his cheeks burning.

'Squeaky clean, too,' said Mackie. 'They get rousted every week by vice. They can't afford any slip-ups.'

'What the hell did they take Catrin to a place like that for?' asked Rhys, his question tinged with mild anger.

Mackie turned her face to him. 'You sound like the gorilla in there. You think women shouldn't be allowed?'

'Whatever melts your butter. You know that's not what I mean. Catrin would have hated something like that.'

'Maybe she did. But she was a little drunk and the guys in the party wanted to go there. There was this big friendly argument and the girls said OK, but they wanted to go too. I think your sister took it as a personal challenge. They sat at a table and Catrin wanted to dance, not naked, just dance. Not many people do that. The floor manager got uppety and asked them to leave. It intimidated the hell out of the guys they were with.'

Rhys allowed himself a faint smile. 'That sounds like her.' He hunched down in the corner and withdrew into himself again.

'So,' said Mackie as they headed downtown. 'You glad you did this?'

'Yes.' He kept his eyes staring out of the window, but added, 'and I'm grateful.'

'You going to be able to pick up your sister tomorrow?'

'Perhaps.'

'What does that mean?'

'There are a few things I need to do.'

'Such as?'

'Talk to a few people. Arrange things.' He turned to face her, his voice peevish.

'Sure. If there's anything I can do . . . ?'

Rhys surprised her by sitting up. 'I'd like to know exactly what drugs Catrin is supposed to have taken so that I can check with her doctors at home.'

'OK. I can get you a copy of the toxicology report.'

'Thanks. Oh, and one more thing. The rep that was with Catrin at the Nelson, and the Planetarium?'

'Yeah.'

'Could I have a name?'

Mackie tilted her head. 'Can I ask why?'

'Because it would save me a lot of phoning around. I'd like to speak to her since she was one of the last people to see Catrin alive.'

'Rhys, please don't get in the way of this investigation. I know how you feel . . .'

'You have no bloody idea how I feel,' he seethed and his anger, so bright, so hard, astonished her.

Mackie hesitated for a long moment then said, 'Rourke. Pamela Rourke.'

It was after midnight when she dropped Rhys off at the Geneva. The spacy feeling was back with him, the discrepancy between his physical tiredness and mental alertness skewing everything and mingling with the burning sense of outrage he felt at all that was going on.

In his room he threw off his clothes and lay on the bed, his legs aching, his brain flying. Catrin's bruised face hung in his mind like a huge balloon. He tried to imagine what she must have felt during those last minutes of her life and couldn't. He forced himself to turn away from it, searching and finding a memory of her clean, pretty face laughing and smiling. But the two images fought, amalgamating into a floating mish-mash of something unhealthy and inhuman.

Mackie got back to her apartment wondering what the inevitable powwow at the restaurant had come up with after she'd left. She checked her answering machine. There were no messages and so her imagination supplied the answers.

'*Leave her alone, she'll get over it.*'

Or maybe just, '*leave her alone!*' – an order from her father. Let her stew in her own miserable juices.

She shook her head. A crappy end to a lousy day. She ran the shower and while she waited for it to heat up, went in to the bedroom she had shared with Nick. She undressed and tried to pretend that she wasn't going to open the blanket box. It sat in the corner, covered with magazines. With her blouse unbuttoned, she told herself it was better that she left it alone. Better that she just had a hot shower and went to bed. And then she was walking over and taking off the magazines, lifting the wooden lid and peering inside, unable to help herself. Drawn to it on this day of sour memories.

Nick's photograph was there, still in its frame – candid, wind ruffling his hair against a background of the boats he loved.

Beneath, carefully folded, some still wrapped in their packaging was the evidence of her folly. Oshkosh, Oililey, Laura Ashley; the names leapt out at her. Pastel shades, not pink or blue. All bought when she had been sure of the pregnancy, unable to resist buying some of the things she had seen, ignoring that cynical voice in her head that told her she was tempting fate. She stopped herself from picking any of the baby clothes up, feeling the emotion bubble and well inside, wanting to step out of the vicious spiral before it got hold. Still on her knees, she put Nick's photograph back, this time face down and closed the box.

In the shower, she cried. After a while the pain eased and she made herself think about Rhys Jacob's hurt and his anguish over what had happened to his sister. It was interesting to find that it bothered her more not being able to help him on that than anything that had happened at the restaurant with her father. And in an odd way, that feeling pleased her.

Rhys had lain there for thirty minutes when the phone rang. He picked it up and the switchboard operator said simply, 'I have a call for you, sir.'

Rhys held the phone close to his ear and sat up groggily, fumbling for a light and not finding it. The line buzzed with ethereal static for a long moment.

'Hello?' said Rhys.

'Jacob?' The voice sounded hesitant, full of trepidation.

'Who is this?'

'It isn't safe. I saw the TV. You mustn't go on again. They watch through the TV. He knows who you are now. The Whistler knows . . .' The sentence stopped, cut off abruptly as if by a shutter.

'You saw me on TV?'

'I knew who you were. I knew before they showed your name and insignia. You look like the Jacob. She was pretty, she was pretty before the hands squeezed . . . I saw her there. I saw her from the planet wall.'

'Who is this?'

'It isn't safe. We are the same, you and me. You have to be careful. I didn't design this communicator it's easy for The Whistler to absorb the thoughts he does it by mode of his ultrasonic beam. He takes everything that's in my head and puts things in there that . . .' A sob emerged, single, solitary.

'Please, who is this?'

'I'm trying to design some alternation but it takes time. It isn't safe you should be careful. I took her insignia. I'll use this.'

'What insignia? What are you talking about?'

'They've taken my memory by mode of the beam. I've been down here so long I can't remember what the words mean. . . . They're on the rear of her insignia . . .'

Rhys heard an intake of deep breath. '. . . h,o,l,l, g,a,r,i,a,d, E,i,r,a.'

'Wha . . .' the breath locked in Rhys's throat. The letters meant nothing except to Rhys, Catrin and his family. An inscription on the back of the brooch his grandmother had given Catrin when she was eleven. A brooch bought new by her grandfather to celebrate their mother's birth. 'With all my love, Eira' was the inscription. Written in the old lady's first language, the one she was most comfortable with. Catrin had worn it constantly, a reminder of the past, a link with the family.

Rhys was wholly awake now. The speech he was hearing was confused, almost unintelligible in a way and yet it was understandable. He had heard such speech before. Not exactly but definitely similar.

'Where did you get . . . How do you . . .?'

'The Whistler sees. I look for him in the chariot. I know it. A chariot of light. And I'll find it and I'll use the words I'll use my specific calculations in designing the alternation. I'll use the words of power. Keep away from the TV, take Jacob back to The Rim. It's too late for me, it isn't safe. They watch me. They have machines that cause alternation in dreams. He sees you by mode of the beam and I don't want those hands around your throat I don't want to get the pictures in my head, it isn't safe.' The voice had risen to a pleading begging yowl. Again the voice shut off as if a switch had been thrown. It returned in a tremulous whisper, as if a great effort of will were being exerted in controlling the flow and volume. 'My mother . . . tell her . . . I couldn't help . . .'

'Hello? Hello?'

The line went dead.

Rhys was on his feet instantly, grabbing for a sheet of hotel stationery and committing everything of what he could remember of the bizarre conversation to paper.

13

AT 8.20 the next morning, Finch called Mackie in to his office. He was smiling.

'I took a call from personnel five minutes ago. You got the exam, Mac.'

For a second, her mind still bubbling with Rhys Jacob and the night before, she stared at Finch in bewilderment. And then his meaning dawned on her with an electrifying buzz.

'The sergeants' exam?'

Finch grinned and nodded. 'It'll take a week or two to process the paperwork, but they thought you'd want to know.'

A big stupid grin slid over Mackie's face and she laughed.

'First time lucky huh, Susan?' said Finch, still grinning himself.

'I thought I'd flunked it,' she said, unable to quell the bubble of jubilation that threatened to burst inside her.

'It'll probably mean reassignment. I'll be sorry about that. You're an asset to the team and I like having you under my command.'

She took two paces into the room and shook his outstretched hand. 'Thanks, Lieutenant.'

She went back to her desk trying to hide the wry smile that played over her mouth. Then she saw that Bek had arrived and was sitting at his desk reading reports. She wandered over to him, a sheaf of papers in her hand. He didn't look up. Not even when her body cast an uneven shadow in the light from the window across from his desk.

'Lou,' said Mackie. 'We need to talk.'

'About what?'

'About the Jacob case.'

Bek put down the pen he was holding, pushed back his chair and looked up, his face giving nothing away.

'How long you been with violent crimes, Mac?' he asked coldly.

'A month.'

'Didn't they tell you anything about me before you joined?'

He didn't wait for her to answer. 'I get results, Mac. But I like to work alone until I'm sure. When I'm good and ready I'll come and talk to you, OK?'

'Lou,' persisted Mackie, 'I ran a check with the DEA guys at Bellingham. The analysis on the residue you found in Jacob's hotel room? It was cut with a little Lactose and laxative, DEA guy said it had only been stepped on once. The mix places the source out of town. Also, the baking soda had a Safeway sales tag still stuck on it. We traced that to a supermarket in Baltimore. I spoke with the hotel. One week before Catrin Jacob checked in, a Tewson divorce lawyer stayed there. He has a possession sheet with Baltimore PD. Frosty the snowman they called him. He had to leave Chicago in a hurry because his wife had a car accident in Milwaukee.'

'So?'

'Aw, come on, Lou. Toxicology on Catrin Jacob was negative for any coke.'

'Maybe her boyfriend was a user, you ever think of that? It doesn't change anything.'

Mackie stared at him in disbelief. The baking soda was a sure-fire sign that this was the paraphernalia of a practised pipe-head. Mackie guessed if they looked close enough, they would probably find some scouring-pad remnants as well, regularly used to wedge into their pipes to trap cocaine vapours in order to maximise the hit and maybe get a second, poorer toke. She could imagine this Baltimore attorney in his three-hundred-dollar suit carefully mixing just the right pinch of baking soda with his fifteen-dollar bottle of stepped on cocaine, heating it up with lighter fluid, or maybe even a bottle of 150 proof rum, until it cooled into the crystalline nugget of smoking cocaine which, she had been assured, was the quickest and purest way to get higher than the Hubble telescope.

'Also, we had three calls through CHTV from Chicago-based physicians who were also at the Planetarium the night of the murder. They said they saw someone answering Catrin Jacob's description asking for a ride. She was anxious to get away. One of them said they saw her leave alone.'

'So?'

'The brother called me this morning. He took a call last night.'

Bek let his eyes drop to the pen he'd put down previously and began tapping the ballpoint on the paper in a hundred dots of impatience.

'Thing is, Lou, whoever rang described an inscription on a brooch that Jacob was wearing. The brother says the caller was off the wall but he thinks maybe . . .'

'He thinks? He thinks?' Bek cut across her. 'He doesn't know his asshole from a hole in the road. I'm listening to this shit but I can't believe I'm hearing it.'

'And I can't believe that you're not interested. With the Lieutenant breathing down our necks like he is you seem pretty cool.'

'You want me off the case, Mac? Fine, go talk to the Lieutenant.'

'I don't want you off it, Lou. I want you in it with both guns firing. I feel we owe it to Jacob's brother.'

'Screw owe it. He isn't going to thank me or you when we find some preppy sadist with a medical degree who lost it and zapped his date because she squealed for help.'

'Is that how you read this, Lou?'

'Yeah, as it happens.'

Mackie's face became impassive. She threw down the reports on Bek's desk. 'Can I ask what line of enquiry you are currently pursuing?'

'Yeah. I'm phoning the list of out-of-town physicians the drug company gave me, talking to colleagues, finding out which of their high-earning friends prefer their muffins English. And you know what? These guys just love shoving in the knife and twisting it. It really warms the old ticker.'

'There were a hundred and ten names. How many have you done?'

'Thirty.'

'You want some help?'

'No.'

Mackie shook her head. 'I'm going to vote, and then I'm going to the Geneva, see the brother.'

'You do that, Mac, you do that.'

She resisted the urge to tell him about her change of rank. He would find out soon enough on the station grapevine. Maybe then his attitude might ease a little. Jesus, she couldn't believe this was just a male ego thing. She hadn't heard that Bek was the resentful chauvinist type, but then you never knew until you had to work closely with someone. So, she contented herself with a secret little smile and left him, for now, to his own devices.

After she'd gone, Bek picked up the report she'd left and read it twice before crumpling it in his fist.

His mind screamed with conflicting emotions and a hint of panic. The drugs had been the anchor to his flawed logic. The girl had messed with her head and got caught up in something – that was what he had wanted to believe. If she wasn't a user then. . . . Bek groaned and began massaging the knuckle joint of his right little finger under the table.

Mackie's news about the crank call worried him even more. Shit, what if it was Jake? Stupid, stupid fucking kid.

He didn't let his mind go further than that, suppressing the questions the clown face was asking over and over.

So if she wasn't a junkie then what?

If it wasn't drug-related then what?

Maybe someone just picked her out of the crowd? Maybe some crazy who thought she was from another fucking plan. . . . No! screamed his mind. No, that was not what happened. Jake would not have done that. Jake was not capable of that.

An image of Rhys Jacob came to him. Bek felt lousy about him. The guy had looked shattered yesterday, probably the way he would have felt if it had been Jake who'd been murdered. A sudden bubble of unfocused anger surfaced and popped. Why couldn't it have been some low-life pipe-head that had died instead of a limey pill-pusher with a crusading brother?

He groaned again and turned to the list of physicians. He had made another twenty phone calls but they were leading nowhere.

He looked at his watch. He'd stay in the office for an hour. The Lieutenant was down at Marquette at a budgeting meeting, would be until at least ten-thirty. At ten-fifteen Lou would disappear for the day, and if they paged him, he'd say he was interviewing a physician. They needn't know he'd be Downtown searching for Jake.

At nine-thirty a.m., Rhys was in the basement of the Hotel Geneva, eating croissants at a table in The Swiss Cafe. The waitress had refilled his coffee cup three times already and his mind was sailing along on a caffeine high, pondering imponderables.

His crazy phone call had rung all the bells in his head at once. After an hour of restless pacing, he'd switched on the TV, craving distraction – any distraction. The fitful sleep he'd eventually found had left him with a muzzy head that only caffeine could clear.

Glancing up, he caught the stare of an elegant, dark-haired woman sitting alone across the room. He'd noticed her before, accepting her glances as curiosity, but there was something else in the stare he'd just seen. He looked at her, expensive clothes, subtle jewellery and a colouring that spoke of a sunnier climate than Chicago boasted. Italian, Spanish maybe? And then he chided his own narrow-mindedness. He was in America. She could just as easily have been Mexican or Brazilian or . . .

She looked across again and Rhys returned his attention to the croissants. He was busy with the blueberry jelly when her arrival at his table took him completely by surprise.

'Please,' she said, her face twisted with entreaty. 'Excuse me. You are the doctor from England?'

Her English was good, the accent European. 'My name is Magdalene Asencio. I saw you on TV . . . I had to talk to you.'

'Have a seat,' said Rhys. 'Would you like some coffee?'

'I have already had some, thank you.' She stared at her hands and then up at Rhys, her face set in anxious resolve.

'I do not usually approach strange men in restaurants.' Rhys tried an understanding smile, but she persisted.

'Please you must understand that. I saw you on TV. It was so sad about your sister, so terrible, *Dios mio.*'

'Thank you.'

'I knew how you were feeling. The police . . .' She shook her head. 'They are so indifferent. My daughter, Anna, she is missing for one month. All the police do is throw up their hands and say they cannot help now.' She shook her head, black hair shimmering in the light.

'Your daughter is missing?' Rhys was still a little unsure of how to read this, still unable to keep the wary, slightly patronising tone out of his voice.

'My daughter is a doctor, a surgeon. In Madrid she is an associate professor. She is very popular, very professional. She tells her mother she must attend the Pan American Congress of Vascular Surgery in Chicago to present her work, her important work. She has been to America many times before and this time for four days, she tells me. Four days away from her beautiful husband and two children,' she shook her head in disbelief. 'But she does not come back after four days. I ring her hotel, they know nothing. The airline knows nothing, the police know nothing.'

'What about her clothes?'

'The hotel say she has checked out. All her clothes gone. But I know something is wrong. I am her mother, but the police care nothing for such things. They look at me and I see their eyes that say Latino. I tell them I am Spanish, my daughter is Spanish.'

'But if she checked out?'

Magdalene Asencio shook her head, her lips a thin line. 'Anna is a good daughter, a good wife and a devoted mother. She had everything waiting for her in Madrid. Until she came here she . . .' She stopped, swallowing hard.

'Is there nothing the police can do?'

'I have given them photographs,' she said despondently. 'She is now a missing person. One of thousands.' Her face suddenly crumpled and tears welled above her lower eyelids. 'I have been here twice in the last twenty days. Paulo, my son-in-law, has also been twice. If my husband were alive, things would be different, he would make them sit up. I have money, Anna had money. There is no reason for her not to want to come home. But when I tell people I see them pity me. I, Magdalene Asencio, do not want pity. Everywhere I go people shrug their shoulders. What can they do? But I know Anna is in trouble, perhaps an accident. And then I saw you on the TV and I saw that you were angry too. The things the newspapers and the police said about your sister, *Dios mio*.' She shook her head again.

'It's very difficult.'

'I was awake all night, thinking. My daughter comes to Chicago and disappears. Your sister comes and is killed. They are both doctors, both travelling alone. I lie awake and think the worst thoughts about this evil city but then no answers come. There is no way forward for me.'

Rhys regarded her with a puzzled frown. 'Where did your daughter stay?'

'The Hyatt.'

'My sister was at the Marriott.'

Magdalene looked away and reached into her bag for a photograph of a tall, dark-haired woman with the face of a laughing girl. Her eyes smiled, and then as she handed it over to Rhys, her face fell. 'I know that she is dead. I feel it. But Paulo? He will not eat, will not sleep. I must find Anna for him, for the children as well.'

'Is there anything I can do?'

She looked up at him with those pleading eyes. 'The police fear you now. The only thing they are scared of are the newspapers and television. Make them tell you the truth. Don't let them treat you like a foreigner, just another *extra anjero*.'

'How will that help Anna?'

'Think of her, that is all I ask.' She got up, smoothing down her skirt, breathing deeply in, composing herself. 'I will go now and ring all the hospitals for news. I do this every day.'

Rhys stood and shook hands with this woman who had summoned up the courage to approach him and who shared his helplessness in the face of a foreign bureaucracy.

'I'll do what I can,' he said and watched her walk away, the posture elegant and proud.

Twenty minutes later, he was in the lobby with Mackie, his mood set and determined. Mackie sensed it from their greeting.

'You OK, Rhys? You seem a little hostile.'

'Do I?'

'Yeah, you do. Looks like I'm going to need to sit down, huh?'

'Can we walk somewhere?' asked Rhys, anxious to get away from the Geneva for a while.

'Sure. You want a Danish?'

'Whatever.'

They walked underground through the Illinois Center's subterranean world, until Mackie stopped abruptly outside an office supply store with a TV flickering above the sales desk. Rhys continued forward ten yards before back-tracking to join her in the doorway.

'What?' he asked.

'Shhh,' was Mackie's brusque retort as she gesticulated towards the screen.

There, they were running some advertisements and Rhys saw the screen fill with a candid still of a smiling man shaking hands with another. They both looked vaguely familiar. One of them, he felt sure, had stared down at him from bills posted all over the city. A voice-over artist with a deep rich timbre was laying on the sincerity with a trowel as the camera blew up the smiling face.

'*The man on the right is John Sheehan*,' said the voice. '*The Republican Party believes he is the man to represent Chicago's central district as congressman in Washington*.' The camera moved across to the smiling face of the man he was shaking hands with.

'*The man on the left is in custody on suspicion of murdering a doctor who was lawfully performing his duty at a woman's clinic in Florida.*'

Rhys said unnecessarily, 'Is that the anti-abortionist guy?'

'Shhh,' said Mackie again.

'*The Republican Party wants you to think that the man on the right has friends in high places,*' said the voice-over before pausing and delivering the killer line—'*Think again. Vote Kervesky. Vote freedom of choice. This advertisement paid for by people for Kervesky.*'

Mackie exhaled and shook her head. 'Wow.'

'What the hell was that all about?' asked Rhys.

'Election day,' said Mackie as she strode on and ducked into a Starbuck's coffee shop. They huddled around a corner table where Mackie tried to explain how the TV had just nailed the Republican candidate for the central district up on a cross.

'But how could they do that?' asked Rhys bemused. 'That was pure character assassination. Those picture might have been taken at a summer fete.'

'It's more likely that Sheehan met the anti-abortion faction somewhere on the campaign trail. The arrestee is a high-profile anti-Pro-Choice activist whose job it was to travel the country looking for political support for his faction. Rather than risk offending, someone probably advised Sheehan to pay lip-service. Feed the slot and pull the handle.'

'What the hell does that mean?'

'Politics American style.' Mackie munched on a large sticky pastry and tried to avoid Rhys's insistent stare.

'Aren't political broadcasts equitably distributed between the parties?' asked Rhys eventually.

Mackie merely laughed in reply.

'And there's no insistence that the contents of the broadcasts remain political?'

'Rhys,' said Mackie, 'this is the USA. We have paid political advertising. That means you need big bucks to win elections. The advertisements are usually nothing more than emotional appeals or character assassinations like we just saw. No politics. Not enough imagery in politics.'

'Doesn't that corrupt the system?'

Mackie grinned and gave him a sad sort of stare. 'Some companies will contribute to their political foes as well, knowing

the incumbent party has the power to influence appointme
public office.'

'That's bribery.'

'By any other name, sure. But there is also free speech anu all
that stuff. What we just saw was some slick action. The guy that
Sheehan was shaking hands with was arrested only yesterday.
Someone put that together very quickly. Someone with a flare for
the kill. We just saw the death knell of that candidate. Someone
will be owed big favours for that piece of work because the TV
companies charge double for air-time today.'

Rhys shook his head. Mackie took in his expression and
smiled.

'Don't worry about it, Rhys. You get used to it, sort of. What's
more important right now is that you tell me about your caller.'

Rhys sighed. 'OK, but first, I need to talk to you about missing
persons.' Between sips of coffee, Rhys explained about Magdalene
Asencio's impassioned plea. When he'd finished, she shook her
head earnestly.

'That's sad.'

'You think it's just a coincidence?'

She stopped munching. 'Rhys, you aren't serious? Have you any
idea how many people come into the country on visas and then
just disappear? This is the land of milk and honey. And everyone
that goes missing doesn't end up a floater in the lake. Some of
them end up with fake papers and steady jobs in Idaho or New
Mexico.'

'The land of opportunity?' Rhys's sarcasm bit deep.

'Yeah,' said Mackie riled, her eyebrows arched in a challenge.

'Not in medicine, Detective. You need to pass exams designed
to thwart all but the most determined. If I wanted to come here,
I would literally have to start all over again. Anna Asencio was
a surgeon. She'd need Boards certification for whatever state she
wanted to practise in. She couldn't simply walk into a job, not in
a million years.'

'Maybe she wanted a makeover. Maybe she wanted to be a pool
attendant in Palm Springs, or saw herself in a hut on Venice beach.
The Dream, Rhys. You ever heard of The Dream?'

Rhys shook his head. 'It may come as a surprise to you, Mac,
but some of us aren't exactly enamoured of a country where you
can walk into a store and buy a hand-gun with which to shoot your
neighbour for cutting down a branch of your tree.' He saw her

begin to protest and held up his hand. 'Even if there is going to be a four-day cooling-off period between buying it and picking it up.'

'Please, Rhys, spare me . . .'

'No, listen. OK, forget the right to bear arms, let's just look at professions. Some of us in medicine actually believe that it is morally wrong to have to pay for health services. Some of us still believe in free health care as a right.'

'Finished?' asked Mackie.

'Yes, thank you.'

'Let's take a step back on this and try and be a little objective. You may not prostrate yourself in front of the Stars and Stripes, but a lot of people do. A lot of people believe in The Dream. Maybe Anna was one of those?'

Rhys's set expression remained sceptical. 'She's female, a doctor and she's missing. One favour, that's all. Check it out, could you?'

Mackie shook her head reluctantly. 'OK, but I'm telling you this is a bullshit road you're going down.'

'Thank you.'

Mackie shrugged. 'What about last night's call?'

'Very disturbing.'

'I did warn you, this city is full of whackos.'

'I didn't think he was a crank,' said Rhys.

'So what? He was ringing you up to sympathise?'

'No. A warning of some kind.'

Mackie picked up the remains of the Danish and took another bite, easing the ring of crumbs that remained on her lips into her mouth with the ring finger of her left hand.

'You aren't making much sense, Rhys,' she said through the crumbs.

Rhys took out the letter-headed sheet he'd scribbled on and swivelled it around so that Mackie could read it. She did do, slowly, her brow creasing as she progressed until she finally looked up, totally perplexed. 'Chinese wasn't one of my strongest suits.'

'I know what it looks like to the layman, but a little analysis of this speech pattern clearly demonstrates thought disorder.'

'Whoa there. You a psychiatrist now?'

'Yes, I am. I've just finished a twelve-month stint. General practitioners need multiple skills. O and G, paediatrics, psychiatry as well as general medicine. I needed to do six months of psych, but I liked it and so I stayed on. And in my opinion, what we have here,' he pointed to the sheet in front of Mackie, 'is the spoken manifestation of thought disorder. Classic examples of derailment and word approximation.'

Mackie's expression remained perplexed.

'OK. OK. Look here. Look, where he talked about someone absorbing his thoughts. . . . "It's easy for The Whistler to absorb the thoughts he does it by mode of his ultrasonic beam." . . . Then again later, "they've taken my memory by mode of the beam". He uses *by mode* several times. It's used in conversation here far more often than its normal meaning suggests. Then there's the destruction of grammar. I've left out the commas and full stops because that is how it sounded. Few adverbs too – this is pure *telegramese*. Look at the way the chain of thought is interrupted by other seemingly unrelated phrases – that's derailment.'

'I'm trying hard, Rhys, I really am.' Mackie took out a cigarette and lit it.

'OK, well then look at "alternation". He uses the word *alternation* more than once. My guess is that this is a neologism – a made-up word which often has a suggested meaning.'

'So what's alternation?'

'I have no idea.'

Mackie frowned and blew smoke in the opposite direction to where Rhys was sitting. 'So this guy has a speech defect. How does that help?'

'Not a speech defect. A thought disorder. He described the inscription on Catrin's brooch which he called an insignia. His speech is riddled with quasi-scientific terms. He sounds deluded. I think he assumed that what was written there was not earthly, but suggested that he should have understood it. He spelled it out. It's written in Welsh. It means he has that brooch, Mackie.'

'I checked with the evidence list. There was no brooch with your sister's personal effects.'

'She would have worn it. She always wore it when she went out. Inexpensive, but seventy years old.'

'OK. But I still don't get what you're saying here. Maybe this isn't a crank call but he's a crazy anyway?'

'Schizophrenic more like. These are classic Schneiderian language traits. All absolutely typical of a schizophrenic.'

Mackie exhaled. 'The perp could be a schizophrenic. That's the best news I've heard all day, Rhys. Now we're going to throw a live one at the mentally disturbed.'

'I'd like to go to the conference centre,' said Rhys suddenly.

'Why?'

'Just to see it, get the feel of it.'

'Don't do this to yourself, Rhys.' Mackie wore a pained expression.

'Do what? Try and find out what happened to my sister? Try and understand why she was murdered?'

'There's nothing out at McCormick Place for you.'

'Then you won't object if I go there.'

'Jesus, are you always this stubborn?'

'Always.'

'OK, OK. But I can't take you this morning. I have an arraignment to attend and then some paperwork I have to do. How about I run you over there this afternoon?'

'Thank you. Now what about my caller?'

'First,' said Mackie holding up an admonishing finger, 'you've got to promise me you'll keep this away from the press.'

He gave her a defiant slit-eyed stare until she shook her head exasperatedly and cursed.

'Jesus, Rhys. OK, I'll try and get a surveillance order arranged through the hotel switchboard and the phone company so that we can trace incoming calls.'

'Does that mean I have to keep him talking for fifteen minutes?'

Mackie made a face. 'Too many bad movies, Rhys. Five seconds and it's all done. Now I've got some news for you. We traced the drug paraphernalia found in your sister's hotel room to a user in Baltimore who'd stayed there a week before.'

'That's great . . .'

'We can't be certain yet, but at least it's a reason for the stuff being there.'

'What did I tell you . . .'

Mackie interrupted him.

'Something went on in that parking lot, Rhys. Something bad. Right now we need to follow up any leads we can find. So, I'll need a copy of your caller's conversation.' She put out her cigarette and stood. 'We passed a computer store with a Xerox machine on the way, didn't we?'

They backtracked and found the store and made copies of Rhys's transcript, emerging a few moments later into cold bright sunlight.

'Looks like it's opening out, Rhys. Got anything planned?'

'You have the toxicology report?'

'You don't give up, do you?'

'You said . . .'

'OK, OK.' She reached into her bag and removed a crumpled sheet of computer paper.

'Thank you,' he said. 'And in answer to your question, I thought I'd walk. Is it safe round here?'

'Of course it's safe. This is downtown Chicago in broad daylight for Pete's sake.'

'Just checking,' said Rhys as he stood on the sidewalk, scanning the busy streets, the El screeching above him. He looked lost already.

'You sure you'll be OK?'

'This is downtown Chicago in broad daylight, isn't it?' he mimicked.

She shook her head and gave him a synthetic over-the-shoulder smile as she walked away.

'I'll pick you up at one.'

Rhys watched her go and followed the flow of human traffic, finding himself on State within minutes. Despite himself, he was beginning to like Mackie. Her candidness took a little getting used to but she was at least willing to listen. Not like that hard-boiled cynic Bek.

State was already bedecked with Christmas and Thanksgiving tinsel; Father Christmases ringing bells and collecting charity donations on each corner. To Rhys, State looked like a street that couldn't quite decide what it wanted to be. Some of the stores were huge and well-appointed, others tawdry dollar stores offering everything under one cheesy roof for less than one dollar in a bewildering array of paper, plastic and yet more plastic. He wandered around Marshall Fields and then meandered back towards Michigan Avenue, across the green Chicago river. The contrast was marked. It was quieter, cleaner, but less vibrant with its huge malls and its consumer-driven splendour. Another Marshal Fields, a surreal Niketown, Nieman Marcus with its exclusive bragging and the malls: floor upon floor of steel and glass stuffed with every conceivable item and all crammed with shoppers. On the street, Rhys felt overawed and crick-necked in this canyon of spending. If there was one thing missing it was elegance; a trade-off for the ostentatiousness of the individual buildings. That was what struck him most, the lack of integration, but then it wasn't something you found too often in flagship areas like The Miracle Mile.

Ninety minutes after leaving Mackie, he sat in an Adirondack chair in Henri Bendel's in a mall called 900 North Michigan watching the people milling around, knowing no one and oddly grateful for the anonymity. He was alone in a sea of 5 million. The physical effort of walking and the visual distraction of people-watching washed over him like valium, freeing his mind, allowing it to wander down its own path.

And on that path he kept tripping over his caller. The schizophrenic that had rung him, that he knew was a link in the impossible chain that led back to Catrin. He knew he had to hang on to that thought, let it shine like a beacon in his heart and in his mind.

He thought of his mother and memory of her suddenly displaced his sense of reality. The air-conditioned showroom was another world to the one he had grown up in. He felt alien, his intelligence and training a thin veil through which poked the raw emotion of allegiance to his family and to his upbringing. His mother had never been to America, had never experienced the overwhelming trappings of capitalism. He was totally incapable of imagining what she would have made of the mall he was now sitting in. Her concerns had been simple in her lifetime. Providing a decent environment for her children had been her life's work. He looked around him at the open magazines on the tables and chairs – advertisements for new lifestyles. It felt obscene to him, this nineties preoccupation. As obscene as the implications that had been made about his sister. The faceless city cared nothing of who or what he or his sister was or where they came from.

And yet he knew he had to try and understand some of this and for that he had to get over his own prejudices and take on board what everyone else saw. In a city where drug killings were two a penny, the natural tendency was to look for the associations. It might even have been reassuring to the inhabitants to have it thus, to have their beliefs reinforced that way – stay away from the evil of abuse and somehow the mindless violence that came with it might stay away too. Because the corollary was there for them to see day after bloody day, laid out by a media whose job it was to scare the shit out of the people. They had to live in this city and the city did its best to make life pleasant for the majority. It was an uncomplicated message, naively altruistic, but if it worked, what the hell? He would have to remember that. He would constantly have to remind himself of the cultural chasm that he was attempting to cross here.

He got up and began the walk back to his hotel knowing that it was up to him to prove to someone that Catrin's case was different.

Back at the Geneva, Rhys placed two long-distance calls. The first was to the UK, to the Chief Pharmacist at his hospital in Gloucester. His name was Davidson, a young guy with big ideas for making the pharmacy department earn its keep. He had caused a few raised eyebrows at the staid Hospital Trust board meetings with his ideas, but he was also a first-class pharmacist. He listened to Rhys's question sympathetically and offered, without hesitation, to help.

The second call was to Atlanta, to the Techrim corporation. No, they couldn't tell him where exactly Pamela Rourke was at that moment. Somewhere in Kansas City, they thought. But she would be ringing in to her office and they would get a message to her to ring him as soon as they could. He sat on his bed, frustrated by his inability to do anything more. Still, at least it was something. A start in his single-handed campaign to make someone care enough about his sister to find out what really happened.

14

FINCH CALLED THE case conference in the same interview room where Bek had met with Rhys that first time. He had decided against the office; with Hopper in attendance, they all needed as much space as they could get.

Each of them clutched the inevitable styrofoam cup of coffee, the white container a virtual badge of office. Hopper sat at the rear, his face inscrutable, a leg or a foot or a hand in constant nervous motion, an open legal pad on his knees. Someone in the station had once said that if Hopper wasn't such a tight-assed son of a bitch they would have sworn that he had a speed habit the size of Mount St Helens. Bek slouched at the desk eyeing Hopper contemptuously, Mackie sat to the side, attentive and expectant.

'Lou? asked Finch, fingers intertwined on the desk, face upturned towards Bek. 'What have you got?'

'Little to tell, Lieutenant. We're doing phone checks on the Planetarium guests. So far zilch. They're all doctors, all busy people.'

'You need more manpower?'

'Maybe.'

'Mac?'

'Forensics say the bullet came from a Smith and Wesson revolver. No semen, perp wore a condom and we're still waiting trace exam results on that. Couple of latents off the victim's wrists – no match so far. She wore a high wing-collar blouse which obscured finger marks on the throat. Quantico are running it through VICAP, but there doesn't appear to be any MO match. This squirrel looks like he's just starting out,' said Mackie.

Behind them, Hopper cleared his throat but said nothing.

'Uh, the brother came up with something.' Mackie spoke into the silence. 'He had a caller who happened to describe an inscription on a brooch Catrin Jacob may have been wearing. The caller was a whacko, and I've read what the guy said on the phone. It's off the wall but it so happens that the brother did some psychiatry, claims what he heard was typically schizophrenic. Even started to analyse it for me.'

'Great,' said Finch dubiously.

'I thought I'd get the transcript analysed,' she added impassively, 'see what an independent expert made of it.'

'Come on, Mac,' said Bek with a hollow laugh. 'The brother is messing with us. He's mad at us and the city. You saw him on TV.'

'He wants to understand what happened to his sister, Lou. I think he's genuine.'

'You think?'

'Lou, what the hell is this? I'm gonna follow it up, OK? I'll get a trace on his calls. No big deal.'

Finch nodded. 'OK. Maybe it'll keep him away from TV stations. Anything else?'

The room stayed silent until Finch stood in a gesture of dismissal. 'OK, keep me posted.'

As she closed the door behind her, Mackie heard Hopper beginning a whining protestation. God, the guy was such a prick. Outside, Mackie turned to Bek. 'You want some help with those phone interviews now?'

'It's OK, Mac.'

'But . . .'

'I said it's OK. I'm on top of it.'

'Really . . .' said Mackie sceptically.

'And I think we're wasting time with this whacko caller thing.'

'Thanks, Lou. I thought I might try reaching out to someone at Cook County anyway.' She saw something swim behind his eyes then, a momentary flicker like the sudden twinging of some deep pain, or the flaring of a desperate panic.

'How's your mom?' she asked with a conciliatory triteness that made her wince inside.

Bek's eyes fell and he shook his head. 'They're calling her condition "unstable". They're too scared to operate. Something to do with her lungs. I don't understand it.'

'Lou, if you really want off this case . . .'

He shot Mackie a suspicious glance which ended in a mirthless laugh.

'You looking for a reason, Mac?'

'What is it with you, Lou? I thought your mom being as sick

as she is would be enough reason. I'm sure Matt would let you . . .'

'And you'd like that, wouldn't you?'

Mackie snapped, 'Is it me, Lou? The fact that I use a different bathroom, is that what bothers you?'

Bek stayed sullenly silent.

'You keep saying you're in on this,' Mackie pressed her point home in an angry whisper, 'but you're doing your best to kill off any leads before they get started. I'm beginning to wonder whether you really want this case closed.'

'Maybe I'm the only one who sees it for what it is, Mac.'

'And what exactly is that, Lou? A shitcan, yeah, I know. I heard you. So did Rhys Jacob.'

Bek shook his head and turned away leaving Mackie to ponder the bad feeling she was having about Lou. She had meant what she'd said about his mother. His mind was most certainly not on the job in hand and she had two options as far as she could see. The first was to go to Finch and tell him that Lou was losing it and run the risk of incurring the wrath and disfavour of everyone in the station and ensure her election as the world's most unpopular person in Area 4. Or, she could ride with it, let Lou fall apart at the seams and run the investigation herself. Shit, she was virtually doing exactly that anyway. And she had a sneaking suspicion that despite all her early misgivings over being roped in as nothing more than a baby-sitter, it was becoming increasingly obvious that Catrin Jacob's murder was turning into a political hot potato and she didn't see it doing her career prospects any harm to close this case on her own. She did, momentarily, consider a third option: to find out just what was bugging Lou and try and help him out of it so that he could get his shit together. It lasted all of five seconds. Jesus, the guy was unreachable, biting people's heads off for just asking the time of day.

She trod on the glimmer of awareness that told her that perhaps, eighteen months ago, she wouldn't even have considered the options. She would have gone to Lou, reached out to him until she knew what was eating him. But some part of her had sickened and soured in that bathroom with her insides running out and Nick watching in oval-mouthed horror as she screamed for his help. It had healed over with time, but underneath the thin frail skin it was still festering.

No, said the confident, flawed thought in her head. This script didn't have her cast as Lou's analyst and saviour. This one had Mackie as the lead.

At two-fifteen, Mackie led Rhys into the Building Security Office on the south side of the lobby level of McCormick Place East. The huge space thronged with thousands of people striding about purposefully, each clutching convention booklets and wearing badges. They were met by a black girl, in a grey uniform, called Joanne Wesley, who introduced herself as security coordinator. Mackie explained that she was involved in a homicide investigation and introduced Rhys.

'How can I help?' asked Wesley.

'Could you run through the security arrangements for me?' asked Mackie.

'Sure,' said Wesley.

'What have you got going on at the moment?' asked Rhys.

'This show began yesterday and is a big one. American Academy of Ophthalmology. We have four or five medical meetings a year. They slot in between all kinds of other expositions and shows. Totals about four million visitors annually.'

'It must be a headache in terms of security?'

Wesley strolled over to the closed-circuit TV screens. 'We have 1.5 million square feet of exhibit space and fifty-two meeting rooms but security isn't such a huge problem for us,' she answered over her shoulder. 'McCormick provides twenty-four-hour perimeter security, but the management for each show has to arrange show security which includes entrances, exits and floors. They usually employ a security company to do that.'

'How many employees do you have?' asked Mackie.

'Approximately six hundred full time and two hundred part time, depending on demand.' She took them over to a wall-plan of the building and ran through the security arrangements efficiently and concisely.

'We're trying to establish what happened to the victim in the hours before she died. Could we take a walk inside?' asked Mackie.

'Sure,' smiled Wesley. 'Let me get you some ID passes.'

They wandered around the exhibit halls, Rhys overwhelmed as Jake had been with the number of companies that existed to support this one narrow field of speciality. He paused for a long moment at the northeastern corner of the enormous hall where seven video theatres had been set up to show hands-on surgery and techniques. He had a genuine interest in what was going on, but Mackie pulled him away, her brow furrowed in disgust.

'If you want me to throw up, you're doing a great job.'

'It's just a bit of surgery.'

'It's some poor guy's eye, for Pete's sake.'

Rhys shrugged and they continued on their way, winding upwards slowly until they could go no further. As fate would have it, they walked right past the odd guy in the trench coat who stared out at the grey day through the bronzed windows, his mind apparently lost in the pleasure of the doughnut he was eating. He was an unremarkable sight except for his hair which seemed to be growing in patches over his head. But this was a medical meeting. Most of the attendees assumed he was recovering from chemotherapy and didn't comment. To them, he was just some poor guy on cytotoxics grabbing a few minutes away from the melee. In truth, most people turned away. Seeing Jake was like opening a jar and staring down at something unpleasant growing on the surface of the jelly. He was an unwelcome reminder of everyone's mortality, nature's little way of telling them that being physicians held no guaranteed immunity from any of the terrible diseases they all knew about.

After thirty minutes of it, they were back at security, handing over their badges, Rhys quizzing the security officer over facts and figures. Back in the car, he sat with Mackie, sensing that she knew it had been a waste of time.

'Feel better?' she asked.

'Yes, thanks.'

'Big place, huh?'

'Very.'

'Maybe if you told me what you were looking for?'

'I just wanted the feel of it. I don't know why . . . I can't help feeling it's all tied in somehow.' He shook his head. 'So many delegates. Catrin could have met any number of people there.'

Mackie shrugged. 'So what? You want to go back to the hotel now?'

'What is this? Are you checking on me, Mac? Scared that I might go back to the TV station?'

'Have they approached you?' she asked a little too quickly.

Rhys grinned. 'No, they haven't. So I am going to go back to the hotel. There's a gym on the top floor. I think I'll work out, try and get rid of some of this frustration.'

'Sounds like a good idea,' she said a little too quickly.

'Do you want me to call you if I decide to go to the bathroom?'

Mackie looked away and then back again. 'Has it occurred to you that this whacko who rang you might decide to come visit? Has it occurred to you that the thought of that bothers me?'

'Mac,' said Rhys with mock surprise, 'I didn't know you cared.'

'Rhys, you can be a real pain in the butt, you know that? This can be a rough city. Treating everything like one big joke isn't a healthy attitude.'

'I don't find any of this the slightest bit amusing, I can assure you.' His response was grim.

They drove back along Lake Shore Drive, behind one of the convention shuttles, a big silver-sided, smoked-glass bus with 'Blue Line Coaches' slashed across the side. It pulled in and began disgorging convention attendees as they passed it on East Wacker, halfway between the Geneva and the Hyatt.

Rhys waved Mackie off and wandered into the hotel. He stood for ten minutes waiting for the elevator surrounded by ophthalmologists, each with their colour-coded name badges which also bore country and place of origin for all to see. He thought of the security guards at McCormick glancing hurriedly at the badges, having to make quick decisions and he realised that the colour-coding was essential. It meant that a quick look was enough to allow access. A simple but effective idea.

He got back to his room, sat down and tried thinking, but found everything kaleidoscoping in confusion. He changed and jogged up ten flights to the Penthouse Health Spa to try and work off some of the excess energy which had made his mind buzz with all those unanswered questions.

An hour later, with his body exhausted but his mind clearer, Rhys came back downstairs to find the message light glowing on his phone. There were two. The first was to say that there was a fax message awaiting him at the desk. The second was from Pamela Rourke. He tried the number she had left and got her immediately. She was in a hospital in Kansas City on a cellphone with lousy reception. But when Rhys explained who he was, she offered to phone him back immediately.

For one anxious moment, once he had replaced the receiver, Rhys felt a pang of doubt that she would return his call, but three minutes later, she came back loud and clear, the absence of background noise indicating that she'd found a discreet payphone.

'Thanks for ringing back,' said Rhys.

'Not at all. It's the least I can do. What happened was so . . . I couldn't believe it. You must be having a terrible time.'

Rhys hesitated. 'Now that I've found you, I don't know what to ask.'

'If there's anything I can do.'

'I wish I could talk to you properly. Just talk to you about that night.'

'You're in Chicago right? I'm flying to Minneapolis tomorrow. Why don't we meet up there? I'll be at the airport Hyatt all morning catching up on paperwork.'

'That would be good. I think I'd really like that. There are things I'd like to get clear in my mind.'

'Sure. I understand. Come on over. I'll see you in Minneapolis at say, ten a.m.?'

Rhys thanked her and sat for a long time on his bed. He had no idea why he wanted to speak to Pamela Rourke. He supposed he needed confirmation that the seed of doubt planted by the newspapers and Bek couldn't possibly be true. He hated himself for even contemplating it, but it was there. The thought that she might possibly have become another person out here, had jettisoned her common sense on the plane over, had decided to do drugs and. . . . He got up and paced. He had to exorcise this thought, rid himself of it.

He picked up the phone and made a reservation on Northwestern for the following morning and then went down to the desk and picked up his fax. It was, as expected, from Davidson in Gloucester. Rhys read it on the way back up to his room in the lift, shaking his head in disbelief.

When he got back to his room, he immediately rang the *Chronicle*.

Just as Rhys and Mackie had stood within yards of Jake on the top of the escalator in McCormick Place and remained oblivious, he too had been too preoccupied to register the presence of the man he had seen on television the day before, whom he believed was another emissary from Catrin Jacob's world and who he was endeavouring, in his own way, to protect.

At five, after walking down to the refreshment area for his third Pepsi and a packet of Reese's peanut butter cups, he stood at his place, scanning the line of taxis beneath as it snaked towards a pick-up point, business beginning to increase now as the day's academic programme drew to a close and, like the embarkation of some huge passenger ferry, McCormick Place began to empty.

He had finished two of the four peanut butter cups when he froze. A brown snail track of chocolate saliva oozed down his chin. It was a Suncab; he couldn't see the licence plate from where he stood. But he could sense it, feel the evil emanating from it.

The cab was inching forward up the ramp towards the line-up of fares waiting their turn. The driver was merely a dark shape, a blur of shadow and to Jake, evil incarnate.

He turned away, letting the soda and the candy fall from his hands carelessly, searching for the steps in a moment of confusion before he was rushing down, flying past the attendees who turned and stared. He flew down the escalators and across the wide expanse of lobby to its north side. Rushing outside, the cold air catching in his throat, trotting to the queue of people, straining to peer over their heads at the taxis approaching.

He ran out along the roadside. It was devoid of sidewalk, but he ignored the whistles and shouts of the stewards that waved him back until, there, he saw it. The three first digits of the licence plate more than enough, the glimpsed silhouette of an hirsute face almost too much. Fear rippled through him, searing his mind, the very air screaming about him like an invisible flock of angry gulls. The world closed in on him, darkness and terror. He turned and ran back, away from The Whistler in his chariot, away from hell.

By the time he reached his car, the panic attack had subsided and a fragile, fearful logic had sprung up. He had to follow, there had to be a lair, and then . . . and then. . . . The small part of his mind that remained untainted by the confusion that barked at him in the guise of a thousand sounds and voices, bombarding him with its incessant artillery night and day, sensed momentarily that there was another way. His brother was a cop. A CPD dick. But it wasn't his brother who had allowed that woman to strike him the other night. Lou would not have done that. And so, alone in the huge city, Jake pulled out into traffic and sat on the shoulder of South Lake Shore Drive, waiting for the taxis to emerge, waiting for The Whistler. Ready to follow him to his lair.

Bek sat at his mother's side. She had not spoken to him that evening and the only noise in the room was the sound of her breathing; a bubbly, rattling wheeze that frightened and revolted him at the same time. He wanted her to be awake, to be the strength he needed to bolster his resolve, but she remained drugged and sick, a silent witness to his haggard, tortured face.

She was still spiking a fever, they said, as they waited for the antibiotics to take hold. But he had seen in their eyes the faint pleading, the one that begged him to acknowledge their words as lies and platitudes, that left the door of doubt open a crack.

He'd investigated a case once; a doctor's wife mugged and raped on the East side, got to know the victim's husband as well as he got to know anybody. They had shared a few beers, got drunk half a dozen times before the guy moved away, his wife divorcing him, the grass greener in Texas all of a sudden. He remembered what the doctor had once told him about his seriously ill patients. All a question of judgement, he'd said. He would never come right out and say it to relatives, he would merely lay the path, let them do the asking, that way it never came as a shock when they said, 'He's not going to pull through this, is he?'

He could see that look in the Asian doctor's face that night.

'Your mother is still very ill, Mr Bek. We are treating her as best we can, but she is no longer young.'

But Lou hadn't asked, he didn't want to give the bastard the pleasure of knowing he'd succeeded in planting the right seed. He wanted him to suffer just like he was suffering. So he had turned away, nodded, feigning gratitude.

And so he sat with his eyes shut in the quiet solitude of the room, letting the day's events run like a home movie in his head. Mackie was good. She had a nose for the truth. His aim had been to stall, not mislead. But it was getting much more difficult, spiralling out of control. He knew with all his instinct that it was Jake that had contacted Rhys. He felt it with every cell in his body.

Frustration ate into him. Goddamn Mackie. She had her teeth in this and wasn't going to let go. Why the hell hadn't Finch assigned a prick like Valdez instead of a bright cookie like Mac? She would crack this case and then the shit would hit the fan and pile on top of him.

Would that be such a terrible thing?

The thought struck him abruptly. That way it would all come to a head and he could stop lying to the others and himself. Then he could tell his mother that he had tried to find Jake. God knows he had tried. Maybe then he could think about the Tackle Store up in Lake County seriously. He allowed himself a momentary flight of fancy. Be great just to let Loretta run it and take off when the mood took him, out onto the lake, or backpacking up towards Canada. There was money to be made as a guide up there. They were always looking for guys with a little knowledge.

He stopped himself, watching the dream fade and crackle. And what about Jake? Where the hell would that leave Jake? Maybe if he took Mackie out . . . the thought struck him like a fist. What the hell was he thinking? This whole mess was getting to his head.

'Jake, Jake . . .' He spoke the words and looked up at his mother's face. A cocktail of hopelessly mixed emotions swirled around in his brain until he felt it was about to burst. In a flash of blistering insight, he wondered if this was how it was for Jake. This times a hundred.

He stood abruptly, unable to contemplate another moment of sitting there. He had to do something, get out of there and back on the street, drive away his demons, pick up a fifth of whiskey. Anything rather than this sober nightmare he was having.

He leaned over his mother and picked up her limp hand before kissing it and turning to leave.

Jake followed the Suncab for five hours, criss-crossing the city, making two runs to O'Hare on the Kennedy Expressway, the hours slipping by as he played the dangerous game of follow the leader, tortured by the fear of losing sight of the man who haunted his dreams and the fear of being seen as he fought to quell the bedlam in his head.

At ten, the taxi's lights went off and the cab took off south. It stopped at a Taco Bell's on Fifty-First. Jake saw him then for the first time properly, a big man, beard and glasses. He wore a chequered work shirt open over a yellow T-shirt. Jake sat in his car and watched The Whistler take his food back to the cab and hunch over towards the passenger seat, eating there in the Taco Bell lot, sipping busily from a huge cup of Coke. Fifteen minutes later he was on the move again, heading west towards the jets coming in over Midway and Cicero, finally turning south on Pulaski onto a street lined with brick bungalows. Many looked painted and fresh as they well might in an area that was in transition from being unpopular commuter outpost to desirable suburbia with the rapid-transit line between the Loop and Midway slashing the journey from sixty minutes plus to less than thirty from front door to Downtown.

The street sign read Cambridge and he watched The Whistler

pull into a driveway and into a garage next to a brick-fronted bungalow with a yellow weatherboard. A porch huddled scruffily under a matching dormer that looked out onto the street. The woodwork on both areas was in dire need of work. Jake didn't follow. Instead he sat in his car and waited for lights to appear. Sure enough, after a few moments, The Whistler's unmistakable silhouette appeared in the window, the arms held up like some great bird of prey before curtains were drawn.

Jake sat and watched for a long time, watched and heard his own lips move to the tune that played in his head in the key of madness.

15

A T THREE-THIRTY on Wednesday morning, Jake was out of his car walking along Cambridge towards The Whistler's house.

For two hours his mind had raced like a runaway train, the voices hammering at him, coercing, screaming, threatening and he knew that most of them were coming from the bungalow. He knew that The Whistler was aware of his presence, that it was The Whistler's mind that was impinging upon him, blacking out all of his own thoughts, issuing these base, degrading ideas that writhed like mating eels in his head.

Out on the street he walked in a long silent lope, pacing up and down in front of the house, searching the pavement for stones or bricks. Finally, he stood purposefully in front of The Whistler's window and looked up feeling the vibrations beat against his face like the powerful rays of some foreign sun.

Within him, in some forgotten corner of rationality, he heard the noise of a voice screaming at him to stop. It sounded like the pleading of a terrified woman left to die behind a bricked-up wall. It appalled him. It froze his marrow, but it was too feeble for him to respond to amidst the cacophony of noises that predominated. He would do anything for that noise, that thronging, urging crowing to stop.

He threw the rock, watched it arc upwards, heard the tinkling crash of shattering glass. He saw lights flick on in adjacent bungalows before The Whistler responded. Jake heard his own voice screaming obscenities, saw faces appear at windows; scared, bewildered early-hour faces. And then, above him, he saw *his* face emerging through the broken pane like some hologram monster.

Jake screamed as if he had been struck and started throwing more rocks, his arm quicksilver, his voice now that of a screeching bird. Above, The Whistler reared back, his voice irate and angry.

'Hey,' he yelled, 'what the fuck is going on?'

Jake kept throwing and screaming, seeing the faces at the other windows, disapproving, accusing, annoyed.

'Hey, you crazy fuck,' screamed The Whistler, but a stone caught him in the shoulder and made him duck down, uttering unintelligible oaths. Jake yowled in triumph. Knowledge that he had struck out and found a target filled him with an energising glee but he sensed too that more lights were appearing, and people were emerging on to stoops to stare at the spectacle. Panic flared and some survival instinct kicked in. He turned and ran back down the street to his car, the screams subsiding as he fumbled for the door and sped off without a backward glance, the voices at last quiet, appeased by his violence, his hands trembling with the adrenaline charge.

Fifteen minutes later, a squad car arrived at 2028 Cambridge and two uniforms got out. They knocked on the door and spoke to a woman in a navy velveteen dressing gown who pointed them in the direction of her neighbour. Normally a very quiet man who kept very much to himself, she had no idea what could have triggered off such a scene. Officer James Piper and Andrew Tanner took her statement, thanked her, walked across and rang the doorbell of 2030. The man who appeared was fair-haired, tall with heavy glasses. He wore a beard that was trimmed and not bushy and stood there in jeans and a stained light yellow T-shirt with a floor-brush in one hand.

Piper flashed his ID.

'Mr Lauden?'

The man nodded.

'Morning, sir. We're responding to a 911 call from your neighbour. She says someone threw a brick through your window and woke up the whole neighbourhood.

'What?' the occupant tilted his head and frowned.

'Did someone throw a rock through your window, sir?'

'Uh, hang on . . .' said Lauden and pointed vaguely towards his left ear.

Piper and Tanner exchanged glances as Lauden walked back into the room and retrieved two small instruments from the table and fitted them to his ears. They watched as he adjusted something and both heard the faint high-pitched whistle of a badly fitting hearing aid before he returned to the doorway.

'Sorry,' he said. 'The door bell triggers a light. That's how I knew you were ringing. But without these,' he pointed to the hearing aids, 'I'm not very good with conversation.'

Piper nodded understandingly and repeated the question.

'Damn right, he did,' said Lauden angrily.

'Can we come in, sir?'

'Sure, come in, sure.'

The policemen followed Lauden in and stood in the sparsely furnished living room. A brown velour sofa sat against one wall with a pile of clothes thrown over one arm of it. Above on the wall, a circular mirror in a Woolworth Bakelite surround reflected back Piper's wary features. Next to it hung a faded sunset in a plastic mock wooden frame. Incongruously, at the same level on the other three walls hung framed black and white photo-prints of young women lounging half naked against tree stumps or pumping iron in half shadow. They were almost tasteful, the lighting shadowy and artful and the three prints had enough in common for Piper to surmise that they might have been a collection of sorts. He'd seen a thousand similar shots on a hundred calendars and postcards, but with less artistic endeavour. The frames look passably expensive compared to the cheap rubbish that filled the rest of the room. Next to the sofa on a side-table with a scratched and stained surface stood a table lamp surrounded by empty cans of Miller and a vodka bottle with an inch of fluid left in it. In the centre of the room on the needlecord carpet stood a neat pile of swept glass from a gaping hole in the window.

'What happened?' asked Tanner.

'I was sleeping. Next thing I know I hear this crashing noise, loud enough even for me to hear.' Lauden shook his head. 'I come in here and find my window in a thousand pieces and some fruitcake in the street screaming up at me. I stuck my head out, fucker started throwing rocks at me.' He stopped and pulled down the shoulder of his T-shirt to reveal a large purple bruise.

'Did you recognise your attacker?'

'Hell no. I caught one look, but then he hit me with a rock. I didn't try looking again. Kept yelling and screaming fit to wake the dead.'

'What was he saying?' asked Tanner.

Lauden shook his head. His unkempt hair stood out at odd angles and lent him an air of befuddlement. 'Guy was a fruitcake. He could of been quoting Shakespeare for all I know.'

'But you could hear him screaming?'

'Yeah. Not real clear, you know, but definitely screaming. I have a hearing problem, but I'm not deaf.'

'You live here alone, Mr Lauden?'

'Yeah.'

'You work, sir?'

'Yeah, I drive for the Suncab company.'

'An independent?'

'That's right.'

'Anyone you can think of that might want to do this thing?'

Piper walked over to the window and the cool night air that was rushing in.

'No. Since it happened I've been thinking, but I can't come up with any names.'

Piper was closest to Lauden. He smelled stale booze coming off the guy's breath in waves.

'No beef with a fare? Nobody who might harbour a grudge?'

'No.' Lauden shook his head.

'You owe anybody money, Mr Lauden?'

'No.'

'And you couldn't give us a description?'

'It's dark out there. All I saw was a tall crazy guy. White guy but crazier'n hell.'

'How did it end?' continued Tanner.

Lauden shrugged. 'Guy ran off. Suddenly there was no more screaming.'

Piper was still at the window inspecting the jagged edges of the glass. 'You have something you could put over this, Mr Lauden?'

'Yeah, sure. I have some plastic trash bags I use for garden waste.'

'You need a hand?'

'No. I'll be fine.'

'Your neighbour gave us a description of a blue Mazda and most of an Illinois licence plate.' He showed Lauden the number.

'Mean anything to you?'

Lauden paused, his mouth dropping in concentration. But then he shook his head. Piper saw that what this guy needed more than anything was a bath. His hands and nails were filthy with grime and one of the reasons his hair stood out was that it was stiff with grease. Even so it glistened red gold in the harsh light of the living room. An unpleasant smell that had nothing to do with Lauden hung in the air pervasively.

'Mr Lauden,' said Tanner, 'we'll file a report but if you can think of anyone or anything that might help, give the station house a ring. The duty sergeant will take a message and pass it on to me. We'll keep you posted of any developments.'

Lauden attempted a smile.

'This sort of thing happens now and again. I wouldn't lose any sleep over it.' It was Piper's turn to try and be reassuring.

'Thanks,' said Lauden. 'I appreciate you calling.'

'No trouble,' said Tanner.

In the squad car, Tanner rode shotgun and it was he who started writing up the report.

'What do you think?' he asked his partner.

Piper shook his head. 'Capital W for whacko?'

Tanner nodded.

'You notice the choice aroma in there?'

'Why do you think I was so interested in the busted window, Andy?'

'I don't think you should make so much out of some poor guy's hygiene problem.' Piper's delivery came from a straight face.

'What the hell is that supposed to mean?'

'It means people in glass houses . . .' Piper grinned.

Tanner held up his pen towards Piper. 'Up your ass, Jim.'

Lauden waited until the squad rumbled by the second time in as many minutes before slumping on the sofa and taking a shot of the vodka. He felt the liquid spread fire in his gut, holding the bottle up and squinting regretfully at the meagre level remaining. There was not enough there to render him unconscious and allow him the oblivion he craved after the night's scary interlude. He took out the hearing aids and put them on the table. He'd got new batteries but it wasn't the electronics that were screwed up, it was the moulds that fitted into his ears. They were rotting through years of use. He'd been meaning to go back to the clinic but . . .

He had an appreciable level of alcohol in his blood already and the swallows he took soon had him buzzing again. Quickly, he split open a green trash bag and nailed and then taped it over the window, watching the wind billow it into the room. But it held well enough and he turned up the heating to combat the freezing night.

The appearance of the police had unnerved him. He felt

unbalanced, his head thick with the alcohol, his pulse thumping in rhythm with the pounding of his head. It wasn't purely the fact that they were policemen that caused his anxiety. It was more that he had been forced into close proximity with two strangers and had no choice but to interact with them. As always, he had found the forced pleasantness and the need to relate excruciating. Shyness, exacerbated by his hearing defect, had been a bane of his life since childhood. The viral meningitis that had struck when he was eleven had spared his life, but irreparably damaged his acoustic nerves. Since that time, he had been on the fringes of society. An outsider might see a tall, well-built bespectacled man with fair hair who had difficulty maintaining eye contact. Passable and unremarkable. But inside, Lauden saw himself with brutal honesty; as a gangling monster.

He thought of the policemen; how everything might have changed if only he had said,

'*Oh, by the way officer, you notice the smell? Want to know what it is, what it really is? Want to come into my bedroom and have a look see?*'

But he would never do that, just as he would never admit to them that he had a damn good idea who had stood beneath his window and tossed rocks at him. For a while after the night at the Planetarium, he had waited in a daze of sick anxiety for the police to come, convinced that the apparition that had bolted from the shadows as he had caught the girl would have gone directly to them. But with time, the image of that silent, running figure began to instil confused conjecture.

With time, he had begun to believe that it had all been imagined, a freakish vision brought on by adrenaline-induced panic. But now, mindful of what had gone on that evening, the whole episode took on a new, even more bizarre connotation. He groaned in frustration. What was it with this guy, some sort of fucking game?

16

MACKIE SAT ALONE in her apartment letting her muffin go stale and her coffee grow cold. The cause of her disenchantment lay folded on the counter in front of her and she seemed unable to drag her eyes away from it. Rhys Jacob's grainy photograph had jumped out at her from the pages of the *Chicago Chronicle* as she flicked through. Candid and poorly lit, it still bore the haggard lost look he had sported the day of the press conference.

The by-line was Tom Bellasco's, a name beloved of his readers. A deflator of bureaucratic egos, enemy of pomposity and an underminer of heavy-handed authoritarianism. Mackie lit her second menthol of the day and for the third time in ten minutes forced herself to read through it all once again.

CPD CRITICISED IN HOMICIDE INVESTIGATION

Rhys Jacob, brother of the Adler Planetarium murder victim, continues his campaign to clear his sister's name after shocked CPD officials at a press conference held after he had positively identified his sister's body heard him accuse them of labelling the crime unsolvable.

On CHTV this week, he repeated in a calm and understated way these denials and criticised police evidence. A positive toxicology report on the victim revealed high levels of the drugs Lidoxine and Temazepam. CPD detectives had suggested that this cocktail had been taken for recreational purposes. But Rhys Jacob finds this suggestion unacceptable. Catrin Jacob was, like her brother, a doctor. Why, he asks, would someone with an extensive knowledge of drugs choose substances which would, at the levels suggested, induce unconsciousness very quickly? Temazepam, when consumed with alcohol, results in an elevation of mood which is short-lived and inevitably spirals down into sleep. But the additional presence of Lidoxine is even more intriguing. An antidepressive sedative, its effect is often only seen after days or weeks of continued usage. Why, asks Rhys Jacob, would his sister chose such a drug in combination with a sleeping tablet when there are now tens of others with far more efficacious effects on mood and little or no side-effects on the market?

Catrin Jacob was drugged. She was on no prescribed medication, had no medical history of depressive illness and no history of abuse. Of that Rhys Jacob is sure. Was this some tragic joke that backfired? Laced drinks that were meant just as a prank? Or something much more sinister?

Fuel was added to the debate late yesterday when Area 4's Lieutenant Mat Finch reported that drug paraphernalia found in Catrin Jacob's hotel room had no connection with the victim. In a new twist to what is becoming a convoluted investigation for Area 4 detectives, Rhys Jacob also revealed that he may already have been contacted by the killer via a phone call to his hotel. In Jacob's medical opinion, the caller's mental state was not entirely normal.

Yesterday, CPD were busy containing the damage. The Superintendent's office hummed with well-rehearsed rhetoric, but the talk between floors is of a political minefield that may yet blow up in the face of the bureaucrats who have supported the President's hard-line crime and punishment programme.

Stringent denials were also emerging from City Hall over suggestions that the mayor's office is footing the bill for Rhys Jacob's stay.

Whichever way this is read, the Jacob killing is proving to be a sharp thorn in the anxious flesh of City Hall. A foreign national attending a convention is not the usual target for crime. Yet, the old adage of 'no such thing as a true victim' is one that field cops repeat to themselves over beers after a long day. A cynical, callous generalisation that is, nevertheless, undeniably the case in a large percentage of crimes where naivety or stupidity takes those unfortunates upon whom some iniquity is perpetrated into situations where predators lurk. But, as with all maxims, there must be the exception that proves the rule and that exception may be unpalatable in the extreme to those hardened CPD employees forced to contemplate it.

Rhys Jacob's refusal to accept City Hall's banal reassurances and his rejection of their trite explanations should be an example to those of us who remain victims of the system long after the crime has been committed.

Wonderful, thought Mackie. She gulped down the tepid coffee, left the muffin unfinished and drove in to work nursing a dull anger. It was only as she pulled into a parking space that it focused and she realised with mild surprise that it was directed not at Rhys Jacob, but at herself and at Lou and at the department. Bellasco was right; suspicion did breed a cynical attitude. Being a cop did indeed bring you nose-to-nose with the worst aspects of the human condition daily. But his implication that it was a deliberate policy was all wrong. It simply became second nature, went hand-in-hand with the territory. Bellasco knew that, he was merely invoking a little journalistic licence. But Rhys Jacob was not that informed. He was coming at this from the other end of the spectrum. People didn't lie to him as a matter of course. In fact it was exactly the opposite in his line of work; if you were sick you told the truth because your survival depended on it. Not so with criminals.

Guilt worried at her. Maybe she should have spent a little more time with Rhys Jacob, maybe each unit should be employing a psych counsellor to help relatives and survivors of violent crimes. Maybe one day the city would fund law enforcement properly. Maybe one day there would be a McDonald's on Jupiter.

As she breezed through the front hall, the desk sergeant handed her a message.

'Detective Mackie? Some doctor phoned. Wanted you to ring him as soon as you got in.'

Mackie took the number and rang it from her desk. The call was short and sweet and by the time she rang off she was almost smiling.

Ten minutes after she had arrived at the station house, she was knocking on Finch's door.

'What've you got, Mac?' said the Lieutenant as she entered.

'Cook County passed my typescript of the whacko caller on to a psychologist at the University of Chicago. I spoke to him ten minutes ago. He wants to see me. Wants to know more about the tone of voice and speed of the delivery, things like that.'

'So give it to him.'

Mackie gave him a lopsided grin. 'I can't, Lieutenant, I didn't take the call.'

'Shit,' mouthed Finch. 'You read Bellasco this morning?'

Mackie nodded.

'I rang Fromm in vice. There's no street trade in Lidoxine. Most people want to be happy and conscious. This stuff puts you to sleep after an hour. Bellasco's right, it doesn't make any sense.' Finch exhaled loudly.

'Maybe that's all she could get a hold of?' offered Mackie.

Finch shrugged dubiously. 'Bellasco has his teeth in this. What the hell is the matter with this Jacob guy?'

'He's just hurting, Lieutenant.'

'Will he cooperate?'

'Sure. He'll do anything to help. That's his problem.'

'Set it up. Get Lou to come along. Don't ask, tell him I want him there and that's an order.'

Back at her desk, Mackie tried Rhys's room at the Geneva and got no reply. After an hour of trying, a desk clerk had a miraculous memory flash and told her that Dr Jacob had taken an airport shuttle at eight a.m.

'Has he checked out?' asked Mackie, confused.

'No, ma'am. We're expecting him back today.'

She thanked the clerk and hung up, unable to rid herself of the anxious little seed of curiosity that germinated in her mind over just what the hell he was up to now.

The phone rang for the twentieth time at eleven and she answered it unprepared for recognising the voice in the incongruous setting of the station house. It was familiar, but for one panicky second of confusion, she couldn't place it.

'Susan?'

'Hello?'

'Susan, it's me. Don't you even recognise your own mother's voice?'

'Mom,' Mackie laughed in embarrassment. 'I didn't expect . . .'

'I know you don't like me ringing you at work, dear, but since you're never at your apartment any more and I refuse to use that Godforsaken answering machine . . .' The tone was prissy, laden with accusation and that touch of distaste that implied that ringing a Chicago police station was certainly not the sort of thing Mrs Lucinda Mackie relished one iota, *dear*. That term of endearment added on, meaning nothing, making her sound as affected as an extra in a forties black and white movie.

Mackie sighed. 'It's just a machine.'

'I don't know which is worse, that or trying to find you at work. Really, it's most inconvenient.'

Inconvenient. Mackie shivered involuntarily and squeezed her eyes against the irritation she felt burning inside. One of her mother's favourite words, up there along with *liposuction* and *Country Club.* Words that were emphasised and lingered over. Vocal status symbols that peppered her conversation with calculated frequency.

Stop it now, OK. Just stop it. Mackie chided herself. *She's phoned you during the day and there's no avoiding that. No point ringing off pretending your beeper just went. Might as well face this and get it over with.*

'How are you, Mom?'

'I'm fine, dear.' Still the slight restraint, the lilt in pronunciation that qualified all she said as some deigning concession. 'I had an appointment with Dr Beacham last week. He doesn't think the cataracts are ready yet and he wants to see me in six months. His wife has just bought a condo in Acapulco, did you know?'

Screaming inside, Mackie resisted the urge to yell, '*No, I didn't know and I couldn't care less, for Pete's sake.*'

'So you're OK?'

'Not really. My golf has gone to pieces and your father is less than sympathetic.'

Father. That was the doozie. The anti-personnel mine amongst her mother's verbal ammunition.

'How is he?' Mackie heard herself say.

'Himself, dear. One of the reasons I'm ringing is that he wants to know about Thanksgiving.'

He wants to know, does he? He wants to know if I will turn up and be cross-examined and humiliated in front of Scott, Michael and Rick again? Listen to Linda's mindless, tactless maternal yammering?

'I don't think I can make it this year, Mom.' She couldn't believe what she was saying, dancing around it, being nice about it.

'Really, dear.' Not a question, more a patronising finger-wagging condemnation. 'I really think you ought to make an effort. Especially since Scott can't be there. He's in Tokyo with the Lansing Corporation. Some big litigation over export restrictions.'

Tokyo! Mackie found herself imitating the word, making a face as she did so, the irritation needle straying into the red zone.

'I've made plans, Mom,' she said firmly. 'I'm going to Florida with some friends.' The lie opened up in her mind like a sunflower blooming.

'Florida, I see.' The comment was cool and detached. 'Anybody we know?'

'A girlfriend, that's all.'

'What about the nice corporate law attorney from Rapid City, oh what was his name . . . umm, Hammond? Did you make contact?'

'No, Mom, I didn't.'

'Really, Susan. Your father and I talked to his parents just last week. We worry about you you know?'

Yeah, worry about still having to tell everyone at the Club that Susan is still just a dick in Chicago PD. Albeit a sergeant now, Mom. But still not like Scott the attorney or Michael the corporate shark or Richard in pre-med.

'I won't be able to make it to Thanksgiving this year. I'm sorry.'

'Will you be coming up to see us before? Your father was most upset about the party but he's prepared to forgive you. I told him that you must be under some strain but I must say I have been expecting you to call.'

'Me to call?' Susan could feel her mouth opening. She forced herself to remain calm. 'No, Mom. I am not coming up.'

'It's still possible for you to . . .'

'I like what I'm doing, Mom. Why can't you just accept that?'

'Susan, dear. The family all think . . .'

'No they don't. They don't all think like Dad. It's only Dad that believes we have to think the way he does and he's brainwashed you into believing the same. But we all don't, OK?'

'I do try and put your side of things, Susan.' Defensive now, unwilling to admit that to survive in the shadow of the overbearing, opinionated husband, she had sold out in the challenge stakes a long, long time ago. 'Are you working too hard, dear?'

Mackie smiled. It was all so trite, so predictable. Blaming work, making it all her fault.

Are you working too hard, dear?

The same line she had used the day she had visited Susan after the miscarriage. Unable to accept Susan's explanations about spontaneity, looking for someone or something to blame.

Oblivious to Susan's psychological pain, pressing for details, accusing almost.

And it was ever there, that accusation. Lucinda Mackie had been brainwashed into believing the family creed that failure was just another word for not trying. Not saying it but implying it in every carping word; her daughter was a failure for not being able to keep the man who might have been an acceptable husband and for losing the child inside her.

'No, Mom, just working,' said Susan in a dry rasping voice, feeling the heat rise and burn her face.

'Will you call?'

'Sure,' she breathed into the mouthpiece. 'I'll call.' Silence crackled over the line.

'Alright, dear. If you're sure.'

Mackie put the phone down feeling her heavy heart sinking in her chest, the mild high of the morning's progress blown away by lack of *convenience* and thoughts of Thanksgiving and her own blood.

At least she had the guts to say no this time. She imagined the banter that would be going on at this moment between her mother and father in the big house overlooking the lake. The sad shake of the head, the brows laden with thunder and frustration at the fact that he no longer could influence her, no longer had the power now that she was free of that house, happy to survive on her own.

They would lunch out as they always did, some charity gig or fund-raiser. The routine rigid and inextricably linked to keeping up appearances befitting the retired head of the leasing and finance corporation he had begun small and which was now huge in eight states with tentacles in the media. That was no accident. Because that was where the power was.

Her mother's censorious criticisms over arranged relationships rankled because her own efforts, since Nick, were always hollow dances with strangers who were never allowed too close, never allowed through her cloak of self-questioning doubts. Some had ventured but all had drowned in the moat of pain that surrounded her emotions. And so, Susan Mackie applied herself to embrace the professional insensibilities of her job with open arms. As a cop, the caring she needed to do was superficial both by necessity and desire.

She hissed out a long sigh and turned back to her work, guarding her pain like a child with a small fire, feeding it lest it sputter and fail.

Rhys took a cab directly from arrivals at Minneapolis. It was a grey November day, low cloud draining what little colour the city offered and reflecting it back in a muted dishwater palette.

The Hyatt looked like a hundred others; grey safety glass and a huge lobby with water cascading over a marble balcony. Rhys walked to the desk and put a call through to Pamela Rourke's room. She appeared after five minutes, tall in heels and a smart suit, slim and well-kept under short platinum-blonde hair and a pale freckled skin. She looked an attractive forty and shook Rhys's palm confidently and then grasped his forearm in both of her hands.

'Dr Jacob, I'm real sorry for your loss.' Her eyes held his and he noted that there seemed genuine pain there. 'You look just like her,' she added.

Rhys nodded. 'Everyone says that.'

'When I heard I . . . I just flipped. I keep thinking what a tragic waste it was.' Her intonation held a lilting Atlanta drawl.

Again, Rhys nodded, not knowing what to say. In truth, this was the first time anyone had expressed true compassion over Catrin's death to him face to face.

'God, listen to me,' said Pamela. 'This is probably the last thing you wanted to hear right now.' She pulled a tissue from her purse.

'No, it's why I came. Look, can we sit down somewhere?'

They sat in a corner of a restaurant. Rhys drank orange juice and Pamela Rourke OD'd on black coffee and nicotine.

'I'm sorry to interrupt your schedule like this,' said Rhys. 'They're saying all sorts of things about Catrin. I had to speak to someone who saw her that night.'

'What sort of things?' asked Pamela.

Rhys told her about the drugs and Bek's narrow-minded approach.

'That's obnoxious crap,' she said, horrified.

'I'm fighting back,' said Rhys, 'but I need all the ammunition I can get. Tell me about the Planetarium. When exactly did you last see her?'

'OK, uh . . . in the lobby. I was with some clients, but I bumped into her as she was helping herself to some hot chocolate. It was definitely a night for hot chocolate. She was fine, her usual self. We talked briefly, she was anxious to get back to her hotel because she was presenting a paper at a satellite meeting in the Hilton the following morning. She wanted to be fresh, she said, because that was where she was going to meet the people she had come to see. It was almost eleven by that time. I told her they were going to arrange for some cabs to come along but that it would take a little time.'

'So that was why she left on her own?'

'I guess so. Everyone was getting a little antsy, but I guess Catrin had good reason.'

'And she didn't appear in any way odd, slurred speech? Overly hyper?'

'Good Lord, no. In fact I don't think she drank much at all that night. I think she was kinda worried over the presentation.'

'And you've had no reports of anyone else being drugged at the party?'

'None.' Pamela looked aghast.

Rhys sighed. 'What about the night before?'

Pamela smiled wryly. 'I guess you heard about the Nelson, huh?'

'Yes, I have had the opportunity of visiting that establishment.'

'It was Tony's fault. Tony Skodol, he's Techrim's sales manager for the Midwest. He had brought two doctors with him from Oklahoma to the Saloon. We were all a little drunk and Tony starts mouthing off about someplace he knew where the girls were just stacked.' Pamela made a vague gesture with her hands. 'The Okies were all for it, slobbering at the thought. I could see Catrin bristling and it wasn't long before she and Tony were having this big argument about pornography.'

'Oh?'

'Tony was saying how harmless he thought it all was and Catrin said that she felt that soft porn was more offensive than the hard-core variety because at least with the hard-core stuff you got to see a good-looking guy as well as the girl.'

Rhys found himself smiling. He could almost hear Catrin saying it, challenging, uncompromising.

'The upshot was that Catrin said, OK, if they were all so set on going we'd all go. There was no talking her out of it. She wanted to see for herself.'

Rhys nodded. 'And was she impressed?'

'As hell. Didn't take her long to figure out who was being manipulated in there and it certainly wasn't the girls.'

Rhys nodded, remembering all those dollars changing hands.

'It looked like the dancers had all the power. I couldn't work out if they were narcissistic or ultra-feminist.'

'They're doing what they have to,' said Pamela shrugging. 'And some of them did have bodies I would die for. But Catrin saw through all that. She just couldn't understand why it was necessary for guys to go to a place like that so that they can whack off in the john afterwards. Why didn't they grow out of that when they were seventeen? She kept saying this to Tony who ignored her although I could see he was getting pissed. Finally, she just decided to do her own thing. They played a Prince track, *1999*? Catrin said it was one of her favourite dance tracks. So she just got up and started dancing. Wanted me to get up too, but honey, I just couldn't. People were staring and cheering, one or two guys got up from other tables and began dancing too. The DJ saw it all and shouted some encouragement. It was spontaneous but it was distracting. Customers weren't paying attention to the dollar dances. Some jerk with a fifty-inch chest in a tuxedo came over and talked to us, said they didn't encourage dancing. The guys were intimidated as hell and Catrin promised to be a good girl. Tony did see the funny side of it eventually.'

'Was he angry?'

Pamela frowned in realisation at what she'd said. 'Hey, don't get the wrong idea about Tony. It was just a little fun. And besides he was with me until long after one a.m. on the night Catrin was killed.'

'It's OK,' said Rhys. 'I know how feisty Catrin could be. Tony must have wished he'd never mentioned the Nelson by the time the night was over.'

'You're absolutely right.'

'And that night, there was no sign of any drug-taking?'

'No, none whatsoever.'

'And she went back to the hotel alone?'

'I dropped her off myself.' Pamela was almost indignant. 'Honey, Catrin was one of the most balanced people I've ever met. She knew what she wanted and who she was. I'd only known her a couple of days, but you know what, I felt as if I'd known her for ever. That's rare in a business where you have to be pleasant to everyone and where you know you're often at best tolerated and never liked for who you are. Catrin wasn't like that. She came over to the Techrim stand at McCormick and we got into a conversation which had nothing to do with the product I was selling. That was the first time in three days I'd had a normal conversation.'

Rhys nodded.

'She was special, Rhys. She didn't deserve any of that to happen to her. She doesn't deserve any of what is being said. It's wrong, honey. All wrong.'

'Thank you,' said Rhys. 'I know it, but it's nice to hear someone else say it too.'

They talked for another half an hour. Pamela Rourke gave Rhys her home telephone number and wished him luck and offered to help in any way she could. He took a six p.m. flight back to Chicago Midway with his resolve hardened into something approaching tempered steel.

Mackie got back to her apartment that evening tired and hungry, still smarting from her mother's call. She opened her mail and played the messages on her answering machine as she did so. There was only one of any importance:

'Susan, it's Audra. I've been meaning to call for days since the party . . . Scott and I, we both thought that what happened wasn't your fault. It was about time if you ask me and I wanted you to know that. The other reason I'm phoning is to let you know that Linda's obstetrician wants her to have an amnio. I thought I'd tell you in case . . .' There was a small pause. 'Scott says I say too much on these things but my invitation still stands and if you want to talk, please, just give me a call. Bye.'

She played the message again, listening to her sister-in-law's genuine concern, filling in the words she hadn't spoken.

In case. . . . In case you hear about it from your mom and fall apart at the seams. Audra was perceptive and she had made tentative overtures – offers of lunches and shopping trips – all of which Susan had declined over the last twelve months because she didn't want to talk about IT to anyone, least of all family. Mackie had a network of friends, some closer than others, who had visited her in the hospital and since Nick's departure had become important props both socially and emotionally. But to them she chose to present a brave face, using work more often than not as an excuse not to go out. They understood, after all they had all broken up with someone during their lives. Her friends liked her and respected her space and the distance she held them at without questioning. But it was only Audra who seemed to see the pain that festered. Only Audra who made Mackie confront her own misguided motivation with her understanding glances and her offers of intimacy. And Mackie shied away from it. Had tried it once and been bitten hard by it.

She wiped the message off and tried putting it from her mind as she warmed up and ate the remaining half of a leftover pizza. Then she threw some clothes in the washing machine, ironed a few blouses and slacks, stacked the dishwasher and sat down in front of the TV for some escapist mindlessness before going to bed. It was a good mundane strategy. By the time ten-thirty arrived, she had almost managed to forget all about Audra.

Managed it with all the ease of a blind man ever forgetting that he was blind.

17

W ILLIAM LAUDEN LIES in his bed between sleep and wakeful-
ness, disturbed by a vague awareness that there is something
wrong. For three nights he has been put to bed early. Not as
punishment in any way, because William is a good boy, very quiet,
content with his own company. The early nights are his father's
idea so as to avoid any undue disturbance to William's mother.
William has not seen her for three days; she has confined herself
to her bed, sleeping most of the day and through the night. His
father describes it as one of her 'off' periods. Hibernating for fear
of turning into something human, William overheard him explain
to someone on the phone a week or so ago. He thought he had
heard a woman's voice giggle on the other end.

William awakes from his slumber and it is still dark. Silence on
the street outside and in the house tells him that it is not yet time
to rise. He hears a noise and realises it is what has disturbed him.
A familiar noise, evocative but incongruous. He sits up, straining
to hear with ears as yet undamaged by meningitis. He is ten years
old and has no fear of walking around his house alone. The noise
comes from downstairs and William pads down in bare feet and
faded Green Lantern pyjamas. In the kitchen his mother is singing
to herself, transferring food from the refrigerator to the breakfast
bar. She sings a song he knows, one about red feathers and a
huli-huli skirt, a little too loud and a little off key. A song she
sang to him when he was a baby. He likes the song. She senses
his presence and swings around, her hair unkempt, a piece of cold
spaghetti hanging from her lips. She pushes it in with one finger
and chews. She is naked except for a pair of panties.

'Hi, baby,' she beams and her smile is like the heat from a
hundred fires.

She turns back to the refrigerator, apparently oblivious to her appearance, accepting his presence without comment. The skin on her thighs reminds him of grapefruit.

'I can't find any pastrami. Where is the pastrami? I know I bought some pastrami.' The irritation in her voice is there without warning, fierce in its intensity. She turns and points an accusing finger at William, her eyes suddenly ablaze with fury. 'Did you eat all the fucking pastrami? Did you, William?' She has a knife in her hand and waves it at him. Her face is suffused with a capricious, dangerous anger. William stares and shakes his head mutely.

She turns back to the refrigerator, frantically pulling things out and letting them drop to the floor now. 'Everything but the pastrami,' she sings out, the pique in her voice loud and clear.

'Peanut butter!' she yells triumphantly and turns holding up the jar.

She comes around and sits at the kitchen table, lounging, aware again of her son staring as she runs a finger in a curve around the inside of the jar and licks it clean.

'Whassamatter, William, you never seen Momma's titties before?' She laughs and does a burlesque shoulder wiggle, thrusting her breasts out. She beckons to him and now William senses that this isn't his mother, not really. This is some creature full of wild abandon that he has never met. An uninhibited creature, simultaneously fascinating and abhorrent.

'Come here,' she orders. 'I'm hungry. Are you hungry too, baby?' William is confused. For what has seemed like weeks his mother has lain in bed, barely wanting to get up, unwilling to acknowledge his presence much of the time. Now she pulls him over to the big kitchen chair and hoists him effortlessly onto her lap. The hands of the clock point to five after midnight. She holds him close to her, singing her song, softer now. Slowly she pulls William's head around until her breast is next to his face. She puts one nipple in his mouth. He doesn't know what to do. The flesh is smooth and warm against his cheek. Inside he is squirming, but this touch, this suckling feel of his mother, the person who has abandoned him for weeks at a time, is magical.

And then he is tumbling to the floor and she is on her feet, yelling.

'Don't touch me. You can't touch me. I refuse to be touched by you. I refuse. I'm eating, feeding my child.'

His father is coming across the room, horror and dread disbelief in his face. His mother screams and throws the jar at his father which he bats off, still coming at her. She fights like a wild cat, gnawing, biting, and the glances William dares to give show her face twisted by some inner glee. His father yells at him to get out of the room and back to his bed. He lays there, confused and terrified. He sneaks to a window and sees a police car arrive followed by Doctor Pascoe's dusty station wagon with the faded bumper stickers.

The following day, his mother is taken to the hospital where there are no children and everything is quiet except for the odd, faraway noise of someone screaming.

When next he sees her she is sleeping, at peace with the devil inside her that subdues her but occasionally unleashes a demon. He stares at her still form, remembering vividly her breast in his mouth, appalled and beguiled, he reaches out his hand and touches hers. She doesn't move, doesn't reciprocate and William feels the love bloom like a blood-red rose inside.

St Louis, 1975

Dave Liebowitz was easy-going with a zit-free complexion and a mop of dark hair which he kept clean. Those two features, added to his prowess on the basketball court made him one popular guy at Meadow Park High School. Dave lived in a low-rent side of Brentwood with his little sister and his mom after his dad never made it back from the Mekong. During the long summer of '75, Dave made a little money stacking shelves at a store called Mellish Mart. His companion during those long boring hours was a boy who lived right across the street by the name of William Lauden.

Dave had been impressed by William's ability to find and to drink beer during the warm evenings. Dave knew his mom would go crazy if she found out he had taken any of the Pabst she kept in the refrigerator for when uncle Jerry called, and he would be grounded until the end of the century if she found out he had been sharing William's supply. But, man, it felt good to swallow one of those ice-cool Buds of an August night.

Dave knew that William never had any problems with his parents because his mom was in the hospital most of the time and his dad worked shifts over at the plant in Kirkwood. William hardly ever talked about it and Dave accepted only what William volunteered. That was cool.

Come September, they were back in school and the boredom of

the summer gave way to homework and tryouts and practice and, in Dave's case, girls. Something had happened to them over the warm, sunny months since he'd seen them last. They were bigger and tanned and better. Dave never really had any problems in that department and he felt for William who curled up and died if a girl so much as looked at him. He just couldn't get past that first hello before hunching up into a ball of frozen embarrassment.

The first weekend of October was always Spanish Lake Fair and Dave decided he needed to help William out. Dave had asked his date, Laura, to fix William up with Sissy Hanson; a new girl who didn't really know William or anyone very well. Laura commented that it was the only way she would get anyone to go out with William because she thought he was creep city but Dave didn't mind because she had the cutest butt and let him put his hands under her sweater the very first time they had necked. Besides, there was a lot in what she said. William agreed reluctantly, not wanting to seem churlish and let Dave down.

The weekend stayed warm for Spanish Lake and there were rides and side-shows and candy-apples and after half an hour, Dave suggested they split up so that he and Laura could get some serious petting done behind the helter-skelter. At nine-thirty, Sissy came running from behind the Millennium ride with its whistling scream, her face streaked with tears, babbling hysterically, grabbing Laura's arms, gasping for breath between sobs.

It took ten minutes to calm her down enough to find out what happened.

When Laura told Dave, he went a little crazy. What the fuck was wrong with William? He felt bad for Sissy who suddenly looked about ten years old. She had trusted him to fix up this date. It was difficult enough being a new kid in school without. . . . He found William slumped behind a generator, the smell of diesel oil not strong enough to hide the stench of beer on William's breath as Dave leaned in belligerently.

'What happened, man?'

'Nothing.' Lauden's eyes were glazed and unfocused.

'Nothing? Sissy's crying her eyes out. Says you left her for half an hour and came back loaded. Look at you, man.'

'I like her,' slurred Lauden.

'She says you wouldn't let her go, Bill. She says you were squeezing her.'

'I only wanted her quiet. I wanted her to be still.'

'You scared the shit out of her is what you did. The fuck you trying to do, man?'

'Don't yell at me.'

'Why not, Bill? Someone sure as hell needs to do something about you. You're a lush, man.'

'Don't yell.' Lauden reached out a hand to grab for Dave's jacket. Dave snapped and threw his fist into Lauden's gut, feeling his hand sink into the soft flesh, his anger erupting into that one blow. Lauden fell to his knees, beer and vomit exploding from his mouth in a gush.

'You're fucked up, man. I've had it with you.' Dave's mouth was an angry snarl as he tapped his head before turning and walking away.

St Louis, March 1976

Jody Hoffstedler had been missing for three days. Her parents had last seen her as she'd left to walk two blocks to her friend Mandy Galetta's house. They were going to study for a biology test. It was almost an hour before Mrs Galetta called to ask if Jody was coming as it was nearing eight-thirty and she didn't want Mandy staying up too late. Margaret Hoffstedler knew then that something bad had happened. She spent ten frantic minutes phoning around all of Jody's friends before dialling 911.

They searched for seventy-two hours around the clock. Heavy rain on the second day slowed them down but the police had called for volunteers and it looked like almost half the population of Brentwood had turned out. Deputy Sheriff Lucas Murdoch had more civilians than he could handle. It looked great on TV but if truth were told, they got in his hair and each other's way. He'd begun turning people away on the second day, politely to start with and then more irritably. Thus, he had no qualms about saying a big No to the tall bespectacled figure of William Lauden. Not only because he was just a gawky kid but because he acted like something was wrong with him, swaying in front of the desk. Almost as if he was drunk. Couldn't have been more than seventeen or eighteen, but Murdoch had too many things to worry about to start hassling kids for ID.

But he really wanted to help, insisted Lauden. Yeah, yeah, Murdoch had heard it a thousand times. Guys in bars, watching the news, feeling bad for the parents, wishing they could do something, maybe catch the bastard who had kidnapped the girl and string him up. Fact was with every hour, the chance of finding this twelve-year-old alive was diminishing. Murdoch told the guy who gave his name as William Lauden to go home. Maybe try in the morning.

Had Murdoch taken Lauden's offer, he might at least have spared Margaret Hoffstedler the pain of years of hoping and searching. The agony of not knowing, the ignominy of seeing her little girl's picture on the back of milk cartons. An hour after he had left the cop, Lauden was sitting with Jody Hoffstedler, holding her in his arms, rocking back and forth, tears in his eyes, his nostrils filling with the stench of her already decomposing body. He knew he couldn't leave her in the trash bags, the smell was getting too bad. He'd only meant to talk to her, ask her to explain to him why he was so scared of girls. But she had looked at him and screamed, for no reason other than her own survival instinct. He had put his hands around her neck and held her until the screams died and she became limp in his hands. It had been so quick, the power to subdue there in his fingers in an instant. He had dragged her fifteen yards into a crawl space under a church on St Martin's Street, not more than two blocks from her house. It had rained, the pavements washed clean within ten minutes.

The next day, the police department dismissed the volunteers and a deployment of National Guard came in and combed the area, concentrating on the woods to the north. A day later, they called off the search.

Thwarted and confused by the police's unwillingness to listen to him, Lauden went back sober to the crawl space, took out the two double lined trash bags and buried them on a construction site for a new supermarket three blocks away.

He was seventeen years old.

Chicago, 1989

The first fifteen minutes were always reasonable if not great. In fact, thought Lydia Crane, the sessions were always of two halves. He would come in and sit down, well-dressed, probably wanting at some level to please her. They might talk about his work at the shoe factory or last week's Cubs game and perhaps, if he was in the mood, he might volunteer a general statement of how he was feeling. She, in turn, would volunteer something about herself, try and inject a little intimacy before she approached the real problem, the reason he was sitting in her office, her brief. The first eight sessions had been useful. It looked like he had made genuine efforts to curb his drinking through AA. But, Crane knew that her feelings were skewed because she hadn't attempted to address the nub of the thing. For some reason, despite all attempts at building rapport, he was becoming increasingly morose and uncooperative. The session had taken place every two weeks for twelve months and if she was going to get any kind of meaningful report back to the court, Crane knew there was nothing for it any more other than to be direct.

She had the psychologists' reports in front of her. It was always easier for them, not needing to establish any kind of relationship, just question and answer sessions designed to assess a variety of emotional and cognitive parameters. It looked as though Lauden had seen them as a challenge. The scores showed above average intelligence but language skills that implied an introversion and isolation that undermined his intellect. The emotional assessment was not enthralling. Marked paucity and restriction of responses across the scale. But the thing that intrigued her most was an analysis of the patient's goals. The phrase 'not rooted in reality' was an unusual one.

Crane sighed. Her own interpretation of all this was complicated by her inability to get behind Lauden's obvious barriers. Any attempt she had made to directly address the circumstances leading up to the charge of lewd and lascivious behaviour, for which he had been ordered by the courts to attend for psychiatric evaluation, had been met with strong resentment.

That he was psychologically troubled was there for all to see, but getting a handle on it . . .

He sat half turned away from her, staring out of the window, his face set in a sullen, disgruntled expression. Crane tried once again.

'How are things at home, William? Did your father come visit on your grandmother's birthday?'

Lauden made a disparaging noise in his throat. 'He was too busy to come over.'

'Did you speak with him?'

'Nnh-nnh.'

'Why not?'

'Because he'd only start asking me things or telling me what to do.'

'What kind of things?'

'Like, why I wasn't going to college. Dumb things like that.'

'Don't you think that shows that he cares about you?'

'No.'

'Why not?'

'Because all he does is preach. Tells me what I should be doing.'

'Doesn't your grandmother?'

'No. She doesn't have to.'

'You get on well, don't you? You have no regrets in moving in with her?'

Lauden turned and fixed her with a big false grin. 'Is that all you've found out after twenty-five wasted hours of this?'

Crane sighed. 'Would you like to talk about when your father left?'

Lauden turned to stare back out of the window.

'Were you visiting your mother at that time?' She glanced at her notes. Mrs Lauden's Bipolar I disease would not have been easy to live with. From the brief summary Crane had, the manic episodes appeared to have been extreme between the depressions. By his early teens, Lauden's mother had drifted down from a morose, melancholic sensitivity into a tranquillised depression and his father had simply wanted out.

'What did you feel about him leaving?'

Lauden's fingers were drumming out a tattoo on the table.

'Did you feel angry?'

He shrugged a reply.

'But you didn't feel you could go with him?'

'No.'

'Do you still visit your mother?'

'Sometimes.'

'It must be painful visiting her?'

No response.

'But your parents were divorced by the time your father left. You were aware that things were not going well and that he had stayed for your sake.'

'Ask him.'

Crane decided to grasp the nettle. 'Did you have any girlfriends a year ago, William?'

'What does that mean?'

'I'm trying to find out a little about your social life prior to the incident.'

'What incident?'

'The reason you're here.'

'To make you money, you mean?' His grin was unpleasant.

'No. The reason that you've been asked to attend. I'd like to know.'

'Why? So that you can tell them?' His response was abrupt and Crane thought she heard a hint of panic in there.

'I have to write a report. I've explained all that. It would be good to indicate that we had made some progress.'

The look he gave her was full of defiant indifference.

'What about now? You told me two months ago that there was a girl at work . . .'

'No girl.'

'But there was someone called. . . . uh, Jody.'

'No girl.' Lauden's voice had dropped low.

'Didn't things work out between you and Jody?'

'There is no Jody.'

Crane could almost hear his teeth grinding.

'It is difficult sometimes to make friends. I can put you in touch with some groups that meet just to talk.'

Lauden's head snapped up. 'What for? To talk about me?'

'Your problem is not unique, William. A large number of people get frustrated.'

Lauden's face went pale with anger. He stood and turned his chair around so that he was facing away from her.

'Ignoring me won't help. It isn't the answer.'

Lauden's fingers found the leg of the chair and began drumming again.

Crane tried for another twenty minutes without eliciting any further response. At the end, Lauden stood and walked out of the room without a backward glance. The report that Crane finally sent to the court contained the following conclusion:

'. . . . this patient's deviant behaviour seems intractable and without intervention will, I'm certain, continue. The marked paranoid tendencies and negativity indicate schizoid traits which could degenerate into full-blown sociopathic behaviour compounded by alcohol abuse. He is at risk from developing marked sado-masochistic behaviour and may already have committed unnatural acts in satisfying his sexual preoccupations.'

What the judge didn't see was the underlined comment in Crane's own hand on the report. A comment that she felt was inappropriate for official inclusion, but which summarized her own feelings concisely as a postscript to her signature:

'This man is a ghoul.'

Chicago, 1992

They buried Mary Francis Lauden on December 10th. She weighed sixty-four pounds. There was a service in the church and later at the cemetery in Palos Hills. It was a quiet dignified affair, marred only by William's dread of the family get-together afterwards. As it turned out, his father was more than willing to shoulder the burden of grieving host and Lauden spent most of the afternoon mending a broken faucet in his neighbour, Mrs Sacks' bathroom. Something he had known about for weeks, but it made a fitting reason to stay away from relatives he hadn't seen for years and had no desire to become reacquainted with.

At around eight that evening Lauden's father left with his new wife Christina to drive an aunt the dozen miles to Calumet City and then on to the airport for a late flight to Detroit. Lauden made appropriate noises and actually thanked them for coming. His father asked him once more to go with them for a few days, but Lauden declined. He'd obtained his chauffeur's licence and the cab company did not feel inclined to give him any time off. At least that was what he told his father.

He turned from waving them off and shut the door behind him, alone in the house. It was not the first time of course. There had been periods over the last few months when his grandmother had needed to spend weeks in the hospital but the air of finality that came with that slam of the door was undeniable and hit home with the force of a recoiling rifle. He stood with his back to the door, the house still except for the popping of the occasional timber in the roof and the thin wind outside.

The silence enveloped him, blanketing him, transporting him. From an early age, Lauden had learned to be stealthy, to creep lest his mother's fragile moods were disturbed, another migraine triggered. Silence and solitude had been his companions.

A strange burble of anticipation coursed through his veins. It frightened him, as a man might feel fear before he leaps out from a cliff side into a bottomless sea.

Ever since he had learned that his grandmother was dying, the brooding darkness of his primal urges that somehow had been tethered and subdued by her undemanding presence had begun to fungate in his head. With her death, the tenuous strands of decency and restraint had snapped like paper ribbons. And a part of him welcomed the release, this evolution of his true self.

The doorbell took him by surprise. There stood the priest that had overseen the morning's service, smiling sadly.

'William, I called to see how you were.'

'I'm fine,' mumbled Lauden, making no attempt to invite him in.

'This is such a difficult time,' said the priest, pulling his coat about him. 'Often I find that a little companionship is all it needs.'

'There is no need, thank you.'

'It may seem that way. It may seem now that all you want to do is grieve alone but . . .'

'There is nothing here for you any more,' said Lauden

The priest frowned. 'Surely, now is not the time to turn your back on us. We are your friends, William. Your grandmother would be very disappointed.'

'She's dead.'

'You're clearly upset. Can't I come in and we could talk? You have lost a dear friend today.'

'I have no friends.'

'Yes you do, William. The Church . . .'

Lauden shook his head. 'The Church wouldn't want me.'

The priest seemed appalled. 'How can you say such a thing?'

'She's gone. That's all there is to it. Don't make it into anything else.'

'William, please . . .'

'Good night, Father.' Lauden shut the door in his face. The priest rang again, Lauden heard him through the door, pleading for it to be opened. After a while, he went into the kitchen and tore off the list of AA meetings pinned to a cork-board there.

Four years ago, before he had moved in with his grandma, he had stolen a mannequin from a boarded up, bankrupt store. For days he had lain with this inanimate object, its skin smooth and cold, unyielding to his hand, talking to it, loving it, until his desires and urges became blunted by the knowledge that beneath the painted torso there was nothing but a hollow body, no real pulsing warm organs for him to possess. He went down to the basement and retrieved it now, taking it to his bedroom and lying with it until the noises from the porch died away.

Lauden waited another ten minutes before walking four blocks to a liquor store and buying three bottles of vodka. He needed fuel to begin his journey into hell.

18

THE HEADLINE IN Thursday's *Chronicle* announced the re-election of Congressman Ted Kervesky Dem. Ill. for the sixteenth consecutive term. Only 40 per cent of voters turned out. Congressman Kervesky polled 52 per cent. The mayor sent Kervy a telegram and faxed copies to all the city newspapers. Not one of them printed it. The one thing people in the central district would remember about the tedious campaign was how they had narrowly avoided voting in that other guy whose friends included fanatics that killed doctors.

Mackie tried the Geneva again at nine a.m. on Thursday morning and got through to Rhys first time.

'Nice trip? she asked drily.

'Very helpful, thanks.'

'I read Bellasco's piece about you yesterday. Thanks for the drug input.'

'Don't mention it.'

'It would have been nice to have heard it from you first.'

'Before reading about it in the papers, you mean? That's the way it goes sometimes, isn't it?'

'People abuse all kinds of . . .'

'Catrin was a doctor,' he insisted. 'Lidoxine is a tricyclic antidepressant with a list of side-effects and contraindications as long as your arm. If you OD on it, you die because it makes you comatose and stops your breathing. It would be crazy to mix it with sleeping tablets. It defies all logic.'

'Junkies don't usually worry about logic.'

'Maybe junkies don't,' said Rhys darkly, 'but we're talking about my sister here. Christ, there are a hundred better drugs I can think of off the top of my head. Prozac for one. Happy pills, you know? The sort that Sergeant Bek could do with half a dozen of.'

His sarcasm wasn't lost on her. There was a long pause before she said 'Can we start over?'

'Try me,' said Rhys.

'I'm calling to ask for your help. I've set up a meeting with a psychologist this morning. He'd like to speak to you about our caller.'

'My word, don't tell me you're actually taking some notice?'

'Rhys,' warned Mackie.

'You know me,' he said, 'only too pleased to oblige.'

They met at eleven a.m. Bek sat in one of the folding chairs hunched up like a bear with a hangover. His face was sullen, orbits dark and sunken from exhaustion. Mackie and Finch appeared serious and preoccupied. The only person in the room Rhys didn't know was a trim, muscular mahogany-skinned man with a runner's physique and an infectious grin whom Mackie introduced as Dr Dean Lavalle. He sat in the cramped chair with an irrepressible good humour. He gave Rhys the impression that he was glad and slightly excited to be there.

Mackie explained how Finch had felt it a good idea to bring everyone together to hear what Lavalle had to say and to answer any questions he might have. Lavalle had looked across at Rhys when she'd said that, his expression unreadable. Rhys had glanced at Bek, but his mind appeared elsewhere, his expression lost and troubled. God, how the hell did this man get to be heading the investigation? he thought to himself. He appreciated how the violence that was almost a way of life for these street cops might make them battle hardened. They had to be able to stand off, even make jokes about the dreadful things they saw, but Bek didn't appear to give a monkey's tit about anything.

Rhys's pondering was intruded upon by the sight of Lavalle opening a large envelope folder on his knees. As he did so, he beamed.

'I should explain that Detective Mackie's brief was passed on to me at the University of Chicago by Dr Aldridge at Cook County. He knows that I have a particular interest in forensic psychology. To reassure you all, I have assisted Chicago PD in the past with some profiling. David Aldridge felt that this was a natural extension of work I'd done before.'

Finch nodded and Mackie smiled, their eyes anxious for him to get on with things.

He took out some typed pages and set them on the file on his knees.

'Firstly, I have no doubt that this is a genuine example of a grossly thought-disordered individual. I understand that a preliminary diagnosis has been offered by uh, Dr Jacob?'

Rhys nodded.

'I agree. The example I examined clearly shows gross language dysfunction and the most likely cause is schizophrenia, although there are a few other potential diagnoses that might just fit the bill. What I was unsure of from the cold transcript were associative factors. Was this shouted? Was it rapid delivery? Was it all completely intelligible?'

'It was rapid and mostly of high to normal volume. I clearly heard everything that was said.'

Lavalle's pearly grin widened. 'Great. There didn't seem a manic element, but I wasn't sure.'

Finch tapped a finger on his desk. 'English please.'

Lavalle bowed his head slightly in apology. 'Lieutenant, you'll have to excuse some of the jargon. It would take too long to explain all this in layman's terms, but I'll get to the point. I applied a simple "Cloze" test procedural analysis to the text. This is where we omit every fourth or fifth word of the text. Under normal circumstances, such an omission does not appreciably alter the meaning of a sentence. Most intelligent readers could infer the meaning from what is left. For example . . .'

He scribbled some words down on a clean sheet.

'Imagine you were ✳✳✳✳ this for the ✳✳✳✳ time. Already you ✳✳✳✳ filled in the ✳✳✳✳ and understanding is ✳✳✳✳✳✳'

He held it up and looked at Mackie. 'Would you like to read the sentence and best guess at what is missing?'

'Imagine you were *seeing* this for the *first* time. Already you *have* filled in the *gaps* and understanding is *unaffected*?'

'Great. You could have chosen reading instead of seeing and complete instead of unaffected, but it would not substantially alter the meaning of what you inferred from the remaining sentence. Predictability is the key. In schizophrenics, the predictability is low and the example I was given showed very poor predictability. Look . . .

He scribbled on a new sheet and held it up:

'The Whistler sees ✳✳✳ look for him ✳✳✳ the chariot. I ✳✳✳✳ it. A Chariot ✳✳✳light. And I'll ✳✳✳✳ it and I'll ✳✳✳✳ the words I'll

'*** my specific calculations **** designing the alternation ****
use the words *** power. Keep away *** the TV take *** back
to the.'

'Care to try again?' asked Lavalle.

'Uh, The Whistler sees you look for him and the chariot. I love
it. A Chariot with light. And I'll read it and I'll decipher the words
I'll deduce my specific calculations to designing the alternation
and use the words and power. Keep away from the TV take it
back to the. . . .'

'OK,' said Lavalle, taking the paper back from Mackie. '"You,
and, love, with, read, decipher, deduce, to, and, and, from, it",' he
said, scrutinising the words he'd written down and making some
rough calculations. After a few moments, he looked up.

'Your best guesses are lousy. The substituted words are: "I, in,
know, of, find, use, use, in, I'll, of, from, Jacob."'

Finch was shaking his head in bewilderment.

'You scored 60 per cent the first time in the example I gave
you,' continued Lavalle, 'and your substitutions on the remaining
40 per cent were apposite. On the second example from Dr
Jacob's caller you scored about 10 per cent but your substitutions
were meaningless. The predictability in the second example is
almost non-existent. This degree of derailment implies rapid,
uncontrollable thoughts. Wild flights of ideas from one topic to
the next. These patients have an inability to apportion or weight
their thinking. We all think a hundred thoughts a minute but we
can concentrate on one and pull ourselves back from overload.
Not so schizophrenics. Every idea crystalises, every thought fights
for expression, like having twenty TVs on at once.'

'What we really need to know, Doctor Lavalle, is if this is the
guy we are after?' Finch's voice cut through the air.

Lavalle's smile almost disappeared. 'The reference to thought
extraction, the preoccupation with surveillance – all point towards
paranoia. His delusions seem to revolve around space culture, but
this is often the case amongst the more imaginative. Schizophrenics
find science fiction excellent material with which to feed their hyper
fantasies. In this instance, it has added significance with the links
to the Planetarium. It could turn out that our caller has been there
more than once.'

No one saw Bek's neck burning.

Lavalle said, 'Dr Jacob, he described an inscription in great detail.'

'Yes.'

'What does it mean, out of interest?'

' "With love, Eira," my maternal grandmother's name. Given by her and written in her first language,' Rhys said.

Lavalle nodded. 'A language professor at the University told me that Welsh is the oldest language in the UK.'

'Yes.'

'It would fuel our caller's delusions that he was dealing with an alien culture, of course.' Lavalle smiled.

'Does it put him at the scene?' hissed Finch.

'Unless he had prior knowledge of that inscription, then undoubtedly, yes.'

'No one has seen this brooch, except Dr Jacob,' said Mackie and out of the corner of her eye she saw Bek snort and toss his head.

'What else can you tell us, Dr Lavalle?' asked Finch.

'For me the neologisms and stock words are the most intriguing.'

'Neologism?' asked Finch.

'Made-up words like alternation. As for meaning your guess is as good as mine. This is his own invention and has its own idiosyncratic meaning. Chariot of light could mean anything – again a suggestion of religious overtones that implies transportation or mythology. But Whistler or The Whistler is a stock word – one that is used repetitively. It has meaning for us in terms of its intrinsic connotation of sound, but it seems heavily connected with his paranoia and as such, I suspect, has a symbolic meaning too. I can't offer much more in the way of explanation. I may have applied the term "thought disorder" to these utterances, but this is usually a reference to how hard we must work to understand them. Even the most disordered speech is, in general, very meaningful. But his delusion will be impossible to analyse without interviews. I can only state that Dr Jacob here is inextricably tied in with them, as probably was the victim.'

'Can you work up a profile based on what you have now and the case details?' asked Mackie, leaning forward.

'I can try,' grinned Lavalle enthusiastically.

Finch thanked him for coming in and Mackie found a uniform to escort him to the street. When she came back in, Finch's eyes were glittering.

'This is progress, Susan. We have to work off this.'

Mackie nodded.

'Lou, got anyone on your list with a mental history?'

Bek shook his head.

'OK. Try the Planetarium. Talk to the attendants, see if there is someone that springs to mind. Possibly a regular visitor.' He turned to Rhys. 'Dr Jacob, thank you for your input. I know it isn't exactly the message you've been getting, but perhaps it might be a good idea if you hung around a day or two in case this fruitcake rings back.'

The irony of it brought a sour little smile to Rhys's face as Finch stood and slid on a jacket over his white shirt. He didn't wait for Rhys's reply. 'Liaise with Detective Mackie,' he muttered as he left.

The room descended into silence when he'd gone. After a long moment, Mackie turned to Bek. 'Lou, I'm sorry I had to put you through this.'

'It's OK, Mac.' He kept his eyes away from her penetrating gaze.

'I was sorry to hear about your mother, Sergeant Bek.' Rhys's statement took both detectives by surprise but Bek was the first to respond, his tone belligerent and truculent.

'So this is common knowledge, huh?'

Rhys shrugged. 'I'm still sorry. I know that you don't like me, but that doesn't alter the fact that I feel for you. I suspect you think I'm interfering in bringing all this to your attention, but I didn't ask for that phone call. Maybe if you tried to empathise a little, put yourself in my position.' Rhys spoke evenly, untroubled by Bek's aggression or the irascible way his eyes narrowed.

'It's my job to put myself in your position, Doctor. That's how I catch scumbags.'

Rhys nodded affably. 'The thing is, I can't honestly class the poor bloke who called me on the phone a scumbag. He's disconnected from reality. His world, the one he inhabits, has its own rules. It's a world taken apart, disrupted, reduced to anarchy. People talk of the soul in schizophrenia, whether it can exert any spiritual restraint on what the confused mind makes the body do. I think he has a soul. Schizophrenics do murder, but for their own logical set of reasons. If it turns out that this man is the killer, it'll be tragic.'

Mackie frowned. 'You hope the guy who called you isn't the perp?'

'Hope doesn't come into it. I've done enough work in psychiatry to know what happens to attitudes when mental illness rears its ugly head. I come from a country where almost seventy thousand long-stay patients have left the confines of mental hospitals over the last thirty years. Some clearout, eh? The public concept, fuelled by our even-minded friends the media, is that they have all been "released" from some sort of concentration camp existence. But I know what happens to patients outside in the community, patients whose control of their illness is precarious at the best of times. Certain kinds of mental illness instil a wanderlust, a sort of constant searching in these patients. They drift from one place to the other because they have no roots. The chain of the anchor that family provides has been shattered for these people. For many of them, the people that love them appear as strangers. But this wandering makes responsibility for care a thing of shadows.'

'You're on the side of the bag ladies?' Bek tried to be caustic but the laugh that accompanied his barked statement was hollow.

Rhys sighed and shrugged. 'I have no idea what happens to the mentally ill in this country, but in the UK they find it incredibly difficult to obtain medical and psychiatric treatment. The suicide rate amongst schizophrenics discharged from hospital is scandalous. We have a "community care" policy and it reeks to high heaven. It's all about limited budgets for an unglamorous sickness.' Rhys stopped himself, hearing his voice rising on the tide of his well-practised and deeply felt argument. He saw the look in Bek's face and mistook it for disdain.

'Sorry, Sergeant. As you will have guessed, a hobby horse of mine made out of soap-box material. My point is simply this: if our caller turns out to be my sister's killer, it will be as a result of a deluded, misguided act of violence.'

'They don't see it like that over here. A whacko is a whacko. Lock 'em up and throw the key off of Navy pier.' Bek spoke to no one in particular, his tone bitter, his gaze focused on that faraway place.

Rhys stared, seeing the face of a man fighting an inner battle. But the moment passed quickly. He said, 'Let's just say that if this is the man, somehow, I will find it a lot more acceptable than some of the scenarios that have been thrown up to me.'

'We're grateful, Doctor.' Bek pushed himself out of the chair abruptly but the usual sardonic ripple in the delivery was absent this time as he shambled out.

'I think you're beginning to wear him down,' said Mackie when they were alone.

'Really?' grunted Rhys sceptically.

'All this stuff about mental illness still gets to him.'

'Why?'

'His brother has problems.'

'Really? Have you met his brother?'

'Once. Looked like an ordinary enough guy. Came to pick Lou up for a family dinner. I saw the way Lou greeted him, caring, protective, maybe even overprotective.'

'I suppose he has reason enough to feel that way.'

'Whatever. But it was nice, what you said to him.'

'It's true, all of it.'

Mackie smiled at him. 'So, I'd better tell you about the phone trap. Someone will go along to your room and set up a voice recorder. It'll be activated the moment you pick up the phone and start speaking. I've already contacted the phone company. They'll monitor all calls to the Geneva. I've spoken to the switchboard operators there too. All male callers will be traced to source.'

'Isn't that going to take a long time?'

'Traps are almost instantaneous. The phone company simply reprogrammes the Geneva switchboard computer. The operator gets a male caller, she presses a button on her console, the phone company gets an automatic read-out of the source number. Takes three seconds. If the caller gets put through to you, I'm gonna leave you this mobile. Just press mem. one and it'll dial through to the phone company and they'll get an address on the number and contact us right away.'

'Sounds complicated.'

'It isn't.' She handed him a small phone. 'Leave the mobile in your room. If he calls, press mem. one.'

Mackie opened the door for him, but he made no move to exit.

'Look, could we talk?'

'Sure,' she answered, letting the door swing shut again.

Rhys glanced at his watch. 'How about I buy you lunch?' Her eyebrows arched in surprise, but she held back the smart remark that threatened and fetched her coat.

They drove a mile to the edge of the financial district, to a deli busy with Brooks Brothers suits and girls dressed to kill for the office. The day was full of the promise of rain. Mackie ordered sodas and sandwiches and they sat in the corner.

'You got your appetite back?' asked Mackie watching Rhys eat. He shrugged. 'Yes. I found it yesterday at the Hyatt in Minneapolis.'

'What were you doing in Minneapolis?'

'I went there to meet with Pamela Rourke. We had a long talk.'

Mackie nodded, noting the gleam in Rhys's eye. 'I'm not going to ask because I have a feeling you're going to tell me anyway, right?'

'First, can I ask if it was Bek that took her statement?'

'Yes.'

'Now why doesn't that surprise me?'

'What, she wants to change it?'

'No, not at all. I suspect it's very concise and factual and devoid of the things that make all the difference.'

'I'm waiting,' said Mackie.

He told her what Pamela Rourke had said and she listened with her brows furrowed in concentration.

'Catrin had an excellent reason for wanting to get away from the Planetarium as soon as she could,' said Rhys finally, 'and it had nothing to do with drugs or illicit liaisons. I checked through her papers yesterday evening. It was all there, slides, lecture, all of it.'

'It doesn't alter the toxicology report,' said Mackie.

'You already know my feelings on that.'

'Rhys, drugs and violence go hand-in-hand in this city.'

'God,' hissed Rhys. 'How many times do I have to tell you that Catrin wasn't from this bloody city? I'm begging you to throw all your preconceptions out of the window.' He paused and shook his head. 'Pamela Rourke had only met Catrin the day before. It was she that invited her to the Saloon. It was Catrin's idea to go to the Nelson with the men, Catrin that wanted to dance. She did it just to prove a point.'

'What point?'

'She wanted to show how ridiculous it was sitting there watching nude girls wiggling their tits, I suppose.'

Mackie was nursing a dull anger. She was mad at Lou for not telling her any of this, but she was even more irritated to hear it from Rhys. 'Hey, you've been there, Rhys, you think it was ridiculous?'

'I can see her point of view. My own opinion is that we forget that there is this big difference between men and women. The easy answer is to quote "hormones" and run for cover.'

'So are you saying it's OK?'

'If you're asking me why men wish to go there in the first place, I think it has something to do with fantasy and a lot to do with fear. These are girls your average Joe wouldn't dare even think about getting close to because they're so stunning. So maybe the men who go there believe that they want a little of everything. Home sure, wife absolutely, family inevitably . . . and then to be able to play adulterer in their minds with these real, live women dancing six inches from their faces. It's a hell of a lot safer than *Fatal Attraction*.'

'Is that all it is with guys? Just flesh?'

Rhys eyed her appraisingly. She had her teeth into this, that was obvious.

'Why are you so angry about this?' he asked.

'Am I angry? I'm just interested to hear it from a man's viewpoint, that's all.'

'OK. Then mine is that the Nelson is something shallow and superficial that appeals to men's fantasies. And that's it. We're straying from the point.'

Mackie shook her head as Rhys put up both hands.

'Look, I didn't come here to argue with you. I'm just telling you that I spoke to Pamela Rourke and it's obvious from what she said that there is a perfectly logical reason as to why Catrin went to the Nelson and why she left the Planetarium alone that night.'

Mackie stayed silent, waiting for Rhys to continue.

'I thought long and hard about telling you all this.'

'Why?'

'Because if Bek gets to hear of it he might try twisting it around, making out that Catrin and Pamela Rourke had something going, I don't know. I wouldn't put anything past him.'

'He wouldn't do that.'

Rhys eyed her sceptically. The door to the deli opened and three people came in wearing coats over their suits. Each sported a name badge on his lapel.

'Look at that,' he said. 'You can spot them a mile off.'

'Conventioneers,' commented Mackie, taking a bite from her sandwich.

'They seem to be everywhere.'

'The Palmer Hilton is across the road. Probably has special rates for conventioneers.'

Rhys pondered this information and then asked, 'This convention business must be worth a lot of money to the city.'

'Quick turnover, regular bucks.'

'Hence the pressure from above on the investigation?'

'You're catching on real quick.'

Rhys continued to stare at the group in the corner. 'Strange though, don't you think? I mean you'd expect they'd want to tear off those badges as soon as they left the convention hall. But not this lot. It's almost a status symbol.'

'Maybe some people like everyone to know that they're attorneys or doctors. Saves on conversation.'

'Smacks of insecurity to me.' Rhys looked off into space for a moment and then added with a frown, 'You want to know something strange? When I went through Catrin's things, I couldn't find her namebadge. That's odd, isn't it?'

'Is it?'

'What's more there's a tear in both lapels of her jacket.'

'Signs of a struggle, Rhys. There were plenty.'

'But it must prove she was wearing something in her lapels. I knew about the brooch, but why take the namebadge.'

'Squirrels collect things from their victims, Rhys,' said Mackie darkly.

Rhys let it go and sipped his coffee. 'Any joy with the missing person's angle?'

Mackie made a face. 'Chicago had 24,000 missing person reports last year,' she said in a jaded voice.

'Doesn't that bother you?'

'It bothered immigration more. A hundred were foreign nationals.'

'You don't find that odd?' he asked after a suitable pause.

'The American dream,' whispered Mackie.

'Any doctors?'

'Last eight months we've had ten reports of missing doctors.'

'Ten?' asked Rhys. 'Nothing specific on Anna Asencio?'

Mackie lit a cigarette and took a long pull, careful to blow the smoke away from Rhys. 'One had a history of depressive illness. My guess is he's in the lake. The others . . .' She shrugged.

'Nothing to link any of them?'

'No. Six were foreign nationals, all from different countries. Uhh . . . Spanish, one Brazilian, one New Zealander, one Mexican and one Swede. The other,' she fished out a small notebook, '. . . was a Canadian, but of British descent. Moved to Saskatchewan two years ago.'

'What about the year before?'

Mackie frowned. 'Five. And one of those was a Greek dental nurse with relatives in Alberquerque. She turned up ten months later as a nanny to some big-shot orthodontist in Seattle. Bad call on her part. Immigration shipped her back to Athens.'

'Sex distribution?'

'All female.'

'And of the six this year?'

'Five to one female to male. The male was the depressive.'

'Ages?'

'Between twenty-four and thirty-one.'

'Physiognomy?'

Mackie put down her fork in exasperation. 'I don't have that kind of information.'

'Can you get it?'

Mackie leaned forward in irritation. 'Just what are you trying to establish here? Some kind of link between your sister's death and five green card desperados?'

'I thought I already explained that to you. Even if they manage to evade immigration, they will not be able to work as doctors.'

'Yeah, yeah. But they all paid their bills and checked out of their hotels with all their luggage. Now does that sound sinister to you? There is no conspiracy, Rhys. Nobody is going around murdering doctors, OK?'

Rhys scowled and remained sullen and restless.

'Rhys, I'd think seriously about seeing that mortician,' said Mackie after a long period of silence.

'What about "liaising"?' he said caustically.

'It wouldn't do any harm to get the ball rolling.'

Rhys became silent and pensive. He waited for Mackie to finish eating, stood up and left twenty dollars on the table.

'You want a ride back to the hotel?' asked Mackie as he walked away.

'I need some air,' he said shaking his head.

Mackie watched him go, sighed and called for the bill, annoyed with herself. It wasn't Rhys's fault that Lou Bek hadn't seen fit to do his paperwork properly. It wasn't Rhys's fault that men went to strip joints. And she certainly couldn't blame him for wanting to talk to one of the last people who had seen his sister alive.

Then what, Susan? Is it because he reminds you a little of Nick? Is that why you let him get to you?

She shook her head. He wasn't anything like Nick. Nick would have come up with something smart about the Nelson. Something mildly derogatory that she would think about later and realise was a put-down of her, the way she looked, the way she acted, her intelligence or lack of it. That was his nature, always chipping away at her armour. Funny most of the time, but occasionally vindictive and snide as hell.

Then maybe it's because he isn't like Nick at all, eh? Thought about that? If he was, you could have hated him so easily. But that's not so easy is it, hating him?

She got up, drained her diet soda and walked out into a bright windy day, not liking the paths her mind was taking one little bit.

It took Rhys half an hour to get back to the Geneva, his mood sombre and deflated. He didn't see Magdalene Asencio until she stood almost right in front of him in the lobby.

'Have you any news?' It was an open question that could have meant anything but he knew it was aimed at Anna.

'No,' he mumbled, caught off guard. 'But I have spoken to someone about Anna. I don't know how much good it'll do, but . . .'

Her smile widened as she cocked her head. 'I am so grateful, so very grateful.'

'Not all policemen are unfeeling,' he said by way of reassurance.

Magdalene nodded, the grin still there. 'No. And she is pretty.'

'How did you know?'

'I saw her in the lobby with you the other morning.'

'Detective Mackie is a good person.' *I think*, he added mentally.

'Then let us hope that she can help both of us, eh?'

19

L AUDEN WOKE UP on Friday with his usual pounding headache. His eyes moved sluggishly in their orbits, their surfaces dry and rough. He didn't complain, it had become a normal state of affairs for him – a side-effect of the booze and the medication he used to get himself to sleep.

For a while he let his mind dwell on Linda Panicik. He often woke up thinking of her. She had marked the beginning of his 'new' existence and she was still the one he remembered most. Almost three years had gone by since he had first read about her in the newspaper and seen her featured on TV. A near drowning, seventeen years old. An athlete, she had been skating on the lake in January when it broke beneath her and she was plunged into an icy Michigan. She had been in the water for forty minutes before they dragged her out. Lauden had studied photographs of the girl taken in the summer, a smiling, tanned semi-naked snap. It had been only two months after his grandmother had died, but it had been the trigger that had spurred Lauden on.

For weeks he had visited Linda in her hospital room at Rush medical, mostly in the early mornings, masquerading as the girl's teacher. Hard-pressed staff had been unquestioning after the first few times, accommodating Lauden, quietly admiring the quiet-natured devotion of the man. Lauden was left alone with Linda for long periods. Soon he began to learn the pattern of the ward staff. Between nine-fifteen and nine-thirty was one of the quietest periods. He found that he was hardly ever disturbed during that time. He would sit quietly, close to the girl, reaching out for her hand, running fingers up the warm but unmoving flesh of Linda's smooth arm, pulling the fingers close, resting her hand on his thigh, sometimes other places, gazing in rapture at her expressionless face and barely moving chest.

It went on until the morning one of Linda's sisters turned up on her way to work with a birthday card. She had met Lauden and had accepted his explanation, suspected nothing sinister of this retiring fellow who had backed out of the room apologetically on her arrival. He could have gone back, he supposed, but her intrusion had spoiled it for Lauden. Her insistence on engaging him in *conversation*, her gratitude, the way she said she would do anything to get Linda *back*.

A month later, he had read of her death. Lauden attended the funeral, standing well back, watching from afar. Two days later he returned to the graveyard, digging down into the soft earth to find Linda as he had remembered her, but this time still and cold. He lay on top of the body for a long while, caressing and stroking, shedding tears of joy and genuine feeling. As the hours passed, Lauden became distraught at the thought of leaving her, knowing that after that night, he could never return. It was then, in a moment of supreme inspiration, that he decided to remove Linda's head and hands with the linoleum knife he kept in the glove compartment of his car, before reinterring the body.

He kept the skull for weeks, watching with helpless consternation as the flesh began rotting away. Finally, he boiled it away in a mixture of wallpaper remover called Solvefast and bleach, finally ending up with the skull and skeletal hands as aids to his fantasies, totems of his distorted sexual desire.

He got up and treated his headache with a beer from the refrigerator as he wandered around the ground floor. Recollection of the disturbance still beat at his head. The police, shit!

Fucking whacko ranting and raving, waking up the whole fucking neighbourhood. The guy was certifiable, there was no doubt about that.

Surveying the billowing plastic-sheeted window, Lauden glanced at his watch. It read eleven a.m. He realised that he felt vaguely hungry. In the kitchen, he toyed for a short while with a stale pizza but after three dry mouthfuls he spat it out, his stomach churning. He pushed himself up from the kitchen chair and wandered restlessly from room to room, finally finding himself at the door of the locked rear parlour. He retrieved the key from his grandmother's sewing box behind the sofa, unlocked the door and stood contemplatively on the threshold looking in. This was a room that his grandmother kept clean and unsullied by occupation. On Sunday afternoons, she would unlock the door and Lauden would sit in the big rocker and listen to her playing the black upright piano that held pride of place against the wall.

She played hymns and folk tunes, making the same mistakes over and over. But Lauden had never minded. It had been peaceful and soothing. The room still smelled of polish from the glistening furniture. Once in a while, Lauden would come in here and do all the things his grandmother used to. Dust the ornaments, polish the chairs and the black piano, rearrange the photographs; things he never dreamed of doing to his own meagre and scruffy possessions. Those he deemed unworthy, items that he preferred to let decay and fester in the dust and grime. But the rear parlour had a power that drew him and a presence that demanded his dutiful abeyance.

He would find himself drawn to unlock the door during the extremes of his mood swings. Rarely, it would be because he felt at ease with himself. More commonly, like now, he would seek solace when the depression and fear weighed heavy. In both instances, the room acted as an escape, a doorway to other times. Times of relative innocence, when his thoughts alone were the things that tortured him, before the deeds themselves took on the monstrous proportions in his memory.

He never sat in any of the furniture now, didn't deem himself worthy of it. His grandmother's rules still held sway in this room three years after her death. Lauden turned his gaze on the piano, bedecked with photographs and mementoes, the centre piece flanked by a framed photograph of him as a child, with his family around him; grandmother, parents and brother.

As he gazed at the photographs that illustrated his past life, little or no emotion stirred in Lauden's heart until he saw one of himself aged sixteen with his dog, Leo. His constant companion for ten years from the age of eight, the dog's death had signalled the end of the only relatively normal relationship in terms of affection that Lauden had ever had with another living being. Together they had prowled the woods and fields during the long summer vacations in Clearwater, Missouri. Images of endless, golden afternoons glittered in his head, but even these normal, warm recollections were tainted by the memory of some of the things he and Leo did. The small animals they found dead by the roadside, Lauden's preoccupations and experimentation with the corpses, and the large animals they trapped and caught and played with unto death.

A portrait of his grandmother dominated the cluster on the piano lid. It had been taken just nine months before the cancer had really taken hold, her face smiling above the gnarled hands ravaged by arthritis, the disease that had made her housebound for three years. Lauden gazed at the picture, vaguely disturbed at the fact that he felt nothing, memory of her persistent and caring attempts at getting him to attend Alcoholics Anonymous and Lutheran services at her church just an echo of the aggrieved and empty anger he had felt at the Church's inability to rid him of the conviction he held that he possessed not an ounce of decency inside him.

There had been periods of remission. Twice, Lauden had found and received help in treating his clinical depression. For a short while, medication had checked some of the fog of negativity that dulled his every waking moment. But his craving for drink and the sheer power of his darker side had led to an abandonment of hope and a final, uncontrolled dive into despair and deviance.

Inexorably, his eyes drifted over to the glass case that had stood atop the wooden locker in the corner for as long as he could remember. Countless times as a boy, he had stood at the threshold, as he did now, staring at the contents of that case in wonder. For the thousandth time he supposed it should have belonged in a museum, but he had never voiced these thoughts, never burdened his grandmother with questioning its presence after she had explained that his grandfather had brought it with him from Austria.

Inside the bronze-framed display case stood the skeleton of a gull. It looked large and powerful, its stark beauty a cantilevered masterpiece of organic engineering as the empty skull stared down at a large speckled egg. It held an almost surreal fascination for Lauden and always had. He would spend hours wondering about the absent flesh and organs, of how they fitted and functioned inside that framework, the cogs and wheels that made the inert bones move and live.

He stepped into the room and stood at the piano, staring at the skeleton, the room's potent, charged ambience mingling with the twisting memory of the stalker that had disturbed him the night before. It was all one, all part of the same nightmare. After a long while, he went back into the kitchen and finished the cold pizza, the need for a fresh beer growing in him. He went to the fridge and pulled open the door.

Anna Asencio's face stared back at him accusingly, the lids slightly open, the yellowed whites of the eyes showing between them. He picked up the head, now blue-black from lividity and decomposition after two weeks of death despite the near-freezing temperature of the fridge. Holding it up, he kissed both the eyelids and placed it on the table while he opened another beer and drank from it thirstily.

Clutching the bottle, he went into his bedroom. There on the floor under a blanket that he now swept off were the haphazardly arranged bones of Anna Asencio's skeleton. The sternum ribs and spine had already been glued back together and sat upright against the wall, like some abandoned prisoner in a long-forgotten dungeon. Lauden surveyed the severed neck parts and tried to envisage Anna's skull attached to the framework he had. It sent a thrill of anticipation through him. He went back out to the rear of the house to a small outhouse adjacent to the garage. He ran water from a faucet into a large stainless-steel cauldron. It was large enough to boil a sizeable ham, at least that was what the advertisement in the cookware section of the store he purchased it from claimed. But Lauden had never boiled a ham in it, nor was it the biggest he possessed. He also had one large oblong aluminium bath that could take four folded legs if he was very careful. He hoisted the cauldron onto the old stove that his grandmother had used to make jelly and turned up the flame. From a cupboard beneath he took out a carton of Solvefast. Lauden didn't know what was in there, hadn't read the label that said 'enzymes, surfactants, dipropyline glycol and propyline glycol'. All he did know was that it was fucking A at doing what he wanted it to. He emptied half the contents into the cauldron with the water and then went back into the kitchen.

Gently, he took Anna's head into the bathroom, setting it high on top of a cabinet from where he could observe it as he showered and abused himself. He dressed and finally, regretfully, placed the head into the cauldron.

At one-thirty, he crossed the littered concrete path between his house and the larger bungalow next door, depressed the lever on the back door and entered without knocking.

'Hello, Mrs Sacks, it's William,' he sang out as he entered. The house was dark and gloomy, curtains drawn, letting in precious little light. Columns of dust motes danced and waved in the beams that did find a way in to reveal rooms that had remained untouched, furniture undisturbed for decades. But this bore the cob-webbed hallmark of abandonment rather than the squalor of habitation that pervaded Lauden's lair. Everywhere, dust lay thick on shelves and surfaces, most of which were laden with manuscripts and music scores.

'William, is that you?' The voice that rang out from an inner sanctum still resonated with a trace of the power that had held audiences enthralled in its time. Lauden knew that voice well. Had spent many an afternoon listening to it accompanying his grandmother, seated on one of the padded sofas munching candies and revelling in the music.

'Yes, Mrs Sacks, it's me.'

She was sitting in front of a brick fireplace, her swollen legs stretched out towards a glowing electric heater, the skin flaked and cracked from being baked day after day. She had grown obese with the blindness and age, but a shadow of the grace of old was still there in her face. Her head came up as he entered, eyes searching without seeing behind thick glasses. Lauden held his hand out and she took it, transiently, in both of hers before asking petulantly, 'Have you made my lunch?'

'Just making it,' he said, walking directly to the kitchen. He took out a frozen lasagne from the freezer basket in the refrigerator and popped it into the microwave before putting water in a kettle and fetching the Indian Tea she liked so much, which he bought from the Asian market.

'It'll just be a minute, Mrs Sacks,' he called out.

'Good,' she said. 'I'm hungry.'

'You're always hungry.'

He smiled to himself. She had been his grandmother's neighbour and friend and he had taken it upon himself to help out. No one had asked, it had just happened this way. And there was no resentment on his part. She had been good to him, a spinster who comforted herself by announcing frequently that she had no time for family or children of her own, but was always ready with candy and milk whenever he called.

The microwave beeped out its finishing tone and he put the food onto a tray and took it in to her. She ate greedily, not spilling much today.

'How are you?' he asked.

'Cold. When is the summer coming? It seems so long since it was here. My legs ache so in this cold.'

The room seemed stuffy and warm to Lauden.

'It won't be long,' he said, wiping away food from her chin. She still managed to find her way to the bathroom and her bedroom. Still managed to dress herself in the housecoats and the un-laced sneakers that were all her swollen feet could bare.

'When is Mary coming in to see me?'

The question always brought a pang of regret to his heart.

'She isn't here any more, Mrs Sacks,' he said, knowing that she would ask again tomorrow. Every day she would ask for his grandmother.

'You're a good boy, William.'

There was no doubt in Lauden's mind that he was still fourteen years old to Mrs Sacks. That was his age when the degenerative condition first struck a blow to her eyes. Her mind followed quickly, but there was still enough there to allow her to function and Lauden liked the fact that he could come in here and do the things he had done for her for years. It was almost like walking into his grandmother's parlour, a connection with the past.

When she'd finished, he took the tray away and put the tea in her hand. He fetched bread and potato chips and some cookies and put them within Mrs Sacks' reach. They would all be gone by the morning.

'I'll see you tomorrow, Mrs Sacks,' he said as he left.

'Send Mary in to play for me, William. I want to hear her play.'

'She isn't here any more, Mrs Sacks.'

'Please.'

Lauden sighed and sat at the piano. He played for her; a Gavotte followed by a little Schubert, the simplistic arrangements ingrained in his fingers and in his head. Mrs Sacks was smiling toothlessly by the time he left and shut the door behind him.

Back in the bungalow, with the flesh now running off the skull like milk-coloured jelly, he used a coping saw to remove the top of the skull and spooned out the majority of the denatured brain matter, boiling it for a further ten minutes before rinsing it thoroughly and setting it in some bleach to soak overnight.

At three-thirty, he was backing the Caprice out onto the street. Thirty minutes later, he was picking up his first fare, but not until he'd stopped at a liquor store. Under his seat sat two bottles of Smirnoff 100 in brown bags. Between fares, on the quiet side streets he knew so well, Lauden would stop and sit with his cab light off, sipping steadily from the bottle, pondering what he should do about the fruitcake.

*   *   *

Bek went back into the station house at three after another fruitless extended lunchtime search for Jake. He had gone by the warehouse and spoken to the manager, ostensibly to explain away Jake's absence to pre-empt any enquiries that the man, a portly Italian who actually cared about Jake, might make off his own bat. Bek explained about his mother and listened to sympathetic outpourings from the manager, his secretary and wife who happened to look after the business books. They had last seen Jake two days before the Planetarium incident, Bek learned. He reassured them, said that Jake might be away for a while but that he would keep them informed. They understood totally and he knew that there would be a big bouquet of flowers at his mother's bedside when he went in to visit this evening.

He hated lying to these good people, hated the slyness of what he was doing but he felt helpless, trapped in a precarious spiral. At the station house, he went directly to his desk, glad to see that most of his colleagues were out on the street, but he hadn't sat there for more than three minutes when Mackie appeared from the floor below clutching a report in her hand and wearing that determined look on her face which he was beginning to be a little scared of.

He'd left her and Jacob in the interview room yesterday morning, wanting to get away, unable to listen to any more of the kid's knowledgable words. He had an old head, understood about things in a way that was rare. Bek found himself wishing for another opportunity to chew things over with this young doctor, talk to him, hear his views, share a little of the pain that he had experienced for Jake over the years. He shook his head, another time in another place there might have been a chance, but in the middle of this mess . . .

Mackie greeted him from across the room.

'Nice lunch, Lou?' There was a little too much sarcasm in the banter for Bek to let it slide.

'At least I was eating, Mac. I guess you were playing nursy with Doogie Howzer, huh?'

'None of your business, Lou.'

Bek nodded sagely. 'Sure. He is kinda cute though, huh?'

Mackie attacked a sheaf of papers on her desk, riding the jibes.

'Girl has to get her exercise, right?' added Bek.

Mackie looked up, unsure now as to how much of this was sourness and how much was an attempt at good-natured ragging.

'You beginning to mellow out, Lou?'

'This is a tough break for him.'

Mackie smiled. It was the nearest she was going to get to a conciliatory remark. 'So, want me to question the staff at the Planetarium?'

'Nah,' said Bek. 'I know one of the guys there. I'll take it.'

'You sure? We could go over there together.'

Bek kept his tone even while all the time a voice in his head was screaming not to let Mackie anywhere near the Adler. It would take her thirty minutes tops to get Jake's description out of them. He felt the despicable slime of his mendacity bubble up to the surface and spread over his mind. It was so easy this lying, so easy when they were not expecting it.

'It's OK, Mac,' he said reassuringly, 'I'm on the case.'

'OK, Lou.' Mackie proffered a smile of reassurance that was almost brittle.

Bek got up and retrieved his jacket from behind his chair, hearing his beeper go off at the same time. He read off the number and frowned anxiously.

'What is it?' asked Mackie.

'The hospital,' sighed Bek as he dialled the now familiar number. He mumbled some words and held on while they found whoever it was that wanted him. Finally he put the phone down, the frown still present on his now pensive face.

'Lou?' asked Mackie.

'I have to get over to Christ's, Mac.'

Mackie heard the desperate foreboding that he couldn't quite hold out of his voice. 'Your mom?' she asked.

'Yeah. It's not good,' he said thickly. 'Could you cover for me for a while? Tell Finch I'll put the paperwork in for a little personal time.'

Mackie waved a dismissive hand. 'Go, Lou.'

'Thanks, Mac, thanks.'

She watched him go, all her misgivings evaporating at the sudden foreboding that filled her mind.

20

LAUDEN SAT IN the long queue leading up to the pick-up point at McCormick, sipping occasionally from the Coke cup he'd half filled with vodka fifteen minutes before. His hands and feet drove the taxi automatically, his mind traversing a different plane. The radio played seventies rock and absently, Lauden's hand tapped out the beat against the dashboard, his eyes sluggish from the alcohol, their glinting mirrored surfaces giving no hint of what writhed behind in the mind that was so full of dark and wretched monstrousness. The music was a link to his past, a time when his life and soul had been malleable. When some small encounter or deed might have changed everything.

In terms of insight, he was a blinkered runner. Lauden did not consider himself a necrophiliac.

In his heart, the adolescent fantasy still existed. He wished he could retain the warm and pulsing body of a living, but unresponsive being without danger of it ever waking, ever intruding upon his desires.

To that end, on the shelf of his bedroom next to the hard-core videos with titles like *Teenage Rear Entry* and *Wild Desires 2* were books obtained from the University bookshops and some direct from the publishers. Their titles might innocently suggest the reading matter of a third-year medical student or perhaps an intensive care nurse specialising in neurology. But Lauden had a darker agenda. He had read and re-read these volumes; *Care of the Long-Term Coma Patient* was light reading compared to the two-volume set of *Illustrated Neurosurgery* that he pored over in his darker moments. He knew little of the jargon, but he had bought a medical dictionary and had taught himself enough to nurture the thought that one day he would achieve his ultimate goal. . . .

After twenty-five minutes in the queue, a black steward in a fluorescent bib waved him forward. A solitary passenger entered and asked, politely, for the Meridian Hotel.

As Lauden manoeuvred out of the exit that led to Lake Shore Drive, he glanced in the mirror. The passenger was female, Asian possibly, he thought. She was short, smooth skinned, boyish almost with thick-rimmed unfashionable glasses. She wore a badge on the lapel of her jacket. Lauden had long ago taught himself to mirror read. The passenger's name was Dr Agarawal and her point of origin was Goa in India. And as Lauden joined the afternoon traffic heading north, he felt the terrible, insatiable hunger overcome him. The thoughts that were always just under the surface erupted afresh, fuelled by the alcohol.

'Your first trip to Chicago?' Lauden's voice was deep and friendly.

'I am sorry?' said Dr Agarawal leaning forwards to hear better.

'Ever been to Chicago before?' Lauden rearranged the question.

Dr Agarawal displayed a dazzling array of good teeth. 'No, this is my first time.' She spoke good, but heavily accented English, her head shaking slightly from side to side as she spoke.

'You're at the congress, right? You an ophthalmologist?'

'Yes. I am a resident at the University Hospital in Goa.'

'Long way from home, huh? Did a bunch of you come over or you travelling alone?'

'I am here only. There is a bursary and I was lucky enough to have won this trip. My university has been very generous as have some of the companies who sponsor our work in Goa.'

'So, what do you think of the city?'

'It is a beautiful city. So many cars and shops and restaurants. But I am not so used to the cold.'

Lauden watched in the rear-view, feeling that terrible cocktail of desire and hunger. He wanted this smiling girl, he wanted to run his hands over the flesh, wanted to hold her, feel the bones beneath the skin. Inside him, Lauden felt that part of him that was itself dead stir and wake. There were no choices here.

He took a right on Streeter Drive, looping back under on Grand and after fifty yards began to pump the breaks intermittently.

'Damn,' he said from the front.

'What is wrong?'

'Feels like a flat. Goddamn roads. They haven't gotten round to filling in all the holes from last winter and it's Goddamn November already.' He pulled over and eased out of the cab, leaning down to inspect the tyre on the offside before sticking his head back through the door.

'Yeah, looks like a flat. Third Goddamn time this year.' Dr Agarawal eyed him from the rear, her expression one of mild concern.

Lauden grinned. 'Don't worry, meter's on hold. It'll take me five minutes, I promise.'

'Five minutes?'

'Sure. Just need to change the spare.'

'Can I help?' Agarawal made as if to get out.

Lauden put his hand on the door. 'No, ma'am. You stay right there. Transit authority regulations forbid passengers exiting on this road. There's no sidewalk. I'll get into trouble.'

'Oh,' said Agarawal anxiously.

'Tell you what. I've got coffee in a Thermos here. Got it half an hour ago from a deli on Wabash. Why don't you sit back in the warm and have a cup while I get on with the spare?'

Agarawal grinned, pleasantly surprised by this courtesy that flew in the face of all she had been warned about in coming to America. She had expected rudeness and had found nothing but kindness.

Lauden went back to the front and took out a Thermos from a rucksack on the floor.

'Cream? Sugar?' he asked as he poured.

'Just cream please.'

'Sure. Here you go.' Lauden handed her the cup and watched her sip.

'Good?'

'Very good, thank you,' beamed Agarawal.

'OK, Doc. You sit tight and we'll have you back in your hotel in ten minutes.'

He went to the trunk and took out a jack and toolbox, his face intense, his mind screaming in jubilation. This was the best way, no mess, no danger. Five times he had used the flat tyre routine and four times it had gone smoothly. The only time it had backfired was with that jumpy Brit doctor at the Planetarium. He'd had to use a gun that time, use it to force her to lie down on the back seat after making her drink the coffee. Memory of it still stung. He hated to admit it to himself but the bitch had outsmarted him. Lauden had been so excited by the prostrate, unmoving body that he'd lost it and begun to pull the bitch's clothes off, wanting to touch the warm buttocks and thighs, push his fingers deep inside. But the bitch had been kidding all along, pretending to have passed out. Lauden had found the coffee on the floor later. Somehow the woman had pretended to drink it while letting it dribble out onto the floor in the darkness of the cab.

As Lauden leaned on the trunk, recollection burned in his face, feeling still the deep pain the bitch had inflicted in his thigh as she had lashed out with her feet, sending Lauden sprawling on the wet asphalt of the car park, the rain spattering his face. He had staggered up, his mind filled with a black rage, seeing the fleeing form in front of him, no more than fifteen yards away. He had fired once, blindly, the noise of it deafening, sure that he would have been heard for miles. But the wind and the rain had carried the noise out towards the lake, to the silent witness of nothing but the black waters. The woman had gone down with the shot but had struggled up again and hobbled off. Lauden had pursued her into the building, no choice open to him but to catch the bitch. His rage had been immense, an unfettered force that had made him squeeze and batter. In a frenzy he had pummelled until there was no more fight, no more movement beneath his fingers. With the body free of life, Lauden's emotions had changed. The frenzy was spent, the desire returned and with it a sudden yearning sorrow for what might have been. It was the only remorse he felt.

He began fitting the jack. It was only when he'd removed two wheel nuts that he noticed the blue car parked thirty yards behind. It had not been there when he'd pulled over, he was sure of that. His breath locked in his throat and his arm jerked away from the spanner. He peered at the car, just able to make out the shape of a figure in the driver's seat before his eyes filled with tears from the keening wind.

His first thought was that it was the cops. But the car looked real beaten up, too beaten up even to be a cop's car. But it was blue and there was some connection between the cops and a blue car, wasn't there? He struggled to get his mind around it, trying to put these two seemingly unconnected pieces of information together.

The cops had come that night in a blue and white, but they had said something about a blue car. The neighbours had told of a blue Mazda, yeah, that was it. Shit, he couldn't tell from this distance what the make was. But he also knew that he couldn't take any chances. Quickly, he replaced the two wheel lugs and let down the jack.

Without speaking and with all pretence at civility now gone, he took back the mug from his bemused passenger and took off for the Meridian, one eye constantly in the rear-view. For three blocks, he saw nothing, his mind bubbling with relief, but at the next set of lights, he saw the blue car cresting a ridge and drifting slowly up four cars behind. It stayed with him as he wound northwards, making several detours to appease his frazzled mind that this indeed was a tail and not some figment of his overworked imagination. He hardly noticed the way Agarawal in the rear kept yawning.

At the Meridian, the doctor exited and left Lauden a large tip along with her grateful thanks. She was only slightly puzzled by the sudden indifference the taxi driver showed to her effusiveness. This was America after all. She went straight to her room and lay down on the bed, wondering slightly at her light-headedness but explaining it away by the awe the vastness of the conference centre had instilled in her. She must have walked miles. She tried counting how many times she had walked up and down the exhibition centre. She got to four before unconsciousness arrived. Agarawal slept for fourteen hours and awoke with a headache which she misinterpreted as a sinus inflammation from the dehumidified atmosphere in the airliner on her flight over. Had her religion allowed alcohol, she might have recognised her symptoms as a mild hangover, something akin to a moderate skinful. But this ache was not alcohol-induced. It came from the eight or so Temazepams and Lidoxine Lauden had laced the coffee with.

Lauden watched his victim disappear into the entrance of the hotel in angry disappointment. He knew he dare not take the risk with someone following him. The blue Mazda had become his nemesis, an instrument of torture like a hot coal held inches from his face by some madman, the promise of terrible damage emanating from it in hot waves.

He pulled out and picked up a fare on Dearbourne, trying to behave as normally as his nervous, tense mind would allow. The delicious image of Agarawal's body at his mercy was fading fast. Panic flared. He didn't know what to do. Fucking blue Mazda.

What the hell did this guy want?

Why hadn't he gone to the police? Was this some kind of sick fucking game?

He dragged his mind back to what the police had said the night the wacko had thrown rocks. He'd been half-drunk, only half-listening to what they were saying. He should have listened better, should have paid attention. He took another slug of the vodka and felt better momentarily. He was being stalked here, for Chrissakes.

The thought burgeoned and grew. And far from being intimidated by it, he felt his mood lightening somewhat. If this turkey really was a fruitcake, maybe he could do something about it.

Yeah, that was it. Play it cool. Make some moves on the fruitcake. He drove around, picking up at every opportunity, running a scheme over and over in his head. After a while, anxiety was pushed out by angry determination. He needed to get mad, it helped him concentrate, see things clearer. People had no right to mess with his head. Worst thing of all messing with someone's head. That was why he never talked in the cab. He hated the stupid little games people played with their mouths. Empty talk about nothing. Lauden only spoke when it was necessary, or when it was part of the scam. And then he was in control, laughing it up a good one like with Dr Agarawal.

Goddamn that blue Mazda.

Goddamn that fruitcake.

At six, he put the cab into an all-night lot on the northwest side, exited at the rear and circled the block on foot. The Mazda sat on the street opposite the lot's entrance. Lauden hurried to a rent-a-wreck office on Kingsbury. Fifteen minutes later, he sat in an Oldsmobile a block behind the Mazda, sipping Vodka from the second bottle of 100 per cent Smirnoff in its brown paper bag.

Fuck him, his mind kept saying.

Two could play at that game.

B EK STOOD AT his mother's bedside, staring at her open mouth, listening to her breathing, listening in despair to the way the rhythm changed, slowly getting deeper and deeper and then, twice now, for a long heart-freezing moment, stopping altogether before resuming again. She looked sick, really sick, her skin the grey pallor of dish-water, the hue of a failing circulation.

The Asian doctor came in behind him and Bek pivoted, his eyes nailing the white-coated figure to the wall. To his credit, the doctor didn't flinch, standing his ground, looking steadily into Bek's desperate face with a sad, knowing expression.

'What's the matter with her breathing,' barked Bek.

'It's called Cheyne-Stokes breathing, Mr Bek. The pneumonia is spreading . . . and we think she had a small CVA this afternoon.'

'CVA?'

'A Cerebrovascular accident. You might understand it better as a small stroke.'

'Jesus. What the hell are you people doing to her?'

'We are doing our best, Mr Bek. She is immobile, she cannot cough. The pneumonia saps her strength. We think a small clot from the heart may have caused the stroke.'

Bek's eyes opened wide in horror. 'What are you telling me here? Are you telling me she's going to die from a broken fucking leg?'

Dr Batta sighed in compassion. 'Your mother is a very sick woman, Mr Bek.'

'She is going to die, isn't she?'

'There is nothing more we can do.'

'There must be . . .'

Dr Batta said nothing more. Bek's face was a grotesque contortion of pain but his voice had lost its anger when he spoke again. In its place was defeat and helplessness. 'You're just going to let her die?'

'There is nothing more we can do,' repeated Batta in a quiet affirmation.

Bek turned back. He took three steps forward and sat at his mother's side, clutching her still hand, wishing he could blank out the noise of that terrible breathing. He sat there with his mind flooding with memories of his childhood. His father coming home from work grimy and tired but still keen for basketball in the yard. His mother calling to them from the kitchen steps; his and Jake's breath jetting out of their hot faces in steaming plumes. The fall dusks when it wasn't too cold yet to go out, the yard strewn with leaves that they swept and threw at one another. The smell of the spicy soups with sliced sausages floating on the surface. His father's hands calloused and hard, his mother's soft and as familiar as they were now.

Where the hell had it all gone to? He found himself yearning for those past times, yearning for his mother's calm insistent voice telling him what was right, what his duty was. Without her he felt weak and devoid of direction. A pinball careering off surfaces in chaotic motion. But there was always Jake at the back of his mind, staring out through the drawn curtains of his responsibility.

Jake.

Bek shook his head in angry frustration. There was a part of Jake that would be devastated when he found out.

She died at six-thirty p.m. quietly and without fuss, the long quiet moment of apnoea in her breathing extending into infinite silence. Bek stayed with her for twenty minutes, shedding his tears before he left to call neighbours, aunts and the mortician. He'd done it all a hundred times before for the victims of countless murders whose ID showed them as just names until someone at the other end picked up a phone. It was then that the name became husband or son or wife or lover.

By eight, it had all been done. His mother was on her way to a chapel of rest, the mortician briefed, the aunts dealt with expediently if intolerantly; their moaning weeping ritual too much for him to bear. He felt beat both physically and mentally. Dead-beat, his emotions stripped bare by the loss, the welcome mental occupation of the arrangements over, leaving nothing in its wake but a black void. He got in the elevator and pressed the button for the ground floor. God, he needed a drink.

The front hall of the hospital was busy with visitors and the pleading faces of the sick and their relatives. Quickly, he left via the front entrance and paused, trying to remember where he'd left his car. As he stepped out to cross to the parking lot, he saw the lights of an approaching vehicle. He faltered, waiting to let it pass, barely aware of the car at some subconscious level as any pedestrian might be. He didn't notice the way it seemed to slow down.

It was only as the car was abreast of him that he glanced at it and saw the face that stared back at him, saw the terror and confusion that reigned there.

'Jake?' The words escaped Bek's lips in a whisper of incredulity. He stepped forward, no more than five yards away from the brother he had been searching for for days. But as realisation spurred the adrenaline in Bek, so Jake's foot found the accelerator and Bek's outstretched hand met the trunk with a slap.

'Jake!' yelled Bek. 'Jake, JAKE!'

He saw Jake turn around, his face shaking, the eyes wide with fear, denial paramount. Already the car was accelerating away as Bek ran after it, his feet slapping the asphalt.

'She'd dead, Jake. Mom's dead, did you hear me?' His screams were loud in his own ears. 'She's dead Goddamnit. DEAD!'

Ahead of him, he saw the Mazda hit its brakes, the tail lights glowing, tyres squealing. But as Bek started forward, his heart surging with hope, it accelerated away again and he was left in the middle of the road, his breath heaving and burning in his lungs. He turned and ran for his car, not seeing the vehicle that was behind him until the Oldsmobile was almost on top of him. He sidestepped it, held a hand up in vague apology and sprinted for his car. He didn't take any notice of the driver who ignored the wave, wouldn't have recognised William Lauden in any case.

By the time Bek got out onto the road, there was no sign of the Mazda. He sat at some lights, engine running, letting red turn to green and then back again as he sat with his head resting on his hands as they clutched the wheel. Drivers behind skirted him. One of them stopped and asked if he was OK. Bek nodded and muttered a thanks through his veil of tears.

Lauden followed Jake to the motel. He watched from across the street as the fruitcake got out of his car and fumbled for a key to a ground-floor room. He looked agitated and jumpy. Lauden had no idea of what had taken place at the hospital, but he was disturbed to know that someone had recognised the fruitcake. The big guy who had screamed after the Mazda didn't look like someone to mess with. But it looked very much as if the fruitcake was running, maybe even hiding out in this flea-bag motel.

Lauden re-examined the idea that had occurred to him immediately he had seen the big guy at the hospital. He looked like a cop. Another fucking cop. He grinned to himself. What the fuck did it matter anyway? In a way it was a real laugh, wasn't it? The fruitcake running from the cops. He felt a surge of confidence wash through him as he took a shot of Smirnoff. This might all work out after all.

He drove into the motel, paid cash for a room on the ground floor at the corner so that he could watch the fruitcake's room and sat in a battered chair at the window with the TV on low and settled down to wait.

Mackie put a call through to Rhys Jacob at eight p.m.

'How would you like to buy a girl a drink?' she asked when he answered.

'Delighted,' he said with that hint of wariness that pervaded his responses. 'Come over, I'll meet you downstairs.'

Mackie found him at a corner table in the discreet end of the hotel bar, away from the lobby's public scrutiny under soft wall lights and posters of Alpine landscapes. His expression softened as she slid in opposite.

'You look tired,' he said.

'Thanks.'

'Well you do.'

'You don't look so hot yourself.'

'Think we're losing sleep over the same problem?'

'Probably,' she said, but the smile that she tried felt false and uncomfortable on her lips. 'Look, Rhys, I came because I thought you deserved to know what's happening. I've been at the Adler this afternoon. Talked to the staff there and then to the caterers who did the food the night of the dinner.'

'And?'

'And two Planetarium guides told me they'd seen a guy hanging around the place for two days prior to the murder. A regular who they classed as a little "flaky" but harmless. Also, a caterer gave me a description of someone she saw leaving through the kitchen exit as they were cleaning up after the dinner. She thought he might have been Planetarium staff, so she didn't challenge him. Truth is, I think she was a little scared by what she saw. Her description –

tall, thin guy with patchy hair, mid to late thirties in a White Sox jacket – tallies with the guides'.'

'You think this is the man we're after?'

'I've talked to the personnel people at the Adler, they have no one in their employ who fits that description.'

Rhys's jubilation faded into a sudden wary anger. 'Why is it that it's now you're finding all this out? I mean, talking to the caterers should have been one of the first things on your list, shouldn't it?'

All she could do was sigh a feeble apology. 'Rhys . . .' And then she saw realisation dawn in his eyes.

'Bek,' said Rhys sourly. 'This is all down to him, isn't it? He should have done all this, shouldn't he?'

'Rhys, I . . .'

'Jesus, I thought you said he was *good*.'

'Rhys, listen to me. Lou's mom died tonight.'

She watched the anger die in his face then, saw the sudden compassion in his eyes.

'Oh, Christ. I'm really sorry to hear that, Susan.'

His use of her first name disarmed her. A young black piano player was getting started in the lobby. Rhys ordered beers and Mackie found herself talking, opening up about the Department, the city, Bek. She apologised for him, defending him, unaware of her fingers tracing the label of the Miller bottle incessantly, her eyes downcast. She didn't want to look at him, didn't want to feel that penetrating gaze stripping her bare. Finally, after a long pointless invective about overtime, she stopped herself and looked up.

'Rhys, Jesus, listen to me.'

'No, it's OK. Sometimes it's necessary to talk.'

'Oh yeah, I forgot, the psychiatrist, right?' She made it sound derogatory but there was no bitterness to her words. 'Or are you all like this from, where is it again, Wales?'

'Don't pretend you've ever heard of it.'

'Sure I have. My grandfather was a Scot. I'm planning to make the UK some day.'

'Most of your compatriots go to Wales hoping to bump into Lady Di,' he said with a sneer.

'Rhys, come on. There must be more to it than a glossy wannabee.'

'There's no gloss where I come from. Only sky-high unemployment and a burning desire to get out and succeed that drives those who have the foresight to look beyond their generation. Catrin and I are not from a monied background, or a professional one. As kids we played on river banks where the water ran red with effluent, fields where the grass was sparse because underneath was nothing but heaps of mining waste. I know where I'm from, I know where Catrin was from. And I can't forgive anyone who labels her a whore and a junkie.'

'Some speech, Rhys.' She tried to make it light.

'You asked.' His eyes smiled but his face remained stern. 'Yes, and I know what it sounds like. I don't walk around with a banner announcing it but neither do I apologise and pretend it never happened. I've seen too many people cut off their roots once money and success appear on the scene.' He tapped his shoulder with the index and middle finger of one hand. 'This isn't a chip here, just a private truth that I won't allow myself to forget.'

They fell into a preoccupied silence. Finally, Mackie spoke. 'I'd better go.'

'Don't be stupid. Look,' he added contritely, 'I have this dour party-pooping Celtic temperament which sometimes breaks through my sunny disposition.'

She glowered dubiously.

'It's OK, really,' said Rhys. 'And you look like you could do with a couple of beers.' He sipped his own and took a handful of nuts from the fresh bowl the waiter had left. 'So, when you do go home from the job, where exactly is it?'

'Clybourn. I have an apartment in a building that overlooks a school hall, a block from the railroad tracks. Half an hour in traffic from here.'

'Nice place?' Rhys tried to hide the vacillation in his voice.

She laughed. 'The train comes once a week, delivering sugar to a confectioners' factory in Northern Illinois so I don't get kept awake by the railroad.'

'Not exactly busy then.'

She leaned forward and whispered, 'Lincoln Park's almost next door.' When she saw it meant nothing to him, she laughed again and shook her head. 'One day you should come over and listen for the train. I'll cook you a seafood ravioli that you would kill for.'

'Your Italian side?'

Mackie's brows furrowed. 'How did you know that?'

'I asked around.'

His reply nonplussed her. 'So how was your day?' she said after a pause.

'Well, Susan.' He watched her face stretch in surprise. 'I thought I'd call you Susan, if that's OK?'

Mackie shrugged. 'You and my mother, what the hell.'

'I walked and thought and came up with the same big empty bucket full of answers.'

Mackie shook her head sympathetically.

A waiter came over and took an order for more beer and began wiping spillages off their table. A TV played on a shelf behind the bar, volume low, unobtrusively showing highlights of that evening's Bulls/Knicks game while the piano player started a Gershwin medley. *Embraceable You* went in to *Bidin' my Time* seamlessly. Mackie sipped the cold Millers and felt the buzz between her ears. Mixing it with the couple of shots she'd shared with Finch after they'd heard about Lou's mom earlier was not the brightest of ideas but she didn't care. She'd come over to tell Rhys about her progress at the Planetarium, guilty over Bek's dilatoriness and a little down over his loss, expecting anger. Rhys's sympathetic and conciliatory mood had thrown her. Now the music transported her back to her teenage. Her mother at the piano playing the songs her father liked, the ones from the shows. Outwardly, she had scoffed, flowing with the late seventies wallpaper rock that was what the rebellious teenager was meant to like. But she had grown up with these forties and fifties tunes in her subconscious. She knew every word, every evocative nuance. She felt like there were a dozen ants crawling on her skin, tingle factor of a hundred plus.

Nick had never liked any of them. Middle-of-the-road mediocrity, he called them. Elevator music that was no better than valium. He'd tried to introduce Susan to the obscure jazz instrumentalists he said he loved. Music that held no meaning for her and made Thelonius Monk sound like Gospel music. It struck her then how much Nick had tried to change her, to make her into something of his.

She only half heard Rhys asking a question and repeated it distractedly. 'Thanksgiving?' She looked into his face, seeing the confusion there, hearing the piano's notes trilling with such splendid familiarity in her head.

'Yes, I just wondered what all the fuss was about. It's not even a holiday where I'm from.'

'It's a time for families. Time for everyone to get together and reminisce . . . or argue.'

Rhys's brow furrowed.

'I uh . . . I usually go up to my folks' place in Michigan, but not this year.'

'Should I ask why?'

Mackie snorted. 'This year I figured I didn't want to ruin it for everyone else. They're all happy as clams at hearing I'm not going to be there.'

'Don't you get on with your family?'

'My dad. Specifically, my dad.' She heard the words emerge from her mouth unable to stop them. Hearing them trickle out like water through a hole in a bucket. 'He thinks I'm wasting my time playing at being a dick in Chicago.'

'Does he not like you being a cop because it's dangerous?'

Her eyes came up, smiling at him. 'That's a nice thought. But it has more to do with fitting an image.'

She thought momentarily of telling Rhys about her time in the Academy. The guy that turned up from some downtown major-league attorney's office, looking for talent to join as para-legals. The money incredible, the carrot; tuition fees to law school for the lucky few. She had been tempted and flattered by his attention. But a sceptical streak had made her want to check him out because he kept on trying a little too hard. A friend who knew someone in the DA's office found out that the guy's firm also represented one of her father's companies. She had made him admit to the scam under threat of misrepresentation. The memory burned indignantly into her cheeks once more. She couldn't tell him that. It was one of her private pains.

'You can't go through life trying to please other people all the time. It tears you apart,' said Rhys.

The piano player was into Rogers and Hart now. *My Funny Valentine*, haunting and bittersweet.

She stared at him, her expression one of perplexity. He had this way of twisting things around, making you look at things from a different angle. He was right though. He was right about a lot of things. Then it struck her. The thing that was so different about him, that set him apart from Nick was that he listened. He had the gift of making you believe that you were the most important person in the world when he listened. Not like Nick who always gave the impression of intolerance, of barely disguised boredom when the subject wasn't of his choosing.

Shit, said a voice in her head. *What the hell were you doing with the guy anyway?*

It made her smile inside. The first time she had admitted to herself that maybe all of it wasn't all her fault.

The piano player segued into *Where or When,* that lilting evocation of uncertain déjà vu. It had been and was still one of Mackie's favourites. She began singing the words softly, her eyes far away.

Rhys smiled. 'You know these tunes,' he said.

'I know 'em all. Have done since I was a kid. Unfashionable as hell, but they still get to me.' Her eyes narrowed in mock suspicion. 'You didn't set this up did you?'

'Of course. The piano player is a personal friend of mine.' Mackie laughed and hummed another line before focusing on Rhys again, the music intoxicating her as much as the beer.

'You're a nice guy, Dr Jacob.'

'Nice? And here I was thinking I'd been doing a great job of being a bastard.'

'No, you'd never swing it. Believe me, I've known a few in my time.' She looked at him for a long moment. 'Maybe it would be better if you went home, Rhys. With Lou out of action this thing could drag on and on.'

'Susan, I know I've been a pain . . .'

Mackie shook her head. 'Just a hurting brother.'

'What I was going to say was that perhaps when all of this is over . . .' He let it hang, not really knowing what else to say.

Mackie smiled ruefully. 'This is real bad timing, isn't it? You're shot to hell over your sister, I feel like shit because I've let the investigation disintegrate . . .'

The waiter interrupted her. He approached from behind, leaned in and said, 'Dr Jacob? There's a call for you, sir.'

Rhys looked across at Mackie and they both stood at the same time, their eyes wide with expectation.

'Where can I take it?'

'There's a phone at the bar, sir.'

'No, we need somewhere quieter.' Mackie flashed her shield. 'There is an office at the rear,' the waiter offered.

'Ask them to put it through there,' said Mackie hurrying Rhys along through the bar.

Rhys let it ring once and picked up the receiver.

'Hello?'

'I went to the healing place he was there he was screaming at me about death. It isn't safe . . .'

Rhys's eyes went wide and he nodded wildly at Mackie. She took out a mobile from her purse and punched in mem. one. Within seconds she was issuing instructions to the phone company before leaning in close to Rhys, her ear to the receiver.

'I know him I found his nest by tracking the Chariot of light. I broke through his shields by mode of rocks that roll. It isn't safe. It stopped the noise for a while when I saw his face. He looked down on me and saw me as a Rim with a Jacob face.'

Mackie stepped away and took a message on the mobile before holding up her thumbs triumphantly and leaning back in to listen.

'He knows my face he must know yours. I heard the beam drill a tunnel into the filtering channel of my brain. He knows it all he will use it to find you . . .'

She heard the voice accelerating, the tone anxious and whining now.

'. . . It isn't safe. You must escape the gravity field before he finds you and takes the Jacob. The alternation isn't ready it isn't ready.'

Mackie pulled back and turned troubled eyes to Rhys, shaking her head in disbelief and mouthing, 'Wow.'

The voice fell to a whisper. 'I've placed strips over this communicator mouthpiece to deflect the beam but I can't shut off the thoughts they fly out like moths on a lighthouse beam. The Whistler is a demon not a man. It isn't safe. I know I must do this alone for the Rim – it must be a fine place. She was beautiful wasn't she?' Suddenly, to their surprise, the voice ceased abruptly.

Rhys attempted a hesitant, 'Hello?'

But all they got in reply was the muffled sound of movement and the harsh clatter of a receiver being dropped. And then there was the noise of furniture scraping across a floor and a high-pitched keening; the noise of a frightened bird suddenly confronted with its natural enemy. The keening ended and in the silence there came the tinny noise of a TV jingle for medical insurance increasing in volume. The gun shot, when it came, made them literally jump back from the phone, the receiver thrust at arm's length away from their ears. When it died away, all they could hear was the obscene noise of the TV playing out its incessant mindless chatter and the echoey hiss of static on the line.

Mackie was up on her feet and talking into the mobile again, Rhys staring at her mumble as she became the policewoman she was trained to be.

'I have to get over there, Rhys. It's a motel out near O'Hare.'

'What the hell happened?'

'That was a gun.'

Rhys stared after her as she bolted from the room. He stood in the office with the phone in his hand, unsure of what exactly he should do. Hesitantly, he put it back to his ear, half expecting at any moment to hear Mackie's voice as she burst in. It was a ridiculous thought. All he could hear was the maddening TV and the static. After three minutes, he put it down. He couldn't stand it any more. He was beginning to believe he could hear the sound of breathing on the other side.

Lauden stood in the motel room looking at the corpse of the man he'd just shot dead, toying with the idea of utilising it but put off by the glistening blood on the walls and the gory exploded mess that was left of the face. He moved forward and quickly put the gun in the corpse's hand, pushing the fingers firmly around the trigger guard after wiping it clear of his own prints.

The room was a shambles, half-eaten bits of food, junk, wrappers, strange drawings and plans plastered over the walls. Fruitcake, thought Lauden, card-carrying fruitcake. It was only as he was about to leave that he noticed the phone off the hook and his mind reeled in panic. Had the fruitcake been talking to someone? Fear surged through him. What if he had been wrong? What if this guy had been a cop or something? He went to the phone and picked it up, hearing nothing but background noise and then, to his consternation, hearing a phone being put down on the other side, the dialling tone purring in his ear as he tried desperately to think.

He put the phone down on its cradle with a crash. He needed to get out of there, needed to get as far away as possible. But someone had been listening, someone had heard . . . what? What had they heard? He hadn't spoken, merely tried the door on a whim, finding it unlocked. The fruitcake had started to scream and Lauden had shot, once. There was nothing much to hear in all that, was there? But who? Who the hell?

He stared down at the phone and an idea came to him. Using a clean part of the bedclothes, he picked up the hand piece and pressed the redial button, listening to the numbers flick through their sequence until it began ringing. On the fourth ring, he heard a voice answer, 'Hotel Geneva, how can I help you?'

Stunned, he clattered the phone down. Hotel Geneva? What was this shit? And yet, somehow he felt he knew that name, felt that somehow there was a connection that he wasn't quite making. He turned and left the room, looked back at the phone, cursed and went back over to it, tilting the handset off the cradle and letting it hang before hurrying to his car, seeing no movement from any of the chalets or the office. A single gunshot from a room with the TV on loud would not raise too many eyebrows. Not many people were going to get excited about that.

In his car, he took some good swallows from the blue-labelled Smirnoff and drove. Hotel Geneva . . . Hotel Geneva. . . . And then it came to him. He'd heard it on TV. The girl at the Planetarium's brother had been on TV. He'd told the fucking world that he was staying at the Geneva. Was that who the fruitcake had been talking to? Again he felt a surge of panic at the thought that the man he'd killed was more than just a crazy guy. What if he had been a private dick? He fought the urge to return and go through the fruitcake's things. He should have done that, should have thought of that . . .

An image of the squalor and the bizarre contents of the motel room came to him then. That was no PI's room. The Geneva, shit! It was too much of a coincidence to imagine that there was no connection. As he drove, Lauden began to wonder what secrets the Geneva held and the more he thought of it, the more he began to feel the empty void of fear fill his gut. Out of control, it was all spiralling out of control.

By two a.m., he was back in the cab having parked the rental and posted the keys back through the office's mailbox. As he drove home, he drank three beers and ate some stale bread, all the while thinking of the Hotel Geneva and the guy with the odd accent who had appeared on TV.

22

THE HONOLULU MOTEL was swarming with cops by the time Mackie arrived. This was an Area 5 investigation and Mackie recognised one of the detectives hovering outside. Kenny Buford was a big coloured man with a loping stride and a speckled moustache and he was listening unenthusiastically to one of the motel residents as she pulled up. She flashed her shield and strolled over to him, lights from squad cars and the whole motel block turning night into false, stark, neon day. The blacktop of the motel lot glistened slickly with puddles from the drizzle the night had brought with it. Buford made out Mackie from twenty yards, eyeing her with a mixture of surprise and vague, good-natured wariness.

'What you got?' asked Mackie.

'Looks like a suicide with teeth. There's a guy with his face all over the pillow and a thirty-eight in his hand. But guess what we found as keepsakes on the windowsill?'

'Surprise me.'

'A namebadge with Dr C. Jacob written on it.'

'And he's D.O.A?'

Buford nodded.

'Shit,' said Mackie. 'Looks like I've got a dead suspect.'

'You gonna fill me in, Mac?' asked Buford drily. 'I get the impression that all this does not come as a complete surprise to you. Maybe you could explain why we found two squads sent by central despatch already here.'

'I've been working the Adler homicide,' explained Mackie. 'We trapped a call from here to the Adler victim's brother. I was listening when the shots went off.'

Buford nodded. 'So, you give him last rights?' he asked grinning.

Mackie snorted. 'How did you catch it?'

'Motel owner got a complaint about a TV on too loud. Found the door open and called it in.'

Mackie shook her head. 'This guy was a grade A whacko. You ought to hear some of his conversation. Sounds like someone reading four books out loud at the same time.' She inclined her head towards the motel room. 'Can I take a look see?'

'Sure, detective.' Buford took her across to the hotel room. They stood on the threshold watching the crime lab going through their routine, her eyes focusing immediately on the corpse sprawling in undignified disarray on the bed, knees drawn up, one arm flung out. Mercifully, the head was turned away from her but she took in an open-necked shirt stained with blood and God knew what else, the skin beneath pallid and doughy in death. She let her eyes scan the walls and saw the surfaces strewn with drawings and sketches full of details that meant nothing to anyone except the dead man. The floor looked like someone had rushed in and emptied out the contents of three trash-cans full of packaging, soda cans and half-eaten food. A White Sox jacket lay discarded over a chair. Here was the burrow of some confused animal gone to ground.

'You have a name?' asked Mackie without looking at Buford.

'Sure,' he said, thumbing open his pocket-book. 'Manager has him registered as one Jacob Bek.'

Mackie swung around, her face instantly draining of colour, her gut turning to ice water.

'What?' she croaked incredulously.

'You know him?' Buford asked.

But she didn't answer, couldn't answer as her brain filled with a thousand instantaneous thoughts. She threw another involuntary glance at Jake Bek's crumpled flesh, the hard-boiled detachment of a moment ago suddenly frangible as glass.

Lou's brother! It had been Lou's brother!

Dark suspicion dawned as she turned and walked out in a daze, back towards her car, numb with denial, shrugging off Buford's restraining hand angrily. Could it really be Jake Bek? But the logic of it seemed suddenly undeniable. It explained why it was that Lou had taken the call about the Planetarium killing in the first place. It would have been an obvious choice for Jake to make. She sat in her car out of the cold for a long fifteen minutes, ignoring Buford's knock on the windshield, waving him away and holding up her hands with the fingers widespread, only half-seeing the exasperated shake of his head.

Finally, she took some deep breaths, got out and walked back across the wet asphalt, smelling the night in all its damp decaying splendour. Buford watched her approach from outside Jake's room, his face set in a wary suspicion, devoid, this time, of any trace of good humour.

'Do you have any ID for this guy?' Mackie asked.

'What the hell is going on here, Mac?'

'Please?'

'OK, OK. We got a driver's licence from his billfold.' He held out an evidence bag. Mackie stared at the photograph through the clear plastic. The face she recalled from the time Lou had been picked up at the station stared back. The features were gaunt, but even so the resemblance was obvious. She remembered him as normal enough, except for the eyes. There had been something about the eyes, something strange that she remembered even from her brief encounter. Finally, she looked up into Buford's attentive face.

'This is Lou Bek's brother. Lou is my partner in this investigation.'

Buford's expression changed from curiosity to disbelief.

'Lou Bek's brother?' he whispered, glancing around to see if any of the other cops had heard. Mackie nodded.

This was a cop's nightmare; a crime that came too close to home, second only to a cop being killed. It stripped away all the objectivity, peeled off all the hard-nosed attitudes that they depended upon to survive on the street and in the sewers. The good ones always tempered their detachment with a little compassion, others dealt with it through sheer aggression or tasteless humour, reducing the horror to a few cheap laughs that inevitably appeared callous to any outside observer. But this was different. This brought it all home to roost.

'You better wait in there,' he said, nodding towards the manager's office across the car park. She trudged across and sat in the manager's cheap swivel chair surrounded by plastic houseplants and wind-chimes until the crime lab had finished, her eyes beginning to burn with weariness as she swallowed three cups of bad coffee. Eventually, she went back into the motel room, not wanting to tell Lou yet, knowing that it was going to be her job to do it. She was going to be his eyes and ears on this one. She didn't want him anywhere near this charnel house. Buford had begun to sift through the room and Mackie watched as he turned out Jake's few belongings, the atmosphere now changed.

Buford had told the others. The uniforms were all subdued, the talk hushed. This was no longer just some poor fruitcake. This was a cop's brother.

They convened at eight a.m. at Area 4 Headquarters in Finch's office. Mackie delivered her report in a concise, detailed monotone. Finch listened with one eye on Bek's slumped form. He looked as if he hadn't slept for days and even Mackie, who had showered and changed in the locker room, was suffering from the effort of concentration.

'Cause of death was a single gunshot to the head. Area 5 are calling it a likely suicide and in view of the medical history, it's more than a possibility. The spatter pattern was a little odd is all. Crime lab and ballistics are running a check on angulation.'

Finch put up a hand to stop Mackie for a moment. 'Lou? I'm not going to keep you here. I've heard enough and so have you.' Bek couldn't meet his gaze and kept his hooded eyes down. Finch had last seen a similar look on the face of a car-wreck survivor whose family had been wiped out by a drunk.

'I'll stay,' said Bek monosyllabically.

The phone call broke the tension. Finch picked it up, listened and handed it to Mackie. She took it, turning her face away from the men.

'Susan, it's me,' said Rhys, his voice was high with tense excitement.

'This is not a good time. I'm in the middle of a . . .'

'OK. Just tell me this. Is he dead?'

'Yes . . .'

'Was he my caller?'

'We found the brooch and the namebadge.'

The line went quiet for a moment.

'Hello?' said Mackie.

'He killed himself?'

'Looks that way.'

'You're sure?'

'The autopsy isn't done yet, but . . .'

'I heard something after you left.'

'You were listening?'

'I had to.'

'OK. So what did you hear?'

'Breathing. Like somebody listening on the other end.'

'The TV was on in the room, Rhys.'

'No, it wasn't the TV. It sounded like breathing, close to the mouthpiece.'

'Rhys . . .'

'Susan, listen . . .' He was speaking quickly now, not letting her interrupt. 'We've all assumed that this man was so deluded that everything he said to us was gibberish. But what if it wasn't? I know that schizophrenics have depressive phases and his delusions could have turned downwards enough for him to take his own life, but . . .'

'Rhys, stay out of this . . .'

'You're sure it was suicide?'

'He had a gun in his hand and a bullet in his head. Crime lab report will take a little time but . . .'

'There was someone on the end of that line . . .'

'Rhys, that's enough. Jesus, I don't want to hear this right now, OK?'

'But I'm sure I heard someone breathing . . .'

'You think you did, Rhys. That's all. You're standing there with the phone to your ear having just heard someone shoot himself and your imagination has the gain turned all the way up. That's what happened, Rhys.'

'Susan . . .'

'I can't talk now. Let me clean up the mess. I'll be in touch.'

She put the phone down before he could say any more.

When she turned back, she knew her face was flushed. Finch was looking at her, impatient for her to continue.

'The uh . . . the gun found in Jake's hands was a Smith and Wesson 38, consistent with the weapon used in the Planetarium killing. Ballistics are looking at it now.'

She glanced across at Bek and saw his jaw working.

'Is this enough to clear the case, Mac?'

'I'm talking to the DA's office in half an hour. There may be a few wrinkles but I'll let them chew over it, see what they think.'

'Thanks, Mac,' said Finch. 'Keep me informed. You'll work with Buford on this one, OK?'

'Sure, Lieutenant,' she said as she got up to leave.

Finch waited until the door closed before saying his piece.

'We have to go all the way on this one, Lou.'

Bek nodded, eyes down.

'I'll do everything I can to limit the damage, but I don't have much straddle here with so many brass-hats breathing down my neck. I don't think you ought to be around here much for the next few days. IA are bound to come sniffing. Take some compassionate leave. If I don't know where you are, I won't be able to tell them.'

Still Bek didn't speak. He merely stood and nodded, reaching out for the door, pulling himself through it. Outside in the corridor, people averted their eyes, unwilling to meet his. Everyone, that is, except Mackie. She was waiting for him: she took his arm firmly and pulled him into the female locker room.

'I have to guess at what you're feeling, but we have to talk.' She spoke quietly, insistently.

When they were both inside, Bek slumped on a bench while Mackie locked the door and stood with her arms folded, regarding him gravely.

'Lou, I'm sorry about Jake. But there are things that have to be said before this goes any deeper.'

'Such as?' Bek's voice was a growl.

'Such as if I were working for IA, I might interpret some of your actions during this case as being a little suspect.'

'You would, huh?'

'Yeah, I would.' Mackie smouldered with anger. 'Like you knew a little more than you were willing to volunteer.'

'You're entitled to your opinion, Mac.'

Mackie rubbed her face with both hands. 'Lou, I respect you as a cop. I don't know what has been going on with you personally and maybe I don't need to know it all, but I also have to go and explain all this to Rhys Jacob. I'm trying to look at it from his point of view and if you have anything to say, I'd rather hear it now.'

'Back to lover boy, huh?' Bek's mouth held an ugly grin.

'Lou, this is me OK, not some IA Apache after your scalp. You're better than this and we both know it. Jesus, maybe we could even have helped Jake if . . .'

'If what, Mac?' growled Bek. 'If I'd told you he'd come home covered in blood mouthing off about fucking men from Mars? What would you have done? Told the guys that they were hunting down a killer but to go easy on him because he's Lou's brother?' He shook his head. 'I still can't believe he did those things. Where the hell did he get a gun, for Chrissakes?'

Mackie shrugged.

'What about the junkie paraphernalia you found in Catrin Jacob's hotel room?'

'I didn't queer any evidence,' Bek said fuming, his face flushed, smashing the steel wall of a locker with his fist. 'The baking soda and the cocaine residue were in that hotel room. OK, they turn out to be the Baltimore low-life attorney's weekend habit. I was trying to find Jake for Pete's sake. . . .'

Mackie remained silent.

Bek sighed. 'Do what you have to, Mac. Don't worry, I'll make sure none of the shit sticks to you.'

'What are you going to do now?' she asked quietly.

'I'm going to go type up my notes on the investigation into the Adler killing and then I'm going to sit in a bar and drink until I fall off the stool.'

'I'm sorry about Jake, Lou,' she said to his departing back as he walked out. He didn't answer her and she felt the thin walls shudder as he slammed the door shut behind him.

Bek tried typing, but his mind kept stalling, his fingers clumsy and unresponsive as if they belonged to someone else. He tried forcing his mind away from Jake. At nine, the phone rang.

'Bek,' he said into the phone.

'Lou, this is Jim Piper from Area 8.'

'Hey, Jim. How're you doing?'

'We're feeling for you, Lou. You cut a rough deal. Your mom and then Jake . . . shit, man, that's tough.'

'Thanks, Jim.'

'Lou, I called to tell you that we took a code 415 on Wednesday morning down on Cambridge in The Lawn. Someone threw a brick through some cab-driver's bay window. Time we got there it was all over. We thought it was a fare with a beef but the licence plate and the description of a vehicle leaving the scene came back as a Mazda registered to your brother. Sounds like Jake was losing it, huh? I'm sorry for that, Lou. I'm calling to say that we're going to lose the paperwork on this one. You have enough grief.'

'Thanks, Jim. I appreciate it.'

'And uh, the guys want to know if you'd be taking flowers for the funeral.'

'Yeah, yeah, flowers'll be fine.'

'Take care, Lou.'

He hung up and within half an hour he'd fielded another dozen calls. By ten, he couldn't stand it any more. He walked out, feeling Mackie's eyes on his back, exiting into the sunlight of a crisp day, the light searing his eyes. He welcomed the pain of it, wrapping it around himself like a blanket.

Lauden had spent a restless night, his sleep plagued by dreams that went way beyond his understanding. He dreamed that he was a wandering shaman doomed to some nomadic life, capable of great acts, miraculous acts, but ones which carried a fearful price: a dreadful storm that followed him wherever he went. A storm of apocalyptic proportions and massive destructive power. In his dreams, he saw ahead of him a vision of unsullied loveliness, a landscape of breathtaking beauty, but behind him and to either side there was nothing but darkness and a howling, keening wind.

The vividness of his nightmare remained with him when he awoke. As Mackie was challenging Bek for information, Lauden was struggling back to consciousness.

All the way home from the motel, he had fretted over the fruitcake's connection at the Geneva. He couldn't recall the face of the man he had seen on CHTV asking for witnesses. But he knew there was a man. Shit, what had the fruitcake told him?

He had driven around for ten minutes, desperately searching for any sign of cops, convinced that they would be waiting for him. But eventually, satisfied, he had parked and entered to find nothing but the ever-present ghosts of his victims in the quiet house. And as the night wore on and still nothing happened, he fell into a fitful, sweaty sleep with the question gnawing at him. The dream gave him no answers, but the threat of destruction hung over him. It stirred some survival reflex inside him. He had killed the fruitcake without pity but cold daylight brought with it the knowledge that it was not enough.

Now, lying on his bed with the stink of the apartment all around him, awareness of the things left undone crowded in on him, mingling with the afterimage of the dream to leave him anxious and irritable. He needed a drink. He reached out and found a half-full can of stale Bud on the small table next to the bed. He drained it in one and lay back trying to let his mind drift along more pleasant paths, recalling those sweet moments with his comatose lovers, his hands straying down into his shorts to help raise the flag. He spent a fruitless ten minutes trying to squeeze a little music from his own oboe, but the notes were discordant, the arrangement all wrong. He lay back, feeling damp sweat cooling under him on the bed, disappointed, his arm aching with the reciprocating effort of it. It was then, as his mind switched from imagined pleasures to mundane thoughts that memory tripped. An article he'd read in the *Chronicle*. It came to him like a static charge, sudden and shocking. He got up, and shambled to the kitchen, mixing himself a vodka and Pepto-bismol and cramming some Fig Newtons into his mouth as he stuffed a shirt into his stained jeans and found unlaced boots to slip on his feet. He went out to the cab, feeling the cold wind wash over his skin like a giant hand and found Wednesday's copy under the front seat with the rest of that week's. The name was there, Rhys Jacob, brother of the woman that had almost got away from him, telling the whole city that some nutty caller had been in touch with him. He took the paper back inside and spread it on the kitchen table. Seeing the photograph brought back memories of the girl. The similarity was unmistakable. He sat down and finished the vodka, chasing it with a couple of beers, thinking things through, beginning to enjoy planning it as he always did, careful, imaginative. Perhaps there was still a way out of this.

He went over to Mrs Sacks' house and made her lunch early. When she complained, he told her that he had to go out and wouldn't be back until late. She whined a little but ate the meat balls he prepared hungrily. He finally left the bungalow at ten-thirty. At ten-forty-five, he stopped at a Seven-Eleven on Halstead to get some coffee and to make a call.

23

A FTER BEK HAD left that morning, Mackie busied herself in chasing up loose ends, all the while knowing that what she was really doing was avoiding the inevitable confrontation with Rhys. She tried telling herself that she didn't have enough facts on the case to really tell him anything he didn't already know.

Like it was Bek's brother, you mean, Susan?

Her conscience kept up a constant battering stream of sardonic questioning. To avoid it, she went up to Grand Central on the northwest side. It was a huge building that housed the 25th police district and Area 5 headquarters. There she found a wary Kenny Buford. She spent an hour chewing over the bones of the case with him. He'd been busy.

'I ran a check with the Planetarium management half an hour ago. We got a positive ID from one of the attendants. He confirmed that Jake was a regular visitor and put him there on the 5th at closing time. A security guard at McCormick also made him from the photograph. Claims he'd seen someone looked like Jake around the convention centre last couple of days.'

Mackie nodded. Her eyelids felt raw and hot. Buford needed to interview Lou Bek as the next of kin, but after a couple of phone calls to Eleventh Street, it was obvious he was nowhere to be found and he never once asked Mackie where she thought he might be. She saw it all for what it really was, a closing of ranks. It left an unpalatable taste in the mouth of all involved, but it was an unwritten law. They all knew that Bek would come in and face the music sometime. It was a question of giving the guy a little space.

The call from Hopper came at eleven. She answered her beeper and dialled an unfamiliar number to hear Hopper's voice, for once reasonable, asking if they could meet and talk over 'certain aspects' of the case. When she pressed him, he didn't offer anything else by means of explanation, just that it was pertinent to the investigation and it would be best that it took place away from Eleventh Street. She thought about saying no, but in truth she had little choice. If it was about the investigation she had to go.

He was sitting at a counter in a coffee shop on Belden, his coat on the stool adjacent to him, his hand on the one adjacent discouraging anyone from occupying it. His naked skull glistened like polished ebony, his eyes showing a lot of white as he eyed Mackie over the rim of a coffee cup as she threaded her way towards him. She sat, looking around her nervously, hoping that no one would recognise her there.

'What's the problem, detective? Scared of being seen with me?'

'Don't flatter yourself. I'm merely paying some attention to my credibility here.'

Hopper sat back. 'We're both employees of the city, detective.'

'Sure. It's just that for me the law is a little more black and white, maybe,' hissed Mackie swivelling her head around behind her at some squabbling kids.

Hopper laughed. 'You certainly know how to put a man at ease, Detective Mackie.'

'Is that why you wanted to see me?' said Mackie drily. 'So that I could put you at ease?'

'No. And since it's obvious you don't want to be here any longer than is necessary, why don't you listen while I talk?'

'Sounds good to me.'

He leaned in low and looked up at her from lowered brows.

'You're on our list as one of the "women most likely to . . ." in this city, Susan. You've just got your sergeant's exam with the best test score in ten years. The need for reassignment has been brought to our attention.'

'Our attention?'

'Let's just say interested parties Downtown. Politically, there is going to come a time within the next five years where it will be necessary to appoint a female officer to a high-ranking position of authority. The feminist lobby has a shrill and persistent voice and we need someone who can take the heat of such a high-profile job.'

'Are you propositioning me?'

'I'm merely pointing out that the time may be right for you and that your continuing cooperation in this sensitive homicide involving a foreign national would go a long way in helping your case. The mayor has a long arm.'

'What are you talking about?'

'I'm talking about being a player in the *big* picture, Susan.' Hopper leaned forward. 'Let's say you spend a year, maybe a year and a half, over in violent crime or narcotics and then make Lieutenant. Couple of years max ass duty at a desk and then if things work out . . .'

Mackie felt the hair on her neck begin to prickle, her breath coming in quick short bursts. This was appalling, listening to this suit patronising her was making her squirm inside and yet . . . and yet he was right. It would be so sweet, the real heart-stopping content of what he was saying sparkled in her brain like some huge unattainable diamond that suddenly, through some quirk of fate, had drifted to within her grasp.

'I thought the election was over,' said Mackie in a dry voice. Hopper watched her, seeing the idea mushroom in her head.

'There is always another one just around the corner. The mayor wants to reorganise. He's looking for another three terms minimum and wants to surround himself with people he can trust. So let's say you keep your nose clean, maybe in four years you might get a call from the Superintendent. Susan, this city is really looking hard at appointing a female C of D before the end of the decade.'

Mackie felt her jaw drop open. Her thoughts were racing. A woman Chief of Detectives! She could only barely imagine the consternation it would cause on the 'good old boy' network. And what it would do to the 3,000 detectives. She felt the elation build inside her just imagining it. Seeing all those snooty, ultra-chic, manicured too-cool boys in suits having to swallow this. It was guaranteed to curdle their cappuccino. And here was Hopper talking to her – actually talking to her about this job!

There was so much she could do, so much she wanted to do. There was such a need for better relationships with the media, and she knew how important it was to project well. And beneath it all, pulsing away like a living entity was the knowledge of what it would do to the occupants of Portland House. She would be out there, undeniably in their faces. She felt herself flush at the realisation of how much she wanted that. How much it would compensate for what she had been through after the baby. No one knew what it had taken for her to keep things together without falling apart, desperate not to let any of it show to her CPD colleagues or her family. Putting in all kinds of extra hours for no pay. So perhaps she was owed. And maybe these weren't the highest of motives, but hell, people did things for worse reasons. She had nothing to be ashamed of here.

Really, Susan?

She told the cynical voice in her head to go screw itself for just one minute. She wanted to relish the excitement that surged inside her, screaming along in the seat alongside her coursing imagination. But then she caught Hopper's smug expression and knew that he had caught her out, hooked her with his bait.

'You're a cheap bastard,' she said.

'Hey, no promises. All I'm saying is what could happen and I wouldn't be saying this if it couldn't. The mayor is owed a lot of favours.'

'Favours yeah. And when would he call in his dues?'

'It's just what oils the wheels, detective. It would be good to have you on the team, but we wouldn't expect you to be anybody's lapdog.'

Mackie tried to read Hopper's eyes, tried to fathom out what was behind all of this. 'So what's the catch? Something simple like whacking the Pope?'

Hopper laughed. A genuine guffaw that he had to restrain with his hand. 'Like I said, everyone appreciates your cooperation, that's all. Publicity is a delicate thing. Adverse publicity is something we're used to handling. But when this Jacob case blows up we need to arrange some damage control, deflect the blast away from the fact that it was a cop's brother, pet the fur of a few nervous businessmen jumpy about the conventioneer angle.'

'And I'm the shield?'

'Yeah. A case like this starts off like a stone in your shoe and ends up with an amputated leg if you're not careful. The mayor made a few promises on the back of last week's elections but it isn't going to take long before someone takes a close look at the way Bek handled this case and finds a bad smell. See, people identify with Rhys Jacob. He comes to the city, hears all sorts of bad things about his sister, blames the city, blames everybody. He looks good on TV, has a cute accent – the voice of affronted righteous indignation. People love that. He's already pointed a finger at conventions, scaring people off. That means trade and that means bad news for the mayor at a crucial period.'

Mackie remembered the odd look on Rhys's face after they'd tramped around McCormick Place. He was bound to ask questions about the security at the Adler and conventions in general. The media would be like sharks in a feeding frenzy.

'I can't change any of that.'

'No, but you can help limit the damage. Now that we have a perp, it would be good to get the brother out of the city and away from the media humps. Let him dissolve into the background, let us handle the press. A grateful family, a contrite city – you know the score.'

'But he's become part of the investigation. The calls . . .'

'You have your evidence, detective. Call him back to testify, sure, but we need him out of the city for a while.'

'There are other aspects to this case. We haven't completed the investigation.'

'You have enough to satisfy the press and the DA. Get the brother home, distance yourself from Bek, cooperate with Buford.'

Mackie was shaking her head. 'But Rhys Jacob believes in me.'

Hopper grunted. 'You screwing? Fine. Get it out of your system and then come back to work. Hell, no one would blame you for that.'

Mackie ground her teeth together but held her temper. 'Tell me one thing,' she said. 'Who exactly is paying the bills for Rhys Jacob?'

A dreamy, feline smile spread over Hopper's face. 'You know I can't tell you that.'

'You mean there isn't a magnanimous businessman?'

'Oh yeah, several. And a lot of them want to see this city's administration run for another term.'

'Pin money,' said Mackie.

'A drop in the ocean.' Hopper saw her look of distaste and said, 'Hey, don't knock it, baby.' He paused and then added, 'There is a downside to all of this.'

'You do surprise me,' she managed, suddenly having difficulty swallowing.

He kept his eyes down, tearing strips off a paper napkin. 'The Superintendent and the mayor have long memories. As long as your career in the city, I would guess. I wouldn't want to see your talent wasted, Susan. The thought of you as an overweight dick of fifty still out there on the streets does nothing for me.'

'I won't ever let that happen.'

'No,' he nodded. 'I'm sure you won't.'

Hopper kept the grin on his face. It said everything. He stood and left five dollars on the counter in front of him before leaning low. She smelled expensive cologne as he whispered, 'Welcome to the game, detective.'

At midday, sitting at her desk, she could find no more excuses for not contacting Rhys. None apart from her own emotional reticence at least. As she sat with her hand poised on the phone, she jumped at the noise of her own name being called by Finch.

'Mac, my office.'

Hopper was sitting legs crossed in one of the folding chairs. He didn't get up as she entered, but his thumbs were in his waist band and he was grinning, well pleased with himself.

'Congratulations, detective. Good work, I hear.'

'We got lucky,' said Mackie without conviction, avoiding Hopper's eyes. The euphoria she had felt in the coffee shop had evaporated. It was pay-off time.

'The commissioner and the mayor, I need hardly tell you, are delighted. His hope now is that we can get this whole sorry episode closed and forgotten as soon as possible.'

'We're in the middle of the investigation.' Mackie tried buying a little time.

'But,' interrupted Hopper, 'I am right in assuming that the weapon is the same one that was involved in the murder of Dr Catrin Jacob, am I not?'

'It looks that way, yes, but . . .'

Hopper's grin widened as he launched into the flowery rhetoric he used for the press. 'Detective Mackie, put away your understandable misgivings over the tragic nature of this case. Obviously, Internal Affairs will need to talk to you and Sergeant Bek, but let that not detract from the very real fact that we are near to closing this case.' He sat forward and dropped his voice. 'For myself, and off the record, I could not have wished for a better outcome. That a conventioneer ends up the victim in a whim killing is regrettable, but limits the damage to the reputation of the city, I am sure you can see that.'

'Is that all you care about? What about the damage to Lou and Jake Bek?'

Hopper's face moulded itself into an appropriately conciliatory expression. 'We all regret the emotional fallout on your department, detective, but perhaps morale might get a boost if we got in bed with the press again. Mindful of the *Chronicle*'s bellicose rantings, I feel a response is in order.'

Mackie remained silent.

Finch looked up, his face inscrutable. 'Do you feel up to it, Mac?'

'Me?' said Mackie her eyes wide.

'I understand you were with him when he received the call last night, I merely wondered . . .' Hopper's dead-pan expression implied a whole lot more.

'Hopper wants to fix up a press conference, small, nothing like the circus of last time. He thinks that getting you out there in front might help.'

Mackie shook her head. 'It's more usual for senior officers . . .'

'Sure,' interrupted Hopper. 'But you are the liaison officer between Rhys Jacob and this department. I presume you will be contacting him to inform him of the progress of the investigation.'

'Sometime . . .'

'Then I suggest you do it right away. We need to get him to react to this. Perhaps a small statement before he leaves, delivered by yourself to the media. We need something so that we can begin repairing some of the damage he's done. I spoke to someone at the Metropolitan Pier and Exposition Authority. They've had two enquiries about possible convention dates for '97 withdrawn in the last two days. One of them from the American Society of Plastic Surgeons. Their conservative estimate is of twenty thousand delegates. Have you any idea how much that is worth to the city?'

Finch and Mackie waited expectantly.

'Something in excess of $30 million. Surgeons have a lot of disposable income. They eat out a lot, they buy gifts for their wives. Over a year in this city, you're talking of delegate spending in excess of $825 million, 26,000 jobs in airlines, hotels, taxis, labour. Secondary spending in the State of Illinois directly and indirectly accounts for a total economic impact of $4 billion. You think we can sit back and let your doctor friend put all that in jeopardy?' Hopper was moving in for the kill, knowing he had her. 'The people at MPEA are working hard on reassurances. We need something that they can use. Our friend Rhys Jacob could turn out to be an expensive liability unless we turn this around.'

Mackie stood with her arms folded, listening to Hopper with a calmness that belied the seething anger within. He'd manipulated her, forcing her into making a choice in front of Finch, making out that he owned her now. Was she with his team, or not? Embellish it with as many unbelievable dollar numbers as you liked, it came down to political survival and personal greed. This was all bullshit, but a little sweet part of it had been offered temptingly to her and she heard herself say, 'If you both think it'll benefit the department, then I'm prepared to do what I can.'

She saw Finch's eyes narrow and kept her gaze away from his.

'You sure about this, Mac?'

'Yeah, why not?'

'OK, let me see what you come up with. I'll run over it with Hopper's office before it goes out.'

Mackie nodded and walked out, her head buzzing, the voice inside it bugging her incessantly.

Great, Susan. Give that lady a kewpie doll. Or maybe you'd prefer the thirty pieces of silver, huh? Well don't look in the mirror, Susan. That brown nose of yours spoils the whole of the rest of your f . . .

Shut up, she told it.

She went into the locker room and locked herself in the john, ignoring the insistent voice in her head that kept on bombarding her with questions that were too close to the truth to ignore. She sat down and let her head fall into her hands, wanting to scream with frustration, and ending up slapping the wall with her palm, welcoming the pain.

Hopper with his pimp's voice had dangled the big carrot. God, was she that easy to read? But it *was* all there for the taking. Shit, downtown deals were what made the department run and anyone who said otherwise was a naive idiot. So why all this angst? Why did she have to put herself through all this grief? How was she going to live with herself if she *didn't* take this opportunity?

But what about Rhys?

So what about him? OK, it was perhaps time that she admitted to herself that he was what all this hand-wringing was about. In an ideal world maybe there would have been room for him, for all of it, but the world stank and you got crapped upon, everyone knew that.

'Shit,' she said getting up and unlocking the door. She lived and worked in a stinking sewer. She should have been used to it. And if it was up to Hopper, she would soon be up to her neck in it. OK, a different kind of effluent maybe, one that reeked of expensive cologne and high rank, but effluent none the less. She shut it out of her mind and went back to her desk. She was so preoccupied it was ten minutes before she saw the note poking out from under her phone. It said, 'Phone message from Rhys Jacob at eleven. TV station called, want to do another interview. On his way there unless told otherwise.'

'Shit,' she hissed in exasperation. It was almost twelve-forty-five. She kept repeating the oath as she grabbed her coat and headed for the door.

Rhys was staring out at the passers-by on the street from the lobby of the Geneva. He saw the wind yanking back the flaps of trenchcoats and saw heads bowed against it, the down-turned faces raw and pale. He felt a hand on his arm and heard someone speaking to him.

'Excuse me, sir?'

A busboy stood at his elbow.

'Your cab's here, sir.'

He slipped the busboy a dollar and walked out to the waiting taxi, the door already open.

'CHTV, right?' asked the driver in confirmation.

'That's right,' answered Rhys. He had taken the call at around ten-forty-five. The TV station had virtually begged him to go in for a short interview, just some comments on the night's events, they had said. When he'd replied 'What events?' there had been a long pregnant pause.

'Dr Jacob, we have a source that indicates to us that you had a telephone conversation with a suspect in the murder investigation involving your sister. That suspect is now dead. Are you telling me that our information is incorrect?'

'Where did you get all this?' asked Rhys, surprised, yet amazed at the power of the press in this city.

'I am not at liberty to say, sir. But I'm sure a face-to-face discussion would be of mutual benefit here.'

Rhys thought it over for a long moment. He had no desire to be contentious again. In truth he felt somehow that he owed Mackie and thus the city some sort of balancing redress. If Mackie was right and his caller had committed suicide, everything was cut and dried. It was sickening, but at least there was less blame to apportion. Perhaps he had let his imagination work overtime, God knows he had enough reason. OK, he had vague misgivings over why Susan hadn't come back to him this morning. He knew she was busy, but he had a right to know what was happening, didn't he? If he went to the TV station, he at least would find out what the hell was going on. He said yes and they promised to send a cab. They used a particular company, the caller had said. He would be there within half an hour.

He strode out through the door held open for him and stood there staring at the logo on the cab door; a huge sun with radiating rays of sunlight. He frowned, trying to focus down on a vague flickering idea that the logo was somehow important. It was a fleeting, tantalising moment that was gone almost as soon as it appeared. He shrugged it off and clambered into the cab out of the wind.

'It's a cold one,' said the driver as he pulled out into traffic.

'It is,' said Rhys staring out at the street.

'First time in Chicago?'

'Uh, yes.' Rhys looked up.

'How you finding it?'

'OK.'

'You visiting relatives or here on business?'

'Business of sorts. I have no relatives in Chicago.'

'You work in TV, huh?'

'It's just an interview.' He saw the driver squinting in the rear-view.

'Hey, you're that lady's brother, right? The one that was killed?'

'That's right.'

'I heard about that. Condolences on your loss.'

'Thank you.'

The car lurched suddenly and slowed to a stop. 'Whoa, sounds like I got a tyre problem.' The car pulled over in the poorly lit shadow of an underpass. Rhys saw the tiny model of a skeleton hanging next to the rear-view jiggle and dance to the car's unsteady rhythm. The driver got out and ten seconds later was at Rhys's window with a pissed-off expression in his face. Rhys took in glasses, a close-cropped beard and lank red-gold hair.

'It's a flat. Take me ten minutes. You want some coffee?'

'No, thanks all the same.'

The driver grinned and reached under a front seat for a Thermos.

'Please. It'll make me feel better.'

'No really, there's no need to go to any trouble . . .'

The driver was back filling the doorway, the Thermos unscrewed in his hands.

'I had one just before I left the ho . . .'

The taxi driver put down the Thermos and held out a steaming cup of coffee.

'Really, I couldn't,' said Rhys and watched as the driver fumbled inside his coat. Three seconds later, he found himself staring into the snub nose of a small revolver.

'Drink it,' said the driver, all traces of bonhomie disappearing like the steam that wafted in front of his face.

Rhys looked down at the cup and then back at the driver.

'Drink it, I said,' he growled, roughly smashing the revolver's muzzle into the skin under Rhys's eye.

Quickly, Rhys put the cup to his lips and sipped the bitter liquid.

'All of it,' said the driver.

Rhys complied, his brain racing.

'What did he tell you?'

Rhys frowned at the question, desperately trying to understand so that he would not aggravate this man further.

'Who?'

'The fucking fruitcake. I know he rang you last night so don't play the dummy.'

'Fruitcake?' asked Rhys, his mind suddenly a blank.

'Don't fuck with me,' warned Lauden, thrusting the gun under Rhys's ear. 'He called you from the motel. What did he tell you?'

Realisation exploded in Rhys's brain. 'Nothing. He told me nothing. He was schizophrenic. His speech was bizarre, he didn't make any sense at all.'

'What did he say?' Lauden's voice was low and menacing.

The gun felt cold against Rhys's skin, the wind whistled in through the open door. Cars kept passing to the outside of them, but no one stopped. Rhys thought about screaming but the gun was so close, and this man seemed desperate and dangerous.

'He kept on about a Whistler. Someone he saw at the Planetarium, I think. But no names. Out of all the garbage he said, that's all I think I understand.'

'Don't fuck with me . . .'

'It's the truth, I swear.'

Lauden looked down at the empty cup in Rhys's hand. He thrust the Thermos in through the window. 'Pour another cup and drink it all.'

Rhys hesitated, but did as he was told, the coffee warm in his throat, his mind struggling for understanding.

What the hell was this all about?

'Who are you?' he ventured between swallows.

'You don't want to know,' said Lauden warningly. Satisfied that the cup was empty again, he kept the gun trained on Rhys as he locked the door and returned to the front seat. He sat there, half hunched around as his free hand twiddled with the radio nob until he found some music that he liked.

'They'll be waiting for me at the TV station,' said Rhys after a while.

A slow smile crept over Lauden's face as he shook his head.

'Wrong. I made that call. No one is expecting you anywhere. Let me have your hotel room key.'

Rhys fished out the perforated plastic card and handed it over. Lauden pocketed it and they sat in silence for long minutes, the gun pointing steadily at Rhys's head.

A new wave station was playing softly on the radio, muted and melodious, and to Rhys's drugged mind, it held an almost religious quality. The driver kept flicking gently at the tiny skeleton, making it move in time, the loose joints waving and cavorting. Rhys felt his vision begin to blur. He felt as if a great weight was slowly pressing him down.

'What was it . . . in the coffee?' he asked.

'Something that'll knock you out for twelve hours or so.'

'Who . . . who are . . . you?'

'What'd the fruitcake keep saying?'

'Whistler. He kept . . . the whistler.'

'Yeah, that's me. The Whistler . . .'

Lauden watched Rhys's body slide sideways on to the seat and sprawl there, eyes gradually closing.

The girl had done much the same at the Planetarium, but she had been acting. She had fooled Lauden into believing she was unconscious. But not this time. He would be extra careful. Lauden studied the smooth line of Rhys's jaw and the long dark eyelashes and felt the faint stirrings of desire inside him. Yes, why not? The quietness of Rhys's breathing, the corpse-like repose. He would make use of this one. He had been repulsed by the killing he had done the previous night. The senselessness of it. But here he had an opportunity of using what he had captured. Looking at this object in his cab, he felt the need to touch the beating heart, run his fingers over the bones inside the flesh.

After ten minutes, Lauden drove off and parked behind the Hyatt adjacent to the Geneva. He threw a blanket over Rhys in the back seat and walked towards the hotel, descending immediately to the warren beneath that was part of the Illinois Center. He followed the corridors around to The Swiss Cafe and into the elevator. He pressed thirty and stood staring at his reflection in the mirrored walls. He hated mirrors. After two floors, he shut his eyes to rid himself of the image and rode up in darkness with Rhys's key clutched firmly in his hands.

24

A T FIVE AFTER one, after negotiating the lunchtime traffic on the Loop, Susan Mackie was striding across the lobby of the Geneva. She spoke to a desk clerk by the vowel-rich name of Stephaniee; a petite clear-skinned girl with tressed chestnut hair held up with combs. Stephaniee looked hassled but friendly as she patiently explained the intricacies of room tax to a Japanese guest.

'Excuse me,' said Mackie stepping up in front of the demanding press of people and showing her badge. Stephaniee saw it and tilted her head enquiringly.

'I'm looking for Dr Rhys Jacob. Could you page him for me?'

Stephaniee turned her eyes down to the VDU at waste level and pressed a few buttons. After a moment, she frowned and said, 'I'm afraid Dr Jacob has checked out, ma'am.'

'Say again?'

'Yes, according to our records he issued instructions to be automatically billed. Officially he is no longer staying here.'

'But . . . what did he say?'

'He didn't say anything. He would not have needed to come to the desk.'

'Stephaniee!' The voice came from a room behind the desk.

Stephaniee made an exasperated, apologetic face and excused herself by holding up one manicured finger. Mackie stared after her in complete confusion, a hundred questions on her lips. When Stephaniee finally reappeared Mackie beckoned her out and took her by the elbow to a quiet corner.

'I don't understand. Didn't Dr Jacob have to check out?'

Stephaniee took a deep breath and began. 'Some guests want to leave in a hurry, or they don't want the hassle of having to join a line-up for the desk. We have a system whereby guests can check their bills via the PayTV system in their rooms.' She paused, seeing the look of perplexity on Mackie's face. 'It's nothing more than a small box with letters or digits in the form of buttons on it. You can punch in a number to choose which video you want to see or if you want information about shopping or verify your bill. If you want to check out quickly you just confirm your bill is correct on the TV screen and then tell the computer to charge your credit card account. We always take a credit card imprint when people check in. It's standard policy.' Stephaniee lapsed into a practised grin.

Mackie's face went white. She was remembering a conversation over lunch with Rhys. She was remembering the way Rhys's face had fallen with disappointment when she'd told him that his theory about the foreign missing persons was unfounded. She was remembering glibly announcing to him that they had all checked out of their hotels and paid their bills.

'Is the system standard in most hotels?' she said quickly.

'In most of the big ones, sure.'

'I need to see your manager right away.'

Five minutes later, Mackie stood impatiently outside Rhys's room, waiting for the manager to open the door. Inside, the bed was unmade but his suitcase, clothes and toiletries were all gone.

'This doesn't make sense,' she said looking around in bewilderment, opening the closet and switching on the bathroom light as if in expectation of seeing some sign of the occupant. 'Could you, uh . . . check with the concierge if they remember Dr Jacob leaving? Find out if he took a cab or an airport shuttle?' she asked the manager.

'Of course. I'll go down immediately.' He left Mackie alone in the room with her chaotic thoughts. Her eyes went to the rumpled bed. Why did she feel such panic? It was unfounded and illogical. But then his checking out was illogical. She stared at the phone and suddenly, cursing, remembered the trap.

She pulled out her mobile and dialled the phone company.

'I need to know what calls came through to this room this morning.'

'Only one this a.m. Pay-phone in a Seven-Eleven in Gage Park.'

'Pay-phone?'

'That's right.'

'Nothing from a TV station?'

'No.'

She felt the panic open up like a dark flower inside her. 'Uh, thanks. And we can dispense with the trap.'

'Good,' said the tech. He sounded young and cocky. 'Know how many calls this hotel receives from males in twenty-four hours?'

'Send me the read-out.'

'You got it. I'll highlight the two from the motel. Hate to think of someone with such a foxy voice wasting her busy time.'

Mackie had time to be vaguely annoyed by the fact that this guy, who she had never seen, was coming on to her before the implication of what he had said dawned.

'You said two calls from the motel?'

'Yeah. One at uh . . . twenty-two seventeen lasting three minutes twenty and one at twenty-two twenty-two lasting thirty seconds. The second call didn't ask to be put through to the destination room. In fact it was the switchboard at the Geneva who triggered the trap. They thought it was a heavy-breather. They didn't actually hear a voice. Could have been anybody I suppose. Still, one hell of a coincidence, huh?'

Mackie didn't answer.

'I said one hell of a coincidence.'

'Yeah, one hell of a coincidence,' mumbled Mackie as she ended the call and sat on the edge of the bed trying to get her mind around this new piece of information. She hated coincidences. They had as much place in a murder investigation as a clown at a funeral. It couldn't have been Jake Bek, could it? No one with his injuries could have survived for any length of time. Certainly not long enough to have redialled the number. And the phone in Jake's motel room had been off the hook, she was sure of it.

On impulse she reached for the phone in Rhys's room, but her hand stopped three inches from the handset. Inexplicably, she didn't trust it any more. Instead, she picked up her mobile and dialled Area 5 headquarters. After three minutes, Buford came on the line.

'Detective Mackie, what can I do for you?'

'Just running through some details, Detective. When the uniforms arrived at the motel, the phone was off the hook, right?'

'Uh,' she heard Buford rustling through his pocket book. 'Yeah, phone was off the hook.'

'OK, thanks.'

'Is that it?'

'Yes, for now.'

'You got a new angle on this, Mac?'

'I don't know, Kenny, give me some time, OK?'

'Sure, some time,' said Buford drily. 'Take all you want. Keep me posted, Mac.'

Mackie ended the call and dialled the number of the Honolulu Motel she found in the phone book. She heard the manager's voice and envisaged him, a nervous Laotian named Phekse with lousy teeth. She explained who she was and listened intently to his terrible English.

'Mr Phekse. You have an automatic call monitor for your telephone network, am I right?'

'Sure, automatic, sure.'

'Please check your print-out of calls made last night,' she said slowly.

'Calls, what calls?'

'Check your print-out. How many calls were made from room 51?'

'OK, you hang on a minute, detective?'

Mackie hung on for a long two minutes hearing guttural conversation in the background.

'Hello?' said Phekse. 'Two calls.'

'Are they timed?'

'Sure they timed.'

'Give me the times, Mr Phekse.'

'OK. First one twenty-two seventeen. Second one twenty-two twenty-two.'

Mackie was silent, listening to her pulse quicken, feeling the growing confusion settle down into hard-edged suspicion tinged with fear.

'Hello?' asked Phekse.

Mackie mumbled. 'Yeah sure. Thanks, Mr Phekse.'

'When can I rent room out?'

'What room?'

'Room 51. When can I clean up? One he was shot in.'

'Soon now, Mr Phekse, soon.'

She terminated the call, sat down and tried explaining all this away. OK, so the first call might have been to someone else, the second call was to Rhys. It was the second call that they heard, right? But she knew even as she gave these thoughts their head that it didn't add up. The second call had lasted only a matter of seconds, or so the phone company tech. had said. Then what?

Simple, Mac. There he is, Jake Bek with his brains all over the wall. With his last dying breath, he puts down the phone he was holding, redials the Geneva and gurgles to the operator there who assumes it's a nuisance call. It's obvious, right? Anything else is going to be very inconvenient, isn't it?

She told the sarcastic voice that sounded just like her mother to shut its stupid mouth. It sounded ludicrous hearing it that way. But it *was* ludicrous.

The manager appeared in the doorway, clearing his throat to attract her attention.

'The doorman says a cab called for Dr Jacob. It was a Suncab and the driver asked for him by name.'

'What time?'

He shook his head dubiously. 'Late morning he thinks.'

'Thanks,' said Mackie.

The manager hesitated on the threshold.

'Could you give me a minute,' said Mackie, and watched him back out.

She made one more rapid phone call to CHTV, fighting the growing tide of anxiety that was rising up inside her. No, they were sorry, they had no one there by the name of Dr Rhys Jacob. Yes, they were certain, yes they were sure they had not phoned him at his hotel, yes they were sure they had not sent a cab for him. Why, was he missing?

It was at that point that Mackie jabbed her finger on the button that broke the connection, her heart full of a cold dread. There was no escaping any of this any more and she felt herself trembling uncontrollably. She looked at her hands in disgust. She was a cop, for Pete's sake. What the hell was she doing shaking like a scared puppy in some downtown hotel room?

It was impossible for Jake to have made two calls from his motel room. He was dead when that second call was made. She had heard the shot herself, for Pete's sake. She had seen what was left of his head. She had marked down the time exactly in her notebook. Twenty-two seventeen. That second call had been made at twenty-two twenty-two. Either that call had been made by a dead man or someone else had been in that room. Someone else had picked up the phone and dialled. She looked again at her mobile, saw the complex arrangement of buttons and focused in on one marked R for re-dial.

What if Rhys was right? What if he had heard someone breathing on the end of that line?

A hundred thoughts galvanised her into movement as she sprang off the bed. But even as she stood the *really* terrifying thought hit her. It had been there skulking in the back of her mind for hours and now it stuck its ugly head out of the pitch-black cave it wallowed in and screamed at her.

What about the alternative, Susan? What about the or? Or? she screamed at it mentally.

There is always an or, isn't there?

'Or what?' she hissed to herself.

Or just sit back down on the bed and think for a minute. Accept the fact that Rhys has booked out and taken a hike. Left you and Chicago. It was what you wanted, wasn't it? Shit, you almost came close there to establishing some sort of relationship, Susan. Jesus Christ. You don't want to let that happen. Mountains would crumble, the seas would rise up, the ground open under your feet. So why not just accept that everything you've just imagined is nothing more than fanciful creative thinking?

Jake was fruitcake,
Crazy as a loon,
Blew his fucking brains out,
And spread them round the room.

The ugly head came up with the rhyme. Kept repeating it. Kept saying it knowing that if it did so enough times she might start believing it. But why? Why did she want to even begin to think that way?

Come on, Susan. Hopper is the answer. Hopper and a sweet job that would jump you twenty steps up the career ladder and let you give the finger to everyone that deserves it. All this crap about phone calls and doctors who book out of their hotels – just chicken feed, just a bunch of hominy grits in the great scale of things, right?

RIGHT?

She sat down heavily, depressed and discomfited in the face of the dilemma that had so suddenly precipitated. It would be so easy to take what was already there and let it flow. Let them crucify Jake and Lou, let them file this one away in the whacko drawer. She could fudge the phone evidence. Imagine Jake's arm flying out to hit the phone in his death throes, breaking the connection and hitting the redial button a second later. It sounded like shit, but sometimes things were shitty. And in five years she would be out of it, sitting in some plush office with a secretary and lunches every other day with the commissioners and the moneyed strata that really owned this city instead of mingling with the scum that hung in the filth of the underbelly. And she deserved it, didn't she? Everyone knew she was too good to be nothing but a plain dick. She deserved a chance at last to put the past couple of years behind her. And people did it all the time, suppressed things, ignored things, got the collar and moved on. It had all worked out just fine without her having to do anything. Rhys gone, the case sewing itself up. She began to let the acceptance flow in a mellow stream into her head, projecting, imagining, dreaming of the success. It felt and sounded good, it felt like the best balm she could imagine to her bruised and aching ego.

Susan Mackie, success!

So why was she even bothering to question it? Because, she yelled back at the ugly head. *Because? Because of fucking what?*

Because of what it meant she would become. She would become what her father had always wanted her to become. A part of the establishment. She half felt that he might even approve of the way she would achieve it, stepping on a few little people, becoming aloof, separating emotion from the need to succeed.

Joining the establishment.

It was almost Thanksgiving. A time for family. *Family!*

God, why did anyone need families? They clung to you, burdening you with memories, things that had moulded you, triggering responses in you that were powerful and over which you had no control.

Lou Bek had got himself jammed up because of misguided loyalty to his family.

Rhys Jacob was so defiantly proud of his dead sister, it made him think he was indestructible in a city that oozed violence. And now, again, here she was, Susan Mackie, tying herself in knots because of her family.

She shook her head, alone in the bedroom. Alone suddenly in this huge city. If she did this it would screw up Lou, it would irritate the hell out of her father, but it would also mean abandoning Rhys.

Abandoning him? Wasn't it he that had walked away from this?

Believing that was the most difficult thing of all. Shit, Rhys didn't deserve these thoughts any more than his sister had deserved to become another homicide statistic. Any more than she had deserved to lose the baby that had grown inside her. Memory of the pain swelled and throbbed again – but she saw it for what it truly was. Not anything physical, more some corrupting emotional tumour that she had never really got rid of. Something that had germinated in those formative years in Portland House and had mushroomed, feeding on her guilt at the way that Nick had reacted in the bathroom door and Hopper's slick patronising grin.

Sitting on the bed with the cold sun on her hands, she suddenly saw everything for the sham it was. In five years sitting in her new office with her name on the door, she would begin thinking of other ways of turning somersaults. It would never end. The self-deception so destructive and ultimately unsatisfying. Wasn't it time to admit that there was an inner being that had to be looked after here? She couldn't go on just careering around in defiance of what she wanted and at the same time secretly kidding herself that she didn't give a shit. It was juvenile, it was stupid, but more than that, it was wrong.

This whole train of thought was wrong.

She got up then on trembling legs, looked around Rhys's empty room and felt an ache inside her. It was all fragmented in her brain, little pieces of a floating jig-saw that bobbed just out of her grasp. But the glimpse of the whole picture that was emerging was unwholesome and terrible. All she knew was that Rhys Jacob was not where he was meant to be and she felt in her gut that it wasn't he that had booked out of this hotel room. At least not voluntarily.

She also knew that it could not have been Jake that had made that second call to the Geneva.

As she hurried down in the elevator, catching a glimpse of her tired face in the mirror, the image that predominated in her racing brain was an odd one.

She saw a frightened, sick man in a motel room surrounded by images conjured up by a tortured mind. A mind twisted by a sickness that made him trust no one except a stranger with the same name as him. She felt the merest twinge of the terror Jake Bek must have felt and a fraction of the loneliness and it scared the hell out of her.

25

LAUDEN DROVE SOUTH out of the city towards Chicago Lawn with Rhys and his suitcase in the rear of the Caprice. He felt much better. Calmer, now that he was back in control of everything. They might look hard for this one, his face was known. Being on TV had that drawback. But then again the others had not provoked a public outcry.

The need for a quick kill and rapid disposal that had driven him to this audacious act was waning. Suddenly, he had all the time in the world to think about what best to do, didn't he? And there was so much he could do in twelve hours with this semi-corpse. He had laced the coffee with a heavy dose of Lidoxine and Temazepam as usual. He used the drugs himself only intermittently, preferring alcohol for modifying his own moods. But he had his physician's prescription which meant he could purchase them whenever he wanted. Twelve hours of unconsciousness was the minimum he would expect from such a load of the drug.

Threading his way through afternoon traffic, Lauden's thoughts began to meander down the paths of his imagination. Perhaps this time . . . A corner of his mind still harboured a belief that perhaps *this* time he would be satisfied. But a part of him knew too that it wouldn't happen. However unpalatable what he was contemplating seemed to be – and somewhere in his consciousness remained the awareness that his lust was tainted and fettered by these obscene preoccupations – the compulsion dominated his control. As he snaked and weaved through the traffic, his vague apprehensions were swallowed up in the all-encompassing fog of his sickness. Ten minutes after leaving the Geneva, he was already planning on how to make Rhys Jacob last as long as he possibly could. He looked like the girl at the Planetarium, same slim build, same fine features. There were of course the obvious differences; there was no getting away from the fact that this was a man. He thought about it, and, far from finding it totally abhorrent, he began to feel a knot of excitement grow. There were modifications to the body that he could make once he had the control he wished for. He had head skins from other 'partners' which he could dress Rhys Jacob with. He could make him into anyone or anything he wanted as long as he could retain the fragile, submissive status of unconsciousness that was Lauden's pinnacle of erotic fantasy. With that in mind, the drugs were a short-term answer. What he really yearned for was another Linda Panicik.

When he reached Cambridge Street, he parked the taxi in his garage and closed the doors behind him. Carefully, he lifted Rhys Jacob's unconscious body onto his shoulders and carried him up to the attic room which served as his pantheon. With an almost mystical reverence, he opened the door. The room was in complete darkness, the windows boarded up and covered by black drapes. His fingers found the light switch and flicked it on.

He had abandoned the harshness of a central pendant, preferring instead the muted glow of red-shaded wall-lights that cast interesting shadows. They provided enough light for Lauden to move around, but when he was in residence, he would light candles for some of the more intimate activities he indulged in. And for when he was dismembering, there was a powerful angled halogen lamp on a moveable stand bought from a surgical supplies outlet. Other pieces of equipment lay in a chest against the wall, all bought cheaply from pawn shops and specialist outlets.

As he laid Rhys down on the cool stainless-steel table he had found in a liquidation sale of abattoir equipment, Lauden switched on the halogen lamp. Suddenly there was more than enough lurid light for him to gaze and wonder at the idolatry he had created in that quiet room.

On shelves set at head height around the walls stood the skulls of his victims, some decorated silver or gold. These were his silent witnesses, his lovers, those who had, without choice or volition, helped him in his dreadful quest for understanding of himself. They gazed down with hollow sockets, angled such that their empty stares fell on the table; some with candles as yet unlit in their bases, their crowns removed, others whole and bleached white. But it was the wall at the foot of the table that held the focus of the room and which was, in effect, the centre of his psychosis. A being occupied this wall, had merged and become part of it like some dreadful fusion of plaster and calcified bone. Twelve feet high with three backbones, huge arms with treble joints and double humeri and widespread legs of composite construction. This nightmare amalgamation was stuck to the wall with expansile foam that bubbled yellow like some decaying fungoid ectoplasm. The legs were thick pillars of heavy femurs one piled on top of the other, taken from unwitting victims and now thrusting outwards in some revolting sexual pose. The skulls, three in all, facing ahead and to either side had been fused and wired into a monstrous three-faced horror.

This being had emerged out of Lauden's imagination, created by his own hands. Searching for some way to at least assuage some of his guilt, he had hit upon the idea and belief that here was a means of celebrating and preserving the terrible waste his 'love' had resulted in. The ultimate totem of his murderous actions.

From the ceiling a pulley had been rigged from a reinforced joist. Beneath it hung a steel bar in a long 'H' shape with chains attached to both ends. This was a new addition, something he had rigged up only a week or so ago. This was yet more fuel for the fantasies that drove him. With it, he hoped to levitate his victims, have them hang in space, legs and arms manacled to the bars, suspended like floating corpses in some limbo state between life and death, awaiting the final acts that would free the soul. Acts that existed only in Lauden's corrupted imagination.

From a closet he removed a battered motorcycle helmet. It had once been blue, but the paint had scuffed and chipped off as a result of the holes that Lauden had drilled into it. They were positioned precisely and carefully. His dalliance with Linda Panicik had led to research in libraries and medical bookshops. From the books he had bought, Lauden had read about stereotactic surgery: the way that brain surgeons positioned and constructed frames around their patients' heads so that approach to dangerous and delicate brain parts was precise once the head was fixed by reference points and the frame pinned to the temples of the skull. His understanding of this was vague, but the principle was one he grasped.

He had known that he would never be able to afford or get hold of anything like the correct instruments and so his imagination had come up with the motorcycle helmet. Positioned, it would hold the head firm and orientated. It meant that with his crude understanding of basic anatomy, he could at least attempt to ablate some parts of the brain. He knew that the reticular activating system was responsible for maintaining the mind in a state of responsiveness. He knew that the reticular formation was a network of connections and centres that defied precise location, but he knew too that it was situated in the brain stem.

Everything that he had seen and read had emphasized the precise and extensive work all neurosurgical patients underwent before any surgery was attempted. Computerised tomography, magnetic resonant imaging and carotid angiography were all used to create a three-dimensional picture with precise location of major vessels and structures. From this, stereotactic localisation of the structure or lesion was possible and an optimal trajectory for the probe or instrument calculated so that its passage would induce minimal damage. But Lauden had none of these luxuries. His approach had been basic, opting for a hands-on approach with the cadaveric heads of his victims. The helmet he had modified to fit with the chin straps in position and a line of holes over the crown. He had also calculated that to get to within the area he wanted to destroy, he would have to insert an instrument to a depth of eighteen centimetres. The hole through the skull would be via the right frontal region, an inch behind the hair line. Lauden had calculated that if the damage that he would induce was not enough, he could use the same hole to insert a long needle on a syringe containing some of the wallpaper remover he had used to deflesh the skull. That way he could attempt a graded destruction.

After gazing at the helmet, he put it down on the trunk and went back to Rhys. Carefully, he arranged the body on the table and took off his shirt, admiring the defined torso and the smooth, almost hairless, chest. He photographed it with a Polaroid camera and then took the photographs downstairs. He was hungry, he had not eaten since his late breakfast. He was also very thirsty, the craving for alcohol strong, fuelled by the dreadful things he was contemplating. Glancing in the fridge he was dismayed to see that he was low on beer and almost out of food. At four, he left the bungalow and drove six blocks to a market for provisions, safe in the knowledge that his victim was drugged and incapable of escape.

Mackie spent a frustrating hour cruising Bek's known haunts and finding him in none of them. She tried his beeper and got no reply. She rang him at his apartment and got no answer. Via the hospital she traced the mortician handling the Bek funeral arrangements and from him learned that Bek had rung forty minutes before from an Antioch number. She rang it in and got an address listed under L. A. Bek as owner. At a little after two, as she walked out of her office, having decided that there was no choice open to her other than to drive up there, Finch called to her from his office.

Inside, she took in Hopper's smug expression and feared the worst.

'Susan,' said Finch with a resigned air, 'Mr Hopper is here about the press conference. How did the brother take the news?'

'I can't find him, Lieutenant.' From the corner of her eyes she saw Hopper's grin, his eyes sparkling. She felt like smacking his complacent mug. 'He's checked out of his hotel. Nobody has seen him.'

'You get a comment from him?' beamed Hopper.

She shook her head.

'Fine,' he grinned magnanimously. 'We'll make one up.'

'What's the story, Susan?' asked Finch calmly.

Mackie's eyes were on Hopper's supercilious grin. He was still congratulating himself over her capitulation.

'Susan?' repeated Finch.

'Something's wrong, Lieutenant. Rhys Jacob left the hotel at the request of CHTV.'

'CHTV?' interrupted Hopper, a cloud over the sunny disposition.

'But CHTV deny all knowledge. He's checked out but . . . I think he may have left under duress.' She glared at Hopper.

'Hey, don't look at me.'

'Lieutenant,' said Mackie, 'there is some evidence to suggest that Jake Bek's death is not as wrinkle-free as we all thought.'

'I'm listening.'

'No soot or powder tattooing around the wound means the gun was held a foot or more away from the head. The spatter pattern and the entry wound are consistent with a frontal shot, which is unusual in suicides. I'd like to get an NAA done on Jake's hands.'

'NAA, what the hell is that?' asked Hopper belligerently.

'It's a Neutron Activation Analysis,' explained Finch. 'It'll tell us whether or not Jake Bek actually fired that gun as opposed to just holding it.'

'I don't believe I'm hearing this,' blustered Hopper, the smug grin fading fast now as he hissed out his interpretation of the facts. 'The guy blew his brains all over the wall. What the hell more do you want?'

'Also,' said Mackie, 'the phone company trapped a call from the motel after we heard shots. I confirmed today that the call came from Jake's room.'

'So he tried to ring for help,' said Hopper.

'With his brains all over the wall?' Mackie said smiling coldly.

'How does this tie in with Rhys Jacob's disappearance?'

'Rhys Jacob believed that his sister's death had something to do with missing persons. Someone at his hotel was missing a daughter, a doctor like Catrin Jacob. It sounded off the wall, but I did some double checking. Five other medical conventioneers have disappeared over the last eighteen months under similar circumstances; booking out of their hotels and never being seen again. I think that maybe Catrin Jacob was attacked at the Planetarium because she was a conventioneer. The Planetarium guides put Jake Bek there and later at McCormick. Maybe Jake saw something and it finally caught up with him. Maybe that something caught up with Rhys Jacob too.'

'This is bullshit,' yelled Hopper. 'The DA will laugh you out of his office. Missing conventioneers? This isn't the fucking twilight zone, detective.' His eyes hardened. 'How much of this is Sergeant Bek's theory, tell me that?'

'None of it,' said Mackie. 'It's all mine.'

'What's the matter, you and the limey doctor have a lover's tiff?' Hopper sneered.

Finch shot Hopper a glance full of thunder but he didn't speak.

'Lieutenant, I think I made a mistake in agreeing to participate in the proposed press conference. I don't think it's appropriate and I don't think we're ready on this. There are too many loose ends.'

'Detective,' sneered Hopper, 'I thought we understood one another.'

Mackie inclined her head dubiously. 'Obviously we don't.'

'Don't screw me around, Mackie. They warned me that you liked squeezing shoes, but you're way outside your territory here.'

Mackie made a great show of sighing. 'Lieutenant . . .' Hopper bulldozed on.

'Lieutenant Finch, the mayor wants and demands that this investigation be brought to its natural conclusion by tomorrow morning. The suicide of a deranged murderer is regrettable, especially when it involves a department employee's family, but that is how I read this and that is what the press are going to hear tomorrow. I have a meeting with the Superintendent in an hour and that is what I am going to tell him. The conference goes ahead with or without Rhys Jacob's contribution. If this district cannot separate personal interest from its professional duty, we will arrange for the investigation to be taken off your hands.' He paused and turned a sick grin on Mackie. 'Hope you like traffic, detective, because that's what you are going to be dealing with for the next five years if Internal Affairs doesn't fry you first. And when you meet up with your boyfriend again, tell him from me that the tab is closed. It's time he flew back to wherever the hell he's from with his stiff sister.' Finch's eyes were downcast, but Mackie could see his jaw muscles tight as a drum.

'Do we have to listen to this crap?' she breathed, her mouth a thin line of anger.

'Hopper,' said Finch calmly, 'could you excuse us for one second?'

Hopper's bug eyes didn't budge from Mackie's face.

Finch took her outside and into the interview room.

'Susan, he's a triple A pain but he's the Super's right arm. He can do the things he says he can. Now I need to know how sure you are of what you're saying here.'

Mackie held his gaze. 'This case stinks, Lieutenant. I think you ought to know too that Mr Hopper arranged to meet me earlier today and suggested that if I could nail Jake Bek to the Adler case it would help with my forthcoming career prospects. I won't say any more except that the offer was very tempting.'

Finch's eyes blazed anger for ten long seconds before he finally said 'Fine,' through clenched teeth. He took Susan's elbow and gently led her back to the office and Hopper's annoyed thyrotoxic glare.

'OK, Hopper, thank you for your input. We will do what is necessary to achieve a speedy end to this case.'

'What the hell does that mean?'

'It means that we've finished our business here today.'

Hopper pushed himself out of the chair and stormed to the door under Finch's baleful glare. 'You better be aware that until the Area commander tells me otherwise, this investigation runs out of *this* office,' said Finch. The Lieutenant's tone was deceptively even given that his face was white with anger. 'Give the mayor my regards and on your way downstairs, ask the desk sergeant for a loan of his night stick so that you can use it to shove your pissant attitude up your ass. Plus, I don't want to hear or see you in this office or even asking the time of day of any of my command again without an appointment, do your hear me?'

Hopper had pivoted and was staring up at Finch, his jaw hanging an inch above his tie. A strange, gurgling noise rumbled around in his throat but his eyes fixed unwaveringly on Mackie.

'You stupid bitch,' he snapped. 'You're dumber than I thought you were. You've just blown the best chance you ever had in this city.'

'Hopper, you better leave now,' said Finch angrily.

'I'm going, but Sergeant Mackie better know that this was a one-off sale and there won't be another for a long time.' He paused and allowed a slow hyena smile to distort his features. 'But we are grateful to daddy.' He fixed Mackie with one final glittering stare. 'Tell him that we can always use a good hand-shake story. Especially one with pictures.'

Finch pressed the intercom on his desk and seconds later a big coloured officer appeared and took Hopper's elbow. He went without argument. As he left, Finch spoke into the intercom again.

'Sergeant Neuer, when Mr Hopper passes you on his way out, do me a favour and wave your night-stick at him, OK?'

Finch looked up and said without smiling, 'You've got work to do, Susan.'

She didn't speak, couldn't. Her eyes were riveted on the closed door that Hopper had just gone through. She felt herself curdling inside, aware of how stupid she had been. Of how ready she had almost been to fall into the trap like a blind, narcissistic idiot. Of how obvious it all suddenly was. She reached out to the table edge and grasped it.

'Susan, you OK?'

'Bastard . . .' she whispered, her lips white with anger. 'That bastard . . .'

'Susan?'

'Yeah, I'm fine,' she muttered, her mouth devoid of any saliva, indignation burning in her cheeks. Hopper could have been lying, getting at her, knowing which lever to pull. But she had never given him that lever and there was no way of him knowing anything about her father unless there was some truth in it. And it reeked of the truth. Her instinct told her it had all the hallmarks. She imagined Mr Ewan Mackie sitting in his hallowed study, taking the call that nailed Kervesky's rival, Sheehan. Some staff reporter on one of the papers her father owned remembering the photograph . . . knowing it was dynamite . . . checking with his boss. She saw in her mind the big self-satisfied smile, the magnanimous offer of making the politico's video for nothing, perhaps even paying for the opportunity, for the cause. All for a small favour. Getting Kervesky elected against the tide of Republican upsurge with the wave of a powerful hand in return for . . . Mackie shook her head. It would have made him gleeful. The thought that he could, despite her defiance, still influence her life. Reaching out across the miles like some disembodied puppeteer. She tried to imagine how sweet her self-deception would have tasted, her believing that she would have succeeded off her own bat, deluding herself that her success would impress him but at the same time refute his lack of faith in her. And all the while he would know that it was through his bribery and machinations that she had been granted her opportunity. Her mind boiled, threatening to erupt in a hot spurt of rage. Would he have told her? Would he one boozy Thanksgiving dinner have spat it out in her face in front of her siblings?

'Mac?' asked Finch.

'Yeah,' she exhaled, 'I'm fine.'

'Hopper had it a long time coming. I take it that last remark was meant for you?'

She nodded, her eyes bright with anger.

'I don't know what it means and I don't want to, Susan. But the fact is we're all out on a limb, so you better get this right, and fast.'

She turned away from Finch, hiding her face, hiding the pathetic tears that welled there, feeling her resolve harden. 'I am right, Lieutenant. I know it.'

She got to her car, her cheeks still burning. The screaming voices of exasperation clamoured to be heard, but she screwed them down, squeezing it all up into a tight ball of anger somewhere in her heart. This thing between her and her father was a sickness that would never heal. But now was not the time to yield to its sapping power. She needed to concentrate. Now was Rhys Jacob's and Lou's and her time.

She drove north out onto the Kennedy Expressway and then onto the Edens, forcing herself to focus down on the case. But it was difficult. Secondary employment was the rule rather than the exception amongst her CPD colleagues. It didn't matter what else cops did as long as it didn't involve a licensed premise, or livery in the form of taxi or limo driving. She knew that Lou had something going, but she had never enquired exactly what.

Kennedy was reasonably traffic-free as she headed north out of the city. The day was gloomy with drizzly rain, the spray thick and persistent behind the big trucks heading up towards Wisconsin. But as she went north, the rain faded and gaps appeared in the clouds, the hint of a late sun beginning to warm the air with no chilling wind to cool it. Fifty miles north, she turned west on 137 through Greyslake. Everywhere, clapboard frame houses were springing up in developments off the highway. All painted in muted blues and greens with lawns that ran straight into the woods of the undeveloped surrounding land. The late fall was decimating the foliage on the trees but still, the yellows, browns and reds mottled the landscape as she sped by. Outside a restaurant called the Vault in Antioch, she spotted a State Trooper's car and interrupted his pancakes long enough to get directions to Shannon Avenue.

It was a tree-lined street, amidst the deciduous woods, bungalows and some larger houses, all wooden, all with stacked chopped wood in the yard and most with motorboats under tarpaulin. Several small jetties jutted out into Channel lake at the end of the street and as she got out of the car, the call of half a dozen geese overhead made her look up into the clearing sky. The impression she had of tranquillity and escape grated against the turmoil inside her head.

She found Lou's place easily enough. His was more cabin-like with a log construction, a well-kept yard and leaves piled into two corners. But, she saw no car in the garage and no sign of occupation as she pounded on the door. In the yard of an adjacent property, and elderly man in a hunting jacket was loading up a pick-up and glancing across at her phlegmatically.

'You looking for Lou?' he asked finally.

'Have you seen him?' asked Mackie hopefully.

''Bout an hour ago. Said he was going up to the store.'

'What store, sir?'

'Name's Burt,' said the man laconically. 'Called the Tackle Store. You know, shooting and fishing gear? That's what we do up here. Need a tackle store for that.'

'Has Lou gone fishing?' she asked making a face.

'Nah. He owns the store.' Burt paused, thinking he had said enough before asking, 'You a friend of his?'

'I work with him in Chicago PD.' Mackie flashed her shield.

'Yeah? Sure didn't have cops that looked like you when I lived in the city,' said Burt with an inane grin. 'It's good having Lou around. Everyone knows he's a cop. Has a sort of calming effect on the excitable types.'

Mackie walked over to him. 'I need to find Lou quickly. Could you direct me to the store please?'

Burt gave her directions and waved her off. The store was in a small retail block standing on its own next to a large boat-repair shop called Bil's Marina off route 173. It was of cabin construction, lots of glass and wood and a shingle roof, in a prime spot opposite a gas station and a camping goods outlet on the other side of the road. Behind, as the ground dipped down, Mackie could see the ripple of sun on silver water.

She parked and hurried into the store. It bristled with fishing and hunting equipment and a distinct absence of guns. A thin, angular woman with weathered features under a Bulls baseball cap stood behind the counter sorting some packages and keeping an eye on some people browsing over a glass-topped counter with a sign above it that read 'Sinkers, bobbers and lures'. The woman looked up as Mackie approached, took in the city clothes and arched her eyebrows questioningly.

'Guess you aren't here for the fishing,' she offered perspicaciously.

'No, I'm looking for Lou.'

'Well he was here.' She took a few steps back and yelled upwards. 'Lou? You there?'

From above, Mackie heard a muted, 'Yeah?' in Bek's growl.

The woman turned back to Mackie. 'He's up in the storeroom. Doesn't sound like he wants to come down though.'

'Can I go up?'

'Kinda dusty up there, but, sure. Through to the back and up the stairs.'

She stood back to let Mackie pass. The narrow stairway smelled of resin and sawn wood. Mackie pushed open a door on a narrow landing and stepped into a converted loft. The smell of pine was even stronger up here and she felt the prickling of dust in her nose. The room ran the length of the building, the eaves low on either side, rough textured to her touch. On either side boxes were stacked neatly in rows up to the roof leaving a narrow central passageway. Halfway along, a space had been left open. There, several low locked steel chests sat snugly in the space between floor and roof. Sitting on one of them was Bek. He held a yellow cloth in his hands with which he polished the stock of a shotgun. He looked up at Mackie, no sign of welcome under the lowered brows.

'You took some finding,' she said.

'I'm off the case, Mac. Didn't you hear?'

'Yeah, I heard.' She paused, looking around. 'Didn't know you had this place, Lou.'

He didn't answer immediately, just stared at her with open hostility. She returned it, arching her eyebrows challengingly, making it clear that she wasn't simply going to walk away.

'I've been sinking money into it for five years or more,' he sighed eventually.

Mackie sat on a chest opposite Bek, relaxed pose, trying to take a little heat out of the situation. 'What you doing up here, Lou?'

'Stocktaking.' He started polishing the gun again. Mackie saw that there was an open box of shells at his feet next to a small bottle of walnut oil.

'You always clean and polish a loaded gun when you're stocktaking? The instructors at the academy would go crazy.'

Bek didn't stop polishing. 'What do you want, Mac?'

'Does it matter?' She didn't try and hide the sardonic tone in her voice. 'Is this how you really want this to end? Three paragraphs in the local paper about the cop who shot himself in the loft of his sporting goods store?'

He threw her a glance full of seething anger and she knew that she'd hit a bull's-eye. Read the scene with a cop's intuition in one easy second.

'I'm stocktaking, Mac.'

'Yeah, Lou. And I'm performing thoracic surgery here. I know what you're contemplating, so do you. So let's cut the crap OK?' Mackie held up her hands and gazed around her. 'This is your future, Lou.'

Bek laughed mirthlessly. 'My mother's dead. My brother shot himself after killing some innocent girl that he thought was from the fucking red planet. Great future, Mac.' He ran his fingers over the gun's stock almost lovingly, his eyes oddly unfocused. 'You have no idea what it's like having someone like Jake in the family. He's there even when you're a hundred miles away. You worry about what he might be doing, what he might be thinking. And then you get to wondering if maybe one day those voices might start appearing in your own mind. See I figure that maybe somewhere down the line I might go a little crazy too. Maybe when I've left the Department. Maybe when I'm up here with some family from Wisconsin out for a little fishing, a quiet week on the lake. Maybe I'll turn up with this pump-action and wipe them off the face of the earth because I've finally worked out that they are really zombies from Venus. It scares me, Mac. I don't want to go to sleep scared for the rest of my life.'

'I came to ask for your help, Lou.'

'I can't even help myself, Goddamnit. Go back to the city, Mac. Read about it in the papers.'

'No. This is wrong. All of it is wrong.'

Bek rubbed hard on the stock and then stopped abruptly. He kept his eyes on the polished wood. His voice, when it spoke, was quiet and dry, as if he hadn't swallowed in a long while. 'I saw the blood in Jake's car the night he tipped me off, Mac. He ran out of the house and pushed my mother over as he did it. She broke her leg so I couldn't go after him. She begged me not to give him up. She begged me to find him. I let myself believe that Jake wasn't capable of doing it despite all the evidence. Jesus, how I wanted to believe that. So you know what I did? I sat back on my hard ass and span you all some bullshit story about a shitcan when all the while I was searching for Jake. I looked for him everywhere I could think of to look. And now she's dead and he's dead and that's what I'm going to wake up and think about every day.'

Mackie stood and walked over to where Bek was sitting but he looked up and shook his head. 'That's far enough, Mac. Don't make me pick this gun up, OK?'

'You threatening me, Lou?'

'Please, Mac. Don't do this.'

She saw tears running down his face then, his lips twitching, his mouth curved into an ugly ribbon of misery.

'Lou,' she said softly, insistently. 'Listen to me.' Bek started polishing the stock again.

'*Listen to me.*' Her anger took them both by surprise.

'I knew something was wrong. At first I put it down to your mom because I knew how it was between you and her.' She shook her head. 'But don't think you've cornered the market in guilt over this case. Since it's confession time, maybe you should hear me out too.'

Bek didn't say anything, but his eyes narrowed in suspicious interest.

'Tell me what you see when you look at me, Lou? Susan Mackie, the woman most likely to? I'm a sergeant now,' Mackie snorted. 'I went into this case hungry and knowing after a day that I'd be carrying you, Lou. But I thought that was OK, because if I cleared the case then it would all be down to me. Another step up the slippery slope.'

Bek sat motionless.

'I'm ambitious, Lou. Lately I've come to realise that it isn't an altogether healthy ambition.'

'There's nothing wrong with amb . . .'

'There is when it means you step all over people. Yesterday, Hopper virtually offered me a lieutenant's post and a lot more if I nailed this case down to Jake, made you look bad and got Rhys Jacob out of the city's hair.'

'Sounds like you'd only be doing your job, Mac.'

'That's exactly what it doesn't mean, Lou. This case stinks. But the worst thing about it is that until I sat in a hotel room two hours ago looking around at an empty wardrobe and an unmade bed, I was prepared to go through with it. I was prepared to screw you and Rhys Jacob and a hundred others for the sake of a lousy promotion. Bastards like Hopper don't give a crock about what's right. But Rhys Jacob does. We're here to protect people like him, not dance to Hopper's tune. The worst thing of all is that Rhys Jacob trusted me and God help me, I like the guy. For a while there . . . God, this sounds pathetic, but he made me feel clean. Like I didn't have to be anybody but myself for him. Sounds crazy? Tell me about it, I've only known the guy a few days. Sounds like the kind of thing some screwed up female might say, huh? Well that's me. This job makes it difficult to really like anyone, doesn't it, Lou? You're always looking for some shitty reason to argue because some scumbag has ruined your day. But Rhys Jacob was prepared to go out on a limb because he believed in his sister and I almost sold him down the river. It doesn't make me feel too good about myself, Lou.'

Bek smiled sadly. 'I've watched you work. You're a good cop but whatever it is that drives you has a sour taste. I've seen it in your face. Like you're getting a kick out of screwing someone all the time.'

Mackie dropped her head. 'Is it all that obvious?' she whispered.

'Mac, most people have some good in them. Our problem is we never see that in anyone and after a while it becomes impossible to see it in ourselves. Don't end up being sour about everything. It's negative and destructive and will eat you up. Believe me, I know.'

Mackie looked up, her face drawn in pain. 'Rhys Jacob couldn't have picked a worse pair of dicks, could he?' There was a long pause before she added, 'Thing is, I don't think it's over.'

'It is for me, Mac.'

She shook her head.

'You believed in Jake, didn't you?'

Bek didn't look at her, but after a while, he nodded, his head down.

'Then I need your help, Lou. I've just come from the Geneva. Hopper sent me over to sweet-talk Rhys, be his little messenger like a good ambitious girl and break the news to him about Jake. You know, how the case is folding up neatly? How Jake didn't really know what he was doing, so now could he please go back on TV and tell everyone how we serve and protect.' She paused.

'When I got there, they told me he'd checked out.'

Bek nodded. 'So he changed his mind.'

'No. It's got wrong written all over it.' She got up and started pacing, the movement helping her put it all together in her mind.

'The phone company trapped the call from Jake last night. I took the address and left for the motel. When I spoke to the phone company this morning, they said they trapped another call from the motel five minutes after I left. Five minutes after I heard the shot. The motel manager has confirmed that call came from Jake's room.'

Bek leaned forward, his brows clouded in bewilderment. He was concentrating now, his cop instincts kicking in.

'Rhys called me to say he was going to CHTV for another interview. When I called them, they denied all knowledge. They hadn't set anything up.'

'This is crazy stuff, Mac. Maybe he's just stringing you along . . .'

'Rhys is smart, Lou. He figured Jake for a schizophrenic right from the whistle. He wouldn't accept anything we told him, remember? Had to find it all out for himself. He went his own way on this. He had this thing about missing persons of the foreign doctor type. I thought it was bullshit, but I worked it up just to keep him happy, gave him the crock about them all disappearing to California to be *Baywatch* extras. Thing is, I told him it was a crock because they had all paid their bills and checked out of their hotels just like Rhys has just done. Five of them were conventioneers.'

'Mac, maybe the guy got scared . . .'

Mackie shook her head. 'No one saw him. You can check out from your room. There's this thing called a video check-out facility. What I'm saying is that it might not have been Rhys that packed those bags and pressed those buttons, Lou.'

Slowly, Bek looked up and put his hand to his forehead. 'Whoa, hold it, Mac. You're losing me here. What are you saying? You think Hopper deported him?'

'That I could swallow.' She hesitated for a long moment before continuing. 'I'm going to tell you something that I didn't want to until I was sure but . . .' she shook her head unhappily.

'Remember I told you about the spatter pattern and the entry wound. I didn't see any powder marks on Jake's skin either.'

Bek stared at her.

'I was going to push for an NAA, but now I think I might not need it. Why would Jake hold the pistol two feet away from his head if he was going to blow his brains out, Lou?'

Bek exhaled loudly twice in reply.

'Think about it. What we heard on the tape? He was talking to Rhys, then he stopped, then the shot. Shit, Rhys even thought he heard someone breathing on the phone later. I told him it was probably just the TV noise. But someone rang the Geneva from Jake's room five minutes after Jake was shot. Someone else came into that room, Lou.' She paused, her eyes bright and fierce.

Bek stood and started shaking.

Mackie kept her gaze on him. 'The second phone call? Jake's paranoia?' she said pressing the point home. 'Someone gets into that motel room while Jake is on the phone. He shoots Jake and sticks the pistol in Jake's hand, but then gets jumpy over the phone being off the hook, listens and hears Rhys breathing, panics and slams it down. Realises what he's done and panics again, wants to find out who Jake was talking to. Presses the redial button and gets the Geneva. Everyone in this city knows that Rhys is at the Geneva.'

'You think that he's grabbed Rhys?'

'Yeah. I think he's grabbed Rhys.'

Bek put the gun down on the floor, his eyes now wide.

'Mac, if you're right on this . . . I've been walking around with my head up my ass.'

'We all have, Lou.'

'God, Jesus, God . . .' Bek's breath came in short bursts. He sat down again, his head slumped on his chest but when he turned his face up, there was a fire burning in his eye. 'I was right. I was right all along . . . Jesus, Jesus . . .'

He let his head hang between his knees for a long while and then slowly looked around him at the storeroom, as if seeing it for the first time.

'This is my life. This is what I'd planned for. Another four years to my pension and then I'd be fishing every day. I was going to get Jake up here, let him work in the business. Maybe all he'd want to do was throw stones in the lake, it wouldn't have mattered. But now . . .'

'It isn't too late for you, Lou.'

'Me.' Bek shook his head. 'What the hell is left for me?'

'Maybe finding out who killed Jake?' The statement hung in the air between them. Bek's eyes were flint.

'I came here to ask you to help, Lou. Help me find out where Rhys Jacob is.'

Long seconds passed in the stillness of the warm storeroom with the redolence of the walnut oil mingling with the pine resin. Bek stood, then stooped to pick up the pump-action and raised it to waist level, his hand reaching expertly for the trigger guard.

'Guess it's decision time, huh, Mac?'

'Lou?' Mackie's question barely had time to emerge from her lips before Bek deftly ejected two cartridges from the breech of the gun and put them in his pocket.

'Loaded gun is a dangerous thing, Mac.'

She nodded and said nothing more about it. She followed him downstairs and as he passed through the store, she heard him say, 'Be gone for a while, Loretta.'

'OK, Lou,' said the woman as she carried on unpacking the deliveries unperturbed.

Back at his house, Mackie waited for him to change and sat in the living room watching the trees outside swaying in the breeze.

'You've checked the airlines?' asked Bek from somewhere in a bedroom.

'Nothing,' answered Mackie. 'He wouldn't just leave like that, Lou.'

Bek appeared at the living room door buttoning his cuffs. 'You seem pretty sure.'

'I am sure.'

He nodded. 'I like him too, Mac. Kinda feisty, but he seemed a good kid. You better ring the hospitals from here – the usual.'

His words filled her with icy dread, but she did as he asked and came up with nothing new. She shook her head at Bek's inquisitive glance when he re-entered with his jacket on.

'I feel like Magdalene Asencio. She rings the hospitals every day.'

'Magdalene who?'

'Spanish lady staying at Rhys's hotel. Her daughter went missing just like Rhys. No one's seen her since. This is what she does every day, rings the hospitals, does the rounds.'

Bek walked to the front door and held it open for her. She walked out into the cooling afternoon air, turned as she reached her car and saw Bek stand on the threshold of his cabin and look around inside, musing on things that might have been. Finally he turned and walked towards her, his big, open face sorrowful.

'Come on, Mac,' he said gruffly to hide it, 'let's go to work.'

26

L AUDEN ARRIVED BACK at the bungalow with his 'groceries';
beer, crackers, three frozen dinners and a water melon and
busied himself with putting them away, trying all the while to contain
the coiled spring of sexual excitement in his gut. He got as far as
unpacking the dozen beers he'd bought when he felt a sudden urge
to run upstairs and check on his trophy. He needed reassurance that
his new acquisition was still there. In the attic room, Rhys Jacob lay
where he had left him, naked and peaceful. Lauden ran his fingers
over the smooth warm skin, caressing the flaccid genitals, strutting
around the room proudly viewing the body from all angles.

He skipped downstairs and retrieved the Polaroid camera.

Grabbing a beer he ran back upstairs and took some photographs before relocating to the kitchen, clutching the drying snaps
like a kid with a much sought-after baseball card. Placing the
Polaroids propped up against the salt cellar and steak sauce on
the table, he put away the remaining groceries and slid a TV dinner
into the microwave.

He ate quickly, barely tasting the food, aware only of his need
for sustenance, his eyes glued to the Polaroids. He popped a second
beer as the remains of the dinner dried and congealed on the table,
drinking from it automatically. When it was half empty, he picked
up the photographs and took them into the small study next
to his grandmother's parlour room. This stuffy enclosure, laden
with memories and a musty odour of old paper, was where his
grandfather had read newspapers from the old country and where
his father had retired to complete his homework and read his books
as a teenager. He flicked on an adjustable lamp and surveyed the
tiny room which in effect was little more than an alcove. In contrast
to the pristine room adjacent full of mementoes of family and
happier times, the study was shabby and in need of cleaning,
furnished with nothing more than a simple chair and roll-top desk
and a crude filing system in cardboard boxes lining the walls.

Pinned to a cork board were the few bills that were the inevitable and necessary intrusions that Lauden had to contend with in order to exist in the society he chose otherwise to ignore. As such it mirrored many rooms in thousands of homes. A place where things were stored and bills were paid. But this corner of Lauden's house contained much much more than innocent accounts.

He placed the Polaroids down on a pull-out reference slide and slid open the cover. Inside covering the writing surface and stuffed into compartments were hundreds of Polaroids, some neatly bundled together with rubber bands, others loosely crammed into the available space. He pulled a handful of prints down and spread them out next to the one of Rhys. The violation of privacy that he had perpetrated in photographing Rhys Jacob was as innocent as a child's drawing compared to those he had retrieved from the desk and which were now displayed in front of him. These were a record, a homage to his necrophilia. For Lauden, photography was an intrinsic and absolute function of his disease. Corpses, organs, heads, tongues, they were all preserved in time on the shiny paper. Mostly, he could not recall what prompted him to capture those particular moments. The majority had been snapped as he proceeded with the actions of dismemberment and butchery that were both stimulus and the necessary means of dispersal of remains. Opened abdomens with billowing entrails swollen by the foul gases that corrupt the lifeless corpse in putrefaction, a decapitated torso sitting up in the bath, here a flayed leg, there an arm devoid of corporeal connections draped almost carelessly over the edge of a sink. These were terrible enough. But there were some where whim or sickness had injected an even more obscene element of orchestration. Looking at them, Lauden always frowned in wonderment and sometimes even distaste that he could have thought up such a thing. His understanding of his frame of mind at those moments of capriciousness a mere transient and insubstantial shadow of the black morass that was his madness.

One showed a freshly decapitated head with an apple in its mouth, the eyes half closed as if in swollen moribund ecstasy. Another showed a skull with a candle projecting through the empty eye socket. He looked at all of them, feeling no remorse, conscious only of the power and strength of his control. They existed, these portraits of butchered souls, because of him. Talismans all; necessary and vital evidence of the rationale of his actions. For Lauden, there was no pleasure in the living being, only the dead inanimate object. The photographs he possessed were an intractable part of that, abrogating participation. As inanimate as the bodies he lusted after, the absolute embodiment of objectivity, taken as an affirmation of authority and omnipotence.

Others had kept similar, dreadful trophies. But Lauden knew nothing of Brady and Hindley's sadistic leanings, and if he had read of Leonard Lake's snuff movies, the memory had been absorbed into sub-consciousness long ago. There were minds, some great and some ordinary that had wondered, through history, whether such a bizarre preoccupation was mere paraphilic fetish or something deeper and darker – a throwback to the pagan psyche that lurks in us all. Certainly, in Lauden's case, there was no trigger, no turning point. The motivation for the abominations he perpetrated remained hidden in a dark spiritual recess that was closeted even from his own understanding.

He stayed in the study for a long time, staring at the photographs, returning to the kitchen for more beer, making himself linger, aware that he had bought time. He loved this part, anticipating what was to come, the feeling of possession he had over the sleeping form upstairs.

After a while, he turned to one of the stacked boxes and dragged it across the littered floor towards him. Inside were books and reprints. He reached for a battered tome, the pages of which smelled musty and faintly of mould, feeling the paper rough to his touch. Published in the sixties, it was out of date by the time it reached the bookshops but it served Lauden's purposes well. Illustrated by lavish artist's drawings, it was an atlas of neurosurgery. Lauden had pored over it a hundred times and lost himself in it again now, willing himself to believe that he could do it, feeling his confidence grow with each swallow of beer.

Eventually, he went out to the garage and took a cordless DeWalt 9.5 volt power drill out of its steel case and took down the extra long drill bits he'd bought to go with it. He carried it carefully back into the study. It felt strong and sturdy in his hands. He had never used it for any home improvements. But his mind was not bent on shelving or deck-work. This was a surgical instrument in his eyes. He leaned back over the atlas and fingered the carbon-tipped bits lovingly. These, Lauden believed, were the instruments of his liberation.

Mackie drove them back to Chicago; seventy miles through the pale afternoon sunshine. She talked for half an hour, trying to keep Bek from brooding. But he wasn't really listening. He sat at her side with a far-away look on his face, and she could only begin to guess at the torture he was putting himself through.

Eventually, Mackie lapsed into silence as she joined the Tri-State Tollway heading south. They were quiet for a long time, letting the miles roll past until Bek finally said, 'I'm sorry I lied to you, Mac.'

'We all make mistakes, Lou. There's no point punishing yourself.'

'You want to tell Internal Affairs that?' He let out a hollow laugh.

'I'm telling them zilch. We never had that conversation at the Tackle Store.'

'They're going to want to do some Q and A.'

'Fine. I'm a big girl, Lou.'

'All I'm saying is, don't perjure yourself for me, Mac.'

'If we can find out what the hell is going on, maybe we can head off the Apaches at the pass.'

Bek shrugged and nodded. 'OK. You're calling the shots here.'

'You up to letting me run this by you once right from the top?'

Bek nodded and slowly, painstakingly, Mackie spelled out what she knew from the beginning from Bek finding the body through Jake's apparent suicide right up to finding Rhys checked out.

Bek sat with a pen in his hand and his pocketbook open on his knees, occasionally jotting down salient points, but largely without speaking.

'OK,' said Mackie when she'd finished. 'Now tell me about Jake.'

Bek kept his eyes straight ahead and his voice low, fighting to keep it free of emotion. Mackie sensed that he was a man in great internal pain, the mental turmoil of his guilt tearing him apart.

'There isn't much. Let's just say I wasn't surprised to hear he'd been to the Adler. He loved it there. He was a class A Trekkie, went to the Starshow twice a week. Spoke better Vulcan than Spock. I hadn't seen him for a few days, but I knew his doctors were trying out some new medication.'

'Wasn't it working?'

Bek shrugged. 'They lucked out. He started thinking that I wasn't really his brother, that someone else had taken over his mom. Weird stuff. I spoke to his shrink, put up a theoretical scenario on the basis of knowing someone who was having trouble, you know the scam. Shrink came up with misidentification syndrome. Even had names for it, Fregoli's syndrome, Capgrass syndrome, I wrote them all down.'

Mackie's face was frowned in concentration. 'If he was confused about you and your mom, maybe he was confused about other people too.'

'He didn't know me any more.' Bek shook his head. 'Maybe he was right to disown me.'

Mackie winced at the heartfelt pain in the words but she wanted to get Lou thinking, break him out of this negativity.

'You said Jake phoned you afterwards?'

Bek looked up. 'Couple of times. Kept repeating the same crazy stuff Rhys Jacob told us about.'

'You've heard what Lavalle said about The Whistler. My guess is he's our man.'

'Could mean anything.' Bek's brows furrowed and Mackie saw him start to sink into the murky depth of despond again.

'If only we knew what Jake had been doing these last few days. Where he went, who he saw . . .' she said. 'The motel interviews came up with nothing. It's a flop house for whores. It'll take days to track them all down. Most of them breech Disney Corporation copyright when they fill in the register anyway.'

'Wait a minute,' said Bek, his face frowning with concentration. 'Maybe we do know what Jake had been doing. At least part of the time.' He told her about his phone call from Jim Piper regarding the disturbance on Cambridge Street.

'Why would Jake smash windows and yell at some guy down in the Lawn?'

'I don't know, but maybe we should try and find out. Give me your mobile and pull over as soon as you can. The reception on those things is shit in the car.'

Briefly, he told her about the call from the uniforms the day before. They were on the I 94 Tollway in Northbrook by this time. Two miles further on, she saw a sign for a Wayside – a roadside park and picnic area. She pulled off and parked in a largely deserted lot. Bek was dialling before she'd stopped the car. There was an information booth with a vending machine near the lot entrance. Mackie got out and bought two coffees. A chill wind blew leaves around the deserted picnic tables as she hurried back to the car. Bek was off the phone. He took the coffee she offered

263

gratefully and she saw a light behind his eyes that told her he was back in the game.

'So?' she asked impatiently.

'Jim Piper and his partner didn't see anything themselves, but they took a description on a blue Mazda with a four-digit match up on Jake's licence plate. Some guy that could have been Jake went apeshit and started throwing rocks through some other guy's windows.'

'Was there no description of Jake?'

'Vague. The neighbours said the guy was acting crazy, shouting gibberish.'

'It's another long shot, Lou.'

'Sure, but now here comes the interesting part. The guy whose windows got smashed has a rap sheet and a couple of stop and frisks for losing it in a few bars with a load of booze on board.' Bek gave her an icy smile. 'This guy also had a severe hearing problem, Mac.'

'Is that significant?'

Bek ran his fingers through his thin hair. 'When Jake and I were kids, we had an old aunt who used to come and slobber all over us on Sundays. We hated her. Thing was she was partially deaf. Wore these battered hearing aids that were always falling out. We used to be able to hear her coming on account of the high-pitched noise those things make when they're too loose-fitting. We had a name for her, Mac, we used to call her Whistler.' He shook his head like a man unable to believe his own incredible stupidity. He looked up at Mackie then, his eyes challenging.

'What does this guy do?' she asked.

'Drives a cab.'

'Who for?'

'Suncabs.'

Mackie went pale. She was staring at Bek like he had just developed a hole in his head.

'What?' demanded Bek.

'Suncabs. Chariot of light. Jake told us right from the start.' Bek stared at her, frowning in concentration.

'Also,' continued Mackie, 'it was a Suncab that picked up Rhys Jacob from the Geneva.'

Bek's eyes opened wide. His voice, when he spoke again, was cracked and dry. 'I spoke to Valdez at the station house. He's pulling the rap sheet and ringing me back. I asked him

264

to run the latents we found on the girl's wrists against this guy . . .'

The phone rang before Bek could finish the sentence. Mackie watched as he listened to the information coming across, offering only the odd 'Yeah' or 'No' in reply. Finally, after what seemed an eternity to Mackie, he ended the call and turned to her.

'Guess what the cab driver was carrying the night they picked him up for a lewd and lascivious, waving his fishing rod outside some mall.'

'What?' asked Mackie breathlessly.

'Twenty capsules of a prescription drug called Quelldane. Its proprietary name is Lidoxine. You want to wait for those prints?'

She didn't answer. She was too busy throwing the coffee out of the window and burning rubber as she roared off.

27

A T A LITTLE AFTER six p.m. that Saturday evening, Lauden took the drill and two unopened beers upstairs. He made two trips, the second time retrieving the large water melon that he'd bought that afternoon and the atlas of neurosurgery.

Rhys Jacob was lying as Lauden had left him, deathly quiet, his breathing shallow but regular. Again, Lauden felt compelled to touch him. Stripping off his own shirt, he climbed on to the cool table and held the unconscious form in a tender caress. He lay there for a long time, feeling his arousal grow, moving against Rhys's quiescent, cool flesh, his whole being transported by contact with this living shell.

Afterwards, he flipped Rhys onto his stomach to photograph him before flipping him back again onto his back and covering him with a white towel before going over to the far wall and pulling out the large wooden trunk. He got onto his knees and took out the motorcycle helmet. From the bit case he selected a 1/8 inch bit and attached it to the drill with a chuck. He needed a lot of concentration, cursing as his hands slipped over the slick metal, knowing that the buzz from the alcohol had its downside in terms of the lack of fine control it induced. All around him, he felt the presence of the ghosts that he had entrapped in this room, feeling them watching, his family, his life. He saw them grinning, felt the air chill with their grimaces of anticipation.

The drill whined with power as he depressed the trigger, holding it up, seeing the bit blur as it cranked up to speed. He put it down again and slid the large watermelon into the helmet and placed both on the trunk with the open face downwards. He opened the atlas and placed it on the floor next to him. It was a large book, full of statistical detail of the number of specimens used and the frequency distribution of the position of structures in millimetres away from specified reference points. Most of this information Lauden found incomprehensible, but what he did understand were the illustrations that accompanied the structural analysis. In each instance, a case report was included, complete with radiographs of the actual surgery employed with thin instruments entering the skull cavity. It was from these that Lauden made his own calculations in a rough-and-ready way. In some, he had even bothered to work out the angle of penetration with the number of degrees written in a careful hand. The book fell open at the twenty-eighth page; a graphic description of the removal of an airgun pellet from the brain of a fourteen-year-old male.

With one hand on the helmet to steady it, he positioned the drill and sent the bit whirring into the soft flesh of the melon. The power was deceptive. Before he could stop it, the drill had sunk in to the hub. He pulled back angrily. He would have to be more careful. He was being sloppy. Control was the thing. Total control.

He got up and went back to the kitchen for a large bread knife. He used it to slice the watermelon in two before sliding one domed green end back into the helmet. This time he held the helmet between his knees, both hands on the drill for better control, feeling the juices run down and onto his legs, cool and sticky. This time, he judged the penetration well, holding up the melon with the helmet still attached, seeing the bit just emerge from the raw red cut surface of the fruit at the angle of penetration he had chosen. Carefully, he stuck some tape at the point that the drill disappeared into the skin of the melon and sat back in satisfaction, letting his eyes drift over to the unconscious form adjacent to him.

He opened another beer, drank half of it, belching loudly as he tried to calm his racing pulse. What he was about to do would determine his destiny, he knew it. He could feel the enormity of it. This time there might be a chance that he might hold on to his desires, prolong the fantasy for ever. He gave no thought to what terrible damage he might inflict on Rhys Jacob, no thought as to how he might nourish and sustain a brain-damaged body. These were not his immediate concerns. The depth of his madness was such that he functioned in a state of total depravity. Damaged flesh and organs were items to be used. The idea of Rhys Jacob's body wasting away and decaying in front of his eyes was something he would deal with. If he could delay it for even a few days it would be the fulfilment of a dark and dreadful dream.

He put the beer down next to the mangled fruit and went over to Rhys. He smoothed down the hair and angled the head away from him before slipping on the helmet. The drill felt sleek in his hands as he climbed onto the table, his knees astride Rhys's head, one hand firmly holding the blue helmet. He put the bit against Rhys's head, heard the high-pitched whine change its note as it met with resistance from the hard skull. He touched it gently, gingerly, barely leaving it in contact for more than a second or two before he pulled back. The smell of charred bone filled his nostrils and he withdrew, seeing blood ooze. But not much. Not anywhere near as much as he had expected. He used his discarded shirt to dab away the blood and again took up the drill, pushing gently, gingerly depressing his finger in bursts of power as he drilled a hole into Rhys Jacob's head. He was pleased to see that his victim didn't stir. The tranquillisers did at least induce a mercifully deep level of unconsciousness. It was as he depressed his finger on the drill for the sixth time that he heard the knock downstairs. He leaped up off the table as if galvanised by an electric rod. He never received visitors, never answered the door to anyone except policemen. The thought paralysed him. And there was something about this knock, this insistent, authoritative knock. He knew they would see no light. Light did not intrude upon what went on in there. Again the knock came. Carefully, Lauden tripped to the door and crouched there, listening.

Bek and Mackie stood at the front door of Lauden's bungalow. Dusk was falling quickly, the street gradually disappearing into deepening shadow. Twice Bek had knocked and twice they had had no reply. Mackie tried once again, this time adding, 'Mr Lauden, this is Chicago Police. We'd like to talk to you, sir.'

After several long moments, she shook her head.

'Swear to God I heard something when we walked up here . . . sounded like a power tool,' said Bek.

Mackie shrugged. 'This door's locked just like the rear. I don't see any lights. Lou, maybe he's out?'

'Cab's in the garage though, so he isn't working.'

Bek put his hand out and peeled a fleck of blistered paint off the door. 'Place needs fixing up. You've taken a look round back, huh?'

Mackie nodded. 'Nothing.'

Bek walked back to the front gate and gazed up at the building. A woman in a hooded thermal jacket was walking a dumb-looking Doberman on the street. When she got to Lauden's house she stopped and stared at Bek.

'You from the health department?' she asked in an aggravating whine.

'No, ma'am,' said Bek turning.

'Someone should do something. I ring every week and every week they promise to send someone out.'

'To do what?'

'Something about the stench. Can't you smell it?'

Bek sniffed the air. 'It is kinda high around here.'

'It's better now with the cold weather coming on. Sometimes I walk past here. I have to take Timmy across the street.'

'Timmy your dog, ma'am?'

'Yeah. I walk him twice a day. Live right in the corner.'

'You remember anything about some crazy guy waking up the street a few nights ago.'

'Yes, I remember.'

'Was it you called the cops?'

'No. Mrs Elder did that. I just saw it from my window. I didn't want to go out. It was too cold that night.'

'You remember anything about the crazy?'

'Sure. About your height. Thinner than you. Needed a shave.' She eyed Bek suspiciously. 'Say, it wasn't you was it?'

Bek showed her his badge. 'No ma'am.'

She pulled on the straining dog's leash. 'Timmy wants to go pooh-pooh.'

'That's OK. He gonna lay his loaf in the park, huh?'

'Sure. Can you do something about the smell?'

'I'll see if I can get the health people out here. Thanks for talking to me.'

'You're welcome.'

Mackie came out and joined him. 'Anything?'

'Lady thought the crazy guy looked a lot like me.'

Mackie sighed. 'What are we going to do?'

Bek looked up at the house in the dying light. 'This place is wrong. You can feel it, so can I. We got a Suncab in the garage. We got the noise of power tools in a house that hasn't been fixed up for twenty years or more. And we got bad smells. Jim Piper told me about the smell too. Told me that was the most memorable thing about the joint.'

'Maybe there's a problem with the sewers.'

'Yeah, maybe,' said Bek distractedly. 'Could we take another look round back?'

They walked around the side of the house, the path littered with rusting cans and large cartons of wallpaper remover. The yard was unswept, weeds poking their heads through concrete. Against the garage stood some large drums with their lids clipped down. Next to them were three plastic heavy-duty garbage sacks with wire wrapped round the necks as seals. Bek walked across. The smell hit him from fifteen yards away.

'Check this out, Mac.'

Mackie made a face and exhaled through puffed cheeks.

'It's coming from the sacks, I'm sure of it.' He reached into a pocket and took out a small red pocket knife.

'You going to open one of these, Lou?'

'That would constitute an illegal search, Mac,' said Bek in a reprimanding tone at the same time as he opened out the knife. 'How could I possibly do that?' He knelt down to one of the bags.

'Lou?' Mackie's voice held a warning note.

'Remember Timmy the wonder dog out in the street? Dobermans love garbage. They have these real long claws. I had a Doberman live next to me for a while. They can unzip a trash sack in five seconds. Worse that a whole squad of racoons.'

He slashed twice at a bulging sack. They both stopped to inspect the result of his handiwork. Bek peeled back the plastic with the blade and shone in a small pencil torch. The beam illuminated a grey chunk of glistening flesh and the smell redoubled.

'Jesus, what the hell is this guy butchering, here?'

But Mackie's attention was caught by something she had seen further in. She stooped lower and took the torch away from Bek. There behind the hunk of flesh, gesticulating at her in an obscene wave was a human hand. She reared up, gagging, leaving Bek to find it for himself. He joined her a moment later, breathing hard, his mouth and nose covered with a handkerchief, his eyes hard with anger and justification.

'I suddenly don't like the noise we heard, Mac.'

She shook her head, her own eyes wide with dull horror.

'You OK?'

She nodded without speaking.

'OK, we can either call this in and wait for backup or we can go in ourselves.'

'We don't have a warrant, Lou.'

Bek strode across to the back door and knocked hard.

'Rhys? You in there?'

Only the wind answered him. 'You hear that, Mac? I distinctly heard a cry for help.'

'Lou?' said Mackie dubiously. She had heard nothing and she knew that neither had Bek.

'This asshole killed my brother.' Bek spoke through clenched teeth. 'We go in there now, we need due cause. Now did you or did you not hear a cry for help?'

'I heard it,' said Mackie, her face hard.

Bek nodded and put his foot to the back door. He kicked twice. The lock broke on the second attempt. Bek went in low, Mackie covering, her eyes wide with an adrenaline charge. They swung into the squalid kitchen, keeping low, both hands on their guns. It was empty. The living room too, with the window still covered in plastic sheeting. They both stood, jittery and staring at the Spartan furnishings, the smell now all-pervading. Mackie nodded in the direction of the bedroom. She went in, Bek behind her. The bed was filthy, stained with God alone knew what. She pulled open the wardrobe and stepped back in horror as three skulls stared out at her. She called to her partner but received a vague, distracted acknowledgement in reply as Bek contemplated a rib-cage propped against the wall.

'We gotta call this in, Lou,' whispered Mackie in a tremulous voice, her gaze glued to the skulls.

Bek nodded. 'Phone was in the living room, right?'

They had to pass the one remaining door on their way back. Bek pointed to himself. He put his hand on the handle and burst into Lauden's grandmother's parlour room. He had two seconds to take in the contrast between the squalor of the house and the clean, unsullied warmth of this room before something hit him in the face. He saw it only as a white blur as it launched itself from behind the piano, throwing his hands up to fend it off. As it struck him it broke into a hundred shards of brittle bone. The two slugs that followed hit him in the chest, both exploding into his lungs, the force blowing him backwards against the wall where he crumpled in gurgling shock, his face registering only surprise before the terrible, crushing pain hit him. He barely heard Mackie's gun as she fired low at the man that had emerged from behind the piano waving a gun at her injured partner.

The man screamed in agony and collapsed to the floor clutching his shattered leg. He fell heavily against the piano, sending photographs and ornaments flying everywhere. Mackie moved into the room and kicked away the gun that had fallen with him, screaming at him to keep still, swinging Lauden roughly onto his stomach and cuffing him before turning back to Bek.

She knelt and held Bek's face, hearing his ragged breathing, not understanding the words that bubbled through the frothy blood oozing from his mouth. She was begging him to hang on, begging him not to give up. But the burning pain in Bek's chest was insistent and unyielding. His breathing hurt, it hurt like hell. He tried to tell her, he tried to explain. But she wouldn't, couldn't listen. He could only squeeze her hand and let himself get away from that dark bubbling pain. He forced a smile onto his lips and saw Mackie's eyes reciprocate in sad, sorrowful understanding.

Her tearful smile was the last thing he saw.

She held him for a while, ignoring the pleas and sobs of the injured man behind her. Then she stood and looked down at her dead partner. In her mind she heard a voice repeating, *It shouldn't have happened, none of it should have happened.*

She glanced down at the blood oozing from Lauden's leg and decided that she could not touch it. Her body trembled and sang with hot emotion. She felt the gun in her hand and knew how easy it would be to point it at this moaning thing. And a part of her wanted to do that very badly. A part of her knew that she would be doing the world a great service if her finger exerted just the right amount of pressure. She swallowed hard and wiped liquid away from the corner of one eye as she turned and walked to the phone and called it in, calmly and concisely. When she put the phone down, she stood alone in that house of death trying to shut out the noise of William Lauden's whimpering pain. She went back to her partner, saw the stairs leading up to the loft and noticed that there was light spilling out from a doorway at the top.

Dread overtook her grief in a black tide. Holding her gun in a trembling hand, she took the creaking steps one at a time. And even as she walked up those steep stairs, she heard, in between Lauden's groans and whimpers, the high-pitched whine of the hearing aids whistling at her. The noise seemed unfocused and eerie to her straining ears, ululations of a monotonous lament.

At the top, she pushed the groaning door open with a foot, her face suddenly bathed in the sickly light, her body in a low crouch, both hands on her gun, her eyes flying up to the calcified skeletal monster with the three faces as her bowels iced in fear. It was such a grotesque, abominable creation, affording a glimpse into the private world of whatever it was she had shot downstairs. And then she saw the table and the naked form lying on it with blood running down the neck in dark streaks from under the helmet.

She walked across as if in a dream, letting her gun fall to her side, defeated at the last by the dreadful evil of this room. Reaching out a quivering hand to touch the flesh, she saw the bloody drill nearby and despite herself, heard a small cry escape her lips like the bleat of a young animal. Her hand wavered, her brain not wanting confirmation of what her eyes were telling her, not wanting to know. And then her hand was on his naked arm, her fingers miraculously finding his flesh still warm, still living. The touch broke the spell, rupturing a damn of relief that rushed out in a sob of garbled gratitude to Jesus, Mary and a whole host of suddenly remembered saints and martyrs. She had expected coldness and death and instead here was wonderful, living warmth.

She reached up for the neck pulse. It beat there, strong and slow. She fell to her knees then, unremittingly grateful that he was at least alive, willing herself not to think about what damage the ghoul had done. She was still sitting there with Rhys's hand held up to her face when the first two squads arrived outside in a wail of sirens.

28

THE FUNERAL CORTEGE marched through the city. People lined the streets to watch as it marched up Washington, past City Hall and Daley Center, across State and on to Michigan Avenue. A sea of dark blue in sombre magnificence.

Chicago loves its heroes – especially cops. The march was made even more poignant by the fact that there were three coffins and there would be only one stone on the family grave. It would bear the name of Bek proudly. The commissioner read an obituary, congressman Kervesky flowed with the uniforms and the mayor looked sober in black. People cried openly.

Later, the press spent several hours searching for Sergeant Susan Mackie, the dead cop's partner, but she was nowhere to be found. They had been equally frustrated in the days leading up to the funeral. They had not known that Mackie was as far away as it was possible to be on the other side of the Atlantic, on a windswept mountain-side at another funeral. A much quieter affair, but charged with as much emotion. No intrusive glare of TV cameras, just the intimacy of a chapel where she had listened to a service in another language and felt the singing sear her heart without needing to understand the words.

After Lou's death, she had insisted that Finch handle the press on the clear understanding that Hopper came nowhere near. The Lieutenant had done so with tight-lipped factual comments on the case. The press didn't mind. They had enough to write about with a murderer whose neighbours, in the clear light of retrospection, were only too delighted to supply all kinds of florid detail.

So far, they had found the remains of ten young women, all listed as missing. Seven of them were foreigners, seven conventioneers adjudged by Lauden as the easiest targets in his compulsive need to feed his dark and monstrous habit. Among the mourners at Bek's funeral was Magdalene Acensio.

Mackie had come back to Chicago for Bek's memorial service,

but had been whisked away by car afterwards, back to her apartment where she now stood in her corner bay, looking out at the busy streets below. She had switched off the TV after they had cut from the mayor's address to a spokesman for CPD, one Boyd Hopper, who announced with nauseating sincerity that both Sergeant Bek and Sergeant Susan Mackie had been commended for bravery. He had spoken earnestly and with so much conviction that Mackie had to leave the room to stop herself from throwing something at the TV. The service had left her with a mixed set of emotions; grief tempered by a strange pride that she never knew she could feel. There was, she was glad to admit, little sadness. Lou Bek had given her strength in those few hours between finding him in the Tackle Store and apprehending William Lauden.

Southport Street in Clybourne buzzed with activity as people hurried to and from the shopping centre in Webster Place in preparation for the holiday. Mackie gazed down, letting her eyes drift across the decorated facade of St Ignatius School and Hall opposite, her thoughts lost and meandering. Below, a figure hesitated on the street before entering her building. The movement caught her eye but she saw only the top of a head and shoulders from her vantage point. For one tantalising moment, she thought she recognised who it was before the ludicrousness of it slammed home. She shook her head and smiled. Stupid of her.

'Get real, Susan,' she muttered chastisingly.

The buzzer, when it rang, took her completely by surprise. She hesitated at the intercom, toying with the idea of ignoring it, praying that it wasn't one of those low-life reporters. It buzzed again. Cursing, she pressed the talk button.

'Yes?'

'Susan, is that you?'

Her mind reeled. 'Who is . . .?'

'It's me, Rhys. Can I come up?'

She buzzed him in and for a long second stood there in bewilderment before the truth of it sank in and she began running around the apartment throwing things into the laundry basket and loading the dishwasher with a day and a half's soiled crockery. The knock on the door, though expected, paralysed her. She walked over to it slowly, opened it to find him standing there, sheepish and full of self-doubt.

'Susan, I'm sorry to turn up like this. I stayed for some of the service but I couldn't stand it any more.'

She nodded. 'You don't have to explain. Come in.'

He walked in and stood awkwardly, admiring her taste: sisal flooring dotted with big textured rugs and large patterns that flowed over the sofas. The walls discreetly stippled complemented by generous soft fabric draped over windows. It was tasteful and very individual.

'You gonna take your coat off?'

He didn't answer, preoccupied as he was with what he had come to say. 'I wanted to thank you for coming to Catrin's funeral. You should have said something. I didn't even know until afterwards.'

'I didn't want to intrude.'

'My family can be pretty daunting,' he acceded. 'But it was nice of you and we . . . I'm grateful.'

'I'm glad you could make it for Lou and Jake and their mom too.'

Rhys nodded, his mouth a tight smile. 'Right,' he said uncomfortably. 'I wanted to say it face to face. I'll leave you alone now . . .'

'Did I tell you I was telepathic?' said Mackie as he turned away.

He swung his head and stared at her in bafflement. Or did she dare to believe there was a flicker of hope there too?

'I know what you're thinking,' Mackie said. 'You're thinking that if you tell me the other reason for you coming here, I might laugh in your face. I won't, Rhys. You're just full of guilt because you think it's selfish of you to even consider yourself at such a terrible time in your life. Like I said, our timing is lousy, but it maybe the only shot we get.'

He dropped his eyes and she could see confusion and doubt in his expression.

'Oh, God. I'm sorry,' she said with chagrin, squeezing her eyes shut and turning away, hearing the voice in her head screaming, *Wrong! You got it all wrong again, Mackie. What does he want with a loser like you? Loser with a capital L. Lost your baby, lost its father, lost your partner. Loser, loser . . .*

She balled her hand into a fist and felt the nails dig into her palms. The pain helped and as she turned away from Rhys's dreadful, bewildered expression, more to shut out the voice in her head than anything, she managed a trite, embarrassed little apology. 'My big mouth. Maybe my telepathy is off today . . .'

She felt his hand on her arm, gently restraining and she turned back to see him shake his head, his eyes clear, a slow smile spreading over his mouth.

'No it's not.' He held her gaze long enough for them both to understand his meaning before adding drily, 'I take it you won't mind if I do take my coat off then?'

Sometime later, she stood by the window again, this time in her bedroom. The bed lay unmade, sheets rumpled and twisted by their lovemaking. She'd last shared that bed with Nick, but it was as if it had taken place in some shadowy dream. The reality was now and it felt more real than it ever had. There was a bare patch on the floor in the corner, noticeable to no one but her. A patch where the blanket box once stood. She had gone with Audra to visit their sister-in-law in the hospital. Linda's amniocentesis had been uncomplicated, the tests negative. She'd told Linda not to open the box until the baby arrived, tied it with ribbon and had it delivered. She remembered the look of shining pleasure on Audra's face when she had said that. The way Audra had looked at her, approvingly, a single tear glistening before it was wiped away. The shake of her head when Linda asked if Audra had a cold.

Mackie smiled to herself. They had talked over a long lunch and into the afternoon. Or rather Audra had listened. Still Mackie was amazed at how much she had unburdened, how understanding Audra had been, how much it had made her realise that hers was a pain that needed sharing.

Dusk was encroaching as she looked at her watch and said loudly, 'You better hurry up.'

Rhys emerged from the bathroom wearing nothing but a towel and clutching a pair of boxer shorts.

'Can't a man have a shower?'

She looked him up and down. 'You've been in there so long, I was beginning to wonder.' She went to him and pulled him into the living room, held him, pushing his straying hand away from the still livid scar under the hair at the top of his skull left by Lauden's abortive attempt at pithing him. She could still see the look on the neurosurgeon's face as he had told her that less than half a millimetre of bone had remained. There were things that she could not forgive Lou Bek, like abandoning common sense in going into that house and for getting himself killed, but she would always be grateful to him for that half millimetre. They both would.

'So what's the hurry?' asked Rhys.

She led him to a comfortable armchair, pushed him down and sat in his lap, enjoying the feel of his hands on her back and midriff.

'Listen,' she said, holding onto his wrists to stop his fondling for a moment.

Outside, they heard the eerie whistle of the sugar train on its once-weekly journey north. It was an evocative sound, a noise that had always caused goosebumps to prickle her flesh and one that she had told his unconscious form that he would share with her one day as he had lain in that hospital bed, still drugged from Lauden's concoction.

She eased the pressure on his wrists and they lost themselves in one another for a long, lingering while. Later, she got off his lap and went over to a hi-fi. *Bewitched* filled the room with Mackie grinning like a kid and sashaying towards Rhys before jumping back onto his lap. Rhys held her while she nuzzled his ear and sang the words in a husky whisper.

'*I'm wild again,*
Beguiled again . . .'

She stood and took away the towel, eyeing him with a wicked grin.

'Just wanted to check that everything still worked, Doctor,' she said running her hands over his bare skin.

'Oh, yes?' Rhys said. 'It was working well enough half an hour ago, wasn't it?'

She laughed and went over to the sofa where she picked up his shorts and threw them to him, watching him put them on with the greatest of pleasure.

'So', said Rhys in exasperation, 'dinner out or in?'

'Thought we'd try Steve B's. We ought to sink one or two for Lou. I hate wakes, but Lou would have wanted it.' Rhys nodded.

'They play good music there too,' added Mackie. 'More progressive blues than we heard in that shack the other night; a little John Lee mixed up with Latin rhythms.'

'Sounds wonderful. And then you said a stroll somewhere?'

'You betcha. Blow away the cobwebs. And tomorrow, I'd like to get out of the city for a while.'

'God, it's Thanksgiving. I almost forgot. You're not going to Bleak House, Michigan then?'

She made warning eyes at him and he grinned. She did the same, amazed at how easy it had become to laugh at herself in his presence. She was laughing now at the joke they were sharing. Not so long ago she had believed she could never have laughed at anything remotely connected with Portland House.

'No,' she said softly. 'I thought we'd go north. Just seventy miles or so. There's a place by Channel lake I want to visit.'

'Relatives?'

'Sort of. I want to throw some stones in the water for someone I knew.'

Rhys saw the brief flash of pain in her face and simply nodded in acceptance. She would explain in her own way. He sensed that they would have plenty of time. And that perception filled him with a glow of wonder that eased away his own pain like a warming salve.

F
JON

Jones, Dylan,
1955-

Unnatural acts.

$22.95

DATE			